WE SHALL
NOT ALL
SLEEP

TONY WOODLIEF

WE SHALL NOT ALL SLEEP

a novel

SL/NT

BOOKS

WE SHALL NOT ALL SLEEP
A Novel

Slant Books
P.O. Box 60295
Seattle, WA 98160

www.slantbooks.org

Cataloguing-in-Publication data:

Names: Woodlief, Tony.

Title: We shall not all sleep: a novel / Tony Woodlief.

Description: Seattle, WA: Slant Books, 2024

Identifiers: ISBN 978-1-63982-175-4 (hardcover) | ISBN 978-1-63982-174-7 (paperback) | ISBN 978-1-63982-176-1 (ebook)

Subjects: LCSH: Coming of age--Fiction | Fathers and sons--Fiction | Fathers--Fiction | Southern States--Fiction

For Mama

I WILL TELL YOU the story of my father, and I will begin with the day we killed the boy. I never received my father's visions, nor his savagery, nor even his ability to find good water in the earth. For a time I saw shades of what he saw, and this is enough to tell you the truth of his life. Or perhaps just as much truth as a man was meant to bear. In memory my father is hell-kettle diver, shore-wandering oracle, tunnel wraith. All the earth is filled with his terrible glory. But my father is also deliverance in the blood-clouded depths, and he is laughter, and he is salvation borne through smoke and ash. The memory of my father is a shadow, and a boy chasing the shadow, and the shadow is his name.

On the day we killed the boy, in the summer of 1972, Daddy told Mama he intended to drill a well. "Sweetwater," he promised her that morning in our kitchen. "Cold as winter."

Mama nodded without looking up from dishwashing. She was likely thinking of a dozen tasks more important than a hand-pumped well on a back acre we didn't even use. Sometimes Daddy knew Mama as if she were his own flesh. Other times he acted like he didn't know the first thing about her. I reckon both can be true.

"I bet not as sweet as an RC," I said. I was hell-bent on riding to town with Daddy when he went to get his drill bits sharpened.

Mama shook her head. Whatever Daddy's ability to read her thoughts, my mother knew exactly what *I* was thinking at all times. "Absolutely not," she said. She gave the dish she was washing an extra-furious scrub. "Those old men at the Esso talk like sailors."

"Sugar, how much time have you spent with those old boys? Or sailors, for that matter?" Daddy winked at me.

"I've bought gas there my whole life, and my whole life there's been old men perched on stools in there like a pack of wrinkled possums, grinning sideways at each other."

Daddy sauntered over to Mama like a man looking for trouble. "Looks and grins ain't filthy talk, baby-cakes."

Mama whipped her head around, chestnut hair whirling like a swing carousel. "Don't you take on like a lawyer with me, Ray

Waterson! I know how men talk!" With her eyes she cut him stem to stern. "And I know what they talk about." She turned back to the sink. "My son will not set foot in there."

"I've never heard anything filthy in the Esso," I said. I realized my blunder when Mama dropped a handful of silverware into soapy water and turned to fix me with her stare. "Boy, why don't you tell me how you came by your extensive knowledge of what constitutes filth?"

I knew she was thinking of my best friend, Calvin Pruitt. She believed he was a slick talker, which was true, though he came by it honestly, what with his father one of the biggest merchants in town. Whenever I acquired a soul-eroding habit—like rolling my eyes, or faking stomach problems that required me to stay in the bathroom for the entirety of Reverend Hardison's sermon—Mama assumed I'd picked it up from Calvin. If she was thinking Calvin was instrumental in my acquisition of cuss words, she was absolutely right.

"Come on now. Let's hear it."

"Shit, sugar," Daddy said. "Anybody who watches the news with your mama is liable to get his ears melted. She's even taught *me* some words."

If Mama had been washing steak knives, she might have skewered him right there. Instead she lit into him with a stream of abuse that was no less frightful for being profanity-free. Her missiles in this fusillade were his heathen Indian lineage, his no-good slut of a mother, and his ongoing contribution to the delinquency of my grandmother, most recently in the form of buying her a new spittoon. Mama said things to Daddy that no man would ever dare utter.

"Now sugar," he said, a grin on his face.

"Don't you sweet-talk me!" Mama's emerald eyes had narrowed to slits. Her people came from Scotland; she said it's why her eyes were so green, her temper so hot. Daddy liked to say her eyes are what kept him from making good grades in high school. He'd say her eyes reminded him of four-leaf clovers, and horse pastures, and other things. Mama would slap his chest when he said *other things*. Right now her hands were serving as punctuation for her sharp sentences. Tiny soap suds flecked Daddy's beard.

With a speed that seemed unnatural for a man so big, Daddy darted under her gesticulating arms, seized her waist, and put his teeth to her throat like a wild beast. Mama yelped and beat his shoulders. "Ray! When are you going to trim this scraggly beard? It feels like I'm being molested by a hillbilly!"

"You are, baby," he murmured into her throat.

Mama shrieked and slapped his back as he burrowed into her neck and lifted her onto the counter. She tugged the hem of her dress toward her knees and with her other hand yanked his thick black hair. Daddy's laugh became a howl. He gripped her waist, put his lips to her ear, and whispered something that evoked outrage and laughter. I felt embraced between them, even though I sat at the kitchen table, my toes just touching the linoleum. I was nine years old.

Mama glanced my way, and her face became that of a mother again. She ordered Daddy to put her down. "Ray," she said. "*Now.*"

Daddy kissed her neck with loud, wet noises. Mama yanked his ear like it was the starter cord on our lawnmower. He yelped and backed away. "God*damn* woman. You're mean as a snake."

"Don't you blaspheme under this roof, you godforsaken heathen." Mama said it so meanly I thought maybe she meant it, about Daddy being godforsaken.

Daddy looked at me and shook his head. "It's the prettiest ones that hurt you the worst."

Mama narrowed her eyes and shook her head at his bullshit. I wondered if she was literally thinking *bullshit*, though she would never say it. She slid off the counter, adjusted her waistline, and walked over to where Daddy stood massaging his ear. She stood on tiptoe, kissed him hard on the lips, then slapped his chest with such force that tiny soap suds flew across the kitchen and lodged in the peach fuzz of my forearms. She turned back to her dishes. "I suppose the boy can go with you." She said it as if she'd tried her best to keep us from perdition, and was now resigned to letting us ruin our lives.

The matter of my RC Cola wasn't settled, but I knew Daddy would make a more sympathetic court of appeal, so I waited until we were bouncing along our dirt driveway in his Jeep. I sat back, interlaced my fingers behind my head, and let out a satisfied sigh. It was a sound intended to convey that, so far as I was concerned, we were all on the same page. "That RC sure is going to go down good in this heat," I said.

Daddy adjusted his rear-view mirror, which I'd tilted while pretending to drive.

"Yessir, a cold drink is what you need on a day like this."

Daddy grunted as he steered onto the blacktop. We accelerated, lurching as he shifted gears. I could feel the tires' vibration in my teeth.

"I brought a quarter."

"We'll see, boy."

"You talked her into it. That kiss meant *Yes*." The truth is I wasn't sure what Mama's kiss had meant, but it sure hadn't looked like *No*.

"Daniel."

I stilled myself and took in the smell of burning oil and gasoline. Daddy's musty Army duffel slouched between my knees. I knew it held two Delco batteries and a scattering of dirt-caked rotary bits, but I pretended it still contained the killing tools I imagined he'd once carried in it: long magazines packed with bullets, knurled hand grenades, rope for scaling cliffs.

Daddy was no longer a soldier, he was a water witcher. He did other kinds of work, but he was known for witching. Farmers from all over North Carolina called him. People imagine a witcher finds water, but in truth it was always the water that summoned Daddy. Maybe this was why he meant to plumb a well on our own land—because it was calling to him. All manner of hidden things called to my father. I hadn't yet come to understand that, but this day was probably the beginning of my understanding. Years later Daddy would tell me that the dead themselves are like a river beneath the soil.

I turned my gaze to his arms, which were brown and hard, like knotted cords. They stretched the sleeves of his T-shirt. Sometimes, when Daddy sat with his newspaper or his coffee, I would lean against him, rest my head on his shoulder, and take his arm in my hands. I would move it up and down, left and right, like I was operating a crane. I wondered if that was what it was like to be a man. To sit up in the cab behind your eyes and maneuver the big arms and legs you'd waited on so very long to arrive.

His right forearm bore a thin scar, white as a fish's underbelly, extending from elbow to wrist-bone. Whenever I held his arm in my hands, I ran my fingers along that pale wound and shivered at its straightness. If I asked he would say: *Aw, now*; or, *It's nothing*. Sometimes he was silent, his face that of a man who was trying to remember himself.

I reached to where his hand gripped the gearstick and traced his scar with my fingertip. He let go of the gearstick and brushed my hair from my eyes. The Jeep roared in the afternoon sun, its tires thrumming like a jet engine. It seemed to carry us forward of its own volition.

I considered the thick, red skin of Daddy's neck, his patchy beard and long black hair. He had the longest hair of any man in church. Nobody whispered about it like they did about Eddie Gilchrist's big brother, home from Chapel Hill for the summer, whose stringy yellow hair was shorter than Daddy's. I knew they treated Daddy differently because of the war.

Sometimes I heard people utter the name of that country that was unmentionable in our house. I wondered what they would say if they saw the medals he kept in black boxes, lined up like little coffins, at the bottom of his dresser drawer. There were two bronze stars, a silver star, and three thick hearts of purple and gold, bearing an image of George Washington. On the back of each heart was a mysterious descriptor in thin, raised type: *For Military Merit.* I wished I could ask him what that meant, but I didn't dare admit I'd gone through his belongings.

I reckoned Daddy's right to long hair, and that Bowie recon knife on his belt, and the wide perimeter most people afforded him, all derived from *Military Merit.* I imagined his long hair gave him power, like Samson. I wanted to let my hair grow like his, but Mama kept it clipped short. One day I was going to leave home, grow my hair long, and gather my own scars. I was going to prove that I had *Military Merit* too.

As we hurtled toward the outskirts of Hickory Shore, a thick rat snake slithered onto the road like it intended to bar us from town. Daddy accelerated, and the snake drew back its upper body and struck as we reached it. There was a clang on our bumper and a tumbling sound beneath. I twisted in my seat to see the snake whip along the asphalt in our wake. It came to a stop and lay unmoving but for a twitching tail.

I have driven thousands of rural miles, and I have never since that day seen a snake attack a car. I got the impression it didn't surprise Daddy at all. That he was used to creation behaving unnaturally in his presence. Or perhaps revealing the fullness of its nature.

We slowed as we reached town, rolling past brick-front stores, the post office, my school beginning to stir in preparation for a new year. I imagined we were in a parade, Daddy and me. I envisioned the people of Hickory Shore lining the sidewalks and fenced yards, cheering for Daddy with his cabled arms and long, wind-tumbled warrior's hair, and me beside him, my arms thin and smooth, but destined to one day be like his. As we rolled past the shops on Main Street, I imagined the crowd waving flags, beckoning us onward to glories yet unrevealed.

When that bundle of green and blue exploded from behind a car parked along the curb, my brain tried at first to incorporate it into my parade fantasy. It was a wayward balloon, maybe, or confetti shot from a cannon.

Daddy stomped the brake pedal so hard I thought his boot would punch through the floorboard. I lurched forward, smacked my face against his extended arm, felt the smooth hard line of his scar against my mouth. Our tires made a scrubbing noise on the pavement and there was a *thump* that sounded like a potato sack tumbling from a cellar shelf.

I would come to think of that boy as a bullet fired long after Daddy thought the war was over. I suppose to the boy's mother, who stood in the Red and White pondering a roast for dinner, or maybe examining a honeydew for soft spots, and who heard that sound and probably thought, for just a second, that a car had hit another car, until realizing it wasn't the bright crunch of metal striking metal, but the sound one hears when an animal gets hit, and who remembered, with a lightning bolt through her chest, that she'd just told her seven year-old son: *Yes, you can go across the street and see about getting some construction paper*—well, to that poor woman, it was Daddy who was the bullet.

Daddy yanked up the parking brake and jumped out of the Jeep. When he saw what lay before our bumper, the muscles in his face seemed to melt. He dropped to his knees. I pushed my shoulder into the door and scrambled out to see Daddy holding a brown-headed boy. Half the boy's face seemed asleep, the other half was swollen and open-eyed, leering at me from my father's arms.

"Daniel," Daddy said. "Get back inside."

People spilled into the street. Daddy shouted for somebody to call an ambulance. "Daniel," he said, "please."

The boy's mother squeezed through the crowd and let out the beginning of a cry that disappeared back down her throat. She knelt beside Daddy. Prayer tumbled from her mouth. Daddy shouted *Somebody call an ambulance for Christ's sake.* He pleaded with me to get back in the Jeep. I just stood there, watching him and that poor whimpering mother cradle her child between them as if together they'd made him, all he was and ever would be, she giving him life and my father taking it and this dead boy peering into the space between them with just one eye, because to consider the short span of his life unflinching is too much for a boy to bear. I wondered if he could feel Daddy cradling him through his paling skin. I wondered if death takes all of you instantly, or by degrees.

A hand settled on my shoulder. Clay Tompkins, our assistant pastor, stood holding a brown grocery sack. He crouched to get his eyes level with my own. Golden hair framed his face, which was smooth and youthful, even to a boy who thought everyone over the age of 20 was old. "Come along, child," he said. He walked me to the sidewalk, sat me down on the curb, and handed me his grocery bag. He went to kneel beside Daddy and the dead boy and the boy's mother.

The boy's mother screamed. She hurled her scream upward past silent faces and downturned eyes. In the distance there was a siren. The cloying scent of peaches wafted up from Clay's grocery bag. I wondered why he'd bought so many. Did he have a mother who was going to bake him a pie? A woman was screaming in the street for Jesus, and the sirens were drawing close, and I wanted my mama.

Clay returned, eyes downcast. "C'mon, Daniel. Let's get you home."

"I threw up."

"It's okay, bud."

"I didn't get it on your peaches."

He stepped behind me, gripped me under the arms, and helped me stand.

"I want my Daddy." I was light as smoke. I was going to drift upward into the cloudless sky with that mother's screams.

From the street came the sound of a slap. A man said, "Why in hell d'you do that?" Another answered that he was trying to calm her down. There was scuffling, then a man was shoved onto the sidewalk a few feet away from us. He scrambled to keep from falling, straightened himself, looked over his shoulder, and walked quickly away. The boy's mother was weeping now, calling for Jesus from the depths of her throat. *Jesus, Jesus, Lord Jesus help my baby.*

I suppose you could say the rest of this story began with what happened next, though maybe you could say it began with what my father did in Vietnam, or with what happened to him as a boy, or with some deeper mystery rooted in the history of his people. Our people.

What happened next is that the dead boy stood up. His mother still crouched over the emptiness where he had lain, mourning the nothing in her lap. Daddy still shook his downcast head. But now that dead boy stood over them, as if he were just another member of the witnessing crowd. Only instead of looking at them like everyone else, he turned to regard me with his one good eye. You can't imagine, unless you've seen it for yourself, how a single eye can contain so much sorrow. He looked at me as if he expected me to say something. To justify myself. I felt my heart dissolve in my chest.

"Are you okay, bud?" Clay squeezed my arm. "Can you walk?"

I looked up at Clay, then back into the street. The boy was a corpse again, lying between his mother and my father.

"Come on, bud. This is no place to be."

"Daddy."

"He'll be along later."

"Is he all right?"

Clay thought I was asking about the boy. "No, child. He isn't."

Mama stood on the bottom porch step with arms wrapped around herself. Clay walked me from his VW slowly, as if girding himself to tell her what happened, as if she hadn't already heard the news, as if half the town hadn't by now called the other half. Mama's eyes brimmed with tears. She pulled me to her chest.

"Did he see it?"

"Yes ma'am, I'm afraid so."

"Lord have mercy."

"It . . . it wasn't as bad to look at as you might think."

"Still." A quake ran through her body and into mine.

Our dog Bailey—*Beagle Bailey*, Daddy called him—pawed at my pants leg.

"Let's pray." Clay sounded mildly surprised when he said this, like he'd just remembered his profession. He cupped Mama's shoulder and the back of my head with his hands. He prayed for that dead boy and his family, for Daddy, for me. In the years to come, I would wonder if Clay prayed it wrong, like when Aaron's sons offered up strange fire to God. I would wonder if his prayer, instead of rising to heaven, slipped through a crack in the earth and tumbled down into hell. If it was demons, rather than God, who answered, slithering upward to afflict that dead boy's earth-creeping spirit and my unraveling father and me.

Daddy told me once: "History's not written until the dead have their say." We wrote some history in the coming years, the dead and me. Understanding them was not the power I wanted, but it was the one I received.

And that Army duffel in his Jeep, the one I imagined once carried my father's weapons of war? Ten years later I would shoulder my own and realize that a soldier's duffel holds mostly food, clean socks, and letters from his mama. But between the day we killed that boy and the day my own death summoned my father's wraith, I would come to understand that the man everyone else knew as Ray Waterson had no need of weapons. My father was the killing thing.

———

```
Interview with Chief William ("Little Will")
Holland Thomas of the Qualla Cherokee. Fa-
cility for the Mentally Disabled and Insane,
                Butner, N.C.
              June 14, 1887.

Q: Did the Qualla believe their burial grounds
were sacred?

A: You have so many questions about the dead.
How can I help you see? To us, every living
being is holy. Do you understand? This means
every place a person dies becomes holy. See?
Where they fall is holy ground. And by us, I
mean the Cherokee, and many human beings be-
sides. The people of my heart, is what I mean,
not the people to whom I was born -- though my
white mother and father loved God as much as
any Cherokee.

Q: What did it mean, that the places where
they fell became holy?

A: Why, it meant we buried them where they
died. My friend Little Moon fell taking a
deer, just as his father before him. On the
very same hillside, can you believe that? On
the very same hill. So we buried him there,
beside the bones of his father. And we believe
Little Moon and his father had many great
hunts after. Fools Cree -- the great warrior
about whom I have already spoken to you --
he collapsed while speaking his peace in the
meeting house in Paint Town. So we pulled up
the boards and buried him. And how many fell
at Baptist Gap, and at Cedar Creek, fighting
the Yankees? So many. So many.

Q: You didn't bury your dead in graveyards?
```

A: (Laughs.) Goodness, no. What truck do the dead have with one another? Do they join a different tribe in death? Do they leave their families, their mothers and fathers, their children, after they have passed over? No. Of course not. They are still bound to their people. And so we bury them where they fall. And sometimes . . . because they are so close, they forget that they are dead.

Q: What do you mean, "they forget"?

A: (A long pause.) They rise. They rise and move among us.

Q: You're saying the dead come back?

A: (Laughs, then begins to weep.) Yes. Yes. Even a white man knows, in his inner heart, that the dead are not nearly so gone as he might wish.

———————

The morning of the funeral, Mama dragged me into the upstairs bathroom and took a washcloth to my neck, my mouth, the backs of my ears. She peered into my face as she scrubbed, like she'd lost something behind my eyes. Daddy stood behind us knotting his worn tie. He'd trimmed his beard and slicked back his hair. Lines spread from his eyes' corners like runnels gouging a riverbank. He noticed me watching him in the mirror and left the bathroom.

Mama knotted my tie, though I knew how. "Your breakfast is on the table," she said. In the kitchen, a bowl of scrambled eggs waited on the table across from Daddy, who sat still as stone, eyes on his mug of coffee. He'd scarcely looked at me since killing the boy. I slid onto my chair. I felt like I had on that curb, seeing the dead boy rise. Like I occupied a body that wasn't mine. My church shoes thumped against the table legs, causing the surface of Daddy's coffee to tremble. He stared at his untouched cup and winced at the clatter of Mama's heels. She entered the kitchen, sighed at my uneaten breakfast, and carried my bowl to the sink. "Ray," she said, "we should get going."

Daddy gripped his cup, his gaze on the tabletop.

"Ray." Mama turned from the sink. Her voice lowered. "Ray?"

"We're not going."

My legs jerked when he said it, though his voice was thinner and softer now than hers.

"Ray, we talked about this."

"No, *you* talked about it."

"You're already dressed."

Daddy stood. "I killed their son. Those people don't want me there." He glanced at me. "They don't want any Watersons there."

Mama stepped closer and jabbed his chest with her finger. "It was an accident. How will it look if we aren't there?"

"I don't give a good goddamn how it looks, Lee Ann."

Mama began to speak, but bit her lip instead. She turned to me. "Daniel."

"I'm not going if Daddy isn't."

Mama's eyes flashed like green lightning. "You'll get your behind up from that chair right this instant is what you'll do."

"Goddamn it, Lee Ann, you can't take our living child to watch them bury their dead one."

Mama shook her head. "All those medals in your drawer don't mean a thing if you can't muster the courage to go pay your respects to that child's family."

Daddy sat back down before his coffee cup. He gripped it so tightly I feared he might shatter it. Mama looked from one to the other of us. "Cowards," she hissed. She snatched up her purse and stomped out the front door. Outside was the slam of our truck door and its engine firing and the rumble as it tore down the driveway.

I waited for some words from Daddy. *She'll calm down by the time she's back. You know her storms blow over quick.* He eyed his cooling coffee. He was poised at the edge of an unfathomable chasm, and I feared by moving I might tip him into it. When the last wisp of steam had risen from his mug, Daddy stood and walked out the front door. I waited for the sound of his Jeep engine. Was he going to the funeral after all? Did he expect me to follow?

I heard a *thwack*, and through the window over the kitchen sink I saw Daddy, still in his tie, had split a cedar log by the woodpile. He stood up another on our oak-stump chopping block, assayed his distance, and brought down his ax. Two rose-colored cedar lengths tumbled off the stump. He split another log from the pile, then another.

When Mama came home, she didn't bother to change, she just busied herself in the kitchen. Daddy came in soon after. His tie was askew, his white shirt soaked through. Mama stepped aside for him to wash his hands in the sink. He sat in his chair and gulped cold coffee.

Mama retrieved the towel from where he left it crumpled on the table and used it on a pot that was already dry.

"How was it?"

Mama shook her head.

Daddy turned to look at her. "Lee Ann?" He stood and took her into his arms. She rested her forehead against his chest. "The devil could make hell out of nothing but children's funerals," she whispered, "and it would be plenty."

"I'm sorry, sugar."

She closed her eyes, her face pinched. "And the sound that poor woman made when they lowered her baby in the ground . . . ."

Daddy stroked her hair. "Hush."

I left my father holding my quietly weeping mother in the kitchen and slipped down the hall to the back porch. Bailey huffed, scrambled up from where he lay, and got on my heels as I walked into the woods. I didn't know what drew me to the river, only that I should go. The banks of the Crow nearest our house were rounded, clay gouged by runnels, but Bailey and I knew the best ways down. Soon we stood by water churned brown from recent rain. I picked up a rock and threw it nearly to the river's midpoint. I prowled the bank for good throwing rocks and hurled them at the Crow.

My scalp got a feeling like it was crawling with honeybees, even before Bailey growled. He was looking across the river, his hackles up. Directly across from us, amidst the trees growing close to the river on the far shore, was the dead boy. He stood silent and pale in his dark funeral suit. Bailey began to howl. I had to resist a sudden compulsion to dive into the river and swim across. Would the dead boy help me ashore, or hold my head underwater? Bailey elicited howls from dogs upriver. When I took my eyes from the dead boy, I realized Bailey wasn't howling at him. He was howling at me.

Mama's voice came through the woods, calling my name. I turned from the river and ran. Bailey scrambled up the bank and followed with all the speed his short legs could muster. We ran toward my mother and home. Only later that night, in my bed, did it occur to me that I might have shown the dead boy the way.

———

I had known Bobby Doyle by sight but little else, except that he was a boy who played kickball in the schoolyard, who carried a Snoopy lunch box, whose mother covered his schoolbooks with grocery-bag paper. Many things had made him the boy who was Bobby Doyle, but he'd run into the street without looking, so the only remaining truth about Bobby was that he lay in a box under six feet of clotted earth in a graveyard east of town, and his mother and father and brother, his Sunday School classmates and best friend, his grandmother and teachers and preacher—none of them would ever hear his voice again.

By the first day of school, everyone in fourth grade had heard. I knew by how kids stared on the school bus, how they whispered his name. They didn't look at me as if I'd killed Bobby Doyle, but they didn't look at me like I was innocent, either. Children talk about many things on the first day back to school, but all I heard was the dead boy's name on the bus and in the hallways, two grievous words lurking behind the squeak of rubber soles on linoleum, the flat thunder of locker doors: *Bobby Doyle.*

"Was there blood all over the street?" My friend Calvin asked this as he slid behind the desk next to mine. His strawberry blond hair was lightened after two weeks at Topsail with his family, his freckles prominent. Despite having a summer to grow, he was still the smallest kid in our class. In most things Calvin was shrewd and even skeptical, but anything involving death filled him dreadful curiosity. Calvin and I were going to be Marines. We were going to fight wars and win medals stamped with *Military Merit.*

I could feel the other children listening. "Hardly any," I said. Our teacher, Mrs. Stuart, was talking to another teacher outside our classroom door. She shook her head, lips pressed tightly together, then looked directly at me. I traced my fingertip along my desk's pencil groove, lifted it to my nose, smelled metal.

"My mama said it was blood everywhere," announced Mary Taylor, her voice flat and authoritative. Heat flooded my face as the kids nearby murmured a collective *Oooo.* I was going to tell her Bobby Doyle hadn't bled that much because my Daddy nearly stomped his brake through the floorboard, so badly had he wanted to miss that bullet of a boy. But Mrs. Stuart breezed in, wearing a smile and filling the classroom with a cheerfulness like thick perfume. The rest of the morning was times tables and long division, in the midst of which Calvin slipped me a note: *MARY TAYLORS MAMA HAS A BIG FAT ASS.*

At recess Calvin and I went to the tall black oak at the playground's edge and dug marbles from our pockets. From behind us came screams and squeals, but under our tree there was only the soft click of a bumblebee tapping its prey, the dull thump of errant cat's eyes striking oak roots. Branches swayed and creaked as the leaves rustled. In our solitude we didn't notice the older boys draw near.

"Stand up, shithead. Broadus Doyle is my friend." Daryl Ledbetter was talking about Bobby Doyle's older brother. Daryl was a seventh-grader with a wide, mottled face, thick arms, and a posse of stupid-looking boys. "Your daddy's going to jail," one of them added.

"No he ain't," said Calvin. He pointed at Daryl. "And your daddy's crooked as a dog's hind leg." Calvin's father owned the Red and White and a farm supply store, and Calvin paid attention when he talked business.

Daryl ignored Calvin and kept his squinty eyes trained on me. "Broadus and me's best friends. Stand up." Calvin told Daryl to shove it up his ass. One of Daryl's friends warned him to shut his mouth or else he'd get some too. "Your daddy's a murderer," Daryl said to me.

I stuffed marbles into my pocket as I stood.

"I'm gonna beat your ass," he said, "and then my daddy's gonna beat your daddy's ass."

I lit into Daryl Ledbetter like he was the dead boy himself. From the corner of my eye I saw Calvin wrapped around a bigger kid's leg, mouth wide open, trying to bite a chunk out of his thigh. The kid pressed his hands against Calvin's forehead and shouted for help. Then all I saw was Daryl's meaty fists. It was over so quickly that none of the teachers noticed from where they sheltered under the school's awning. Daryl left me lying beside a gnarled root with my face on fire. He and the others strolled away, laughing. They had taken Calvin by his arms and legs and chucked him down a slope beyond our tree. He stumbled up the hill, hotly swearing, twigs and dead grass in his hair. "Don't you worry," he said when he got to where I lay. "One day we'll be bigger."

That night at supper, Mama and Daddy didn't notice the angry red streak beside my eye. I sat across from Mama, whose eyes were on Daddy, whose eyes were on the empty chair across from him. They uttered terse sentences about the weather, about what to plant in our fall garden. We scraped forks across our plates and sipped iced tea and pretended that as the living moved on, the dead would recede from memory.

*I went to the back cause the vireos was set thick on that
fence. Set upright and sideways and upside-down and*

pecking blackberries, watching with their red eyes when I passed that fence you can't hardly see in summer for the vines winded round it. With their red eyes watching, pecking at berries and bugs on the berries cause I guess it's all like salad to them the berries and the bugs, and they was singing back and forth like in Mother Watts's church and I walked maybe long as a football field before the fence was empty and then a little past that the blackberries started up again. Like with degradation only instead of blacks and whites it was birds and boys and maybe I was the colored this time even though Mother Watts says it don't matter what color I am, even if some say I ain't white on account of my skin being browner than theirs, but this time I was the one walking to the back of the fence like a black boy in degradation but the berries there was just as fat and maybe a little buggier then the front of the field, but I'm always hungry and the bugs is small and most come off when you blow em. The Harbor House feeds you but it's always a little less than makes you full. I'm only seven but Mother Watts says I'm in a grow spurt so I'm getting bigger and they don't know where I'll stop.

So I was just walking slow grazing on blackberries but then the Shiver went through me and then it was a shadow and light inside the shadow, kind of like dark clouds right before a storm, but a pole of light stabs down and you can see whatever God's pointing to with it better than you could see when it was sunny out.

It was the Shiver went through me like it does sometimes.

You see this field now and it looks flat but with the Shiver and the light I saw it ain't straight, it kindly falls, but that's not the right word. It's just lower. Like when you go down in a holler and it's cooler and that's how you know. It was lower here and darker here and cooler here, though I don't guess you could tell. It was lower or maybe just closer to the underneath. And it was quiet.

The quiet is the worst and I'm not afraid to be alone but I hate the quiet.

And it was darker except for that light pointing to the place God wanted me to see. I wasn't scared even with the dark. The birds weren't scared neither, they just didn't want to be near it.

I felt the water under my feet like when you walk over a snake. You couldn't see it and my boots didn't get wet but it was there just like the dark and the cool and the shallow. So I followed the underneath water where it slithered to that well cap yonder broke in two like to be by lightning is what they say on account of the scorches. You couldn't see it if you didn't know to follow the undersnaking water, it was hid in tallgrass up to my chest even though I'm big for my age like I said.

I followed the hid water to the broke well cap and I tasted the water not in a cup or my hands I just tasted it the way a bad word tastes bitter. It was sour from the earth which is why I suppose the Doyles dug a new well and forgot about this one and let the grass grow up and didn't tend to a broke well cap you can't even see from their house not even I bet from that top window yonder. So I reckon they forgot and they didn't come back to mow or eat blackberries or nothing and so how would they know the smell wasn't just the water but that poor boy tangled down there in them pipes in the dark with his neck broke. Now the Sheriff is talking to Mr. Doyle like he ought to know something, but Mr. Doyle didn't even know he had a broke-cap well back here.

That poor boy.

I bet his mama misses him, if he has a mama, though not all of us do. Not all of us do and maybe he didn't, and maybe that's why God let him fall in there. Split that well cap and let him fall down in there so he could get up to heaven. Maybe his mama's there. I hope she's there, because what good is heaven if your mama ain't there?

Sometimes I wonder what is this in me that finds the shallow and the dark and the cool and feels sometimes like falling into a darkness like that well.

Sometimes I wish it wasn't in me.

When I tell Mother Watts she says hush, God has a plan. I know she's right because she knows more about God than even the preacher, but sometimes God has a plan for you to fall down a well. I don't want to fall into that room in my dreams, the room with no walls. I can't look at it, but I know it's there and even though it don't have walls I can feel it has a darkness like somehow the light still can't get in. I don't want to fall in there. I don't want to fall.

Granny Watts said they realized Daddy was anointed the first time he went up front at Mt. Olivet, the church she no longer attended, the church that had served the orphans at Harbor House before the state in its compassion dispersed them to foster homes. "I'd had no idea any of my Bible-reading had stuck," she told me. "It was such a remarkable thing, a child lining out."

Lining out is call-and-response hymn-singing people did in those peculiar little churches nestled amongst the hills and mountains above Hickory Shore. Still do to this day, in fact. It's eerie to the uninitiated, that unchorused blending of voices. Haunting, even unnerving. Yet they are among the gentlest church folk you'll ever meet.

"But there that boy went. His face had a glow, I guess you could say, because Brother Tillis got one look and stepped aside. And lo and behold, your Daddy had him a *voice*."

She paused, looked out the window of her kitchen where I was eating a tomato sandwich. She was a big woman, so that when she peered through one of her windows, as she was wont to do, it became inside like a cloud was passing overhead. She wasn't fat, just big. "He was like a prophet," she said. "Or . . . ." She shook her head.

"Granny, why doesn't he go to your church anymore? Why doesn't he line out?"

She shook her head again. "Last time he did was before his first deployment . . . to that place." She motioned with her chin, as if Vietnam were just outside her kitchen window. "He had on his uniform, which disturbed some folks. Most Old Regulars are pacifists, you see. Your daddy sang from the third Lamentation, if I recall correctly."

She closed her eyes. "Remember my affliction," she warbled, "and roaming. The wormwood and the gall. My soul still remembers, and sinks within me. This I recall to my mind. Therefore I have hope. Through the Lord's mercies we are not consumed."

I wondered how much of the Bible Granny Watts and Mama and Daddy carried about in their heads. I could scarcely retain *the Lord is my shepherd.*

"It is good," she sang, her voice a whisper now, "for a man to bear the yoke in his youth." She opened her eyes, put a trembling hand on my head. "And that was the last time your Daddy sang in church. I reckon that war burned it out of him. Or maybe he just lost the heart for it." She sighed. "Or, maybe, it lies in him still." She looked me in the eyes, as if searching for something. "It's alright not to have your father's gifts, child."

I nodded, but inside I burned with shame.

Later at home, while my parents were outside doing chores that I should be helping with, I took down my mother's Bible. One of her bookmarks was placed at Isaiah 61. I envisioned my father as a child, leading that small assembly of aging Old Regulars, crying out: "The Spirit of the Lord God is upon Me." And their croaking, undirected yet harmonious repetition, syllables stretched to savor each God-breathed word like manna: *The Spi – i – rit of the Lo – oo – ord Go – o – od is u – u – u – po – o – o – on Meeeeee. . .*

I read each verse aloud, quietly, repeating each line in the Old Regular sing-song. I imagined the people swaying, even my grandfather, who by then could no longer sing, but who came faithfully regardless, and who'd loved Daddy like a son. This was why Granny Watts didn't go to church anymore, because of Granddaddy's throat cancer. Singing was everything to the Old Regulars. She'd never said anything directly about it, but Granny always took the hurts God allowed more personally than most.

<hr />

Hickory Shore Messenger
August 25th, 1972

HICKORY SHORE, NC—Cantwell County Sheriff Charles Wilson has confirmed that the investigation into the August 15th vehicular death of 7 year-old Hickory Shore native Bobby Doyle is ongoing.

When asked whether his office anticipates filing charges against Ray Waterson, the driver of the vehicle that struck and killed Doyle, Wilson said, "At this stage we are still interviewing people and making determinations about which are reliable eyewitness accounts and which are hearsay. The challenge in a small town is figuring out who saw what, versus who heard what."

Members of the Doyle family could not be reached for comment. Other local citizens, however, are calling for the State Highway Patrol to investigate. "Everybody knows Sheriff Wilson admires Ray Waterson's military service," said one person who asked to go unnamed. "Just like everybody knows Ray Waterson used to live on the wild side. We need law enforcement who can come in here and run an impartial investigation into whether his driving was impaired."

A source inside the Cantwell Sheriff's Office confirmed that no sobriety test was administered at the scene of the accident.

—✕—

I suppose it was witching that got that boy killed, for if water didn't call to Daddy, he wouldn't have gotten it into his head to sink a well out back. People from all over called Daddy to find water, though some wouldn't because they didn't like how he did it. What he would do is take off his boots and walk in slow circles around the place where someone wanted water. After some minutes, or sometimes hours, a spirit would take hold of him. He'd traipse where it beckoned, hips shimmying and arms flailing like he was caught up in a pagan dance, until the spirit showed him where the sweet water vein lay. Then the electricity would leave him, and he'd stand straight and still. He'd stretch out his arms, like Jesus on the cross, or a sword poised to pierce the soil, and that's how you'd know.

The worst of it was the guttural speech, which contorted his lips and sounded to most people like gibberish. Those who'd known him when he was a boy, however, knew he could not only line out hymns with the Old Regulars, but that the Holy Spirit had gifted him with tongues. Mama told me it wasn't any angelic language my father shouted in Granny's church as a boy, it was just plain Cherokee. She knew this because a Cherokee visitor told my grandfather so. When Granddaddy Watts asked what it was my father the child-prophet was up there shouting, the visitor just shook his head. He never came back.

"Who taught Daddy Cherokee?" I'd asked Mama when she told me this. She said he probably learned it from his mother, before she abandoned him at Harbor House. But Granny Watts said that wasn't it at all. She said he'd picked it up in the spirit-world.

The first time I saw him witch was maybe three years before we killed the boy, over at the Floyd farm in Rowan County. Mr. Floyd told Daddy his grandson, who put no stock in water-witching, had given five hundred dollars to an N.C. State hydrology professor, who had brought a seismographic something-or-other to his farm, drilled seven holes and came up dry in all but one. "And that one," Mr. Floyd said, "was sour." He and Daddy chuckled as we stood in the middle of his pasture on a sunny afternoon. Mr. Floyd sauntered off to a pine tree at the edge of his field and squatted to eat a sandwich while Daddy went to work.

I tugged off my boots and followed Daddy, trembling in an effort to emulate his electric-shock dance, stomping like he did, mimicking his gibberish. This made Mr. Floyd laugh, but not unkindly. I leaped to place my feet inside the impressions left by Daddy's footfalls as we glided through arcs and abrupt turns, like bumblebees. My heart was filled up and I could have followed him forever.

Finally, at a dip in the earth so shallow you could feel but not see it, his back went straight as a pine, and he stood crucified. A wind blew hard against us but didn't stir the grass, nor Daddy's long hair, nor the leaves of hackberry and oak standing witness along the field's edge. It felt like the earth was accelerating on its axis. Standing in that spirit wind I turned my head toward Mr. Floyd, who'd fallen asleep with his back to his tree. A sound like the flick of a cigarette lighter penetrated the dreadful silence. Daddy's fingers pointed groundward, to where his knife shivered hilt-deep. "Here," he said, turning to face me. "*Here.*"

For maybe the first time in my life I could see something that my father could not: his dreadful, haunted, prophesying eyes. I knew then that the secrets of earth and water are more terrible than man is crafted to bear, and they creep up through fissured soil to lay hold of prophets. At the sight of those eyes, a warm stream snaked down my thigh and along the back of my calf. I felt ashamed and small beneath my father's gaze. He didn't notice; he stared through me like I was smoke. A shudder ran through his frame, then his eyes returned to the sunlit world.

I kept my distance while he set up his rig. As evening spread across the field, water bubbled from the uppermost pipe. Daddy held a tin cup beneath the tumbling water and tasted it. Then he offered a cupful to Mr. Floyd, who sniffed, tasted, and grinned. I ran over to stomp in the puddles, and we slung fresh-forged water in cold ropes and sheets, laughing and dodging. The water washed away my stink.

Daddy didn't go to Mama's church that often, so in a way, witching was his only immersion in the awful kind of holiness I imagine was more commonplace to the Old Testament prophets than to any of us, no matter what our hymns say about power and blood. I think the hillbilly church of his childhood had done that for him too. The church we went to—Mama and me and sometimes Daddy—was full of believers, but you never had to worry about running smack-dab into God there.

Mama and I went to church not long after school began, for the first time since Daddy killed the boy. The women gathered round as if it was Mama's son who was freshly buried. I imagined them congregating around my smooth casket, shaking their heads at the sin and death of a fallen world. I wondered if Bobby Doyle's family was in their church, or if the taste in their mouths was too bitter for hymn-singing.

We sat on a pew and I felt in the squeezes and cheek-pecks of Mama's friends a peculiar kind of love, the love of what one is not. I was not the killer named Ray Waterson. They loved me for being his son and Lee Ann Watts for being his wife. They loved us for being the people who bore the burden of being his kin. They loved us for being close to him without *being* him.

How I *wanted* to be him, though. How I yearned to be as he was. God help me, I still do.

———✦———

As we tumbled into fall, Mama became like someone who'd been startled more times than her constitution could bear. She snapped at me for shutting the refrigerator door too hard or not shutting the screen door all the way. She griped when I scraped my fork across the plate, or for clomping up the stairs too loudly. She would lay into me for getting on her every last nerve, then shift mid-sentence to fussing at Daddy for some uncompleted chore.

It used to be that Mama's fussing got him happily riled. He might call her a merciless witch of a taskmaster, say, inciting her to sharper remarks, which only provoked him to taunt her more. It was like watching a stormy sea from a house on a cliff, seeing the two of them go at it. You knew, even if you didn't understand the first thing about sailing, that there were deep currents underneath, an entire physics of aquatic motion that a boy could never comprehend. These days, however, Daddy just nodded at her complaints and even apologized before setting about whatever it was that she wanted done. She would watch him slump out of the house, a look of betrayal on her face.

While Mama frayed at the edges, Daddy seemed to wear at his center. Every movement was deliberate and fluid like before, but sometimes, if he didn't know anyone was watching, his face would slacken, and it was like his spirit was draining away, until you could almost see through him. My worn mother and center-frayed father became like two dancers who can't hear the music.

They canceled our newspaper subscription and wouldn't let me fetch mail from the mailbox. The library had newspapers, so sometimes

I would bicycle over there after school. I kept one of Daddy's razor blades wrapped in wax paper in my backpack, and if I found an article I wanted to keep, I would slice it out when no one was looking. That's how it began, I think, my fascination with hidden histories. By stealing stories about my father.

I didn't need newspapers to tell me people thought he was a murderer. "My mama says she can't wait for the election," Mary Taylor announced before class one morning. "So we can vote in a sheriff who does his job instead of letting people off cause they was in the Army." She walked the aisles between our desks, passing out bumper stickers for Sheriff Wilson's challenger.

I wanted to punch her right in her flapping lips, but I couldn't even imagine what Daddy would do to me for hitting a girl. Not to mention what Mama might do, and Granny Watts on top of that. The odds of slugging Mary Taylor and getting away with it were discouragingly low. When Mary got to Calvin's desk, he asked if her mama's ass needed two stickers. Eddie Gilchrist burst out laughing at that, and Mary gave him a punch on the arm. "I'm not surprised you and your friends are rude, Calvin Pruitt. Your daddy overcharges people every day."

"My daddy makes enough money charging your mama regular price for a case of pork rinds every week." Calvin always found the right words for any situation. And he didn't flinch when Mary walloped him with a fistful of bumper stickers.

━━━━━━

When the state police cruisers crept up our driveway that evening, Mama sent me to my room. I lay on the floor and listened to the officers' flat voices questioning Daddy in our kitchen. I couldn't make out what was being said. I wondered if they would try to arrest him. I couldn't imagine Daddy letting anyone handcuff him. My stomach became an anchor. I thought about that deadly recon Bowie on his belt, its handle of long, banded wood long ago fitted to his palm. Did they see it? Were they keeping their hands near their guns, just in case?

The litany of question and answer continued for a few minutes, then I heard the screen door's twang. I turned off the lamp and crept to my window. The officers walked to their cruisers, turned them around in our side yard, and drove away. I heard Daddy's boots on the porch below, then a grunt as he settled on the porch swing.

"You know who sent them, don't you?"

"We don't know that for sure, Ray."

"It was Ledbetter calling in a favor."

Fred Ledbetter was the father of the boy who'd beaten me up the first day of school. He was a contractor, a town councilman, and an elder in our church. He was as ugly as his ape of a boy. The swing chains creaked as my parents rocked.

"You know what he's after," Daddy said.

"The one doesn't have anything to do with the other. Even if it was him that sent them." A dog barked upriver, and Bailey huffed in response.

"Everything has to do with everything."

———————✂

Most of us think our dreams are more fascinating than they really are, so I'll say only this: in the weeks after we killed Bobby Doyle, each dream was the same, and this dream was a darkened staircase. I stood at the bottom of that staircase with feet shod in iron, and the world on every side was not our world, but a darkened mirror of our world. I stood at the base of that stairway and took in the darkness enshrouding its upper steps, and my heart overflowed with dread, for I knew the only way out of this darkened plane was up. Up into the room without walls.

I realize now that if I'd shared that dream with my father, it might have changed things. When you are a boy and you have a father who loves you, the space he inhabits is something holy. You become his shadow, and because he loves you, he allows you underfoot and against his skin even though you're clumsy and you talk too much. Sometimes he waits for you when you chase after him, and sometimes he seizes you up with his strong hands and sets you on his shoulders so that you can have a turn in the sun. All this is how he tells you that a man with no shadow isn't really there and that you make him fully there. In the months and years after we killed that boy, I had to search for my father. And often when I found him, it seemed there was no longer a place for me in his presence. As if he were covered in darkness, where shadows can't persist.

Sometime after school started, Daddy scrubbed the grill of his Jeep until it shined and drove into town to get those drill bits sharpened. Usually when he came to town on a school day, he would get me at lunchtime. We'd sit in the park and eat sandwiches Mama sent him with and I would tell him about things that are important in the

life of a boy. He would ask questions, and sometimes he would laugh
at parts of my stories I didn't find funny, but never in a way that made
me feel small or stupid.

On this day, though, I didn't even know he'd been to town until
I got home. When I asked where he was Mama rolled her eyes and
said he was drilling that useless well out back. "I don't need two men
getting nothing worthwhile done around here," she said, "so tend to
those chickens before they peck each other to pieces."

I ran down the hall to the back door.

"And don't forget to pick the butter beans I asked you to take
care of yesterday!"

Outside, the chickens gathered at their fence and squawked in
outrage when I bypassed them. At the edge of our back yard I slipped
through blackberry bushes picked clean by the birds and by me and
dashed across the sloping field that led to the back of our land. I crept
up to a stand of chokeberry through which I could see Daddy. It was
always a game, trying to sneak up on him, and well-nigh impossible,
no matter how quietly I moved, how carefully I placed my feet like
he'd tried to teach me. He always seemed to know when anything or
anyone approached. But not this time. Not me.

He sat on the battered tailgate of our pickup, a length of pipe in
one hand and a long gleaming bit in the other. Bailey snored beneath
the truck. A beer can sat beside Daddy and empties were scattered
across the ground. Mama didn't allow drinking in our house, not by
anyone, not even when her cousin down from Pennsylvania pulled a
champagne split from her luggage on New Year's Eve. Daddy threaded
the bit into the pipe's end, then dropped the pipe to the ground and
examined his palms like a fortuneteller. With his head bowed and his
palms upturned, he reminded me of Mama when Reverend Hardison
would give the benediction in church. Most people just stood there
waiting for church to finally be over, but she always held out her
hands and bowed her head, like the preacher was about to hand her
baby Jesus himself.

"Shoulda stayed with your mama, you little son of a bitch."
Daddy's words were slow and heavy, and they pegged my heart to
the dirt where I lay. He guzzled the remains of his beer can, dropped
it on the grass, and reached for another. He looked about him, as if a
crowd were gathering. Peering through reddening chokeberry leaves
as the sun fell behind the pines, I could almost believe I saw them,
too. Daddy cursed his phantoms. He told them he was glad they were
dead. He said he was happy it was them and not him, happy to be

out here witching a well and drinking his beer. He shouted hoarsely that he wasn't sorry, that every goddamned one of them had had it coming, so they might as well get on back to hell where they belong.

He slid off the tailgate and waved his hands about like he was swiping away cobwebs. He muttered as he wrestled his drilling frame to the place where he intended to pierce the soil. When he was satisfied with its position, he ran a cord from the engine above the gantry to a generator in the truck bed. He clambered onto the bed, crouched, and yanked the generator's starter cord. It coughed and shivered to life. Bailey lurched awake and crawled from beneath the truck. He surveyed the situation, sniffed at an empty beer can, then slumped onto a nearby drift of leaves. The generator's growl filled the cooling air.

Daddy dropped back to the ground with a grunt and lifted the first piece of drill pipe, the one fitted with the machined bit that was as much a cause of that boy's death as anything. He locked the pipe into a joint beneath the gantry and thumbed a switch on the motor. The bit began a slow, ruthless rotation into the soil. Daddy retrieved another beer and sat on his toolbox to watch the violence.

From our separate places, Daddy and I listened to the generator's hum, the drill pipe squeaking in its frame, the hiss of an air hose forcing loosened dirt up the pipe to tumble at the feet of the rig. Daddy lit a cigarette and stared into the gathering dark. He was deathly still until the pipe attached to the bit was itself almost submerged. Then he stopped the motor, took another length of pipe from a pile in his truck, screwed this into the end of the first pipe, and flipped the motor switch back on. He guzzled more beer. He added pipe lengths as his drill ground past wet black soil, through clay and fragile shale, toward a thrumming subterranean artery that only he could sense.

"It was a place for men," he said, his voice like a rusted fender. "You shouldn't have expected different than what you got."

Through shadow and red-dappled light I could almost imagine I saw someone standing before him. No crowd now, just one person, a person smaller than him, yet somehow more powerful. A sensation came over me like the first time I'd seen him witch. I knew his shadowed face held now those witching eyes, which surveyed someone visible only to him—someone he pretended not to fear. He looked down at his half-empty beer can, then chucked it toward the chokeberry bush protecting me from his gaze. It slung ropes of beer before landing with a clump near my head. Foam oozed from its mouth. Daddy pressed his palms to his face and moaned. "Jesus Christ, what were you doing there?"

I didn't know if he was speaking to Bobby Doyle, to me, to himself, or to someone else entirely. What I do know is that a boy never forgets the sound of his father crying.

———×———

Hickory Shore Messenger
August 28th, 1972

WILKESBORO, NC — County officials say that after early structural challenges, the planned expansion of the Crow River Dam is back on schedule. A spokesman for the Crow River Watershed Authority says the expansion will raise the height of the dam eleven feet, and increase electricity output from its turbines to an estimated 120 megawatts. The 47 million-dollar expansion is expected to be completed by early 1975.

Concerns voiced by local environmentalists about down-river effects have been taken into account by project engineers, the spokesman added.

———×———

The night she told me how the Crow once tried to take me, Mama found me crying in front of the linen closet. I was getting fresh sheets because I'd wet my bed. She calmed me and remade my bed while I cleaned myself up in the bathroom. I was afraid Daddy would wake up and see me this way, but he was snoring hard in their bed. Outside was the dark silence that settles into the air before daybreak. As she settled me back into bed, Mama leaned close and searched my eyes. She pressed her hand to my cheek. "Daniel. What?"

Tears darted down my face as I tried to explain the nightmare about being held beneath dark water, of blood enveloping me like a storm cloud.

Mama nodded. "I guess everything that's happened. . . ." She glanced at the wall, in the direction of her bedroom, where Daddy had begun to turn and moan. "It's brought things back."

"What things?"

She looked at the small clock on my nightstand and sighed. "The three of us were down where you and your father like to fish. You were just four years old. Your daddy was home on leave, and even though there wasn't a thing on this property that didn't need fixing, he insisted on taking you fishing." Mama tried to sound annoyed, but she smiled as she said this. "You layabouts dawdled in the river with your poles, so I gave up on getting any work done and lay on a blanket in the sun."

I tried to conjure a memory of fishing with Daddy. He was probably knee-deep in the water with his long cane pole. I was likely holding the short red pole that now hung like a memento on our shed wall. I would have been too little for fly fishing, which meant I would have stayed on the bank, my eyes alternating between Daddy's fluid casts and my orange bobber.

"Your daddy liked that spot because the river bends there. The water slows and pools around the rocks." Mama made a curving motion with her hand. Her face darkened. "But that river is like a snake. Its deep places rise; its shallows deepen. Sometimes people try to wade it, and it rises before they're halfway across. Like it wants to swallow them." Mama shook her head. "We forgot that it can't be trusted. One second you were standing there, the next second, your little fishing pole was floating in the water, and you were gone."

It was as if Mama's words cracked open a sealed grave. I remembered the sight of Daddy's back where he'd stood on the outermost rocks, his arms whipping his line overhead, false casting to dry his fly, then setting it like a feather atop a swirling pool. I remembered stepping from the bank to a rock shelf, then to another, working my way toward the deeper water. I'd lifted my rod overhead in an imitation of Daddy, but when I waved my rod and released my line, it didn't glide through the air like a spider flying on his strand of silk, it whipped about and snagged an overhanging branch. I'd tried to tug it free, leaning into the effort until my leader snapped, toppling me into a deep pool between the rocks. End over end, a slow somersault through the water. I remembered the river's rush, thrumming in time with the blood behind my eardrums. I remembered the sudden terror as I saw my fishing rod floating overhead. I remembered knowing that something in that crevice had been waiting.

My leg, Mama said, had gotten wedged in a mass of sunken branches. I remembered straining to break free and clamping a hand over my mouth, because I could sense how badly the river wanted in. Down into the warm dark of my lungs. A burning had begun to spread through my chest, then the sky had gone dark. I remembered it all now. It was that darkening sky, more than the breathlessness or even the grip on my ankle, that had filled me with terror in my nightmare.

That darkness, Mama explained, was my father. Neither of them had seen me go in, but they'd both known instantly that the Crow had me. "I went slipping about on the rocks," she said, "but I was looking too close to where you'd *been*, rather than thinking about where a troublesome boy was like to *be*. Meantime there went your father, prancing across those rocks, shimmying and shaking like a shaman, and I thought to myself: *Lord have mercy we do not have time for this man's voodoo nonsense.* I was about to shout at him to *do* something, but he looked at me and . . . ." Mama glanced at the wall separating us from him. "His eyes . . . ."

The witching eyes. In his spirit Daddy had choked that river like a snake in his fist, until it confessed to him where it was hiding me. When the vision had settled on him, he'd turned, run across a rock shelf, and cast himself boots-first into the crevasse that was becoming my tomb. I remembered the violence of his plunge, his fury, how my leg shook as he tore at the branches. How he seized my face, sealed his lips over my mouth and nose, and blew air into my lungs. The life my father breathed into me tasted of cigarettes and cherry soda.

Then a glint of light, and he dropped into the darkness. More ferocious tugging, and I felt my pants leg peel away. A cloud of blood. His strong arms around me. Sunlight and precious air.

"We thought you were dead," my mother told me. "I was so *angry* with the Lord. 'How dare you?' I said to him. 'How dare you take this one, too?'"

Mama's eyes were directed at the ceiling. She was thinking about my older sister, Sarah, buried behind our house beneath a redbud Daddy planted over her grave. Granny Watts told me once that Mama poured breast milk on the grave, in the weeks after Sarah's passing. It's why the redbud rooted so strong, she said.

"So your daddy laid you out on that river bank and blew air into your lungs, and he spoke whatever heathenish spell the spirit had given him. Then your eyes popped open, and you asked him where he was hiding the cherry soda." She laughed.

"He poked you in the calf slicing away your pants leg," Mama said, "but most of that blood in the water came from your father. He sliced two fingers to the bone cutting you free. He would have stayed down there to the last." She frowned, her eyes now on something outside my darkened window. "I would have had to bury you both," she said. "My whole heart, beneath that redbud." She kissed my forehead.

I pressed my fingertip into the gouge in my calf. I wondered if other oddities about me had stories behind them. "Mama?"

"Yes, child."

"Will I ever be able to witch like Daddy?"

Her face hardened. "That's his burden. Not yours." She pulled the hem of my sheet up to my chin. "Now get to sleep." She rose, turned out the lamp, and returned to Daddy where he writhed in their bed.

I lay in the dark of my room, imagination afire. I conjured an image of Daddy standing on the rocks, arms outstretched, interrogating creation until it revealed its secrets. I fell asleep awash in the memories of a blood cloud, of water drawn from the earth's depths, and within these, the awful, haunted eyes of my father. I woke in the morning with a question I dared not ask my mother: That spirit who'd guided him—had it come from above, or below?

———⌇———

That October my birthday fell on a Saturday, and Calvin pedaled up the driveway late that morning. Nobody had invited him, he just showed up the same way I darkened the Pruitt doorway on his birthdays. He dropped his bike in the yard, though he knew my mother hated that, and grinned as he dug a sack of marbles from his pocket. "There's bumblebees in there, and steelies." He poked a clear blue jumbo. "I'll probably win that one right back from you."

"Okay, Mister Big Talk."

He slapped me on the back, a habit he'd acquired from his father. "That's a long damn bike ride. Your mama make lemonade?"

"Probably."

Calvin started toward the house, glanced over his shoulder, and returned to prop his bike on its kickstand beside our porch. He saluted me as he went up the steps. I heard Daddy's ebullient welcome, Mama's slightly clipped *hello*. Daddy asked if he'd brought his fiddle. I knew he was pumping Calvin's arm up and down in an exaggerated handshake.

Tracks from the state police cruisers still marred our side yard. Our house was haint blue, just like my grandmother's. Mostly you find this on porch ceilings, to trick the spirits into believing it's a sky that they should float into and through, rather than tarry on one's doorstep. Some old-timers hold that spirits, unable to pass through water, won't enter a haint-blue house. I surveyed our peeling and faded cladding and thought of the dead boy on the far bank of the Crow. Would water bind such as him?

Someone opened a window, causing the cowboy-print curtain in my bedroom to press against the screen before falling back into shadow. I told myself there were no spirits here. The dogwood tree at the corner of our porch, the shed beside our house, the barn and garden behind, the fields and pond beyond them—all were unhaunted and as they should be.

I heard the pop of gravel and turned to see Granny Watts in her battered green Monte Carlo that creaked as it slumped through the driveway ruts. She honked ten times when she saw me. She laid on that last one, so that Mama came out onto the front porch and put her entire body into a dramatic roll of her eyes. Granny fought free of her car, which was reluctant to part with her wide wicker sun hat. She was tall for an old woman—or any woman, for that matter. She had a square face, and long hair that remained blacker than gray, despite her age. Her eyes were the same green as my mother's. Those two squaring off was like a lightning storm.

Granny shut her car door with a grunt and a curse, lit a Lucky Strike, and wedged it into the corner of her mouth. Her floral-patterned house dress billowed in the breeze. She squinted through the smoke and extended her thick arms. "How's my birthday baby?"

"Good," I said. I sank into her embrace. She smelled of tobacco and liniment.

She hugged me so fiercely my spine popped. "Good? You ain't just good! You're *Ten. Years. Old!*" Each word bore with it a bone-crushing squeeze. "It's double-digits from here on out." She groaned as she stood straight, her veined hand moving instinctively to her lower back. "You'll pray you never reach triple-digits, trust me."

"How old are you, Granny?"

"Old as my tongue and a little older than my teeth. Now help an old woman carry your presents into the house before I give you the first switching of your new decade."

Mama served pimento-cheese sandwiches with homemade pickles because this was my favorite. Granny told stories from Daddy's days in the Harbor House orphanage. In all her stories about Daddy, he was either making mischief or risking his life or both, and she grinned so widely while telling them that I thought her dentures might drop into her lemonade.

"Good God, Mama, don't give these boys any ideas."

Granny put her trembling hand on my head. "He's not near as much trouble as this wild Indian you married."

Daddy's eyes shone. I wondered if Mama could see that. Of course she could. The liquor was like medicine, I told myself. Just a bit of medicine to help him through. Surely Mama could understand that. But did she know about his weeping by the well he'd dug, and his rages against an invisible gathered host? Did she believe house paint could keep them all at bay?

Mama snapped at her mother to stop encouraging Waterson delinquency and stacked my presents on the table. Calvin made an effort to get in her good graces by helping clear plates. I forced myself to open the pliable packages first, the ones I knew bore underwear, socks, t-shirts. Next I turned to the ones I knew to be books. "A man who doesn't read," Granny Watts often said, "will answer to other men his entire life." She'd installed bookshelves at Harbor House herself, ones Granddaddy Watts had cut and sanded in his workshop. She'd also put up a *Fahrenheit 451* display in the town library. Granny Watts was militant about a great many things—gun rights, protecting the bees, keeping polluters away from the river, preserving native dialects, breastfeeding—but chief among them was reading. "I don't need debates," she would say every election year. "Just show me what the sonsofbitches have on their bookshelves."

This time I got three *Hardy Boys* and a book about the Revolutionary War. Next Granny reached under the table and retrieved a slender paper sack containing bottle rockets. Calvin and I voiced our deep approval. "Mama," my mother groaned.

"Ain't fair to bury a boy in books if he can't look forward to blowing some shit up."

"*Mama.*"

Granny Watts reached under the table again and retrieved a bundle of hazel switches tied with twine. She handed these to Mama. Granny liked to provide a fresh supply every birthday. Mama mostly used them as kindling, but my God, the remainder could make an impression on a boy.

More packages from my parents, meaning Mama. An Atlanta Braves cap. A camping flashlight. A set of airplane lithographs I'd seen her linger over in an antique shop. I took the time to run my fingers over them. Calvin murmured admiration, trying yet again to get on Mama's impossibly thin good side.

My final present was a small, paper-wrapped box. I'd shown my parents the Case XX Trapper, with knurled stag-bone handle and three-inch swoop blade, at the Woolworth's in Winston-Salem months ago. "Wouldn't you rather have this nice compass," Mama had asked at the time, "as often as you go roaming off into the woods?"

"Every boy wants a sturdy knife," Daddy had said, plainly and firmly. Mama had pressed her lips together and shaken her head. Short of my father's Recon Bowie, that Case knife was the most beautiful and dangerous thing I'd ever seen.

For my son. Love, Daddy. The note taped to the box was in my mother's handwriting. Calvin nudged my arm. I'd told him about the knife. I tore apart the paper and lifted the lid to reveal a compass. "Why Ray, what a nice gift!" Mama exclaimed.

Daddy stared at the thin curl of lemon in his glass. I knew he was just now remembering. He turned his eyes to Mama, as if trying to discern whether she'd remembered wrongly, or just done what she wanted despite him. He mumbled "Happy birthday, boy," and went into the living room. Mama started to call him back, so I asked if we could have cake, and Calvin seconded my motion, and then Granny Watts was bustling about, distributing plates and forks and trying not to drop too many cigarette ashes in the frosting.

Afterward, Calvin and I played marbles in my back yard. Calvin chattered about everything but the knife I didn't get. When I was sure nobody was looking from a window, I fished the compass from my back pocket, dropped it on the ground, and stomped it. It felt like a stone beneath my rubber sole. I brought down my heel again and felt its glass face splinter. I stomped again and again.

"Daniel?" Lucky Strike wafted through the air. "What's happened, baby?"

Calvin faced Granny Watts and slid his shoe over the shattered compass. "Yellowjacket." He ground the remains of the compass into the dirt. "We got it."

Granny Watts clucked her tongue as she crossed the yard. "Come here, child. Yellowjacket got me on my ankle-bone last week and I liked to die." She swiped at tears I didn't know were on my face. "Help me find my purse and we'll rub some chew in it." As she walked me to the house, Calvin gathered the remains of the compass and chucked it into the woods.

———⤙

Hickory Shore Messenger
November 22nd, 1972

CANTWELL COUNTY, NC—The Cantwell County Commission met in a lightly attended hearing yesterday evening to consider several business development proposals that officials say are promising signs the county can emerge from its economic slump.

... Also receiving unanimous approval was a proposal to change the zoning designation of a land parcel adjacent to the town of Hickory Shore, currently zoned residential, to mixed use.

Hickory Shore businessman Fred Ledbetter said during the hearing that this is an example of town-county cooperation in pursuit of much-needed economic development, and added that it has the potential to attract outside investment, as evidenced by the attendance of representatives from an unnamed commercial development firm who declined to be interviewed. . . .

———⤙

Whenever Granny Watts got animated about whatever conspiracy was foremost in her thoughts, she would lay hold of any nearby papers and thrust them before her, as if the electric bill or her *Reader's Digest* revealed the machinations of the piss-pot chain-gang lawyers and thieving political Judases she said were intent on packing her off to the pauper house in Winston. One Sunday supper in January she grabbed hold of an old insurance invoice and a couple of pages of the math homework I was trying to do on her cluttered coffee table. She insisted she'd seen three different men from the town council drive by her house this past week. "And you know there ain't nothing to see at the end of my road but an old railroad trestle."

Mama rolled her eyes. "Nobody is *taking* anything, Mama. At worst you'll be annexed and get yourself town water and sewer."

"*Annex* is what they used to do to each other over in Europe, and look how *that* turned out! I don't want the government touching my water!" Granny launched into her stock lecture about how fluoridation damages children's brains. She caught hold of my wrist just as

I was about to extricate my homework from her grasp. "That's one reason this child reads so well." She shook my arm so hard I thought she might dislocate my shoulder. "Because y'all are raising him on well water. And because of switchings."

Daddy clapped his hands and told Granny to testify. "You and me will make our stand right here, Mother! They'll need to call in the National Guard before they take nary a fence post!" He wasn't even drunk; he just liked to get her stirred up. Granny started in on the goddamned chain-gang lawyers and ass-kissing politicians and unchurched teenagers while she throttled my homework. "Preach it!" Daddy shouted.

Granny unleashed hellfire against interlopers and backbiters and low-down politician men as Mama came to the kitchen doorway and accused Daddy of trying to give her mother a stroke. He jumped up from the couch, wrapped an arm around Granny's wide waist, and cradled her shaking hand in his palm. He sprang from one foot to the other, his body quaking with a wild, joyful force that ended at his hands which held my grandmother. With those gentle hands he led her in a dance that was half Indian war stomp, half hillbilly waltz.

Mama burst into laughter even as she shouted at Daddy that old women have brittle bones. But her chest was full of hope, because Daddy hadn't taken a drink—so far as we knew—since Christmas. She crossed the room, took my hands, and made me dance a proper waltz with her. I tried to steer her close enough to Granny to snatch my homework, but Mama was not a woman easily led. The four of us whirled about Granny's den, singing a nonsensical chant about four-flushing lawyers and political fat cats until Granny remembered the pot roast.

On the ride home, I pretended to fall asleep between my parents. "There's no reason to annex unless they want something," Daddy said. "You know Fred Ledbetter's only reason for being on the town council is making money, not extending town services to the elderly."

"Nobody is going to push a widow woman out of the home her husband built."

"They'll make her out to be crazy. Senile. That's what they do to inconvenient people."

"You're being paranoid."

"That's what you said when the state troopers came out."

"Nobody's taking anything from anybody."

I could feel the tension vibrating through Daddy's body. I imagined his capacity for violence soaking into my skin. I imagined going to school the next day and beating the holy hell out of Daryl Ledbetter.

"There's just no gain in worrying," Mama said.

Daddy's resolve didn't last, and later that spring he sold three acres to Doctor Moore, who lived on the hill behind our land. Those acres held a dozen apple trees and a pond we'd stocked with bluegill and catfish. "Don't need the water," he said over supper. "Especially with a well back there now." He speared a chunk of ham and ran it through his mashed potatoes. He'd stayed at the edge of drunk that week, cleaning himself up during the day, sinking into a quiet stupor at night. I could feel the fury building inside Mama like a gathering storm. Daddy looked at her for a response. She eyed her plate. "We need the money," he said.

"We fish there," I said.

"Boy, you got a whole goddamned river for fishing."

"You need to think less about fishing," Mama snapped, "and more about schoolwork. Did you know I got a note from your teacher about that paper your grandmother helped you research? She said it was something she would expect to see from a professor in Chapel Hill. And she didn't mean it as a compliment."

"The catfish in the pond are sweeter than river cats," I said to my father.

"In fact, don't you have a math test tomorrow?"

"You can sneak over and fish the pond if you want," my father said.

"Does he know to leave in the barrels we sunk for minnows?"

"Young man, since you seem so uninterested in supper," Mama said, "why don't you get upstairs and study right now?"

"Does he know it'll drain off if he lets the slope get rutted?"

"Daniel."

"We need the money," Daddy carried his half-finished plate to the sink.

"*Now*, Daniel."

I pictured Doctor Moore and his sons standing by our pond, casting lines, reeling in our fish. "I'll not ask again, Daniel." Mama stood with her back to me and stretched plastic wrap across the remains of her baked ham. I heard Daddy turn on the TV in the living room.

I knew he wasn't watching it; he was staring at his upturned palms. Mama shoved leftovers into the refrigerator with a clatter. "*Daniel.*"

I stomped up the stairs, imagining Doc Moore and his sons climbing the hillside to their white clapboard house, a cooler full of our fish borne like a coffin between them. I envisioned them scooping the glistening fish onto the grass, notching each below the fin, and stripping away silvered skin and miasmal guts with the precision of surgeons. I thought of my father pondering his unblessed hands in the blue-lit gloom.

When our house was darkened, I rose quietly and slipped on jeans and boots. I dropped my pocketknife that wasn't a Case XX Trapper into my pocket and felt its meager weight there. It would have to do. I crept over my windowsill, along a short roof span, and down the shaky trellis laden with honeysuckle vines that squeaked beneath my boot soles. I feared Daddy would hear. That something in him could sense my thundering heart.

I surveyed our yard, heard the wind incite the screen door to gently thump in its frame. Overhead came the creak of tree branches, the shiver of pine nettles. I dropped to the ground and crouched like an Army scout. I was unmoored, dangerous.

I darted across the sloped field behind our garden, giving the treacherous chickens a wide berth. I traversed the field where Daddy had set a red-handled pump over that well whose purpose eluded my mother and me. I passed the mound that I was certain, though my parents foreswore knowledge otherwise, was someone's grave.

Then I steeled myself and walked into the whispering cedars beyond. Dead brush snapped beneath my boots. Coming to the pond that was no longer ours, I stood on its small shore and listened to the water chuck against its red clay bank. It shimmered beneath the moon, its surface a wavering reflection of the sky.

Beyond the pond was a tree-covered slope that I climbed until I stood at the edge of Doctor Moore's yard. His gabled house, white in daytime, glowed a luminescent blue wherever the trees didn't shield it from the moon. His black Chevy pickup rested on an even, graveled drive. Behind this was his family's white Dodge station wagon, also blued in the moonlight.

I took out my small knife and extended its blade. Gravel kneaded my soles as I squatted beside the back tire of Doc Moore's truck. I pressed my knife point against its sidewall and leaned forward with all my weight. Nothing. I tightened my grip and stabbed. My knife shuddered to a halt and nearly sliced open my fingers as they skittered along its blade. I sawed at the tire wall, producing nothing but the sound of a faulty windshield wiper. The Case knife would have cut this damned tire to ribbons.

I spat out a quiet curse as I folded the knife and put it back in my pocket. I took a rock from the driveway and imagined Daddy's palm outstretched to receive a sheaf of twenties from Doc Moore. I hurled it at their house and dashed several steps towards the woods before realizing the *thwack* meant I'd missed every blessed window. I snatched up another rock and tried again. Another *thwack*. My third rock produced a satisfying shatter. I sprinted toward the woods and darkness, my skin afire. I was an Indian warrior.

A furious weight sent me sprawling across the grass. I thought it was a dog until it shouted "Daddy!" with a girl's voice. Her fists pummeled the side of my head, each strike punctuated with a shout for her father. I got to my knees and rolled her off, but as I tried to stand she brought me back down. "Daddy!" From the corner of my squinted eye I saw the porch light snap on.

Julie Moore was almost a foot shorter than me and a year behind in school. She was also surprisingly strong. She wrapped an arm around my throat and squeezed until my head felt like a balloon about to pop. I croaked that she was killing me as I crawled toward the woods with her on my back. She leaned backward to put more weight into the choking. I closed my eyes to keep them from popping out of my skull. Breathing began to take precedence over escape.

Someone dragged Julie from my back, and she howled at the intervention. A hand seized my arm and yanked me to my feet. "He did it! I saw him do it!" Julie tried to fight free of her older brother's grip. He was a sophomore in high school. Her other brother, a senior, was apparently a hard sleeper. "Nate, let me go! Daddy!"

Doc Moore had hold of my arm. He was tall and skinny, with thin, graying hair, and ears that protruded as if straining of their own accord to hear better. His Adam's apple shot up and down like a bobber when he talked. He wore a tattered robe, and his grip was like an iron shackle. He turned to consider the shattered window, backlit now. I could see Mrs. Moore's silhouette moving about inside. Doc Moore turned back to me. "That right, son?"

"You don't have to *ask* him Daddy! I told you I *saw* him!" With close-cut brown hair and an upturned nose that looked like she'd tried to run through a door, Julie resembled an agitated groundhog. She writhed against her brother's restraint. "Tell Nate to set me down!" She shot a heel at his shin.

"Kick me and I'll stuff you in the wood bin."

"Put me down!" She calmed her voice in an attempt to sound reasonable. "I'm not gonna whip him. I just want to watch Daddy do it."

"Daniel," Doc Moore said, "answer my question." I stared at his bare feet that were like two fish lying on the darkened grass. His voice grew firmer. "Own up to your actions."

"That pond is ours."

He sighed. "Nate, take Julie into the house and help your mother clean up."

"Whip him Daddy! I'll get a belt!"

Nate hefted Julie over his shoulder like a grain sack and walked to the house. She raised her head to regard her father with a mixture of betrayal and outrage. "Daddy!" She glared at me. "Wait till Monday, Daniel Waterson! I don't care if you *are* a fourth-grader!"

Doc Moore released my arm. I considered breaking for the trees, but he would only show up on our doorstep. What would Daddy think of my inept raid? I shivered in the night air.

"We have ourselves a problem, Daniel."

"Yes, sir."

"You feel like something was taken from you, I suppose."

I wanted to tell him that feeling had nothing to do with it. That if Bobby Doyle's parents had taught him to look both ways before crossing the street, my father would still be working, and we wouldn't need money.

Doc Moore crouched so we were eye-to-eye. "I know you want to protect what's yours, but I have to protect what's mine. You understand?"

I nodded and tried to look reformed.

"Way I see it, you owe me for one broken window, along with the two hours of sleep I'm going to lose by the time I get my household settled." He settled onto his haunches, calculating. "You know how to glaze a window?"

"No."

"Back when you thought you might get out of restitution, you called me *Sir*."

"No, *sir*."

"Keep eyeballing me that way, and we can have this discussion with your father."

"Yes, sir."

"You owe me one window pane, and the time to glaze it, and my aforementioned loss of much-needed slumber."

"How much do you want?"

"I'm not taking your money. You're going to work off your debt. Mrs. Moore has been after me to restart that vegetable garden lying fallow over there." He thrust his chin at a long rectangle of crusted sod beside his house. "You bust up that soil and get whatever it is she wants planted, and we'll call ourselves even. That sound like a reasonable settlement?"

It sounded like indentured servitude. I wondered whether a whipping wasn't a better bargain. But I envisioned Mama's face, were Doc Moore to sit at our kitchen table and tell her what I'd done. It would go even worse for me when she found out he'd offered me the chance to settle things like a man. Doc Moore peered at me with moonlit eyes. "Son, the world is hard on everybody. A man labors through it." He offered his hand. We shook.

He stood, groaning as he straightened his back. "Lord, I thought my nights of getting rousted by unruly boys were over." He looked down, as if surprised to see me still there. "Get on, now. You crept up here well enough; you can creep on back."

I started toward the trees.

"Daniel," he called after me. "I expect Saturdays will work best, don't you?"

I nodded without turning.

"Alright. We'll see you next week."

I stumbled down the hill, no longer concerned with being quiet. I pushed past branches that slapped my face and arms. I lumbered past the shimmering pond, across our back field, through our back yard, and up the trellis. Only here was I quiet again. Back in my room, I pried off my boots and placed my small, boyish knife on my bedside table.

A History of Land Grabs in Hickory Shore
By Daniel Waterson
4th grade, N.C. History
April ~~12ᵗʰ~~ 13ᵗʰ 1973

In school we learn songs like the one that goes "this land is your land this land is my land from California to the new York islands". I believe the man that wrote that song meant it to be good and I'm glad to live here in my town and in north Carolina but my grandmother is always saying you don't really love a place if your not able to tell the truth about it good bad and ugly. So here are some true things about Hickory Shore that I believe everyone should know. I learned these things at the town librbay not the school libray librery because the one in town has better books. I like Ms. Williams our school liberian and I know she does the best she can. I also learned them from the courthouse because my grandmother showed me how to get answers from the registerer of Deeds.

First, I would like to tell you about our town, Hickory Shore. We were built here in a crook of the Crow river because the river was how loggers would send down oaks and chestnut and yes hickory to get milled here. Then our millers would send the boards on wagons to winstonSalem and elsewheres around the state and even the country.

If you know where I live I live with my parents to the east of our town. I know its east because the sun rises in the east and you can look out mama's parlor and see the sun coming up over the trees down by where the river is closest to our house. My granny lives on the far other side of town witch is the west side. If you could fly over top of it you would see the river is like a upsidedown horse shoe and we are on the right side and granny is way over on the left and the town is in between and the bridge that leads to the highway is right where you would hold the horse shoe if you were wanting to throw it. but not if you were putting it on a horse which I have helped my daddy do.

Believe it or not our land and granny's used to be connected in one big stretch that this one rich tobacco farmer had long ago but he came on ruff times and

parceled it out is what the old-timers in the Esso say.
That is how its done in 'this land is my land this land
is your land" country.

If you look in the register of deads you will see
there were 26 property deels in Cantwell County which
is our county the year I was born which was in 1962. But
what you don't see becase they dont have records for it
is that the Pamlico Indians used to own this land and
farm it. The Tuscarora came along and killed most of them
and took the land because the river makes it so good for
hunting and fishing.

So then the tuscarora were in charge and they were
fierce and there were lots of them but then dutch and
also English white people came. They were very devious
and they got the Tuscarora tribes to fight each other
until all their chiefs were dead or enslaves. Then the
white settlers took the land and they were fierce also.
but then the wealthy merchants came over and they were
even more clever and meaner too. And they pretty soon by
hook and by crook took the land, and they put African and
Indian slaves to working on it.

Then after the civil War came the carpetbaggers and
they bossed the land for a while. But then the KKK aka
midnight riders drove them off and that might have been
fine if you don't like yankees. but they were cruel and
murderous also to freedmen which is what you call slaves
who had worked harder than anybody to deserve the land.
The sight of a black man working his own land enraged the
kkk worse even than yankees. Soon all that land was back
in the hands of white farmers and merchants who hired it
out to get worked but you never could get ahead if you
were one of the people working it no matter what they
told you. And a lot of black people got fed up and moved
down to iredell where things were easier but still hard
for a long time, and this is why you hardly see black
people in hickory Shore which most people don't even
seem to notice like how a fish doesn't know he's in water
until he's out of it.

In conclusion, if you go in the courthouse building
you can find the register of deads and the county clerk
office because hickory Shore is the county seat. If you
go there like I have you will see all these paintings
of mayors from all the way back to the civil war. One
of them, Silbey Taylor, stole so much land he got shot

down by who knows how many people. But they never sorted
out who ought to get what. Sometimes even when you put a
thief down you don't get back what got taken. RIght next
door to the courthouse is the sheriffs office where you
will see pictures of wanted felons. Sometimes i think the
only difference between the pictures in the courthouse
and the ones at the sheriffs is that some got caught, and
others got elected.

Monday at school I kept an eye out for Julie Moore. There would be
no winning a tussle—if you beat up a girl, everyone calls you a bully,
but if she beats you, then you might as well move to a different county
and change your name. The third-grade classrooms were around the
corner and down a hallway from ours. To us kids, that was like a
separate country. And yet suddenly there she was, creeping into view
as I bent over the water fountain, her eyes level with my own. She
grinned maliciously. "Been worrying about this moment?"

I wiped my chin and stood straight to emphasize my height
advantage. "Nope." A blue dress that might have looked nice on a
normal girl hung from her narrow shoulders like a sack on two nails.
A girl in a dress would be even worse to fight. She stood with hands
on hips, smiling to display her teeth in all their yellow malice. The
bottom ones had formed no consensus about which direction they
wanted to grow. She looked like a biter.

"Only reason I'm not tarring you right now," she said, "is because my mama said I'd be in trouble if I didn't behave like a lady."

I wasn't convinced she knew how to follow that instruction.

"Otherwise I'd stomp you in front of God and everybody." Julie
had a sharp, flat voice that always seemed a few decibels higher than
what the occasion called for. Some passing kids slowed, anticipating
a fight. Julie stood on tiptoes and leaned close. With her cloudy blue
eyes she glared at me from beneath the fringe of her soup-bowl haircut. "Sooner or later I'm liable to snap," she said. "And then you
won't know I'm coming until it's too late."

"I bet your breath will give you away."

A couple of kids laughed at that. Julie unthinkingly began to rub
a swatch of her dress between her thumb and forefinger. Her manner
of blinking was to mash her eyelids together at unpredictable intervals, like she had to remember to do it. She considered the laughing

kids from behind those malfunctioning eyelids. It occurred to me that maybe something was wrong with her. Like Special Education wrong. That would explain a lot. She returned her gaze to me, scowled, and kicked my shin with the hard rubber toe of her sneaker. I yelped, and she scurried back down the hall to the third-grade realm. She turned to regard me one last time, bared her teeth, and disappeared around the corner.

I went to work at Doc Moore's the Saturday after breaking his window. He looked me up and down when I arrived. "Work boots, good. Jeans, good. Did you bring gloves?"

I shook my head.

"Well, I'm sure we've got extras somewhere."

Their utility shed was set against the house, painted the same shade of white, with the same red-shingle roof. While Doc Moore rummaged inside, I looked from window to window. "Don't worry about Julie," Doc Moore said. He'd emerged from the shed with a hoe, a rake, and a pair of dirt-crusted gloves. "She's more bark than bite."

I wondered if she'd bitten someone. If that's why he put it that way. He led me to a stretch of clumped brown earth. "A tractor would till it faster, but I doubt my old Harvester has it left in her."

It wasn't fair, him taking our land when he couldn't even work the land he had.

"You know how to bust soil?" I lifted the hoe and attacked a fat dirt clod. "Fine. There's a mattock in the shed if anything needs persuasion. And there's gypsum, once you've got it workable. I'm headed to town, but Mrs. Moore knows our arrangement." He considered his wristwatch. "I reckon it's a fair Saturday's labor if you work till noon."

"I can't finish by then."

"There's another Saturday coming next week. And another after that."

I hacked another dirt clod. There were millions of them. Doc Moore drove off in his truck. I found a rhythm, hacking clumps of dirt intermingled with leaves, raking the remains flat, and repeating. A spring breeze blew over my neck and back. Maybe this wouldn't be so bad.

Something sharp bit my hip. Julie stood barefooted at the edge of the garden bed, clasping an armful of rocks to her belly. She palmed a particularly sharp-looking one and grinned with righteous malevolence. "For all they that take up the rock shall perish by the rock."

A screen door creaked open and slapped back into its frame. "I'm setting you a water pitcher over here," Mrs. Moore called. She eyed her daughter's back with suspicion. "Julie Moore, come away from that boy so he can work." Julie pinched her face at me and spilled her rocks onto the grass. She turned to face her mother. "I was just keeping him company."

"Then that would be the first sociable instinct you've shown yet, missy. Leave him be."

Julie stalked back into their house. I returned to my labor. Perhaps it was just because I was on guard now, but I felt eyes on me. Not just from the windows, but from the birch and maple bordering the garden. From the shadows.

That night I woke to weighted silence and knew the dead boy was out there. I went to my window and saw him standing just inside the woods beyond our yard. Wearing the black suit they'd buried him in, he comprised more darkness than visible flesh. And his eyes—my God, his eyes—were black as his suit, like eggs plucked from the damp nest of some unholy night creature. He gazed up at me. Wind blew through shivering dogwood and swaying pine, stirring everything but his clothes and hair. He said not a word, for there were none that could change his being dead, nor my being alive, nor the curse of seeing one another across this expanse.

It was silly that selling our pond made me angry when I'd outgrown it years ago. Daddy and I were fly fishermen, the rituals of which bound us even as life's other litanies dissolved. We needed ponds like chess grandmasters need pocketfuls of checkers.

Movies favor western fly fishing, with long rods and yards of line floating in golden sunlight above the fisherman where he reigns over a wide and unencumbered river. The rivers our people fish afford little room for showmanship. Narrowed and overhung, they demand craftiness if you want to keep your line intact. We use eight-foot rods and cast sideways more often than overhead. Daddy could land a fly wherever he divined the trout were lounging with mouths turned upstream. He didn't use a net, preferring to tail or gill them. The littlest he would cradle by the belly, turning their mouths to the oncoming water, gently moving them side to side to stimulate their gills, until they wiggled free.

Daddy detested nylon for its vulnerability to kinks—*memory*, he called it—so we used silk, just as Granddaddy Watts had. We would unreel it when we finished, dry it with a soft cloth, loop it into big loose coils, and hang it from pegs in our shed. While bait fishermen tossed their rods in corners, or hung them from nails, we disassembled ours with care. Our rituals of preparation and repair were almost as lengthy as the fishing itself. They were holy. They still are.

One morning we were casting upstream, in the river's turn, when Daddy called me over. I thought he was going to make me switch from the Gray Ghost I was stubbornly using because I liked the name, even though it was wrong for the light and the season. Instead he slung his cast, then fished into his pocket and held his hand out until I put my palm under it. "Here, boy." It was the Case Trapper knife. I gripped it tight and threw my arms around him. He wrapped the crook of his arm around the top of my head. "You're getting taller."

"Thank you, Daddy."

"Mind you don't drop it in the river. And don't take it to school. Used to be you could take a rifle. Nowadays they wet their pants if your pencil's too sharp."

"I won't."

"And goddammit, be careful like I showed you. That blade'll cut all the way to bone before you feel it."

"I will."

He looked down at me. Other men wore polarized sunglasses to fish, but not Daddy. I don't think anything could mediate what he saw. He considered me for a moment. "There's no need to go waving that around in your mama's face, you hear?"

"Yes, sir."

He tousled my hair. "Now give me some space. I know you snuck banana bread for breakfast, so take that bad luck back downstream." I moved away, grinning. It was funny how Daddy, seeing all he'd seen, believed bananas were bad luck for anglers. We fished the morning, moving upriver, and didn't catch a thing. It didn't matter; I was with my father on the river, each of us bearing our deadly knives, casting with skill and poise, even if the trout were too dumb to notice.

I didn't know how Daddy kept apprised of the growing threat to Granny's house, but there was a reliable correlation between my razoring articles from library newspapers and him chain-smoking on our porch swing. It seemed to me that this was when he most needed Mama's harsh rebukes, but instead she would go into a slow burn, with occasional explosions over my boots lying in the doorway, comic books spilled across my bedroom floor, my bathwater being too high when I knew full well that spring rains had oversaturated our septic field.

Whenever I snuck out that razor blade in the library, I felt like I was altering my family's trajectory. Now I realize you can scarcely see the arc of your history when you're upon it, let alone change its destination.

People in our church called McAllister the *Drinking Town.* Cantwell County had been dry for as long as anyone remembered, and the liquor business the next county over, across the Crow River, was the better for it. I'd never been to McAllister, though it wasn't far beyond where the river bordered our land to the east. Sometimes, by the riverbank, I could hear noises from McAllister. A dog's bark, a truck engine shifting gears, a strained shout that I imagined to be either the start of a fight, or the bloody end to one. Whenever we read about Sodom and Gomorrah in the Bible, I didn't picture cities in a distant desert, I envisioned McAllister.

Just as razoring a newspaper article seemed to push my parents into their separate corners, it drew Daddy's eyes to McAllister. He would eat whatever sweets we had in the house, and dump extra spoonfuls of sugar into his tea, and steal glances eastward. He'd linger late on our porch swing, cigarette smoke swirling about him like a wraith. Mama and I would become wraiths to him as well.

He kept a skiff shored in a stand of birch on the riverbank. I suppose it was faster than the roundabout drive to McAllister, but even a ten year-old child could tell he didn't row for expediency's sake. Crossing that river was its own ritual. Daddy crossed the Crow many times, but I remember him crossing it after the town council rezoned Granny's land because of what happened when I followed him. Because of the snake, and the story Mama told me later about Daddy and snakes.

I'd known he was going that day not just because he'd slouched on the porch swing late into the night before, but because there was an electricity that ran beneath his skin, like how the air feels before a lightning storm. It was a Saturday, so after I finished at Doctor

Moore's I meandered through my chores, my eyes on the path from our house to the river. When I saw him slip down it, I followed. I stayed well back, because of his unnatural ability to sense things. By the time I got to the birch stand, he was already well into the river, head bowed, bent-shouldered, rowing toward the shadowed trees on the far shore. His paddle gouged the dusky water as he glided away from me.

I was overcome with fear that he wouldn't come back from the other side, so I called to him. The river wanted to swallow my voice, but I knew he heard me because his back stiffened and his oar froze above the water. I called again, and he bent forward and cut the river with a fury, his oar slinging gouts of water that looked in the sunlight like handfuls of sapphires. He quickly reached the shore, dragged his skiff aground, and took the bank with long strides. When he was all but hidden among the birch and ironwood, he looked back at me. I couldn't make out his face, distant and shadowed as it was. Sometimes when I try to envision his face now, this is all I can conjure. Daddy scrambled up the bank and was gone.

Mama had warned me never to go to McAllister, but I knew the way. I dragged my bike from the shed and careened down our driveway, bent over the handlebars, resolved to pretend I didn't hear Mama if she called to me from the front porch. My legs became churning pistons once I reached the state road. I hurtled past tobacco fields and dense pine woods, filled with a sense of dread and freedom. I'd just begun to sweat when I reached a sign pointing to McAllister, across a blackened iron truss bridge that stretched over the Crow where it roared through the narrowed, rocky channel below. I crossed the bridge and pedaled past a cornfield, peering ahead for signs of the town. My ears strained to hear the sounds of saloon music, like what I'd heard in cowboy movies.

Eventually the cornfields gave way to mowed lawns. I passed neat brick ramblers, then rows of smaller shotgun houses, their porches bearing swings and potted plants. I didn't see any drunks lying about. A house with a primer-gray Chevelle on blocks in the driveway looked promisingly trashy, but as I passed, I saw a man with tucked-in shirt bent under its hood. His tools made soft clinks that carried through the still afternoon air.

The center of McAllister was inhabited by a brick church beneath a solemn steeple, a post office, a bank, offices for lawyers and insurers, a VFW post. Behind these were tin-roofed warehouses, a train depot, and a grocery store with evenly spaced signs announcing two cans of peas for the price of one, pork shoulders for twenty cents a pound, Double-Coupon Day. Cars were parked in parallel alongside the clean and unbroken sidewalks. I heard no clinking glasses, no pistol shots, no saloon pianos. From a butcher shop came the sound of paper tearing. Someone slammed a tailgate. A car glided past with a pebble lodged in its tread, tapping out a cadence on the cambered road.

Finally, a liquor store. A woman in pleated white skirt emerged, holding to her chest a brown bag with two bottlenecks poking from the top. A purse dangled from her forearm. She seated herself neatly in her car, buckled her seatbelt, and drove away. I didn't see Daddy anywhere. An old man in overalls ambled toward me on the sidewalk. "Excuse me," I said. "Where's the saloon?"

He evaluated me with sun-yellowed eyes. "Ain't you a mite young, cowboy?"

"I'm looking for someone."

"Ain't no saloon, nor a bar. Feeney's Diner yonder's got beer on tap. But not before supper." He squinted at me. "Where you from, boy?"

"Hickory Shore."

The old man assayed me with his farmer's eyes, a gaze that determines which seedlings get pulled, which younglings in a litter get put down. "Best get home, child." My bicycle chain creaked as I dropped onto the seat and pedaled away from him, down the street, back toward the road home. I passed evenly spaced cars, solid square buildings. I was stupid to have come here. A stupid boy.

I passed an alley down which Daddy walked, a brown bag cradled in his arm. I clamped down on my bike pedals and left a tire mark on the clean-swept street. A car horn brayed, a man shouted. Though I turned and pedaled toward the alley, I felt motionless, as if roots had thrust up from the asphalt and wrapped around my legs. I entered the alley as Daddy reached its far end and set off through a field of knee-high grass. By the time I reached the field, he was almost to the trees overlooking the descent to the Crow.

Grass whipped my legs and snapped in my bicycle spokes as I tore after him through the field. I wheezed his name as he disappeared down the bank. I pedaled faster, seized by a strange conviction that if I didn't reach him before he got in his boat, I would never be able to cross the river home. I didn't brake when I got to the trees; I hurtled forward as if to leap homeward over their secretive darkness, over even my father crouched beside his boat below, drinking from his brown-bagged bottle.

Midair I shrieked his name, and he recoiled like a skittish beast beside a waterhole. Leaves whipped my face, there was the sweetness of birch in my mouth, the crack of branches, and my bike fell away from me like a spent booster rocket. It seemed for an instant that my momentum might truly carry me over the river, but a branch that had no care for a boy's imagination slapped me to the ground, where I lay stunned. A rat snake longer than me slithered along my leg and onto my belly. I felt the weight of it, the reticulation of its skin. Its eyes were black like the dead boy's and I couldn't move.

Then Daddy was above me, speaking a word I didn't understand. His word was to that snake like a blast of frigid air, because it coiled back its neck as if he'd struck it. The snake considered my father with hatred and fear, then slithered into the underbrush.

"What are you doing here, boy?"

"Nothing."

"Are you hurt?"

I lay flat and considered his backlit and darkened face, and above that the swaying treetops. "I don't know."

He crouched beside me. "Does anything hurt?"

"Yeah."

"Well, what?"

"All of me."

Daddy surveyed what had been my trajectory. He helped me up. "You seem a bit wobbly, son."

"I couldn't tell if that was me or you."

Daddy chuckled. He took hold of my bike where it hung in a tangle of branches, its back wheel turning like a clock reversing itself. He tried to tug it free. "Lord-a-mercy. How fast were you going?"

"I don't know."

"Well what was your damn hurry?"

"I was afraid you'd leave me."

Daddy looked down at his mud-crusted boots and nodded. He yanked free my bike and crouched to examine it. "Front rim's bent. Your mama told you about coming here. I oughta make you walk it home." I nodded. "C'mon," he said. He leaned the bike into my hands, went back to his boat, and tucked his bottle under the rowing bench. He looked up at me. "Careful."

I maneuvered my bicycle down to him. He lifted it from my hands, and I sat on the forward thwart. Daddy lay my bike across the gunwales, gently, like a soul in our care. He shoved the boat into the water, climbed in, and took up his oar to ferry us homeward. Midway across, he lifted his oar from the water. The current broached the prow and pressed us downriver. "Do you feel that?" he asked. He stared upriver.

"Current's strong today."

"No, underneath."

"Underneath the boat?"

He put his palm to the water and closed his eyes.

"Daddy what is it?"

He shook his head, annoyance on his face. Then he opened his eyes and forced a smile. "Nothing. You know how I get sometimes." He took up his oar, righted our course, and rowed us home.

Some nights, even now, all these years later, I wish you had let the river carry us away from here, Daddy. Away from here, to the sea, to the sea and what lies beyond.

I don't care if Jimmy Bryson says girls can't play baseball I'm not getting my Sunday dress dirty proving him wrong. I can throw a ball further than most of the boys because Daddy taught me even though Mama told him a girl raking her arm cross her bosoms isn't ladylike. Daddy says ladylike is what you choose not to do, not what you can't do. Today I'm choosing to be a lady by not hitting Jimmy Bryson in the stomach with my fastball and making him wet his pants in front of the whole church. Instead me and Rosalie Taylor are gathering flowers.

Rosalie wants to look in the tallgrass beside the ballfield but I told her there isn't anything worth picking there but ragweed. I wish she'd stop complaining about her feet hurting. I told her take off your Sunday shoes like I did but she says she won't because they make her gingham dress look nicer and now I wish I'd come by myself.

Over here by the riverbank, Rosalie. Look at these here cardinal flowers. See now I told you. Right here at the top of the bank and we don't even have to get our shoes muddy down there.

Down there.

Down.

Oh mother mama mommy.

That boy, all swole up and white and that moccasin slithering across his belly and Rosalie asks me do I see that big ole snake and now her eyes are wide, so wide I see the pink red meat all round them, because she sees him too, that boy in the mud beneath the snake, and see how quick it shoots into the water when she screams. Her scream, her screaming, and my feet won't move, and here they come running from the ballfield, little boys and the big boys and now the daddies and the mamas about to knock the daddies over cause they hear a little girl screaming, scream-ing, screaming.

That boy with eyes open gone to white and skin so white not like cream but like the underside of a mushroom. Why are his eyes open and what can he see with eyes so faded?

"Did you know it was your father who cured me from my fear of snakes?" Mama lifted cooled bacon from a paper towel, layered it onto a plate beside scrambled eggs, and brought the plate to me at the kitchen table. Morning light poured in behind her through the window over the sink. There had been a rat snake curled in one of our hens' beds, digesting her eggs. It was my job to shoo away snakes, but I'd been afraid to get near it. I'd gone to Mama in my shame. She'd chased off the snake without chiding me, which made me feel worse.

I crunched a strip of bacon between my teeth. "How'd he do that?"

"When you talk with your mouth full, you look like an ingrate." Mama moved, as she spoke, through what she called the stations of her cross: stove, sink, refrigerator, table. "Well, I was wandering the woods down by the Watts family's stretch of the river, and I came upon a water moccasin. He was all curled up and reared back, mouth wide-open the way they do. One more step, and my foot would have landed right on him."

I shivered, but pretended I was just fidgeting on my chair. "Did you run?"

"I didn't run, I didn't walk, I didn't even back up. It was like I had no control over my own body. Then your father was there. 'It's afraid,' he said. Him appearing like that broke the spell, I guess you could say, and I was able to back up a step or so. The serpent lost interest in me and shifted its head to show your daddy its fangs. Like it knew what he intended."

"What did he intend?"

"He reached down, faster than a blink, and snatched it up by the tail. He held it out front of himself while it arched and hissed that awful sound moccasins make, snapping at him. But he just walked it away from me, calm as anything. Then he drew back his hand and whipped its head into the side of a tree."

"Did that kill it?"

"Oh yes. It hung twitching from his hand like an electrical wire that's come loose from the pole." Now it was Mama's turn to shiver. "He waited until the last bit of life quaked out of it, then he strung it along a willow branch, like he was putting up a strand of Christmas lights. 'Birds'll eat it,' he said. I asked him why he killed it, if it was just afraid, and he said he killed it because it had scared me. 'Now you see how easy it is to kill one, you needn't be scared anymore.'

"'I ain't picking up a durn snake,' I told him." Mama shrugged her shoulders. "I sounded like white trash when I was ornery. 'Then I'll do it for you,' he said. And that's the first time I fell in love with your father."

"*First* time?"

"Oh, I've fallen in love with that man more times than I can count. Wanted to brain him with a frying pan just as many."

I thought people fell in love and just got stuck that way.

Mama brought me more bacon. "You're lucky I'm feeding you at all, given how long those chickens were squawking before you got out there to tend them." Mama sat, a rarity in her kitchen. "When you're paired with someone, a thousand things can stir love. You glance at him, and it's like you've never really seen all the good of who he is, not until that moment." She rolled her eyes. "But there's also a thousand things can make you want to sink him in the river."

"It seems like with Daddy it's ten thousand things that make you mad at him."

Mama's green eyes flashed, and I braced myself for a tongue-lashing. Then she sighed. "Your father does have a way of inspiring the worst in me. But that kind of fury is only possible where love has taken root."

"So even when you feel mad at him, you still feel like you love him?"

"*Feel, feel, feel.* People tell themselves love is a feeling, Daniel, but it's a *decision.* Don't ever forget that." She stood and returned to the stove. "You wake up, and you *choose* to love. It's commitment that keeps your heart open to someone. Open to being surprised and overwhelmed by how much love's inside you. Even when you think there's nothing in them able to receive it." She cleared her throat to obscure the tremble in her voice and whacked her spatula on the edge of the frying pan. "At the very least, it keeps you from shooting him while he sits there like a big dumb bear, waiting for his supper."

"How old was Daddy when he killed that snake?"

"Twelve. Already as big as some men. And quick."

"Where did he come from?" I asked. "That day in the woods."

"From the trees. From the shadows."

"Did you hear him coming?" I already knew the answer, just as I knew my father could witch more than water.

"Nobody hears that man unless he wants to be heard."

"Because of his Indian blood?" I knew the answer to this, too.

The spoon in Mama's hand rasped across the skillet bottom as she gathered bacon fat. Daddy liked to say—in Mama's hearing—that Indian blood was why he and I tanned, while her people pinked up like piglets. Mama would hit him when he said this and declare that the women in her family were cream-skinned ladies, and that if she'd married a businessman or lawyer like her mother had wanted, she wouldn't be stuck here in the backwoods with a heathen witch-doctor.

I knew full-well that Granny Watts loved my father like the son she'd lost. Daddy would always get down on his knees regardless, whenever Mama lit into him about how she could have married up and be living in Charlotte with a poodle and servants. He would seize her hand, apologize for being such a miserable tramp, and kiss up her forearm with wet lovey-dovey noises until she slapped him for slobbering all over her creamy skin.

Daddy was half Cherokee, half Creek. He was some other things too—there was English blood in there, and Mama insisted there was a wild Welshman in his lineage, along with at least one runaway slave— but whenever I thought about his heritage—and mine—I considered just those two predominant lines, the Cherokee and the Creek. I'd read every book on them in the town library. The Cherokee were peacemakers. The Creek were killers. At least that's what I'd come to understand.

"You know the Cherokee only went to war," Mama said, in that mind-reading way of hers, "when they had no choice. They never let themselves be driven by blood lust like other tribes." Whenever I mentioned Daddy's Indian blood, Mama talked about the Cherokee half. He'd screamed in his sleep the night before. This was how he was when he was sobering back up. Long nights of nightmares. It made me wonder if alcohol is what kept the spirits tamped down.

Mama spooned a pillow of bacon fat and plopped it into a Butter-Nut coffee can. "After the Cherokee fought a battle," she said, "they purified themselves. Because they believed bloodshed made them unclean." She paused, a dollop of bacon fat clinging to her spoon, and looked directly at me. "Did you know your daddy's great-grandfather was a full-blooded Cherokee priest?"

I shook my head.

"I met him once. We drove down to Oklahoma, not long after getting married." A chuckle bubbled from her throat. "That was your daddy's idea of a honeymoon—drive a thousand miles in a rusty pick-up."

"How'd he know where to look?" Daddy had been raised in the orphanage Granny Watts tended. I thought he didn't know any blood kin.

"Oh, when his mother dropped him on the doorstep of mama's church, she left him with nothing but raggedy clothes and her family Bible in a little brown sack. Somebody had inked their little shrub of a family tree inside the cover."

Mama prided her family on knowing themselves all the way back to peat-stained clansmen huddled in the caves of northern Scotland.

"I reckon that Bible hadn't done her much good. So your daddy had it, and when he was older, he went down the list of birthplaces inside its cover, calling their town halls. He had to use Mama's phone, and didn't any of us know what he was up to until Daddy got the bill. When Ray told him what the charges were for, Daddy didn't want to take his money. But your father is so proud." She shook her head. "He stood in my father's living room, so tall and handsome, that raggedy hair of his finally shaved down. He was on leave, about to redeploy. . . ." Her face darkened. She rapped her spoon on the can's edge. "Those calls narrowed it down, but a lot of letters had to be sent. County clerks, Indian reservation offices, hospitals. He went through a treasury of stamps, your father. His great granddaddy was the only one he could find." She scraped the skillet under steaming water.

"What did he look like?"

Mama peered through the window over the sink. Water dripped from her red hands. "He was like your father," she said. "Quiet around people he didn't know. A look on his face that makes people who don't know him think he's mad at them. His eyes were clearest blue, like the sky after rain." She turned to me, her own eyes shimmering emeralds. "Can you imagine your daddy with blue eyes?"

"Daddy says the Cherokee are brown-eyed. Like us."

"Well his blue-eyed Cherokee great-granddaddy was one of them that isn't. Do you mind if I finish this story which I happen to know and you do not?"

"Yes'm. I mean, no."

"Alright then. Well, that old man stood straight, so he could get a good look into your daddy's eyes. And he stood there a long time, like he was reading a page filled with words. Then he nodded, like he'd known all along that we would come roost on his porch at exactly that time of morning, on that particular day. He said to your father: 'You have the *adanvdo*.' It means *vision*, in Cherokee."

I shivered at her savage word. How many others did she possess?

"He told your father that, when he himself was a young man, his eyes had been brown as mud, too. It was the visions that turned them blue."

"Did he say Daddy's eyes would turn blue?"

Mama looked down at her dishes perched on the drying rack. "He said your father would be *adanvdo ditlihi*." She regarded me. "*Spirit warrior*."

I thought of the *Legion of Super-Heroes* comics scattered across my bedroom. "Does it mean he fights ghosts? Does it mean he can become one?"

Mama chuckled again, but this time her voice had a bitter edge. "His great-grandfather told your father to come with him to see the Long Man. And that I should sit for a spell on his front porch."

"Who is the Long Man?"

"I waited there as they walked off together across a field, into a stand of hedge apple. I listened to that hot wind blow, watched a hawk circling overhead. Then I decided I'd had enough of sitting around while the men did their secret and important man things, so I set off after them. They weren't hard to catch, given how slowly that old coot walked."

"Did you see the Long Man?"

"I did."

"What did he look like?"

"Like the Arkansas River." She didn't pronounce it like the state; she said: *R-Kansas*.

"A river?"

"They were standing in it up to their knees. Something about the water made that old man spry, because he danced and hopped around your father, stooping every so often to scoop up handfuls of water and throw them at him. He was chanting God knows what, in a voice that didn't sound entirely . . . human."

"What did Daddy do?"

"He just stood there, his arms out like he was being crucified. Which I guess in a way he was."

"What do you mean?"

"Your father always had the sight, even as a little boy. But whatever that ritual was, it was like handing him the key to a doorway. It was after that he was able to, you know, find water—find anything, really. To see what he needs to see, when he wants to see it. To talk with them."

"With who?"

"God knows. I just know that there's sight and then there's power, and whatever power that old man had, he gave it to your father."

"Does that mean Daddy can do the same for me?"

Mama let her skillet drop into the sink with a clatter. She turned to look at me as if I'd blasphemed in her kitchen. Which I guess I had. "That old man opened the door to Hell and showed your daddy the way in." Her voice was hard; her eyes gleamed. "I'd sooner kill him than let him do the same to you."

"But it's what made him a war hero, isn't it?"

"No mother wants that for her son." Mama turned from me and attacked the inside of her frying pan with a salted rag.

I carried my empty plate and glass to the counter.

"Daniel." Mama gazed out the window above her sink.

"Yes."

"Every son wants to be like his father. And every mother wants better for her son."

Daddy stayed sober for a long enough stretch that he decided to push his limits by attending Mama's church. One Sunday he slicked back his hair, trimmed his ragged beard, and put on his church pants. Mama was back to her sharp rebukes, which bounced off him like sunlight striking an aluminum silo. Her barrages would have withered me, but all those mean words, interwoven with his taunting replies, constituted their litany of love.

I scooted close to Daddy as we three rode to town in the pickup. He smelled of soap and coffee. Mama hunched over her compact mirror with an eyelash brush and laid into him about his unmanly failure to defend her apple trees against the squirrels, which she swore only ripped the budding apples from their branches out of spite. Daddy grinned, stretched his arm behind my neck, and rested his hand on her shoulder. She leaned into it despite herself.

"It doesn't seem Christian toward the other ladies, you making yourself even prettier than you already are."

"Quit your sweet-talking and drive steady."

Daddy laughed. The sun shone in a cloudless sky, and I wished we could ride forever along this smooth, straight road. A weather-bitten steeple loomed over the trees. Nobody had dared ascend it when they'd painted the rest of the church. Reverend Hardison liked to reference it in his sermons, how its grayed and pitted planks signified the battles raging between angels and principalities above, while we all sit comfortable in our pews, imagining we're not at war. Nobody could discern whether that meant he wanted the steeple painted or let be.

They were already singing as we approached the doors, which led Mama to thump my ear once again for mislocating my church shoes and making us late. She stroked the hair above my reddened ear back into place as we entered. We sat in the back, amongst the whores and tax men, as Daddy liked to say. Reverend Hardison's sermon was about the importance of sobriety in a world drunk with pleasures and power. It wasn't because he'd known Daddy was coming; it's just that we were Baptists. Reverend Hardison was in such fine form that even Mama had to root about in her purse for a handkerchief. Husbands up and down the pews draped their arms around their wives and patted their shoulders. It seemed like everyone in the congregation had someone given to the bottle. I tried not to look at Daddy. My face burned.

Afterwards, we were beset by people telling my parents, and Daddy in particular, how good it was to see us. I retreated through a phalanx of hair-touslers and watched Daddy tug at his collar and rub the back of his red neck with a grimace that was the best fake smile he could conjure. How I wished we'd slipped out during the last hymn.

Calvin came to stand beside me. "If people were that happy to see *me* every time I came to church, I'd probably pretend to have diarrhea less often."

"You'd hate it as much as he does."

"C'mon," Calvin said. We exited a side door to the playground and climbed to the top of the swing set. The girls below threatened to tell our mothers. The littler boys begged us to help them up.

"It's good your daddy came to church."

"I guess."

"Don't you think?"

I shrugged as I considered our church, radiant beneath noontime sun, its congregants spilling onto the sidewalk and into the parking lot, shuffling toward afternoon rest and evening melancholy, husbands coaxing their wives homeward to lunch and naps and the Rebel 400 on television, wives leaning away from their husbands and holding one another's hands to share one more story or recipe or prayer, teenagers huddled in tight covens, younger ones chasing each other about, and amidst all of them, a stray brown mutt nuzzling crotches and knuckles.

Reverend Hardison stood beaming atop the steps, shirt collar unbuttoned and tie askew. Somewhere still inside, my parents stood cornered by well-wishers and busybodies. I wondered how Mama would bear their pitying faces during the next long stretch of Daddy's absence.

Fred Ledbetter stood beside his Cadillac in conference with another councilman. "You know what they're talking about?" I asked.

"My daddy says they're up to something."

"They're trying to take my granny's land."

"What for?"

I shrugged. "It's in the papers, if you know what to look for. Plus Granny says Ledbetter's been driving past her house with some man who isn't from around here."

"Those shit-heels."

Clay Tompkins, the assistant pastor who drove me home the day Daddy killed Bobby Doyle, approached. He'd been standing with a group of teens nearby, blending in so well we hadn't noticed him. He shielded his eyes from the sun and squinted up at us. A lock of his golden hair stood straight in the wind. "You boys like camping?"

We nodded warily. Even though Clay had been assistant pastor for over a year now, he was still considered a newcomer. He wore his hair just short of too long, drove a Volkswagen, and played acoustic guitar. Services at Hickory Shore Baptist Church were organ-only, but the older kids said Clay played his guitar during Youth Group. They reported only acceptable Baptist hymns, but there were rumors of extracurricular James Taylor, some Beatles, even Peter, Paul, and Mary. "Well," he said, "you ought to join Young Explorers."

"What's that?" Calvin asked.

"We get together for camping, and field trips, and to learn outdoor skills."

"Sounds like Boy Scouts," I said. I'd been hoping, now that I was ten, that Daddy would start taking me.

Clay nodded, like I'd offered a strong rebuttal. "Kinda. Except we have both boys and girls and no uniforms or badges."

Calvin and I looked at each other. These weren't selling points.

"It's just something I'm putting together."

Calvin made an evaluative sound in his throat, like his father when he scrutinized crates of peaches or corn.

"But at least you don't have to go door-to-door raising money," Clay added. "I'm thinking we'll camp on Saturday nights and have church service in the woods. Every once in a while, at least." He looked about, then stood on tiptoes to whisper. "Outside church is more fun."

We nodded. He wasn't going to last long.

"Ya'll just consider it. First trip is in a couple of weekends, down-river to Overlook. Spending a lot of time on the river this year." He turned and walked away. "Good Bible lessons in rivers," he said over his shoulder. He waved, his back to us. We returned waves he couldn't see.

"Could be fun," Calvin said.

"Yeah, but . . . girls."

"Some girls aren't so bad."

"Name one."

Calvin's house was in town, so whenever he and I camped, it was in the woods west of my house. That spring was dry, and Mama threatened bodily harm if we started a fire. Early one evening we loaded our packs with sandwiches and canteens and, after much wheedling, a thermos of coffee. "What the likes of you need with coffee," Mama said as she saw us out the kitchen door, "is beyond my ken."

Neither of us liked coffee, but we wanted to drink it from enameled tin cups, the way John Wayne always did after his suppers. We set off toward the western tree line with backpacks and BB rifles, Bailey traipsing alongside. Past our barn and its adjoining field was a copse of oak that yielded to slash pine as the terrain coursed upward. The high narrow trees and abundance of rock made it feel like cowboy country. Above was a ridge whose other side tumbled through ash and birch toward a creek, beyond which was farmland and, bordering this, the backs of houses and stores that lined Hickory Shore's Main Street.

Bailey escorted us as far as the hillside before chuffing at our unbroken pace. He parked his behind, barked once at us to stay, then headed back toward the comforts of home. "Grumpy old fart," Calvin said.

We marched upward amongst the pines, across sloping sheets of granite that rose into outcrops as we went higher. The ground was blanketed with pine needles, the sheltered air cool. In a small flat clearing we strung a line between two trees and draped an oiled sheet over it. We gathered sticks and used rocks to pound them through rope loops Mama had sewn into the sheet's fringe. We arranged our blankets underneath, pulled our sandwiches from their wax-paper wrapping, and ate supper before the sun had finished lighting the tree-tops on the ridge above.

"I think I can see your rooftop from here," Calvin said. He pointed.

"That's a piece of kite."

"I think I hear Bailey coming back."

We listened to movement of small animals around us. A turkey made its ghostly warble in the distance. A breeze stirred the darkening trees below. Bugs began their water-sprinkler noise. *Tsk tsk tsk stop.*

"You joining Scouts after your birthday?" I asked.

"I don't know. My pop says it'll be hard for him to make meetings and whatnot. Did you ask your daddy?"

"He said *we'll see.*" We both knew what that meant.

"I already know how to tie most knots anyhow." Calvin's father had been a Marine in the Korean War. Even though Daddy had been in a different branch and a different war, I think they could have been friends, if Daddy were inclined to spend time around people other than Mama and Granny Watts and me.

The shadows of the trees above stretched homeward as the sun sank. "I need a blanket," Calvin said.

"Mama gave us enough to sleep at the North Pole."

Calvin rolled his eyes. *Mothers.* "You sure that's a kite? It looks like part of your roof."

"There are too many trees to see my house from here. Maybe if we went higher." We considered the slope above as it darkened in the waning light.

"You think your mama will make pancakes in the morning?"

"Maybe." I pulled a blanket close. "It's stupid to camp without a fire."

"We're sitting on an acre of kindling."

"You bring your flint?"

Calvin nodded, then shook his head. "We better not."

"She can't see it."

"Local boys who started a forest fire," he said in a news-anchor voice, "were killed by their fathers before they could be sentenced to juvie."

I pulled my blanket closer. I wondered if Bobby Doyle wandered the full breadth of these woods, or just around my house. "Calvin?"

"Yeah."

"You ever see a ghost?"

Calvin got very still. "No. Have you?"

Shadows gathered amidst mounded rock and close-standing pines. I didn't want to tell Calvin about the dead boy out here. "I think Daddy sees them."

"Who are they?"

"People he's killed. Maybe Bobby Doyle, too."

We were now huddled in blankets up to our ears.

"You don't realize how noisy woods are," Calvin said, "until you can't see all that well."

"Maybe we should move to where there'll be moonlight." We yanked up stakes, gathered our things, and stumbled quickly through the trees. The faster we moved, the more it felt like something was following us. We were in nearly a flat-out run by the time we emerged onto the grayed field beyond the base of the slope.

"I still can't see your house."

I pointed into the distant gloom. "Mama hasn't turned on the lights yet. Sometimes she sits on the porch with one of Daddy's cigarettes when she's alone."

"She smokes?"

"Don't tell your mama."

I tilted back my head as we walked. "Think they teach you constellations in Boy Scouts?"

"James learned them from a book." James was Calvin's older brother.

"I only know the Big and Little Dipper." We stopped to look for them.

"If you join the Boy Scouts," I asked, "will you teach me the constellations?"

"Sure."

"Daddy says every Indian used to know how to read the sky." We walked through a drift of leaves that looked like iron shards in the moonlight.

"There's the light in your kitchen."

We strung our line between a cedar and a willow sapling, low, so that the entrance at either end would be small. We pegged the sheet and crawled under. Inside, we spread the blankets into a comfortable mass and stacked our gear at the openings. It wasn't late, but it felt late. We talked about teachers, lethal traps we could set for Daryl Ledbetter and his stupid friends, what countries we'd fight when we became Marines. Every night the news talked about Irishmen bombing England, so Calvin estimated we'd go there. I said I wanted to go back to Vietnam, to finish what we'd started. I'd heard Sealey Price say this during a horseshoe match at the Founder's Day picnic. Sealey had worked at a Navy depot in Norfolk during the Korean War. He'd said we should go back to finish things in Vietnam, and a few men had nodded, then someone had asked whether the brisket was going to be done this Founder's Day or if they were smoking it for the next one, and then everyone had laughed, and nobody paid Sealey any more mind. I didn't know what had been started there, or how we were supposed to finish it, but I figured that meant sending Daddy back. I imagined any war demanded my father. That they couldn't wage one without him.

Calvin fell asleep before me. I lay beside him and listened to animals move through the underbrush. Something skittered across the grass outside, and the owl haunting a nearby tree fell silent. The oiled sheet of our tent glowed beneath the quickening moonlight. I listened until I could hear trucks passing along highway 421. I turned my head toward home. All was silent there, save for the creak of our porch swing. I didn't know where my father was.

Calvin lay on his back, fingers twitching on his belly. Sometimes he fretted a violin in his sleep. He'd been playing since he was four. Most kids' musical education leaves them hating both their instrument and the classical music they're required to mangle. Calvin's mom had found a violinist in Winston who actually liked teaching and was good at it. Calvin's family could afford things like that.

Calvin was good, his mother proud. She always tersely corrected anyone who dared call it a *fiddle* in her presence. She demanded nightly practice, so on the nights I was over, I'd sit in their den in a high-backed chair, with a book or homework on my lap, and try not to make faces at Calvin while he played. He'd roll his eyes at the humiliation of having to practice in front of me, and retaliate by sawing away with no rhythm whatsoever, until his mother shouted from the kitchen that if he didn't play correctly, he'd work through the whole music book while the rest of us watched *The Waltons* without him.

Calvin liked to complain about practice and recitals, but he played the violin like it was a part of him. Once I'd arrived at his house while he was playing a nocturne, and it had filled my chest with such mourning that, instead of ringing the doorbell, I'd crept around the porch to the den window. There I saw his face pressed against the golden wood of his violin, eyes turned heavenward. His face was not that of a child, but of an angel who has witnessed the murder of God and his resurrection and the dread Judgment to come. I watched him play until my heart couldn't bear it, until he was almost so irreparably different that I would never be able to reclaim him as the boy who was my friend. Then I'd crept away, and pedaled my bike home. I never told Calvin what I saw through that window.

This was heavy on my mind as I listened to the scurrying animals and the scribble of Calvin's sleeping fingers on his belly. I wondered if music ever opened his sight to visions. Had he dreamed of darker things? Of the dead who don't know how to sleep? Did his music that was like a holy grieving draw them forth? The moon had conquered the sky, and the shadow of the owl slipped over our tent, quiet as a spirit passing across the desert. In the brush nearby, a rabbit squealed like a baby and fell silent.

You come bearing flags and guns, but you will bleed as we have bled. Your women will wail as ours have. Your pale and rounded eyes see only where light falls, and our land is to you a shallow place. We have lain our fathers in this soil. It gives us food and water, it whispers wisdom. We know its depths as our fishermen know the sea.

The French before you came with their flags, their guns, their shallow-seeing eyes. They saw only fragile huts, rice still green in the fields, peasants in simple clothes. They could not see underneath. They could not fathom how deeply we would tunnel. There we built arsenals, hospitals, even schools. The French rumbled across our plains in their tanks, their hearts haughty. We rose up in darkness and reminded them there is a hell. We maneuvered them in their arrogance to the valley of Chiến dịch Điện Biên Phủ, and there we broke them.

As we will break you. We will break you because a people will give more blood for their land than interlopers dare shed in its taking. You knew this once, but your memory grew short. So enter the tunnels. In this darkness we are vipers, sulphured air, sharpened pike, blinding flash. We will create for you a hell in the catacombs.

Spring rains made for muddy work, but by the end of the school year I'd tilled Doctor Moore's garden and planted it with squash and sweet corn and other vegetables that didn't mind a late start. He kept conjuring additional jobs to pay me for. Now that school was out, I liked having reasons not to be around our house. Sometimes, while I was up at the Moore's, Julie would watch me as I pruned bushes or uprooted cedar volunteers. At first she watched from the trees, but as my presence became more regular, she would sit in the grass nearby. Most of the time she didn't even throw rocks.

If I were there at lunchtime, Mrs. Moore would call Mama to confirm that I could eat with them. This left me no excuse to avoid sitting in the cramped confines of their kitchen nook across from Julie, who mashed together her eyelids in that deliberative blink of hers, and stared with no apparent self-awareness whatsoever.

Her parents were unlike many adults in that they felt no obligation to entertain children with conversation. They preferred talking with each other, about things that interested them. Other adults ended up prying—even if they started with good intentions—into where my father was and what he was up to these days. This always made me feel like the family spokesman, or worse, an informant. The Moores were uninterested in my information or opinions, other than whether I wanted a second sandwich or my favorite knot for tying a leader to my fly line. It was relaxing, even if I did have to sit across from their demented sheepdog of a daughter.

Harlan Carver arrived on one of those days I worked for Doc Moore. I saw his gleaming blue Cadillac parked next to Daddy's Jeep when I came walking home. I didn't yet know who he was.

He lounged in a kitchen chair, a sweating and untouched glass of ice water on the table before him. He was big as Daddy, with thinning blond hair, uneven mustache, and a red complexion. The skin of his throat looked like overstretched taffy. His gray pant leg jutted from beneath the table, and his yellow dress shirt clung to his skin in the humidity. His eyes were faint brown, their whites tinged as yellow as his shirt. He eyed Mama as she worked at the kitchen counter, her back to him.

Daddy came down the hallway as the screen door slapped shut behind me. He held two coffee mugs. Mama turned from the counter and gave me a thin smile. "Go wash up for supper." She turned back to her work. The man at our table looked me up and down. He grinned as Daddy offered him a mug of what wasn't coffee, glanced at Mama's turned back, and winked at Daddy. He pressed his lips together at the taste, then returned his attention to me. "Now Ray, this here has *got* to be your boy."

Daddy put his arm around my shoulders. It was the first time in a couple of weeks that he'd touched me, and I felt myself leaning into him—even though I could smell the liquor wafting from his skin and the danger billowing like smoke from this stranger he'd let into our home. "Daniel," he said, "this is Mr. Carver. We were in the service together." He said it like he was admitting to a crime.

Mr. Carver leaned across the table and offered his broad hand. His handshake was loose, so that my hand rattled around in it like the meat inside a walnut shell. "Any family of Ray Waterson is my family too, boy." He turned to Mama, who'd taken a stew pot from the refrigerator and was furiously stirring it on the stove. "Same goes for you, Lee Ann. Appreciate your hospitality."

Mama nodded without looking at him. "I apologize all I have to offer is leftovers. Had we known you were coming, I could have made something fresh."

Daddy slumped into his chair. Carver took another tight-lipped pull from his mug. "Don't trouble yourself on my account. Last thing I want to do is put somebody out." He cast his gaze around our kitchen before settling it back on Daddy, who stared into his cup. "You done mighty fine for yourself, Ray."

"I reckon we get by."

"You buy all this property with your Spec-4 wages?"

"I worked out a deal with Lee Ann's daddy years back."

Carver smiled at the corner of his mouth. "Looks like you married well." Daddy considered Mama's back, then his cup. Carver tapped his mug against Daddy's. He took another drink, then made a half-hearted attempt to suppress a belch. Mama dropped the lid onto her pot with a clatter. "Should be another fifteen minutes or so."

She hurried past us. "Daniel," she called to me, "wash for supper. Upstairs."

The sun still burned through the treetops as we ate. Our kitchen felt like a swamp as steam rose from our bowls and heat poured off the men. They wolfed stew while I did my best to keep up. "Slow down," Mama said.

Carver told us he scouted land for a commercial real estate firm. "That's how I knew right away," he said to Daddy, "what a sweet piece you got here." He said with price controls ending, there was going to be a building boom. That if we ever thought about selling, he was the man to call. He said he had a list of Special Forces buddies in a notebook, because he liked to call on them when work took him nearby. He named men my father had known. He said who was doing well in business, who'd been arrested or disappeared, who'd put a gun barrel in his mouth.

Mama ground her teeth so hard I thought they were going to snap. She watched the coffee mugs lift and return to the table, lift and return. She watched Daddy carry them empty down the hall to the mudroom and return with them full. He didn't look at her. "Slow down," she said to me.

Carver wiped sweat from his forehead and winked whenever I got the nerve to look him in the face. "Boy," he said, "I hope you appreciate what your daddy and me done over there." Mama stiffened.

"I do," I said.

"I could tell you stories—"

"Mr. Carver," Mama said, "would you like some pecan pie?"

Carver frowned, then the smile crept back onto his face. "Sure thing, Lee Ann." Mama went to the cupboard. Carver finished his bowl and gazed yellow-eyed at my mother as she assembled forks and plates and cut wedges of pie. He leaned toward me. "I could tell stories, boy, would put fur on your chestnuts." Carver glanced at Daddy, who peered into his bowl like he'd lost something in it. He turned back to me. "You know what a tunnel rat is?"

"Mr. Carver," Mama said loudly over her shoulder, "where does work take you next?"

The smile fell from his face again. "Kannapolis."

"That's a long drive. At least you'll have some sunlight if you leave soon."

"What is it?" I asked. "A tunnel rat."

"Ray," Mama practically shouted. Her eyes were on the window over the kitchen sink. "I do hope you're not going to let that west field grow too high again this summer."

"I'll bush-hog it."

"The gooks built themselves these tunnels, boy. Mile and miles of 'em. And somebody had to go down there and root 'em out. Your daddy—"

"Are you married, Mr. Carver?" Mama turned back to us, wearing a bright, brittle smile. She took Carver's bowl and placed a meager slice of pie in front of him.

"No." Carver lifted the pie wedge with his fingers and bit it in half.

"I suppose some men," Mama said with ferocity, "get by better that way. Now my Ray—bless his heart—I think he'd waste away if I weren't tied to his hip. Isn't that right, sugar?" Her eyes pleaded with Daddy.

"Ray," Carver said, "what say you rustle up that bottle?" Daddy seemed to have disappeared into himself. Mama turned back to the sink. Dishes clattered as she washed them. Daddy rose slowly and walked his empty bowl and full water glass to the counter.

"Ray," Mama said, "I'd like to talk to you for a moment, please."

"Later."

"Ray Waterson, I need to talk to you right now. Daniel, get upstairs to your homework." Mama stomped down the hallway to the back of the house. Carver drained his cup. On his way to follow Mama, Daddy paused behind his chair. He looked at me with tormented eyes. "Daniel, do as your mama says." He watched me until I was at the top of the steps.

In my room I sat in the windowsill with my vocabulary book. The sky glowed orange over the western ridge, and the crickets had begun their chatter. Carver's shiny car lent an odd color to our yard. I heard the screen door thump in its frame, his footfalls on our porch. The swing's chains creaked as he settled onto it. Mama and Daddy were arguing in her back parlor. I couldn't make out the words, only their rhythm—clipped, sharp sentences met with long runs of words, murmured responses, awful stretches of silence.

I stared at the pages. None of the words made sense. My belly was full, and I was suddenly very thirsty. I crept downstairs to the kitchen. I heard Mama's vicious tone in her parlor, Daddy's mumbled replies, Carver on our porch swing. Why wouldn't he just leave? I

filled a glass at the sink and gulped it down. I drank another, but my
thirst wouldn't abate.

"Your daddy don't talk about Nam, does he?" I jumped at Carver's words. His face pressed against our screen door.

"No sir."

His blond bristles made a scratching noise as he nodded toward
the refrigerator. "How about you bring out a couple of glasses with
ice? I imagine your daddy will be out soon." He glanced down the
hallway. "Once she lets him off the rack." I brought two glasses of ice
out to the porch. Carver took them, settled back onto the swing, and
motioned me toward the nearby chair. He squinted at me as he lit a
cigarette. Bailey snored underneath the swing.

"You look just like him, boy." Carver took a long drag and blew
out a lazy stream of smoke. "I knowed it soon as I seen you. 'That's
Ray Waterson's boy,' I said to myself. I suppose you ain't got but half
his blood, but I bet you got the fighting part." He grinned and leaned
toward me, the swing creaking beneath his weight.

"Do you have any children, Mr. Carver?"

His face tightened. "One. Lives with his mama." I heard my own
mother's strained voice reach a crescendo at the back of the house.
"You fight at school?" Carver asked.

"Sometimes."

He laughed. "I'll bet you whip 'em, too."

The truth was that I was slow and clumsy. I wondered what it
was like to be Daddy. To move flawlessly. This man wasn't like Daddy
at all. He seemed alien to everything around him, forcing his presence
onto our land, our home, the air itself. Daddy moved through things,
like mist in the treetops. This man was nothing like my father, but he
knew things about Ray Waterson that I did not. "Did Daddy kill a lot
of men? Over there?"

"They could field a battalion with the men your daddy's killed."
I envisioned a battalion of grim and silent ghost soldiers. Carver
glanced at the door, wiped a palm across his mouth. "Hope he brings
that bottle soon."

"He doesn't usually keep it in the house."

Carver grinned. "You know where he keeps it?"

"No."

"Your mama's got him on a short leash, huh?"

"How many battles was he in?"

I tried not to cough as Carver blew smoke into my face. "Who
knows?" he said. "We would go weeks without nothing. There'd be

sunshine, birds singing, nary a gook to be found. You'd relax, like you're just sightseeing. Then we'd find a hole." He regarded the glowing end of his cigarette and shrugged. "It was your daddy usually found them."

My full stomach tightened. "Did you go in with him?"

Carver leaned back into the swing and snorted. "I'm too big for gook holes."

"Daddy's as big as you."

Carver looked me up and down with narrowed eyes. He took another drag and blew it at me, grinning as I coughed. The cigarette's glow was reflected in his yellowed eyes. "Your daddy could make himself small when he wanted. Looked like a snake slithering down them holes."

I shivered in the dimming light. "Did he take his rifle?"

"Ain't you listening, boy? They was holes in the ground. Weren't no room for rifles." He took another drag, tilted his head back, and blew smoke at our porch roof. "How long they usually go on like that?"

"It depends."

He chuckled. "Never expected to see Ray Waterson scrape and bow."

"Did he use his pistol?" I think some part of me knew the answer to the question I was really asking.

Carver turned his eyes back on me. "Your daddy didn't use no pistol, son. Others did, but not him. He took that knife of his. Blacked it with a lighter. Didn't use his flashlight, neither. He had a way of moving around down there, of knowing where not to put his weight, where not to turn. He had a way of getting behind 'em. Sometimes we'd find a hole, but instead of slithering down it, he'd go off in the brush or across a field—sometimes a quarter mile away, drunk-walking, even if he hadn't had a drink. We'd all just set up and watch, because sometimes he'd take awhile. But you knew it was time when he froze, his arms out wide." Carver closed his eyes and extended his arms from his sides. His cigarette dangled from slackened fingers. Its miniscule embers were as a fire raging on a distant plain. He came back to himself, raised the cigarette to his cracked lips. "God*damn* I'm thirsty."

"Why did Daddy look for a different hole?"

"You ever hear of Russian roulette?" I shook my head. "That's what them tunnels was. In some, a gook is tucked into a hidey hole, waiting to spear you in the belly. Or they've filled a dip with chlorine gas that'll burn out your lungs. Sometimes they just wait for you to peek into one of their caves, so's they can blow your brains out. Charlie's a patient little bastard." Carver grinned. "But that's only if you pick the wrong hole, see? Your daddy could always find the right one. He'd shimmy and shake while we all had a smoke. New COs would holler, but he'd pay them no mind. He'd spread his wings, and that's when we knew. We'd leave a few men around the first hole, then gather round the one he'd found. He'd strip gear, unsheathe that blade, and go to work."

I imagined Daddy crawling through damp tunnels, blackened knife in his hand. Carver shook his head. "Sometimes we'd hear them screaming down there." The contents of my stomach shifted.

"What the hell are you doing?" Daddy stood before us on the shadowed porch, like a summoned demon.

"I was just telling your boy about Nam."

"We don't talk about that here."

"That right." Carver nodded toward the house. "That another one of her rules?"

"It's time you were leaving, Harlan."

Carver settled back on the porch swing, pulled a fresh cigarette from the pack in his shirt pocket, and lit it. He squinted up at Daddy. "You know, I seen this happen to other men. Strong men. They hook up with a willful woman, and she drains all the pluck out of them. Much as it pains me to say it Ray, I've never seen a man broke to the plow sweet as you." He blew a stream of smoke in my father's direction. I couldn't make out Daddy's face in the shadows. He was still and quiet. Carver smiled so wide his gums showed. "Turns my stomach, if I'm being honest."

"I'll not ask twice."

Carver's eyes traveled lazily from my father's face to his boots. He drew in his legs and planted his boot heels on our porch floor. He nodded toward our house. "I'd never let a woman shame me like this."

"Daniel," my father said, "get in the house."

Carver put out an arm to stay me. "I think the boy ought to stay. How about you go fetch me that whiskey, then you and the missus can do some knitting while I make a man out of him." I heard the faintest creak of boards as my father shifted weight. Carver stubbed his cigarette into the wood of our swing. Daddy started forward and Carver sprung upward, his fist arcing hard and tight.

Daddy's shoulders and hips twisted violently as his fists pounded Carver's gut and ribs. Carver *oomphed* with each blow. He reached for Daddy's throat and Daddy used his arm as a lever, spinning Carver around, dancing with him almost, driving him against and over the porch railing. Carver landed in Mama's rose bushes with a swish and a thump and then a howl. Bailey stood and barked as Carver extracted himself. He cursed as he stumbled toward his Cadillac, his skin bespeckled by thorn pricks. Mama pushed through the spring door and grabbed Daddy's arm as he strode to the porch steps. He let her stay him.

Seeing my father wasn't pursuing, Carver stood a little straighter as he fast-walked toward his car. He rubbed his jaw. "You got no call to treat me this way! Neither one of you!"

"I told you to go."

"You know how we counted kills, boy?"

Daddy started down the steps, my mother still clinging to his arm. "Lee Ann, let me go."

"He scalped 'em! That's right. Tell him, Ray! Tell him how we gave you a whiskey shot for each one!"

Daddy reached the bottom of the porch steps, Mama hanging on his arm. "Ray," she said, please."

"Like a good Injun!"

"Just go!" Mama screamed at Carver. Daddy moved across the grass as if she were weightless. Carver had opened his passenger door and was fumbling for something in his glove compartment.

Mama turned to me. "Daniel, help." Daddy unsnapped his knife sheath and closed his fist around the pommel. "Daniel," my mother said, her voice now calm and firm. "He's going to kill that man. *Help me.*"

Carver stood straight and trained a fat-barreled revolver on my father. "Come get some, motherfucker." Daddy kept coming. Mama pleaded with him as she struggled for traction on the grass. "I'll blow your goddamned head off," Carver said, a tremor in his voice. His hand holding the gun trembled.

"You know what I'll do if you miss."

"*Daniel.*"

"You think you can dodge bullets now?" Carver pulled back the hammer.

"Daniel, *please.*"

With a lurch I vomited stew all over the porch steps. The adults were silenced. I heaved a second time, then a third. I heard the

Cadillac's engine fire, its tires spit gravel across our grass. I was crying. Mama's hand settled on the back of my neck. I saw Daddy's boots, felt his hand on my head. For some reason this made me cry harder. "Look what you've done!" My mother shouted at Daddy.

My father withdrew his hand. He shooed Bailey away from my vomit with his boot and went into the house. Mama was leading me up the stairs to the bathroom when we heard the screen door slam, heard Daddy's boots tromp down the porch steps. The Jeep engine started. "Is he going to go kill him?" I asked. Mama sighed. "No."

That night I woke to unnatural silence and knew Bobby Doyle stood in our yard. I knew as well that he was nearer than before, that he would close the distance each visitation until he stood not in our yard but on our steps, then in our kitchen, the upstairs hallway, my bedroom. I shivered as I rose and went to the window.

He stood black-suited in our yard and gazed up at me. His flesh shone white in the moonlight. I knew were I to join him, the air around us would be cool as the grave. All the night creatures held silent in the presence of the revenant. I waited for him to speak. He regarded me with the same expectation. The gathered night and the living within the night waited for life or death to speak and all were silent.

My mother crying in her room bade me look over my shoulder. I knew when I did this that Bobby Doyle was gone, just as I had known he was there. In her bedroom, Mama sat forlorn on the bed she had shared with my father all my life. I sat and lay my head against her shoulder. She put an arm around me and stroked my hair. "Sweet Lord, you're cold," she said. She drew a quilt about my shoulders. She whispered *there, there*, like I was the one who'd been weeping.

"I want to show you something," she said. From the top drawer of Daddy's dresser she retrieved two black cases and opened them. She pointed to the Bronze Star. "He got this because his unit was attacked and he retrieved three wounded men under fire. He wouldn't get on the helicopter until they were safe." She pointed to the Purple Heart. "That scar in his shoulder is shrapnel from a mortar that landed while he was saving those men." She stroked the medals' ribbons.

"What about the other medals?" I asked.

Mama scrutinized me. "You've no business going through your father's things." She snapped shut the cases. "Get to bed."

The second time I woke that night was to voices on our front porch. I heard my mother and father, along with a man I didn't recognize. At first I feared Carver was back, but this man's voice was calm. They had a short conversation, interrupted at intervals by my father, who sounded like he was trying to get them to join him in a song. The front door closed, and I heard Mama slowly walking up the stairs with my father. From my window I saw Sheriff Wilson's car leaving.

I lay back down and listened to their voices, Daddy's sung phrases and Mama's gentle replies. I drifted into a dream in which Carver stormed through our house, shouting: "Come get some!" and shooting at us with his shiny revolver.

We went to retrieve Daddy's Jeep the next morning, a Sunday. A square of white gauze covered his eyebrow. He didn't want me to come, but Mama insisted. She drove the truck while he gripped a coffee mug with trembling hands. It spilled over the rim every time she hit a rut, so that the stretched skin of his hand turned an angry red. He didn't even wince. I wondered if drinking made you so you can't feel anything.

His Jeep sat near a little park in the center of town. I unbuckled as we parked, but Mama told me I was riding home with her. I didn't see how Daddy could drive, not with that hand red and blistered. He set the half-empty cup on the dash and as he made to get out I took hold of his hand's burned meat. He yelped. "Daniel," Mama said, "let him go."

Daddy got out of the truck, then leaned down to peer at me. He considered his burned hand. He appeared to be puzzling over something. "Church'll be letting out soon," Mama said crisply.

Daddy walked with unsteady gait to a park bench, around which were scattered beer cans and a bottle shrouded in brown paper. He picked up the bottle, opened its bag's mouth, and began to collect cans. Each time he stooped for one, I thought he would topple. "That's why I don't want you to learn his ways," Mama hissed. She jabbed a finger in his direction. "*That's* what becomes of men who dabble with unclean things." She shifted the truck into reverse as he shambled to his Jeep. People were starting to emerge from their churches.

"Why are we going this way?"

"Hush, child." Mama drove us past houses I'd never seen, despite living in this town my entire life. I turned to see Daddy following, the dead boy beside him. I knew Mama couldn't see Bobby Doyle sitting pale and silent beside my father, just as I knew my father could see the dead boy and many others besides, men with sundered skulls and opened chests, because the dead are bound to those who snap their life's thread like children to parents.

Eerier still than the sight of Bobby Doyle riding in my seat alongside Daddy was the sight of Daddy's burned hand when he got home. It wasn't even pink.

———⌐

Between these worlds lies a veil that Daddy may pass but not you Daniel nor me. Have you heard me call your name? I lie here in this waiting groaning earth and am not afraid. This earth is like a mother like Mama's belly and I wait and I have a long time yet. We cannot pierce the veil Daniel but we have heard the same heart beating in the center of the world. I ponder your name and with it fear, for your path is longer still and darkness awaits and your eyes will deceive you. Your heart Daniel your heart it wants to darken like the eyes of the wanderers. And oh Daniel the river the river don't go in the river. For it craves you still.

———⌐

One night Bobby Doyle led me to the Crow. The air was humid and restless, making our screen door rattle in its frame. The walls creaked with the shifting air pressure. I knew he was there before I opened my eyes. He stood at the foot of my bed, half his face lit by bone-white moon. Instead of a burial suit, he wore jeans and t-shirt from the day we killed him. Someone had washed out the blood. I considered his chin, his night-blacked hair, the smoothness of his whitened cheek, but I dared not linger on his unblinking eyes. They weren't black like before, but neither were they his. They bore a terrible familiarity.

"It's your birthday, isn't it, Bobby?" I don't know how I knew. He nodded. I asked him how old he was, and he shook his head. There is no age in that place. For the first time since we killed him, I wanted to cry for this boy.

He needed me to come with him. He wanted to show me something—something I might otherwise seek for the rest of my days. I feared what it might be, but I feared even more a life of fruitless searching. I slipped out of bed and struggled into my jeans. When I looked again he wasn't there, so I went to my window, where the wind stirred against my face and throat. The moon was full but for a scorched edge. The dead boy watched from our yard. I crawled out my window and down the trellis. A fear crept over me that there was nobody in our house, nor in the whole world—that all had departed but for this dead boy waiting on the moon-fired grass. Wind rushed through the woods. The dead boy walked into them, toward the river, arms limp at his sides. Brush and branch shrank from him. He didn't look back.

I followed. Above us, the treetops battled. Pine nettles slapped my face and arms as I struggled forward. Moonlight darted through the swaying trees, illuminating the dead boy one moment, rendering him shade within shadow the next. He did not look back.

We came to a field of waist-high grass and I stumbled across its uneven ground. The dead boy didn't stumble; death makes you steady. He walked the path of the earth-haunted dead and did not look back. A stab of lightning lit the eastern horizon, followed by a crack. I heard the rush of water, smelled the river's wet decay. The dead boy descended the bank.

From atop the bank I saw the Crow sliding past. The mounds between the bank's runnels shone like coffin lids. Just offshore lay the rock shelf where the river had tried to swallow me. Bobby Doyle waited at water's edge. Lightning struck closer, thunder hard behind. A branch on the far shore cracked as wind raced unabated across the water. Nearby river birches were silvered in the moonlight, their trembling leaves like frantic flocks of small birds. I smelled electricity above the death churning in the river's deep.

Bobby entered the river to his waist. I remembered I was shoeless when I felt cool pebbles beneath my feet, felt the water lap against my ankles. Trees bent before the approaching storm. The moon disappeared behind a fast-moving cloud, then reappeared, illuminating with its cold light the shore, the water, the shuddering trees, the boy in the river. Behind him the water rushed, agitated by the wind, but I was safe here in the company of what cannot be killed. The pebbles made my soles ache, but further in was soft silt. Water warmed my calves.

The water was up to Bobby's shoulders now. He wanted me to come deeper, to show me something. The water at my waist was warm as a blanket. I moved like air, like my father through silenced jungle, like a dead boy through water. He waited. I considered his eyes that I'd seen in some other face. He appraised me with borrowed eyes because the real Bobby Doyle was rotting beneath a mound of dirt, like the dark drifting things on the river floor. I went to him because his eyes held answers to mysteries, because while the world devours you when you're dead, it also groans into you its every secret. Bobby Doyle would speak, if only I ventured a little further.

A girl called my name from the willow copse. She was afraid, but not for herself. I'd never heard that voice but it was familiar, like Bobby's eyes. Those eyes widened now, became as black pools. I was almost close enough to take his offered hand. The girl ashore called my name again, her fear rising like the water.

Bobby glanced shoreward and slipped beneath the water. The water drank up his lips, his nose, his unblinking eyes. I reached for him as he ferried his secrets to the depths. From the willows the girl sang a mourning song.

There was splashing behind me, and I was scooped from the water like a baby mid-baptism. I writhed in my father's grip. Bobby was just beneath the moonstruck water, eyes open, whitened hand still extended. My father carried me ashore, away from those eyes and that hand and whatever secrets the dead harbor from the living. "Jesus," he said. "Sweet Jesus."

I was suddenly very cold. A river once placid now swirled and foamed. Daddy stumbled up the slope and across the wind-whipped grass. Clouds crowded out the moon as lightning crackled. Daddy clasped me close and broke into a run. Treetops flung themselves about with abandon, pelting us with pinecones. I closed my eyes. My father was the forest and the earth and the storm above us, and I was not afraid.

Icy drops struck our heads as we reached our yard. Daddy carried me through the front door as the sky unleashed its torrent. He carried me upstairs, laid me on my bed, and slid my window nearly shut. He left my room to move about the house, closing windows. A fine mist tumbled over my windowsill. Outside was the sound of a thundering river. How could Mama sleep through such violence?

Daddy returned to my room and sat beside me. "Daniel," he said, "why were you out there?"

"Following Bobby Doyle."

He leaned close, like he wanted to be sure he'd brought the right boy home. "Did he say anything?"

"No."

He pressed his palm to my face. "It wasn't really him, you hear?"

"How did you know to come to the river?"

Daddy stood, groaning with the effort. "Go back to sleep, boy." At my doorway he turned. "Daniel." He ran his hand along the doorjamb like he was judging whether it was plumb. "If he comes back, just close your eyes. Don't listen if he says anything, because they lie.

And don't ever tell them anything about yourself. Nor anyone you care about."

"Do you ever see him?"

He was silent for a moment, then he sighed. "I see them all."

"Are they all bad?"

"No. Most are just wandering."

"Where are they going?"

His face hardened. "Where they go is their business. That's why you should never follow them. Not ever, Daniel."

"Daddy?"

"You need to sleep."

"Daddy, where are they going?"

My father peered at me through the shadows. The rain slowed, as if creation itself awaited his answer. "To the room," he whispered. "The room without walls." He pulled closed my door so tightly the wood groaned. I peeled off my jeans and burrowed beneath the sheets. Outside was the tick of droplets falling from the awnings. A distant train sounded its horn. An owl hooted in response. I was suddenly very thirsty.

Downstairs, moonlight filled our living room, where my father sat mumbling. I peeked around the threshold and saw him slumped on the couch, head down, hands clenched. "'The unclean spirit,'" he said, "'passed through waterless places seeking rest, but could not find it.'" His voice was like that of a preacher speaking over a coffin. He exhaled until he seemed to sink into himself, and I realized then how much of a man is just vapor. He ran his fingers over the unburned meat of his hand. "Please," he said. "Let it pass over him."

It hurt me in a way I can't explain to know that my father wanted to deny me what was inside him. I tiptoed upstairs to the bathroom and drank from the sink faucet. It bore the metallic taste of blood, but I drank until my throat felt unstuck. I returned to my room, pressed shut the door in its frame, and made myself a tight ball beneath the sheets.

The water is cold though it's summer but the Shiver and the light and the dark inside the light—I can't carry them no more. It's no longer just light and dark out there, they're in me, light and dark inside the light, which is where storms are born. The Shiver is a storm and the seeing is the eye within and Mother Watts says it's a gift but god damn it god damn me I don't want it I don't want to see the things I see. I don't want this storm inside me this lightning this crackle along my skin this electric sight this god-sight this damnation.

I hold you vipers left and right, I lift you skyward and look at the light swirl within itself there. You black moccasin in my left curled round my forearm and squeezing. You white copperhead in my right whipping your tail at my eye. Your mouths popping open and closed like your jaw hinges are rusty your fangs white and delicate and hard and how you want to sink them deep but I'm stronger now, I'm stronger. I'll crush you both goddamn you dark and light I'll murder you and the vision with you or I'll by God drown us all in this river this water rising or is it me sinking and the Shiver run through me and we three trembling as it takes us. The river will swallow us all. And what is the river but a great viper writhing on its earthen plate?

I'll kill you both goddamn you and this light and this dark in me or the river will take us all.

Who is screaming who is calling my name like she knows me like she would know all of me like she would bear me for all I am? What voice is a homeward calling that breaks this spell? And look, now I've killed one but not the other. I was nearly free, I was almost free, but her voice it calls me shoreward, and now God help us both.

<hr />

"Mama, how did you save Daddy from the river?"

My mother sat on our porch swing, wide porcelain bowl on her lap, shucking peas. It was October, and the weather had begun to turn. She stopped in the midst of tearing open a pod and considered me where I sat on the porch steps. I returned my gaze to the math book open across my knees.

"Why do you ask me a question like that?"

I shrugged.

"*Say*, Daniel. Did someone in town say something?"

Nobody told me anything, but I didn't want her to realize how much I knew because of our walls' thinness, my father's sleep talk. "I think Daddy said something about it."

Mama resumed her labor with furrowed brow. I worked long division and listened to peas tumble into her bowl. The katydids were becoming more confident as the sun sank. She sighed. "So he said something about the Crow, and the snakes?"

I shrugged.

"I didn't *save* him, if that's what you heard. Not like he saved you. It was the stretch of river behind my parent's house. He was out there up to his belly."

"Why?"

She startled, like she was seeing it for the first time. "He held a snake by the throat in each fist. Held them up like some kind of god-awful sacrifice."

"Sacrifice to who?"

My mother shrugged.

"Were they poisonous?"

She answered with dull voice, as if hypnotized. Her hands hovered over her bowl, peapod in her fingers. "A black moccasin and a copperhead that looked like all the color had been bleached from it."

"Why was he out there?"

"I don't know." She looked over my head, to the horizon beyond our barn.

"How old was he?"

"Fourteen. Maybe fifteen."

"Did he kill them?"

"They were whipping like live wires. His arms trembled terribly. The current pressed into his back, nudging him further and further out, like the river was . . . embracing him."

"Did he kill them?"

"I couldn't let it take him, so I screamed his name." Her voice bore something like regret. "I guess that broke the spell. He threw those snakes toward the far shore and waded back. To me."

"They weren't dead, were they?"

"What difference does one dead snake make? Haven't you been listening? He was so caught up in that voodoo of his that he couldn't see he was drowning." She went back to shucking peas. "Just like a man," she muttered. "Miss a river for a snake."

I felt like I was listening to her story better than she was—to a story within her story. I returned to my math. Mama seized more pods from a paper bag beside her leg and ripped them open one by one. A pea missed her bowl, rolled across the porch, and came to rest against my leg.

"Mama?" She continued attacking peapods like she didn't hear me. "Mama."

"Boy, if you ask me one more question about snakes, I'll tar you."

"Why did you go to the river?"

She eyed me like I was accusing her of something. I put the stray pea in my mouth. It was cool and small. She shook her head. "It was silly." She gave an exasperated sigh and rolled her eyes. "I thought I heard a funeral dirge. Like they say the slaves used to sing, down by the water."

"Did you see anyone besides Daddy?"

"What kind of fool question is that? Who else would there be?"

I shrugged.

"Child, the imagination you have. I hope you put it to good use someday."

"Mama."

"Wha-a-a-t." She stretched the word to signal that I was getting on her very last nerve, though whenever I really got on her last nerve, her words got short and sharp.

"Which one did he kill? The black one or the white one?"

She shook her head, exasperated. "How in the world am I supposed to remember that? And what does it matter?"

It seemed to me that it mattered more than anything.

Excerpt from the Diary of Lenora Watts: March 7, 1968

Oh Lee Ann, I know I confound you with inconsistencies, with my insistence a lady should wear dresses but know how to work the smart end of a Remington, with my fine china for Sunday dinner and my pet pig, saying we ought to shoot the flag-burners and leveling your daddy's Sweet Sixteen at those Klansmen who said we ought not take in coloreds and Indians at Harbor House. I know it makes no sense to you, but it's all of a piece to me.

And every Hickory Shore Council meeting I speak at, every County Commission sit-in I organize, none of them are for show, no matter how you roll your eyes and ask what your father would think. Child how you split us in your mind, he the calm and me the storm, but we two were always of a piece and a peace, in life and now in death, and you never saw his storming because the rage of some men is hard to bottle once it's loose, which he knew better than anyone.

Something in my heart knows you'll learn this for yourself one day.

None of it has been for naught, even if every staying action is doomed from the start, was doomed from the moment Adam stood in a stupor while Eve whet her appetite. Nothing is symbolic, child. It's all knit together as we are, and when we forget that, we'll all come unraveled— families, communities, nations.

"I don't see how it's community-minded to stir up trouble," is what you say, but soil must be tilled, and besides, how else will those old boys know their decisions matter, unless somebody shows up to argue from time to time? "You show up every time, Mama," you say. Maybe so, but that's because everything matters. Everything. And so I bring your boy, my brown-eyed baby, and I hold him up and I ask them to explain why they're tampering with his future, which makes the farmers cheer and gets cagey smiles from the politicians because they know a trump card when they see one, and yes there's theater in it, but the boy best learn his part early, for I'm guessing it will skip a generation, this orneriness, and that's fine, daughter, because you've stayed while your sisters fled, and I know, though we fight, we too are of a piece.

And perhaps one day, a peace.

You gave me this baby, and together we'll rear him until your man comes home, and afterward as well, for there'll be healing to be done, you know it as well as I.

And how I love your man, my brown-eyed boy before this one, which is why I swung my hammer at the long-haired snot-nose dragging the flag through the street in Winston and trying to set fire to it with his Zippo, even though we were marching in the same demonstration, each of us wanting to bring your man home, albeit for different reasons. And all you could think to ask, after you posted my bail, is why a lady would carry a hammer in her purse.

Daddy missed most of our Sunday dinners at Granny's that November, laid up in bed with what he called the flu. Granny's house was normally a refuge, but she was becoming increasingly agitated. Like me, she read the newspaper. She discerned the signs.

"Really Mama," my mother said as she mashed potatoes, "when has any Hickory Shore politician ever been a match for you? Anyone in the county, for that matter?" Granny grumbled as she sliced ham. "Mama, you single-handedly staved off fluoridation for two years past when every other county had the good sense to start doing it."

"And I eventually lost!"

"Remember how you extracted a town council resolution that fluoride would never be added to private wells?" Mama turned to me. "Which has *got* to be the silliest vote those poor men ever subjected themselves to, because the town never had that power in the first place."

"Lee Ann, if you don't handcuff 'em before they have the power, you'll never get the cuffs on afterward." She gestured at the television, where President Nixon had just told everyone that he's not a crook. "Every one of 'em is a crooked sonofabitch, from top to bottom. It's the only kind we know to vote for."

"Well Mama, you're making my point. If Nixon and Agnew can be called to account, the politicians in Hickory Shore don't stand a chance against the woman who's had more influence over this town than anyone we've ever actually elected." Granny harrumphed as she pulled down a serving dish. I didn't understand how her wildly varied politics held together, but I hazily remembered being by her side while she chewed out a row of seated councilmen in a fluorescent-lit government chamber, and holding her hand as she led a platoon of farmers to accost the Soil and Water Commissioner.

I vaguely recollected impromptu speeches that blended civilization-spanning prophecies with a fine knowledge of local particulars. She would hold forth about the slow but murderous unraveling of the social fabric, for example, and connect this to a proposal to widen easements on agricultural land. People would sit straighter when she spoke in town meetings—some with delight, others with rolls of their eyes, more than a few with both. Officials singled out for her opprobrium would look about for help, or a sign of insincerity, for surely no one was this opinionated about forbidding bids for park bench installation from businesses outside the county, or truly serious about a citizen committee to assess whether state-approved textbooks comported with local values. These poor men strived to articulate for Granny Watts their small and good intentions, but against her imprecations there was no defense.

My mother tried to reassure her mother that no secret cabal existed, but Granny insisted the world was different than Mama believed it to be. That the forces of oppression had grown more persuasive and powerful, that my mother was misremembering how much influence she'd actually wielded, that she'd never been more than an amusing irritant.

Whatever her doubts about her influence, I knew that Granny Watts was the reason our library had maintained a *Fahrenheit 451* display for years, which she'd kept updated with newspaper clippings that, to her mind, proved Ray Bradbury's prognostications were coming to fruition. But I also knew that the display had been taken down earlier this year, after the town got a librarian with a college degree and no patience for amateurs. So I could see Granny's point about the gathering powers of officialdom.

"I've been a thorn in too many sides," she muttered as she gazed out her kitchen window. I knew that back there, past her garden and my grandfather's workshop and a grove of hickory, was the stretch of Crow from which my mother had drawn my father when they were young. "It's not my land I fear for most," Granny said. "Nor even being stuffed into an old folk's home. It's what he would do to the men responsible." She shook her head. "Lord have mercy."

Mama and I glanced at each other. We knew who she was talking about.

———

Hickory Shore Messenger
November 30th, 1973

HICKORY SHORE, NC—In a close vote the Hickory Shore Town Council tabled a proposal to annex a parcel of land on its western border currently owned by Lenora Watts. Council member Fred Ledbetter spoke on behalf of developers who believe the county's recent rezoning of Ms. Watts's property indicates its economic potential. Speaking in opposition was Ms. Watts's daughter, Lee Ann Waterson . . . .

———

"Lord-a-mercy, Daniel, if you could have seen your mama testify!" Granny Watts stood in the center of her living room, crushing a handful of mail.

"Oh, Mama." My mother was placing silverware on the dining table. She was unable to suppress a smile, so she overrode it with a scowl. "Stop that nonsense and help me in here."

"Wished I'd seen it too," Daddy said. With his knife he sliced out the short article from Granny's newspaper. I resolved to sneak my Case knife into the library and do the same. A mostly empty glass of iced tea rested on the coffee table beside him. "I heard you were just like Jimmy Stewart," he said.

"What you heard," Mama said, pointing at my grandmother, "was from that one. And neither of you is helping me get dinner served."

"Like Patrick Henry!" Granny shouted.

"Mama, please."

"*Patricia* Henry," Daddy said.

"A couple of instigators, both of you."

Granny waved crumpled mail like she was shooing flies. "Oh no, I'm retired from instigating. I've passed on my mantle to my daughter, Mrs. Willa Jennings Bryan."

"Daniel, I hope you have the good sense not to believe anything you hear from these two. All I did was state a few facts during the public comment time."

"Don't you listen to her, boy. *Preach* is what I hear she did. Harsher stuff even than the sermons she gives you and me."

"Well let me see if I can't remedy that," Mama said. "Look at the three of you gossiping while your supposed heroine does all the labor."

"A prophet is never respected in her own town, sugar."

"Quit your *sugaring* and pull the roast from the oven."

Granny lay hold of Daddy as he walked toward the kitchen. "No! Now everyone, just hold on. I have something I just want to *say*. Daniel, you come over here too." She wrapped a finger from her mail-choking hand around my wrist. Mama came to the living room threshold, arms crossed. A smile threatened to spread across her face despite her best efforts. "Now I just need to say," Granny continued, "I'm proud of each one of you."

"Oh, Mama."

"No, now I *mean* it." Granny shook my arm. "This boy is a treasure, and Lee Ann, what you did, when raising a ruckus was always my responsibility, but now, give-out as I am, you just marched down there in my stead and stood up to Ledbetter and the rest of those conniving chain-gang lawyer sonsofbitches—"

"*Mother.*"

"—and while I admire each of my girls, I was just so, well, *proud* of you—"

"Hush before you give yourself a stroke."

"And Ray, you've just . . ." Granny's eyes were wet, and she blinked at Daddy like she'd forgotten what she wanted to say, but that wasn't it at all, she just had *too much* to say, and not enough breath to get it all out.

Daddy put an arm around her shoulder. "It's alright, Mother Watts."

"You're just a *good* man, Ray. I want you to hear that. You're a good man, and I know you wanted to go down there and whup 'em all, and though they deserve it, sometimes a woman's rebuke is better. But I know you're with me, that you'll always protect me and these babies, and it just gives an old woman comfort, son. It gives me comfort." She looked from one to the other of us, eyes wet and blinking. Daddy took her trembling hand and began to dance, yipping as he hopped from foot to foot. Granny kept rhythm with small shuffles.

Mama rolled her eyes. "Ray! For the love of Sunday! Your fake Indian nonsense is like to give me a headache."

"Any yipping I do is real Indian yipping by definition, sugar! *Yee-hee*! *Yip yip*!"

Mama threw a folded napkin at his head and told him to be careful with her mother, who was crying and laughing at the same time. She didn't have to caution him, because he had gentled his every murderous limb, and there was nothing on his breath but tea and mint. I figured this was just a caricature of the dances he knew, dances he'd never show me.

Six months is an eternity in a boy's life, and time passed slower once we thought the danger had passed. As the weather warmed in 1974, Daddy and I fished; I helped Mama and Granny put in their gardens; I worked for Doc Moore and dodged the occasional pinecone from Julie Moore; and Calvin and I endured the rest of fifth grade, including getting pushed around by Daryl Ledbetter and his friends. I waited on a growth spurt.

Daddy had a long stretch with no liquor that I knew of. He witched some wells, roofed a few houses, tended our apple trees, and danced with Mama on our front porch with the radio on. Even I had

the sense to see that gratitude was in order. In the heat of July, Calvin's
parents took him to visit his mother's parents in Savannah. He sent me
a postcard, which is the first one I ever recall receiving. It was a picture
of a two-tiered water fountain, and on the back he'd written:

> *This picture makes me want to pee. I tried to buy one of a*
> *lady in a bikini but Mama said over her dead body. Daddy*
> *says Georgia is hotter than a billy goat in a pepper patch,*
> *hah hah. They talk funny down here.*
>   *Your friend,*
>   *Calvin.*

I couldn't imagine anyplace hotter than here. I sweated through
chores to earn my freedom but had nothing to spend it on. My other
friend Eddie Gilchrist was with his parents down at Lake Norman.
Even when you only had two friends to start with, when they're both
gone you can't help but feel abandoned. I wandered our property with
a stick and a sullen attitude and wound up by the pond that used to be
ours. The sky was scorched white, without the slightest breeze. I stood
at water's edge with the vague intention of spearing a fish.

An empty beer can whizzed past my nose and skittered across
shore pebbles. Here I was nearly half Indian, yet Julie Moore kept am-
bushing me. She stood a few feet away with a crumpled grocery bag at
her feet and a tattered notebook under her arm. She launched the bag
with her foot and it landed between us with a rattle. "Those are your
daddy's," she said. She pointed to a birch tree overhanging the pond.
"He sits over yonder and throws 'em in our bushes when he's done."

I wondered if Mama knew. "You don't know they're your bushes," I said. "The property line runs right through there."

"Those bushes were ours before we even bought this useless
waterhole."

Sometimes I wanted to smack Julie Moore. "Did you tell
anybody?"

"I told my daddy. He said your daddy's got a sickness, but not
the kind he can heal. He said all we can do is pray for him." She
walked to where the bag lay and nudged it my way. "I think you're
both criminals, so I'm praying you get arrested."

"You better shut up."

"I don't have to. You're on my property."

"I don't owe your daddy anymore."

"I know." Julie squatted on a rock and put her notebook on her
knees. "What're you gonna do with them?"

I picked up the can she'd thrown and held it underwater. Air bubbled to the surface.

"What're you doing?"

I chucked the water-laden can into the center of the pond.

Julie pointed to where it sank. "That's littering."

"Go tell Woodsy the Owl."

"This is *our* pond."

"I can still use it. That was part of the deal."

"For fishing, not littering."

I opened the bag, breathed in the sickly-sweet beer smell, and pulled out a can.

Julie waved her notebook. "You know what this is?"

"Don't care."

"It's my spell book." She whipped it open and flipped through the pages.

"You gonna turn yourself into a human girl?"

"It's got real spells, Daniel Waterson, like how to make somebody's fingernails fall out, or how to give 'em permanent hiccups."

"You are the saddest little witch ever."

"You won't be saying that when you've got a serpent's tongue." She stuck out her own tongue. "I hath a spell'll make it thork in two." I tossed the can into the pond. "You're lucky I don't have a cat's liver, else I'd turn your toenails inward." I filled another can. "Stop that!"

"It's magic. I'm making them disappear." I threw the can.

"You throw one more in there and I'll take the next bagful to your mama."

"You would, you little tattle-tale."

"Litterbug!"

I briefly considered throwing her in the pond, but I was pretty sure she'd take me in with her. I snatched up the bag and started toward the woods.

"Where are you taking them?"

I quickened my pace when I saw she was following me.

"If you throw them back in the bushes, I'll just take them to your mama."

Adults say to ignore kids who harass you, and usually that's terrible advice, but in this case it was perfect. We marched through the pines, she threatening me with spells, and I tormenting her with silence. My path brought us to the Crow. We came to the place where Bobby Doyle had led me. There were deep holes here. Julie squatted at the top of the bank as I descended to the waterline. I opened the bag and began filling cans. I tossed them at the place where the dead boy had gone under.

"That's still littering."

"A few cans won't hurt what's laying down there."

There was a ruffling of pages. "I got one here that can shrivel your boy parts to raisins."

"Is that what happened to yours?"

More furious ruffling. "I got another that can give you diarrhea for weeks. All I need is eye of newt and you'll have the squirts till Christmas."

"Do you have any spells that can give someone powers?"

"What kind of powers?"

"Like the ability to find things, or to see things other people can't see."

"You mean like X-ray vision? Because that's just a dumb comic book idea."

"No, I mean like the power to see ghosts. To talk with them and stuff."

"It's not that kind of spell book." She thumbed through the pages, naming afflictions.

When the bag was empty, I climbed to where she sat. Her bare feet were crusted, her legs welted with scratches and bug bites. I dropped the crumpled bag onto her open spell book. "Just leave them by the pond from now on. Beside the dead tree." Julie squinted up at me with her head cocked sideways, like I was some kind of puzzle. "You shouldn't come here by yourself," I said.

"I ain't a baby," she called out as I walked toward home. "And I ain't your maid!" I walked slowly, until I was sure she'd left the river's edge.

Excerpt from the Diary of Lenora Watts: May 19, 1970

Lord, please don't you pester me about church. I've put in my time, and you know Clovis put in his. It's not that I love you less now, though I doubt I'll be able to keep my mouth shut when you finally get around to bringing me home. Why all these years without my man, Lord? Did you truly need him more?

Oh, Clovis. You always did have a heart for the hopeless. You'd have made a fine preacher, except you'd bankrupt the church like you did your own business. It was hard enough on the church, you being a lay elder. Roping in drunks and thieves and sinners until there was barely room for good Christians. You could never admit when something can't be fixed. I suppose heaven was made for such as you.

I suppose I've answered my own question, haven't I, Lord?

But haven't I also served you well? Prayed and switched those girls to your bosom, put in my Sunday School hours, my Harbor House years. You know my heart. You know if there's anything worthy in here. I just can't sit there, not with the Old Regulars nor with Lee Ann's people, now that my man is gone. I can't bear the cool of the seat beside me.

And don't get me started on the preaching. Now Lord, you have to be with me on this. You hear all that prattling on, the puffery, the ugliness and the glibness and the plain wrongheadedness, most of it for ourselves and not you. It's a testament to your grace every Saturday night you choose not to burn us all to a crisp rather than endure another goddamned sermon. (You know this isn't cursing, because I'm saying it just to you.)

That last revival—you were there, same as me. They brought in that pale beanpole with a squeaky voice that couldn't be pushed no further than a three-lagged nag, and I know anyone trying to break into the revival business has to start somewhere, but most people aren't fitted to it, and ought to have the good sense to know so.

And you saw how it went—dwindling numbers each night and nary a response to the altar calls, until the little feller packed up his one threadbare suit and absconded two nights earlier than the church marquee had prophesied. People don't want to entrust their souls to anyone weighing in at less than 250 pounds, and they want him to sound like George Jones, not Barney Fife, because that's just how we are, Lord—small and petty and sinful, and I guess I'm more mindful of that in church than anywhere else. Not my own small petty sinfulness, but everyone else's, and while you didn't erect many barriers to entry, that one is bold and clear; "Ye shall be judged as ye judge," and Lord, you know the last thing I need is you judging me the way I judge them, so I stay away from church to avoid sin, for you also said "If thy eye offend thee, pluck it out and cast it from thee," but even blinded in church I'd still have to listen to it, and I can't very well root out my ears. So I just stay home.

I guess all I'm asking, Lord, is that you understand that I'm trying. I know it looks to those busybody women—and yes Lord, even as I say it I recall full well that I was one of them once, and so yes I'm judging them but I might as well call a spade a pious squinty-eyed spade because that judgment is going to fall rightly on my head regardless—my point is I know it looks to them like I love you less because I'm not there, but Lord, while we've had our differences and I still bear you a grudge in my weaker hours, you know I love you, love you as much as I do my own daddy dancing there with you now, and I know you love me too, and you understand me better than I understand myself, and none of this passes through your hand but for a reason, though sometimes I wonder with this grieving old heart of mine: isn't there an easier way?

Not long before I turned thirteen, in the fall of 1974, Reverend Hardison enlisted a towering revival preacher. Brother Don Dunwoody had long arms that never stopped moving at the pulpit and a tangle of wiry black hair that leaked sweat down his wide forehead. His eyebrows were like thornbushes, his eyes bulbous and predatory. His thunderous voice echoed from a region so southern it made the rest of us sound like Californians. Don Dunwoody was a charismatic horror.

He drew lessons from obscure biblical personalities, pairing their alien names with descriptors to signify the saints and the villains: *Faithful Eliashib*; *Shameful Sennacherib*. The specifics didn't matter; he was carnival sideshow freak and orchestra conductor and gospel singer all piled into a single towering, sweating, raving pillar of holy fire, ordained to ignite the slender kindling of Hickory Shore. He told us that he came to conquer our town for Christ. "And the Lord's Army," he declared, "don't take no prisoners."

Brother Dunwoody knew how to bring men to their knees. He not only did altar calls, he did encore altar calls. He'd stand amidst a brace of penitents on the dais, close his eyes, press a thick finger to his temple, and demand more. "The Lord is telling me there's a broken soul out there in them pews! He's caught up in liquor and lusts! He's gettin' dragged down into the Pit, but he's afraid to ask for help!"

Then he would assay the crowd, as if the Lord had just whispered the wretch's name in his ear. His eyes would bore into each of us in turn. "You know who you are. You've just about give up hope, but the Lord Jesus said: 'My sheep hear my voice—yes they do—and ain't nobody gone snatch them from my hand.' Naw sir! Now you come *forward*, brother! Come forward because the hour, brother, the HOUR IS NIGH!"

When he shouted, three or four men would bolt up from their seats like they'd sat on rattlesnakes and shuffle down to the altar, faces upturned and wet. The very first night of Revival Week, Calvin's father leaned over to his mother and informed her he wouldn't be coming back. He said he had to look these men in the eyes and do business with them, for Christ's sake.

Our mothers made the mistake of letting Calvin and Eddie Gilchrist and me sit together that first night, and Eddie paid the price. While the adults were rapt, Calvin screwed his face into a passable imitation of Dunwoody, and Eddie guffawed so loudly he had to pretend he'd been moved to tears. It was a reasonable camouflage, but his parents, moved by their son's faith, took him up front during the altar call. Dunwoody singled him out each subsequent night—*look at yonder boy with the mustard-seed faith; see ye gathered sinners the faith of this here child*; and so on. Poor Eddie had to sit up straight and pay attention for the rest of the week.

Calvin and I bet marbles on who we thought would crack each night. We didn't include revival regulars like Mrs. Massey, who liked to recount all the betrayals that had weakened her faith, or Mr. Stuckey, who did more drinking than farming, or Mr. Wilkinson, who stood during hymns with hands raised like he was being robbed. A stiff wind could harvest those tender souls, but with a masterful reaper like Brother Dunwoody prowling the aisles, there was no telling who else might succumb.

It held a macabre fascination for us kids, seeing the adults come apart without warning. I was thankful Daddy wasn't there. I thought Mama might go forward, but she never did. It wasn't pride that restrained her; I remembered when I was small how she would kneel with me by my bedside and ask God to forgive her pettiness, her judgmentalism, her failures to trust him. On her knees in my room, she would confess her worry and ingratitude and faithlessness. She would rattle off shortcomings that I didn't even know counted as sins until I wondered how she could ever get into heaven. Then she would put her hand on my head and list *my* transgressions, leaving me certain we were both of us bound for perdition.

My mother often seemed unforgiving, perhaps of herself most of all. And yet she truly believed that God crafted heaven for people like us. I suppose this is why she poured herself into the hymns, her flat voice not singing the verses so much as declaring them. She would smile as if their promises were coming true before her eyes, as if the key really was being placed in her hand, the false things disappearing. "Open my eyes," she would warble, "illumine me." And in asking, she received; my mother would become illuminated. She would stand in a sheen of sweat in our window-cooled church, face aglow, green eyes hope-filled. She was so beautiful in those moments that I had to fight tears.

I was terrified Mama would drag me up front during an altar call, but I wanted her to go receive this salvation being doled out by the bucketful. And if God closed his doors to her, then I preferred hell. It gave me goosebumps to think such an unholy thing in church, but that was the truth of it then and still is today. What I came to understand years later was that her heart was inclined the same towards me and my father. She never went forward for that blessing because she didn't want it without us. She wanted it especially for Daddy, but she knew she could never force such a thing on him. I suppose some people in our church thought differently.

Calvin and I were playing in my front yard when they drove up one afternoon. We'd stuffed feed sacks with cut grass and arranged them into a machine-gun nest. We were strafing Nazis with a piece of driftwood when we saw the car, which we strafed as well, glad to have a live target. We kept strafing, spit flying as our lips vibrated into numbness, until we realized the car belonged to Reverend Hardison and that it ferried three preachers and a church elder. Don Dunwoody unfolded himself from the car and dusted off his suit pants. With his loose and crooked mouth he grinned at us. "You boys playin' army man?"

We nodded.

"Soldiers for the Lord." He turned to offer the other men a silent, slack-jawed laugh.

It made sense for Reverend Hardison to be his escort, but I was surprised to see Clay Tompkins. "Still waiting on you two to come to Explorer's Club," he said in a low voice as he passed.

"Why are all these preachers at your house?" Calvin whispered.

"I don't know," I said, "but it can't be good."

The last man out of Hardison's Oldsmobile was Fred Ledbetter, father of our school bully. He was copper-headed, with long, hairy arms and a divot on his forehead just below the hairline. He scowled as he considered everything in our yard, including me. Reverend Hardison cleared his throat. "Daniel, is your daddy home?"

Calvin looked at me with wide eyes. I pointed to the house. Clay Tompkins winked as he and the others tromped up our porch steps. Reverend Hardison rapped on the screen door, and I heard my mother exclaim in an overly bright voice what a nice surprise this was. The men filed into our house.

"Holy shit," Calvin said.

We ran bent over, like soldiers under fire, to the living room window on the side of the house. It was above our heads, so Calvin dropped to all fours in the creeping Charlie. I pressed my hands against the weather-beaten siding, stepped onto Calvin's back, and slowly stood until I could see over the windowsill. Through the living room entranceway, I saw the church men seated around our kitchen table, where Mama poured lemonade from her glass pitcher. She moved around them, offering a whirlwind of pleasantries.

In the living room, just around the corner from them, Daddy lay on the couch, staring at a television that wasn't on. Why didn't he move? He could use the other doorway, pass through Mama's parlor, then out the back door.

"My back's breaking!" Calvin hissed. I dropped back to the ground. "What are they doing?"

"Sitting in the kitchen, drinking lemonade."

"Where's your daddy?"

"On the couch."

"Should we sneak in there and wake him up?"

"He's already awake. He's just laying there."

"Oh boy."

From the kitchen we heard chairs scraping as Mama's voice grew brighter, offering them pie, maybe some coffee to wash it down. Footfalls crossed to the living room as Reverend Hardison said my father's name like a question. Calvin and I scurried along the side of my house and around to the back door. I pulled it open slowly, wincing at the shriek of rusty hinge pins. We heard the men's voices as we crept through the pantry and into the hallway afire with sunlight that poured slantwise through the front door. At the end I could see my mother standing just inside the living-room entranceway, wringing her apron.

We inched down the hallway on the balls of our feet, then darted into Mama's parlor. Daddy had walled it off from the original living room years ago and painted it a warm shade of yellow. A small writing table stood beneath the single window. A bookcase held hardbound volumes by Elizabeth Goudge, worn paperbacks by E.B. White and Erma Bombeck. There were hymnals, too, and, on the very bottom, books with ambitious titles like *The Greatest Story Ever Told* and *Peace With God*. We crouched behind the partially open door and peered past its hinges.

Daddy was sitting now, leaned forward, face down with hands in his thick black hair. Don Dunwoody crouched so that his shins touched the coffee table between them. The others stood arrayed in silence. Dunwoody placed his blunt-fingered hands onto the table like an offering. "Ray Waterson," he said, "I've come to take you home."

Daddy chuckled.

"I understand your pain, Ray. I know about brokenness."

"Do you now."

"My church in Alabama takes in orphans. Many's the night I myself have rocked an abandoned little one to sleep." I wondered who'd told him my father was an orphan. I wondered what else he knew. "I know pain can linger in a man, Ray."

"It'd be bad for the preaching business otherwise."

Fred Ledbetter stepped forward. "You'd better—"

Dunwoody raised a restraining hand. "I know there's anger, Ray." His face contorted with empathetic pain. The coffee table groaned against his shins. "It's eating you up, son. But the Lord is calling."

Daddy pushed his hair from his face and peered at Dunwoody for the first time. "How come he's telling you?"

Dunwoody's back straightened. "How's that?"

"I mean if the Lord has a message for me, how come he's got to go through you? I'm in the book."

"It's the Book of Life that ought to concern you," Ledbetter said.

"Ray," said Reverend Hardison, "we just want to help."

"I can see that," said Daddy, in a loud, friendly voice. He considered this cloud of witnesses stuffed into our living room. "I can't tell if I should be flattered or worried, what with three preachers visiting me unannounced." Clay Tompkins laughed nervously. "And Fred, ain't you some kind of minor prophet now?"

"Elder."

"Three preachers and an elder. Reminds me of a joke I heard once—"

Dunwoody stood. "Mocking the Lord's servants is unwise, Ray."

"We're just bringing the Word," said Hardison.

"Mother Watts taught me Jesus is the Word," Daddy said as he smiled up at Dunwoody. "You look a mite different than I'd imagined."

Ledbetter took another step forward. "You think Mrs. Watts wants her daughter living with a drunk?"

The smile remained on my father's face, but his voice became like a whetstone. "I'd be real careful, Fred."

"Every drunk is the same. You crawl inside a bottle and only come out when you run dry." Ledbetter glanced at my mother. "Or to slap someone around."

"He's never raised a hand to me," my mother said quietly. "Nor to Daniel."

"Not yet," Ledbetter said.

My father eyed Ledbetter like he was sizing him for a coffin. "Don't stand there pretending concern for the Watts family," he said. "Not when you're scheming to take the home right out from under that old woman."

"Don't try to change the subject!"

"I oughta cut you down right here."

"Let's not be ugly." Clay Tompkins seemed to surprise himself with those words.

Dunwoody crouched back down. "I know about your service in Vietnam, Ray. I was in combat myself."

"Is that a fact."

"I served in the 143rd. Salerno, Anzio, the Rhine. I know what war can do to a man. But it's time to lay those burdens down. The Lord can heal *anything*."

"I've heard that all my life, but I never once saw him seal up a sucking chest wound."

Dunwoody's nostrils flared. "The Lord can't do his work unless you're willing to do yours."

"What is it you think you know about killing?"

"I was a machine gunner. I know plenty."

Daddy snorted. "From a thousand yards out?" I imagined Dunwoody in fatigues, spraying bullets the way he did words.

"Look at what drink is doing to your family, Ray."

"I take care of my family."

"They need spiritual care."

"From a sober man," Ledbetter added. Then, so softly I had difficulty believing it came from him: "They need to feel safe."

"Ray," said Reverend Hardison, "please let us help."

"Well, I'm having a little trouble paying the electric this month. How much cash did y'all bring?"

Hardison cleared his throat and forced a smile. "I mean with your soul."

"Haven't y'all collected enough scalps? I heard it was a banner week for soul-snaring."

Reverend Hardison looked both gratified and insulted. "It's not numbers that matter, Ray. All heaven rejoices when even a single lost sheep is restored." Dunwoody closed his eyes and added a deep and lingering *Amen*, like he was poised on the edge of song.

"So I should get down on my knees, is that how it works? I kneel, and y'all lay on hands to cast out my demons?" My father eyed Dunwoody like he was a wound. "You like watching men cry, preacher? You think their tears float you closer to heaven?"

Dunwoody stood. "Ray Waterson, the time has come to repent!" My father cradled his head in his hands and laughed. Dunwoody leaned across the coffee table and jabbed a finger at him. "Woe be unto the mockers and scoffers for whom the Pit awaits!"

My mother quietly came further into the living room and steadied herself behind an old ladder-back chair that had been a gift from her father. Sometimes, when she was troubled, she moved from room to room, gently touching the oldest things in them, as if they bore some ancient wisdom that might aid her. Dunwoody towered over my father, declaiming, denouncing, invoking the righteous fury of God. My father's fingers in the hair of his downturned head became clenched fists.

"Holy shit," Calvin whispered. My stomach swelled with Dunwoody's imprecations, as if an unclean thing writhed in my gut. I felt a terrible compulsion to burst into the living room, throw myself across the coffee table, and beg them to cut it from my belly.

"Just leave," my father said. Dunwoody didn't hear him. Or maybe he thought Daddy was close to breaking. Tears tumbled down my mother's cheeks as she clung to the back of that chair. "Please," Daddy said. Dunwoody closed his eyes and stretched out his arm like Aaron's rod. Sweat trickled down his forehead, into his untamed eyebrows. He implored God to have mercy on this stubborn, broken man. His words bespoke mercy, but he spat them at my father.

None of the praying men saw my mother heft that heirloom chair over her head and plod toward Dunwoody, jaw set for murder. She closed the distance without hesitation, like this wasn't the first time she'd killed a man in her living room. Perhaps Clay Tompkins felt her passing, or maybe he prayed like I did, with one eye open. He grabbed the chair's bottommost stretcher before Mama could swing. I don't think he cared for the itinerant preacher, but I do know that on this particular Saturday afternoon in September, a lowly assistant pastor saved the Right Reverend Donald Dunwoody from being fed through a straw the rest of his life.

Mama screamed at Dunwoody to get out, for all of them to get out of her house. Every man in the room jumped, even Daddy. Calvin tumbled backwards, but nobody else heard him. The men shrank from Mama who still brandished that chair overhead, her green eyes like a wrathful ocean. Clay Tompkins, clinging to the chair like the tail of a kite, took hold of her shoulder. Daddy stood, and I felt bad that of all these interlopers, Clay was the one he was going to kill. Clay let go of Mama and showed his palm to Daddy. Mama relaxed her grip on the chair and allowed him to take it from her. He set it safely out of reach.

Dunwoody's jaw worked like a stamping machine on an empty assembly line. Before he could feed more words into it, Reverend Hardison said: "Enough." My father was coiled now; I could feel more than see it. I wanted to shout that they'd best not walk but run, that he could kill any of them as easily as gutting a catfish. "Come along, Don," Reverend Hardison said. It was as if the words punctured a hole in Dunwoody. He traipsed wordlessly out of our living room. Shutting up a revival preacher was likely the only miracle Reverend Hardison ever worked, but how many others can boast of doing the same?

Calvin and I crawled to the hallway door and watched the men file out the front door, down the porch steps, into sunlight. Something in me wanted to run after them through that sunfired doorway, but I crouched rooted in this place of my birth as their silhouettes disappeared. There was a thumping of car doors, an engine revving, the crackle of tires on gravel.

Returning to the living room door, I saw my mother glaring at my father, her chest a bellows. Her eyes were splintered glass, and I thought she might take up her chair again. He approached her like she was a wild animal. She trembled, broken-glass eyes cutting him in a way the words of a preacher could never do. "Don't," she said.

Daddy came forward. She slapped his outstretched hands, his face. He pulled her close as she struck him over and over. When she could no longer swing her arms, she clenched his shirt and skin in her fists. She mumbled a word into his chest, her trembling almost like a seizure now. That word remains a mystery to me, and a deeper mystery still is how a solitary word could peg my father in place even as her clutching fingernails pinked his t-shirt with blood.

"What's happening?" Calvin whispered behind me. "They're not saying anything."

That night I dreamed of heaven and the people who dwell there. The ground was misted cloud, and from it grew all manner of bright and vibrant things. Animals moved past in twos and threes and sometimes herds. The animals knew to stay away from the edge of this misted landscape, but some of the people did not. These people wandered paradise, calling the names of wives and husbands, of brothers and mothers, of children.

These searchers drew close to the edge because they heard the cries from hell below, a great chorus of want and hurt and rage, and within that chorus the individual straining throats, crying out for release, for a drop of water, for a word.

I too stood with the searchers as they gathered in mounting horror, and I saw on their faces recognition. Many heard the cries of friends and lovers and parents, yet they turned away in sorrow. But the mothers and fathers, they could not turn away. Arrayed along the edge of this misty salvation, these parents began to hurl themselves into the darkness beneath. Some stepped forward as if into a bath, others dove headfirst, but none hesitated. They cast themselves hellward toward their children.

I saw my mother poised at the edge with those other parents, and I shouted to her that I was here, that she needn't jump. She tumbled forward with the rest of them, adding herself to this overpouring of lovingkindness, and from the depths of hell there came a roar of indignation. I elbowed past the onlookers until I too stood at the edge of heaven, and though I could hear neither my mother nor my father, I leaped as my mother had leaped.

I woke in our home surrounded by the gathered darkness and its quiet. My mother slept and my father slept and there was a peace between them and it pressed outward against the darkness. I asked God to forgive me for what I had chosen in my dream, to forgive us all for loving how we do. As I drifted back to sleep, I knew what my mother knew, which is that the blood of man cannot bear us God-ward. The blood of man is a river bound to the earth, and man is not born Godward, but my mother waits in her pew because God may yet come to us here.

They's all kinds of drunks and daddy is the mean kind. He's as good as any daddy when he isn't drunk, but when he gets liquor in him you don't want to be close enough for him to throw a lug nut, and you sure don't want to be in reach, cause he's faster than you think and he can lift a whole Ford 9 in motor hisself. He gets mean when the liquor gets in him because our house ain't painted and his shop's too small for much work and Mama don't cook like he likes and we kids is loud and there ain't never enough money.

If you put your finger right there on top my head there is the notch from his best socket wrench which I dropped down a McCormick 10-20 on accident and then the flashlight after it, so once he got it back and saw how it was scratched he lit it up against my head and then I was in bed for some days, and how my head hurt, and Mama wanted to call the doctor but he said weren't no money for a doctor. Mama loves me, but she was afraid.

She was afraid, and that's why she begged Doc Willard while he stitched her head there on that same couch, don't call the Sheriff, don't you do it, I got some money saved and I'm gonna take these babies to my cousin's but I can't get it all together before he'd be out of jail. You know what he'll do then, she said, so please just give me some time.

Doc Willard showed me how to hold that gauze under where he was sewing to catch the blood and keep it off the cushions so that's why the only blood you see on there right now is fresh.

He's always better for a time after, so I'll have time to get some money together and leave, is what Mama told Doc Willard. She didn't mind me hearing because she knows I won't say nothing, and you can see my brothers are too little to understand, plus they was crying and pulling on her arms just like now, only that last time she could shush them in between asking Doc Willard not to call the Sheriff.

So Doc I guess he took pity or was just real tired, cause flu was going around plus everybody knows Daddy beats Mama, that's just what he does. You know they all know cause of how they look at you when you go into town. So he gave me some more of that gauze and half a bottle of peroxide and said you take care of your mama you hear.

And I would've stopped Daddy last night but I was sleeping and I guess they were in his shop yonder cause the blood drops run from our living room down the porch steps over the dirt to out there only it was the other way around, she was out there, you know it cause when you go out you'll see that same socket wrench with more blood and her hair tangled up round it and his Packard is gone and he's gone and she's laying here on this couch and I done used up all Doc Willard's gauze and she won't wake up and my brothers are crying and she won't wake up.

"Did you notice anything along the path up to our house?" Julie Moore asked as I raked out the gully bordering their garden. She'd hung old pantyhose from branches, stuffed with God knows what. I knew it was her doing because none of them had been tied higher than four feet.

"Nope," I said.

"Liar. They got roots and moss in them. I cast them with a spell that gives toad skin to anybody who passes by them thirteen times. I've been counting, and after you go home today, that'll be six times. Assuming you've not been creeping up here at night."

My skin suddenly felt itchy, but I refrained from scratching. "Your mama know you're a witch?"

"It took me a month to collect all the ingredients. I had to spit on the mix three times a day and keep it buried under a cedar tree. Then I dug it up at midnight and said the spell over it."

"One night you're gonna say the wrong spell and turn yourself the rest of the way into a skunk."

"I even had to put five drops of my own blood on it." She showed me a red hole in the tip of her index finger. "I used an awl from Daddy's tool shed." I was impressed a girl would creep about in the dead of night, dripping her own blood and uttering incantations in the shadows of trees, but I wasn't about to tell her so. "I couldn't find devil's claw, so I used slimy mushrooms and extra pine needles. It may not make you green, but you'll definitely get warts."

"Is that what happened to you?"

"Once you're all warty-toady, maybe I'll sell you the antidote."

I raked free a clot of clay and matted leaves.

"I got all kinds of spells. Want to know where I get them?"

"Nope."

"I got one from a fairy-tale book. Got another from when Mama took me to see a play in Winston. Spells are everywhere, but most people don't pay them any mind."

"That's because most people don't want to go to hell."

"My spell book is like a jigsaw puzzle. One day I'll have all the pieces."

I hacked at another clot.

"Daniel."

A ringneck snake that hadn't yet descended into hibernation threatened to strike my rake. I tapped its head with a tine and it wiggled away.

"*Daniel.*"

I knew I was the only kid who ever talked to Julie, but I didn't see how I had to be a martyr to that cause.

"Daniel?" It's a simple question, the question of a boy's name. When she concluded that she was getting no more words out of me, Julie sighed in exasperation and stomped away.

Later that afternoon, I met Calvin and Eddie in the dirt lot behind the Red and White. Calvin crouched, spread his arms, and growled. "You're goin down, Hossein!"

"I don't want to be the Arab."

"Well, who are you then?"

"Dusty Rhodes."

"Then Eddie and me are the Valiant Brothers."

"Which one?"

"All of 'em."

"You can't be three guys."

"Watch us!" Eddie shouted as he drove me into a pile of cardboard boxes. We wrestled until he tagged Calvin in. We all lifted boxes over our heads, pretending we'd spilled out of the ring and were about to bash each other with folding chairs.

"Dusty Rhodes turns on the Valiant Brothers like the chickenshit traitor he is!" shouted Calvin. He threw his box at my balls. Everybody knew that Dusty had turned face, and that this is different than being a traitor, but Calvin didn't believe becoming a good guy mattered if the way you did it was to turn on your partner in the middle of a match. Loyalty was important to him. When Mary Taylor had announced to our class that my mother nearly murdered the revival preacher, Calvin had replied that the only reason Dunwoody hadn't gotten what he deserved was because Mary's mother had leaped from the shadows and blocked the chair with her enormous ass. Calvin's loyalty had earned him a slap and detention.

"Dusty Rhodes drops Jerry Valiant with a chair!" I smashed a cardboard box over his head. Calvin dropped and faked traumatic injury.

Eddie climbed a pile of pallets and poised to leap. "Johnny Valiant tags in!" I backed toward the pallets and pretended to scan the ring in search of still-living Valiants. "Get closer," Eddie said. I complied and he jumped onto my back. Calvin staged a miraculous recovery and went for my legs. We battled across the lot, slinging boxes, shaking off pretend dazes, and wiping pretend blood from our eyes, narrating it all at the top of our lungs. Our match got increasingly real, until I had Calvin in a headlock and was making him eat dirt while Eddie pulled my hair.

"Leave that boy alone!" A hand yanked me to my feet. I found myself looking into the angry face of Fred Ledbetter. His thinning copper hair was combed forward, where it congregated over the dent in his forehead. Up close his divot looked even deeper, like you could fit most of a hammer's head into it.

Calvin spit out a mouthful of dirt and blood. "We were just playing."

Ledbetter tightened his grip on my arm. "You like picking on little kids?"

"I wasn't picking on him."

"I'm not little. We're the same age!"

"I'd take you down to Sheriff Wilson, except I doubt he'd do anything more about you than he did about your daddy."

"Turn him loose, you shit-heel!"

"You watch your tongue, boy!" Ledbetter shook his head. "I'd think your daddy would have more sense than to let you go about with a Waterson." He gave Eddie a disparaging glance. "Both your daddies."

"You're just mad because Daniel's mama beat you in the town council!" Calvin shouted.

"And his daddy threw you out of their house," mumbled Eddie.

"You'd best shut your mouths about things you don't know nothing about."

"I know Daniel's daddy is going to give you the ass-whipping of a lifetime."

"What'd you say to me, boy?" Ledbetter grabbed for Calvin, who darted out of reach.

"I also know you're crooked as a dog's hind leg!"

Ledbetter dragged me with him as he maneuvered to trap Calvin in a corner. I heard the underarm of my t-shirt tear.

"I'm getting the sheriff," Eddie said.

"Everything alright, Fred?" Clay Tompkins stood holding a grocery bag in the alleyway. "I thought I heard some commotion back here."

Ledbetter scowled. "Caught these boys fighting," he said. He shook my arm. "And this one was beating on the littler one."

"That's a lie!" Calvin shouted.

"Boy, your daddy's gonna hear about how you speak to adults."

"Fred," Clay said, "when my meeting with the boys is over, I'll be sure to speak with Calvin's father."

"What meeting?"

"Bible study."

Ledbetter scowled. "*Bible* study."

Clay nodded.

"This crew?"

"'Let the little children come unto me.'"

"Behind the Red and White."

"Oh yeah. The dirt here is perfect for it."

"Dirt."

"We're studying the eighth chapter of John. You know, where the Pharisees want to stone a woman to death, and Jesus crouches like so . . . ." Clay squatted and pressed a finger into the fine dirt. "Then he wrote something that turned them all away." Clay squinted up at Ledbetter. "What do you think he wrote, Fred?"

Ledbetter let go of my arm. "How should I know? The Bible doesn't say."

Clay traced a circle in the dirt. "You know what I think? I think he wrote their hidden sins. The things they thought nobody on earth knew about. But God sees everything, doesn't he, Fred?"

Ledbetter scowled. "I don't have time for this."

"Tell your wife I hope she brings her lasagna for tomorrow's potluck!" Clay watched him trudge down the alley, then turned to us.

"You've got to forgive ole Fred. He's got a lot on his mind. Now, since I've delivered you all from perdition, can I assume you'll be joining the Explorers?"

"We're in sixth grade now," Eddie said. "Lots of homework."

"We camp on Saturdays. You get lots of Saturday homework?"

Calvin raised his eyebrows to imply that indeed there might be tons of Saturday homework for sixth-graders.

"We play a game called Stump the Preacher. Y'all ask me Bible questions, and if I can't answer, you get to dunk my head in the creek." It was little wonder people had concerns about Clay Tompkins.

"We can ask anything?"

"Anything Bible-related."

"How long do we get to hold you under?"

Clay laughed. "Longer than I'd like, but not as long as I deserve."

I guess I'll always remember his saying that, because of what happened. No matter how lowly Clay Tompkins thought himself in God's kingdom, he never did anything to deserve what was coming.

<hr />

My father had been demoted to second-most dangerous Waterson in Cantwell County. I knew Mama couldn't stay away from church forever, if only because she hated having people think she was beginning to take after her mother. I figured this meant we'd have to find a church where nobody knew us. That's why, when she woke me Sunday morning and told me to get my church clothes on, I asked where we were going. "That's a stupid question," she snapped.

The church lot was nearly full when we arrived. Inside was the quiet hum of the organ prelude as the choir shuffled into position and Reverend Hardison conferred with an elder. People settled squirming children, waved to one another, considered their programs. There was the familiar smell of wood soap and dried flowers. Nobody seemed to notice us, thank God. But as I tried to slink into a back pew, Mama took my hand and kept walking up the center aisle. Her chin was thrust forward, a terse smile plastered in place. We passed the middle pews. I felt more than heard the growing stillness, because my ears were thrumming, and I was sure my face was a moment away from bursting into flame. Mama kept walking, her thin smile unwavering.

Reverend Hardison noticed us coming up the aisle. I could tell he was wondering about my mother's intentions. I was too.

Mama directed me toward a narrow space on the front pew. She nudged me past turned legs. Eddie Gilchrist and his family were there; he gave me a sympathetic look. Since his faux salvation by Don Dunwoody, he'd learned what it feels like to have the entire church staring at you. Any minute now I was going to catch fire, not just my face but my entire body. *Why, Mama?* Watersons were not front-pew people, and preacher-killers certainly didn't belong this close to a pulpit.

As she sat down, my mother whispered a hoarse hello to Mrs. Gilchrist, who reached across Eddie to squeeze her hand. Mama's eyes welled up, but her smile remained fixed. Reverend Hardison rearranged his notes, eyes furtively taking us in. He seemed to be pondering some question of theology floating just beyond his grasp. Clay Tompkins sat in his usual place to the side, like a relief pitcher who knows he'll never be called from the bullpen. He smiled at us.

Mrs. Colwich leaned forward from the pew behind and gave Mama's shoulder a reassuring squeeze. Mrs. Rose did the same. Mama smiled her tight smile and nodded almost imperceptibly at each gesture of kindness. A single tear struck her Bible's worn leather cover and restored a droplet-sized portion of its luster.

Reverend Hardison settled into the familiar rhythm: hymns, announcements, a prayer, then the sermon. This one was about the cloud of witnesses in heaven, about how nothing we do here on earth goes unseen by those who have gone before. Did he comprehend the truth of this? Does anyone?

That evening was supper at Granny's. Daddy slouched slack-faced on her couch watching *Hee Haw*. An untouched glass of iced tea sweated on the coffee table.

"Mama," my mother called in a purposeful voice as she placed a bowl of creamed corn on the dining table, "you should have seen how gracious everyone was today."

"How's that?" Granny cried from the kitchen.

My mother's brow crinkled in annoyance. "At church, Mama!"

There was a clatter of pans from the kitchen. "Lee Ann, you know church hasn't set well with me since your father died!"

My mother closed her eyes. "I'm talking about us, Mama! Daniel and me! We went to church today!"

Granny peered around the kitchen doorframe. "Took you back, did they?" She turned her eyes to Daddy and me on the couch, then back to my mother, who was rearranging dishes by quarter inches. "Well, I suppose churches can't afford to be picky." She disappeared back into the kitchen.

"There's plenty of churches that make sure you know you aren't welcome. But there wasn't anyone going to look me in the eye and cast us out. Not a one of them is better than us." She eyed Daddy, who watched Buck Owens and Roy Clark duel with guitar and banjo.

Granny steered a tray of ham through the kitchen door. "Well," she said, "I suppose a church that isn't full of sinners is a waste of timber."

"That's what Sarah Gilchrist said! 'The Father welcomes all of us back.' You just have to be willing to humble yourself." Her voice had risen. "You have to ask for his help. Isn't that right, Ray?" I tried to lose myself with Daddy in the blur of Roy Clark's fast-picking fingers. He and Buck Owens were laughing so hard I wondered if they were only pretending. "Ray," my mother said. "*Ray.*"

I leaned closer and closer to Daddy, until my bare elbow touched his arm, giving me a static shock. He didn't stir. His jaw was set, his face blued by the light of the television screen. His eyes were elsewhere. "Ray Waterson," my mother said in a low, fierce voice, "you can cower from the rest of the world if you want, but I'll not be ignored." She took a step into the living room.

"Honey," Granny said, "come help me brew more tea. You know how it clouds when I do it." Mama stood just inside the living room threshold, fists clenched, eyes glinting. "Lee Ann," Granny said in her no-bullshit voice. "*Now.*" Mama followed her mother into the kitchen, and Granny pulled closed its swinging door. Someone turned on the sink. I took care not to let my skin brush Daddy's. His eyes were unblinking.

It was Granny who finally pulled him from his spell. She called me to the table, where Mama sat red-eyed and waiting, then turned off the television and stood beside Daddy, running her gnarled fingers through his hair. She murmured something. "What's she saying to him?" I whispered to Mama.

"What?"

"Granny."

Mama considered her mother where she whispered to my father as she stroked his hair. It was like how Daddy soothed horses, and I realized in that moment that he must have learned how from her. Mama shook her head. "Mama always did have a way with wild animals."

When we were all seated, Granny took the conversation in hand, with me as her foil. She asked about school, about Eddie, about Calvin and his entire clan—aloof mother, self-made father, bitchy sisters, even an uncle down in Atlanta I'd never heard of who was apparently a bit of a ne'er-do-well. There was no staring sullenly at my plate and satisfying Granny Watts with single-word replies. She expected complete sentences, and if I left things out, she prompted me like she was quizzing me on a book she'd already read.

On the subject of my numerous girlfriends, however, she was clearly misinformed. "Granny," I said, "I've never had a girlfriend. And I don't want one."

Granny gasped and launched into a recounting of her daughters' varied romances. "Any given night under this roof," she said, "witnessed the unfolding of a Great Romantic Tragedy. Ole Billy Shakespeare could have used the Watts family for inspiration."

Daddy grinned and cast a tentative glance at Mama. She gave him a tight smile. He straightened in his chair a bit. "Well, now, Mother Watts, all that drama may have been true with your other girls, but surely things calmed down once I began courting Lee Ann." Mama and Granny rolled their eyes in unison and began berating him with specifics. Everything from missed dates because he didn't wear a watch when he fished to promising her a fancy evening and driving her all the way to Winston to sneak into the drive-in movies. Daddy raised his hands. "Time to give all those grievances up to Jesus, ladies."

This had an effect similar to when I would aim our garden hose into the chicken coop. Daddy gave me an incredulous look. I began stuffing food into my mouth. Warm mashed potatoes, sweet creamed corn, slices of smoked ham. I was full of love for them all, though I didn't know how to say it, and perhaps didn't even realize it then. I noticed Granny, too, had begun to eat with more gusto, watching delightedly as Mama laid into Daddy, and he in turn parried with remarks that spurred her on.

My parents left as the sun dropped behind the trees. Mama admonished Granny not to let me stay up late watching TV and to inspect what I packed for my school lunch. Granny and I stood at her screen door and watched Daddy's truck tool down her dirt road, Mama seated close. I know the sight of them easing into the sunset should have made me happy, especially given how they'd been lately, but instead it filled me with melancholy.

Granny patted my shoulder. "Now that the boss is gone, how about a second piece of cobbler?"

"How come he can't stop?"

She led me into the kitchen and sat me down at the table. She spooned blackberry cobbler onto a china saucer, stuck one of her silver dessert forks into it, and placed it before me. One of my tears splashed onto the cobbler crust. Granny knelt and pulled my head to her. A soothing murmur began in her chest, which she stifled by clearing her throat. She gripped my shoulders like she was willing a portion of her strength into me, held me away from her, and peered into my eyes. "Listen, boy. People will disappoint you for the rest of your life. I've lived seventy-two years, and I only ever met a handful worth a damn."

She glanced through the kitchen threshold toward her front door. For a moment I thought I saw my father peering through the screen. "Your daddy is . . . was a fine boy." She pressed her finger onto a stray cobbler crumb and lifted it to her tongue. "And he *is* a good man. Never forget that. But he went down into hell, over there. The stink of it rises up in him sometimes."

"Is that why he has nightmares?"

She shook her head, lips tight, wrinkles arrayed about them like rows of scars. "Lord knows why men dream what they dream."

"How come he never hits us?"

"What?"

"I heard that's what drunks do. Beat up their families."

"Don't call him that." She ran a trembling hand through my hair. "Most men drink because they're powerless. But your daddy . . . ." She stilled her hand. "Well, he has a deep power in him. You know that by now." I nodded. "Sometimes that power—and the memories of what he's done with it—is too much for a man to bear. Drinking is a way to silence it. Kindly like my headache powders."

"He wasn't always this way, was he?"

"People get broke, Daniel. Just like things." She pointed at a thin gray crack that originated near my plate's rim and disappeared beneath the cobbler. "This plate'll probably last well past when I'm dead and buried." She sighed. "But you never know, when you're washing it or setting it on the table, if it's going to snap in your hands. Some people are like that."

"Was it killing Bobby Doyle?"

"The cracks beneath your daddy's skin run deeper, child. You know that."

"Vietnam?" A thrill ran through me, saying that forbidden word.

"Your mama thinks so. But I believe they were in him from the beginning. That God crafted him just a little broken, the way he does people sometimes."

"Why does God do that?"

She wiped her spotless counter with a damp sponge. "You're asking the wrong person. I've not set foot inside a church since your grandfather's funeral."

"But you read your Bible."

She pinned me with her watery gaze. "What makes you say that?"

"Your bookmark's always in a different place."

"Eat your cobbler." She shuffled toward the pantry.

"Granny?"

"Inquisitiveness is a boy's way of asking for more chores."

"Will he get better?"

She paused in the pantry doorway, considered her worn and veined hands. "I don't know, child." She gave an apologetic smile. "Maybe being your grandmother, I'm supposed to tell you different. But I try not to lie." Her look hardened. "Don't waste my cobbler."

A knock at the front door drew her from the pantry. "Who in the world comes knocking on a Sunday evening?"

Harlan Carver stood squinting on the other side of her screen door. He seemed not to see me where I stood on the kitchen threshold. "Evening, madam," he said as Granny approached. "How are you?" His pressed yellow shirt crinkled when he offered his hand through the crack Granny made with her door. She regarded his hand. "What is it you're wanting, young man." Her monotone made it more declaration than question.

"We've been working in your area, helping your neighbors improve the value of their homes, and I wanted to give you the opportunity—"

"I ain't got neighbors." She pointed left. "That there's a junkyard." She pointed right. "And nobody lives in them woods but a family of thieving raccoons."

Carver's smile stayed glued to his pitted face. His unsmiling eyes roved across Granny's porch, her side yard. "I mean neighbors in your community, madam. Now if you'd permit me to walk around your house—"

"What is it you're selling." Her flat voice stifled him like a blanket over a fire.

"We sell exterior protection."

"You mean imitation siding?"

The man's eyes traveled to her other side yard. "High-quality aluminum, yes'm. Now if I could just walk—"

"I've got no more use for imitation siding that I do for imitation cheese, or imitation Bibles."

"Every estimate comes with a free home value appraisal."

"I know the value of this home better than anyone."

"Is that right."

"If you get going now, you can reach the main road while there's still some light."

"Uh huh." Carver peered past Granny's shoulder. His eyes roamed her foyer. He squinted to see further, to where I stood.

"Daniel," Granny shouted over her shoulder, "go fetch Buck and Roy from the barn and tell 'em supper's ready."

Carver showed her his palms. "Sorry to disturb you, madam. Y'all have a nice evening."

Granny latched the screen door as he tromped down her steps. He glanced back toward her darkened barn, then slid into his gleaming Cadillac. Granny pressed closed her door and watched him through a sliver of open curtain until his rear lights were out of sight. "That one should've been bored for the hollow horn," she said. "Oozing out here on a Sunday evening, calling me *madam* like this is a New Jersey roadside whorehouse." She shuffled back toward her kitchen, muttering about chain-gang carpetbagging industrialists.

I told her about Harlan Carver, his fight with Daddy, the shiny revolver in his glovebox.

"Lord-a-mercy. Aluminum siding, my foot. You see him since? With Fred Ledbetter, maybe?" I shook my head. Granny took my chin in her trembling hand. "Child, if you see that man again, I want you to tell *me*, you hear? Only me. And listen. I mean *listen*. Do not tell your father." She glanced toward her empty front porch. "We got to keep those two apart. Understand?"

Oh, Granny. No promise I've kept has cost more.

———————

Whether out of obligation or curiosity, Calvin, Eddie, and I camped with the Young Explorers the next weekend. We agreed the name was exactly what a church would call something to disguise the Jesus part, and sure enough, Clay Tompkins found ample opportunity to preach. It wasn't nearly as painful as we'd anticipated, though.

We camped close to Moravian Falls, where we could hear the tumbling water from our tents. Once our tents were up, Clay led us to a moss-covered log, which he invited us to lift. When none of us could, not even the older boys working together, Clay delivered his point. "That," he said, "is just about the weight of Goliath's spear." Then he pointed to a rock bigger than Calvin. "That's the weight of his shield." None of us bothered trying to budge the rock. Clay pointed to a branch midway up a pine and said Goliath has to stoop to walk under it. His use of present tense was eerie; we were accustomed to Bible stories being relayed as distant history. He asked if we knew any cuss words. "Not just regular cussing," he said. "I mean really nasty curses."

We kids looked at each other and considered the possibility that our parents had been gravely mistaken to let us venture into the forest with this man. Clay told us all the cussing we'd heard in our short lives was just nursery rhymes compared to what Goliath conjures. He dug some pebbles from his pocket and tossed them onto the ground. He asked if any of us wanted to go up against so terrible a man with just a few stones.

Of course we knew the correct answer was *No*, though some of us imagined whirling a sling above our heads, feeling the weight of a river stone there, releasing it into the air and thereby into the vengeful hidden hand of God. Watching it arc hard and fast, seeing Goliath's eyes widen as it embedded into the flesh above them, hearing the crack of his skull, the gasps of the gathered Philistines, the creak of the giant's tumbling armored frame. As if reading our minds, Clay unfolded his pocketknife, stood on tiptoes, and etched a rectangle into the bark of a cedar a couple dozen feet away. He told us the rectangle was roughly the size of Goliath's forehead, though not nearly high enough off the ground. He invited us to hit it with one of the stones he'd provided.

"Y'all are probably about as experienced with regular rock-throwing as David was with rock-slinging," Clay said, "so this is a fair enough contest. Except that the tree won't skewer you with a 12-foot spear when you miss."

We took turns throwing rocks and missing, while Clay explained how much further David stands from Goliath and how little time he has before the giant gets his freight train of a spear hefted so he can hurl it with as much accuracy as Rawly Eastwick. He told us about the killing stone and how David promises to behead Goliath before the fight commences, even though the shepherd boy doesn't have a sword. "He knows," Clay said, "that it's Goliath's own sword he'll take his head with." He told us about the Philistines' panic when they see the giant fall, the great destruction brought upon them for being party to Goliath's blasphemy.

Then he told us about King Saul's jealousy toward David. "The only thing worse for some men than being beaten," he said, "is being rescued." It felt like he was offering this to me as a way to make sense of my father. Only now do I comprehend that it explains something in me, too. I guess Clay's woodland sermon stuck with me not because I hadn't heard the story of David and Goliath but because I *had*, like every other child. A true story lay hidden within the story we all thought we knew, and Clay gave it life despite our knowing. And this makes me wonder: How many stories have we missed because we didn't have someone to tell them true?

⸻

I liked history even though it was something they tried to teach us in school. I didn't like history textbooks, though; they read more like lists of facts than stories and not even the interesting facts at that. I preferred the histories in our town library—shelf after shelf devoted to every conflict that might interest a boy: both world wars, the Korean War, the Civil War, the Revolutionary War, and, of course, Vietnam. Books about that last one I read in the quiet confines of the library itself.

I also read books about our state's history and our town. I began to think of Hickory Shore as a forgetful old man bowed up with age whose attic was piled with journals. You could still form a picture of who he'd been and things he'd done, even if he himself had forgotten most of it. I learned to navigate the oldest books our library contained, to sort through their recitations of rights and wrongs—rights that became wrong the more you learned of the wrongs that had preceded them, and wrongs that may well prove right in the final accounting. Or if not right, then maybe just the very best a man can muster, laboring ill-sighted as he does under his appointed burden. These books harbored lies and misperceptions, just like people, so I had to cultivate discernment by setting them alongside each other—this author's omissions next to that one's worship of an idea next to accounts from people who'd witnessed the same thing and recorded it differently.

I was probably the chief cause of interlibrary loans in Cantwell County between that fall in 1974 and when I left town in 1981.

Perhaps I still am. I aimed to construct something like a house from crooked timber. I suppose you'd need to look down with the eyes of God to decide if what I've built is habitable. The most valuable thing I took from all these books—all this scrutiny—is that history isn't something behind us. It unspools from our very hands and enshrouds us.

I mostly kept my promise to Granny Watts about Harlan Carver, though I did tell Eddie and Calvin about his visit. We three patrolled Hickory Shore on our bikes weekends and after school, paying special attention to Fred Ledbetter's whereabouts. Fred drank a lot of coffee with other men at Marjean's Diner. Calvin was certain any skullduggery directed at my grandmother's place would originate with Ledbetter, so we turned a hollow beneath a holly hedge across from Marjean's into our observation post. We recognized some from church, others by sight but not name. One Saturday Eddie had a flash of inspiration and crawled backwards out from under the bush. "Wait here," he said. A few minutes later he returned with a framed picture of several men clustered at the base of the Town Hall steps, squinting at the photographer.

"What's that?"

"The town council. They pose for a new picture after every election."

"Where'd you get it?"

"The Town Hall lobby."

"You *stole* it?"

"Borrowed it."

Calvin pointed to one of the men in the picture. "That guy's in there with him right now."

"Yesterday he had coffee with *this* guy."

"Maybe it's just regular business stuff," I said.

"My daddy says businessmen talk to customers when they want to *make* something and to politicians when they want to *take* something."

"Fred Ledbetter needs an ass-beating." I considered Ledbetter, his hairy red arms parked on the table he shared with a councilman, his fat-knuckled hand cradling a coffee mug. He laughed at something the councilman said. His body didn't move; his jaw just worked up and down.

Two gray pants legs suddenly obstructed our view. "What are you boys doing under there?" We crawled out from under the holly and stood before Mr. Beasley, our sixth-grade teacher. I don't think he was any older than our parents, but he had liver spots on his face and shiny dark hair that fit his skull like a cap. A thin and uneven mustache trembled beneath his nose, as if he'd gotten a whiff of something unpleasant. "I asked you boys a question."

Eddie held the stolen picture behind his back. "Just playing army," he said.

"Well you look to be spying on people."

"Oh no, sir," Calvin said. "We're *pretending* to spy, but we're not really spying."

In Mr. Beasley's classroom, he kept a row of clean square bins arrayed beneath the windows. Each served as a receptacle for one kind of item. This one for construction paper, that one for crayons, another for bottles of rubber cement. He regarded us as if judging in which bin we belonged. "Do you boys hope to get better grades on next week's geography project than you did last week's book report?"

I answered *Yes*. Calvin and Eddie said *No*. It was a confusing question.

"Young men, I believe in two things: homework and hickory sticks. I'll make sure boys who don't do their share of the first will get plenty of the second."

"Yes sir."

"How you spend Saturdays is your business, but you'd best leave other people to theirs." We dragged our bikes out from under the hedge. Eddie had by now shoved the purloined picture up the back of his shirt. As we pedaled away, I noticed Fred Ledbetter watching us, his jawbone no longer exercised by laughter.

———⟨———

Whether it was because his father said something or simply because he was a jerk like his older brother Daryl, Carl Ledbetter shoved me during recess that following Monday. "My daddy says your daddy's going to hell," he said.

I rolled over to see Calvin lunge at Carl and get headlocked by one of Carl's friends before he could reach killing velocity. The boy told Calvin to be still or else he'd squish his head like a pumpkin.

"Your daddy killed Bobby Doyle," Carl said. "Broadus Doyle's my friend."

"You don't even know Broadus," Calvin said, his voice muffled. "You're a bigger dipshit than your brother."

"I do so know him." Carl sounded like his feelings were hurt. "Get up," he told me.

I imagined Carl's older brother standing over some other kid on the high school playground. I wondered if that boy was going to get up and fight. I clambered to my feet as Carl danced from foot to foot, fists raised. I reared back to swing at him, and in my head I was like Daddy walloping Harlan Carver, but my fist seemed to be coming from another county and stopping for groceries along the way, because by the time it got in the vicinity of Carl's nose he'd already punched me twice. I felt my knuckles bounce off the side of his concrete head as he pummeled my cheeks and nose, and through the din of my thrumming blood I heard Calvin shout from the other kid's waist that he was going to whip Carl's ass, rip his balls off, and so on, most of it inspired by *Sgt. Rock* comics.

Then Mr. Beasley strode into our fray atop his signature gray slacks, seized us by our upper arms, and marched us to the principal's office. Along the way, he told Carl his father had raised him better than that. Principal Blevins warned us about permanent files and juvenile delinquency, then gave us each ten licks with a varnished oak paddle. It didn't make sense to me, giving two kids the same number of licks when one of them had done far more punch-receiving than punch-landing, but that was justice for you.

—————◁

As winter approached, Calvin, Eddie, and I spent our free time building redoubts in the woods around my house. As we worked, we recounted to one another the future legend of my father's last stand. Once this snake of a conspiracy raised enough of its head for Daddy to discern the fullness of where it lay, he'd kill Ledbetter, Carver, a bloody quorum of the Town Council, and maybe some county supervisors for good measure. We knew he wouldn't hurt Sheriff Wilson, but he might cut down a deputy or two, if left with no choice.

All of their deaths would be effected by the Bowie recon knife Daddy wore on his belt; of this we had no doubt. No man could hide from my father. *And after the bloodletting*, I thought, *he'll retreat to these woods. The ones he haunts even now.*

Sometimes we spoke scarcely a word as we huddled in our bivouacs and dugouts, behind our ill-strung screens, beneath our shaky lean-tos. We didn't feel a need to fill the air with words like adults. We thumbed through comics, swapped bottle caps and marbles, flicked lighters, sharpened sticks for traps, even tried our hand at tying flies, though I'd so far manifested none of my father's or grandfather's skill, despite my small fingers.

Other times we talked about the wars we'd fight and how we aimed to whip the entire Ledbetter crew—father, sons, dog, cat—as soon as we'd had our growth spurts, which we assured one another were right around the corner. I wasn't so sure about Calvin, given his father's height, and I figured Eddie would be a beanpole like his daddy, but surely I had to manifest some size sooner or later.

Julie Moore wandered upon us on a warm afternoon in March. We were setting a ridge-beam for a camouflaged hut. She surveyed our work from the slope above. "That had better not be one of our trees."

"We're on our side of the ditch."

"Well it looks like you're dragging limbs from *our* side."

Calvin rolled his eyes. "Are y'all really going to argue about dead wood?"

Julie sat on a rock and opened her spell book.

"How come I never broke out in warts?" I asked.

"Deer ate my herb bags."

"What in the world are y'all talking about now?"

"Julie's a witch."

Eddie walked up the slope and peered over her shoulder. She showed him some of the spells with which she intended to afflict me once she secured the ingredients. "This one I have everything I need for, but you have to cast it at exactly three in the morning, and I don't have an alarm clock."

"Got anything for bullies?"

"You mean those Ledbetters?" We all nodded. Julie paged through her book. "I got plenty of revenge spells. That's my specialty. It just depends on what you want to do to them." After some discussion and page-flipping, Eddie and Julie agreed festering skin lesions would yield the optimal blend of non-lethal discomfort and embarrassment. They started rooting through the underbrush.

"How do I tell what a mandrake looks like?" Eddie asked.

"It looks like a little man. Like Calvin, only bigger."

"You're so funny I forgot to laugh."

"Does it grow around here?"

"Everything grows around here."

"Y'all are gonna get snakebit."

"I found some yellowed fern." Eddie raised it overhead like a trophy.

"Find me a toad."

"What are you gonna do with it?"

"We need its liver."

"Daniel," Eddie said, "find us some reindeer moss."

"I never heard of reindeer moss. Reindeer aren't even real."

"Yes they are," Julie called from beneath a downed log.

"No they *aren't*, you big baby."

"*Santa's* reindeer aren't real. Regular reindeer are, moron."

"I think it's like regular moss," Calvin offered. "Only lighter and fluffier."

"We're gonna get snakebit for sure."

"If you see a copperhead or moccasin, I need their fangs. But don't break them."

"This recipe doesn't say anything about fangs."

"It's for something else."

I searched for reindeer moss with a rock in my fist. We found everything but the toad, so we settled for a crawdad from a nearby stream. Julie put it on a flat stone and smashed it with my rock.

"How can you tell which part's the liver?"

"It's in there somewhere." Julie extended dirty palms for the other ingredients, then ground them all with the smashed crawdad until she had a dull green paste. She spit on it three times. She looked up at us, her face solemn. "Y'all spit too."

Calvin and Eddie hawked three good ones. "C'mon Daniel." Calvin nudged me with his elbow.

"This is stupid."

"Do it."

"I don't want to."

"If you don't do it," Julie said, "the spell won't work. All the wronged parties have to spit."

"Then how come you spit?"

"Carl called me a sheepdog and hit me with a rock, and Daryl jammed a stick in my bicycle spokes and like to broke my neck."

Calvin shook his head. There was nothing he hated more than bullies.

I exhaled loudly. "*Fine.*" I spit three times.

Julie found a hazel switch and directed Eddie to strip the bark. She used it to stir the paste, then she read some hocus-pocus from her spell book. She adopted a foreign accent that sounded like a blend of Scotland and south Mississippi. Calvin shivered.

"Wait," I said.

"What now?"

"Can you add Carl's daddy? Maybe if he comes down with leprosy my daddy won't have to kill him."

More hocus-pocus. "Now we have to burn it," Julie said.

"How are we supposed to do that? It's all spitty."

"We have to build a fire over it. Every little bit has to burn, or else the revenge will land on us instead."

"Shit," Calvin said. "You should have told us that before we started."

We gathered twigs and built a small teepee over the magical mess, then crumbled dry leaves in the center. Calvin handed me his firestarter, and I used my Case knife to scrape magnesium flakes onto the leaves. I struck the flint with the blade's dull edge until tiny sparks spilled from it. Soon the magnesium flakes glowed orange, and I blew on them. Wisps of gray drifted up from the leaves, then a flame emerged with a puff. Eddie crumbled leaves over the top as Julie read more incantations. She walked around the fire in a circle while we fed it. We lay stones around it and crouched to stare into its trembling flames.

"Your spells ever work?" Calvin asked.

"No," I said.

Julie scowled. "How do you know?"

I held up my hands. "I don't see any warts."

She shrugged. "Some spells take time."

"How long will this one take?" Eddie asked.

"It should work pretty fast. Just be sure to burn it *all*."

We fed the flames more leaves as Calvin relayed in excruciating detail the latest *Sgt. Fury* plot, which led to our usual argument. Sgt. Fury and his howling commandos were always stumbling into moral dilemmas, which Calvin enjoyed, but which mostly irritated me. Heroism shouldn't be that complicated.

Julie crouched with armpits on knees and poked the embers with her hazel stick. She watched us like an anthropologist might observe some newfound tribe. Her animalistic crouch and her silent watchfulness and the flames reflected in her eyes lent the appearance of witchiness, though none of us was going to tell her that.

A week later, Carl Ledbetter wrecked his bicycle and broke his arm.

Perhaps the dead rose so easily that day because Reverend Hardison was in the throes of a vigorous sermon on hell. Some churchgoers nodded and others checked their watches, but many sat rock-still as if nailed to the pews. And who knew but that someone's eternal damnation was being undone as a consequence? In his chair off to the side of the dais, Clay Tompkins squirmed.

Outside, mist swirled like clothes in a washer. In the graveyard beside the church, Bobby Doyle walked amidst the headstones in unsullied black suit, brume purling in his wake. He walked over the mounded grass of younger graves and the shallowed soil of our ancestors. Over some he paused, as if to consider not the ground but the bones beneath the ground.

If Mama had seen that pale and grave-treading boy, her eyes would have splintered like thin glass, and the dread of our secret would have settled on her shoulders as it had my father's and mine. How much weight can a mother's frame bear? She kept her expectant eyes on Reverend Hardison and, above him, the heavy wooden cross affixed to the back wall.

The revenant paused before a crumbling gray headstone. He kneeled, and an apparition rose from the soil like smoke from a burn pile. It took on whitened flesh and the unruly hair of a tramp. The wraith followed the dead boy to another grave, and then another, and at each of the chosen places, Bobby knelt in demonic prayer, after which a paled follower rose from the dirt.

Reverend Hardison shouted the way he imagined the dead in hell must even now be howling. He had no idea that their silence is far worse.

The host gathering to Bobby Doyle comprised men and women born across generations. About their legs shambled listless children. The gravewalkers wore wool shifts and faded dungarees, poplin dresses and JC Penney suits. One or two wore little more than rags stitched from coarse sacking. Some of the women wore bonnets, the men embroidered coats. All were barefooted, for the dead walk more softly even than my father.

The swelling congregation moved in widening circles about the graveyard, calling forth some, forsaking others. The graves of those the dead boy did not call to himself darkened when he passed, as if scorched, and somehow I knew that every creeping thing beneath—every snake bedded in its wintering hole and every beetle scratching through topsoil—had fossilized. Bobby Doyle led his congregants to a slight rise near the graveyard's fence. Wind pressed against the church walls, but it disturbed neither the mist nor the clothes of the dead. Bobby knelt, and from the unmarked place rose a man naked but for breeches. What secret violence had placed him so close to the sanctioned dead, yet unnumbered among them? And how many more unknowns inhabit the soil below?

Reverend Hardison shouted that the dead in hell are shackled by chains of hot iron, even as the dead outside walked past our church windows, their ungodly gazes turned inward. With blackened eyes, they considered we gathered worshippers as we pondered hell and the coming Judgment, as we imagined our Sunday dinners, as we envisioned our week's work or whom we may marry or divorce or avenge ourselves upon. They regarded us as they passed, and that's how I know that in the history of rights and wrongs, a man can't know where he belongs until he feels the weight of judgment upon his grave. If salvation truly comes down to the content of our ledgers, the dead will do the accounting.

In a copse of pine just east of the graveyard, I saw my father where he stood watching the dead. Our dog Bailey stood beside him, hackles raised. Daddy knelt to calm him. Bobby Doyle led the gravewalkers toward him. My father turned and walked into the eastern woods, Bailey by his side, the dead in tow. They bore with them the enshrouding mist, and I knew this wasn't a dream because Reverend Hardison cut short his exposition to remark on the blessing of God dispersing the haze in time for Sunday dinner. He praised God for his son and for sun on Sundays, and everyone sighed and some laughed in relief, because hell, so far as they knew, had been returned to its caverns.

<hr/>

Hickory Shore Messenger
April 9th, 1975

HICKORY SHORE, NC—The Hickory Shore Town Council voted unanimously last night to annex several parcels of land west of town limits in what councilmen described as an effort to bring uniform services to more residents. "We are in no way altering ownership of these parcels," noted Councilman Bill Gardner. "Nor are we changing their designation as previously determined by Cantwell

County. Parcels zoned residential will remain as such, while those zoned mixed-use will hold greater value for their owners now that they have easier and more afford-able access to town services."

———

People said gunfire might have been avoided had someone explained to Granny Watts that a land survey is standard procedure after an-nexation. Those who knew her best suspected she would have mur-dered the surveyor outright had she been given time to stew on it. Fred Ledbetter's coffee meetings must have been effective, because we didn't know the town was reconsidering annexation until after the vote. A week later, Granny looked out her kitchen window to spy a man peering through a device atop a tripod he'd erected next to her barn. She had a predictable reaction, which was to snatch up my grandfather's Sweet Sixteen from beneath her bed, hobble down her back steps, and announce to him in her flat monotone that she was within her goddamned constitutional rights to send trespassers straightaway to Judgment.

"The law doesn't let you shoot trespassers," I heard Mama say to Daddy in the retelling, "and she knows it. Sometimes I think she's *your* mama, and it was *me* raised in an orphanage." Mama said the surveyor fished out his identification, but this had the opposite effect to what he'd intended, as Granny fired a blast that cast a spray of dirt and ricocheted birdshot against his shins, removing any doubt about her capacity for murder. The surveyor abandoned his tripod and left a long fishtail track down her dirt road.

Rather than exhibit remorse, Granny demanded that Sheriff Wil-son arrest the surveyor. When he tried to explain that surveys are a legal town pursuit, she demanded he arrest the entire Town Coun-cil for violating the Bill of Rights. That's when Sheriff Wilson called Mama, who repaid the favor by letting him know the next time she took Granny to the grocery store, so that the surveyor could complete his assignment without dying in the line of duty. I could only imagine what Granny would have done, had she discovered her daughter's betrayal. Quote *Julius Caesar*, most likely. *Et tu, Lee Ann?*

At Sunday supper, Granny preached hellfire in the center of her living room, arms raised, their pale flesh quivering like sheets on a clothesline. She said the survey was another step in the town's plot. "Regular brigands just bust in and take what they want," she said, "but government crooks measure it first. That's how they took your father's business back in '61." This she directed at Mama with a squint of her rheumy eye.

My grandfather had been a mechanic by trade and a minor inventor by avocation. For a time he'd branched out from engine repair into plumbing and electrical supply, but this venture folded after a year. Granny talked like it had collapsed under the weight of a vast conspiracy of monopolists and government busybodies. "The truth of it," Mama once told me, "is that Daddy's warehouse was as poorly organized as his workshop."

Grandpa Watts's workshop had been the back half of his barn, a maze of machine tools and tables piled with grease-darkened engine parts and metal whatnots whose purposes had long-ago passed from memory. I liked to wander amidst these ruins, trying to divine their mysteries. His workshop smelled of machine oil and sawdust and was lit by aluminum-housed fluorescent lights strung from the rafters. They crackled and hummed when their switch was flipped, lending the abandoned space an aura of latent power and restless magic.

"They ruined your father," Granny Watts bellowed at Mama. "But I'll not let them take his land. No, by God, I will *not*."

Daddy was hungover but with us, the sweet redolence of liquor still oozing from his fresh-scrubbed skin. He rose from the couch, and I expected him to conjure some energy to dance with her, but instead he approached her slowly, his voice husky and gentled. "Mother Watts," he said, "let's sit down and eat." Granny clutched his arm and looked up at him like he was her sole help in a crowd of strangers. He guided her to the table and pulled out her chair.

"You go to *watch* 'em, Ray! Watch 'em like a *hawk*!"

"I know it, mother."

Granny's forehead was beaded with perspiration, her cheeks flushed.

"Mama, are you alright?"

Granny nodded with a grunt. We all were silent but for the scrape of silverware against plates. Lima beans, stewed tomatoes, and thin strips of liver slathered with onions, which put me in mind of a saying I'd heard from Eddie: *Well ain't this a turd in the punch bowl.* I almost said it, just to get a laugh out of Granny and my father before Mama walloped me into a coma. Instead, I mounded ketchup on my liver serving until she confiscated the bottle.

Mama calmly explained all the work Daddy was going to do around Granny's place now that the weather was turning. She gave special emphasis to the garden he would help Granny put in. She offered this as proof that the town wouldn't be taking anything. Granny nodded and made a show of eating, but her eyes were on the butter dish her husband had brought her from an antique store in Georgia, and the candlesticks he'd fashioned on his foot-pedaled wood lathe, and her own gnarled and trembling hands.

At home, my parents talked on our front porch while upstairs I sat by my bedroom window and pretended to read. The sky was dark and clear, its stars like a fleet of lamplit boats. "It just means town water and sewer," Mama said. "And maybe a paved road for the first time in her life. I just don't see how anyone living next to a junkyard can be so particular."

"You know they're not aiming to see she gets reliable water."

"Well they can't just take it from her." Mama sighed. "Can they?"

"There's no reckoning what men'll do."

"But why?"

"Damned if I know."

The swing's chains creaked, and I knew Mama had tucked up her legs and laid her head on Daddy's shoulder. "I suppose we can worry about that bridge when we come to it." The chains groaned as they settled into each other. In the distance, a train rumbled across its river trestle. Mama sighed, and then there was silence but for frogs chirring at the riverbank and that distant rhythmic rumble.

———

As the weather warmed, my friends and I made plans to defend Granny Watts's home. Calvin wanted to make punji traps like we'd seen in *The Green Berets*, the kind that turn a man into cube steak. Eddie said we needed to prepare for trucks and bulldozers, so we devised traps that required gears as big as tires, barrel-sized springs, wide steel plates. We reasoned we had plenty of time to scavenge these from the junkyard because the wheels of government turned, according to Calvin's father, damnably slow.

I expected Daddy to patrol the perimeter of Granny's property, or to pay stealthy and possibly lethal visits to her enemies, or *something*, but all he did was drink and sleep and walk the river. Sometimes I followed him along its crenulated shore, early in the morning, when the water was thick and blanketed by haze and the waterthrush practiced their descending scales amidst the birch roots. I couldn't see what the

Crow had to do with Granny Watts. Daddy would crouch at certain places and cup his hands behind his ears, like the river's purl was a human whisper. Sometimes I thought maybe it was Bobby Doyle he heard. I wondered what a dead boy might say to my father.

After river-haunting, Daddy would walk the furrow adjoining our property to Doc Moore's until he reached a cedar-walled clearing. From my hiding place, I could hear the *shush* of cans being opened, the chirr of insects congregating the milkweed, the groan of treetops bent by the wind. I would lie in the tallgrass and watch clouds wander across our piece of sky as my father drank himself to sleep.

One afternoon in early summer, Julie sat on a rock and watched me sink bottles and cans in the Crow. "How much can your daddy drink before he dies?" she asked.

"Your daddy's the doctor."

"He says every man is different."

I hurled a Jack Daniels bottle past the Crow's midpoint.

"But he says your daddy will get better one day."

"How does he know?"

"I don't know." She scratched a mosquito bite. "I found a spell that can make him stop. We just need a ground-up newt tongue to brew like tea. Then you pour some in his liquor bottle and pour the rest in a Coca-Cola or sweet tea or whatever you want him to love instead of liquor." I rolled my eyes. "I just have to find a newt."

"You tell your parents about the bottles?"

"Didn't I say I wouldn't?"

I filled a whiskey bottle and held it up to the sunlight.

"You ever taste it?"

"No."

"Why's he drink it?"

"Why don't you go on up to the house and ask him?" I threw another bottle. "Or the woods or wherever he's sleeping."

"Mama says I'm supposed to leave y'all alone."

"Little girls should obey their mothers."

Julie scratched some more. "I reckon one day you'll dam it up." She pondered a patch of red on her ankle. "Do you know how to tell poison ivy?"

"Nope."

"I ain't thrown a rock at you in a long time, you know."

"So?"

"So maybe I ought to."

I came up the bank to where she sat. "Maybe I'd like to see you try."

Julie stood, her eyes squinted in anger. "I'm not scared of you, Daniel Waterson."

"Only because I don't hit girls."

"Give me back that bag." She held out her hand. I dropped the bag at her feet and turned toward home.

"You could say *thank you* sometime."

"Stay away from the river."

A month later, Daddy got a witching job in Black Mountain, and Mama sent me along. She argued with herself as she crammed hat and raincoat and more socks than I could possibly use into a duffel. "I don't know why I'm doing this; it'll likely rain, and I'll have more work washing out mud than I save myself getting this boy out of the house for a couple of days." As I laced up my boots in the mud room, I heard her speak to Daddy in a low, angry voice: "Are you planning to drink while you're up there?"

"No," he said. He sounded hurt. He'd been good about getting the west field's fence mended and the brush-hogging done, and he'd done a herculean amount of pruning in the apple orchard over toward the river. He also hadn't been drunk in our house for weeks.

"You just can't, Ray. Not with him along."

He clattered out the screen door. When I entered the kitchen, Mama handed me a grocery sack filled with sandwiches, potato chips, apples, and half a pecan pie. She put a towel-wrapped loaf of bread on top. She took hold of my arms. Her face was haggard, her eyes red and watery. "If he starts drinking, I want you to call me from the farmer's house." I nodded. "Do you hear me? No matter what time. You get right up and walk to the farmer's house."

"Yes ma'am."

She glanced at the door. "I shouldn't let you go."

"I'm all packed, Mama."

She shook her head and sighed. "Alright. Go on."

Daddy started the truck and turned us around in the yard. The porch's shadow obscured Mama's face where she leaned in the doorway. She looked like a ragged dress hung on a nail. My father was quiet as we rolled through town, across the bridge, onto the state highway west. Pin oaks and poplar crowded the road's edge. As the truck roared over blacktop, I squinted so that the trees became like two walls of water, Daddy Moses and me the Israelites and those dark walls looming overhead, threatening to converge as we raced toward the sliver of light between.

We passed through towns with names like Valdese, Nebo, and Old Fort. I asked Daddy what people in them did for work. It seemed like there were so many people, in so many places, and jobs were getting harder to come by.

"They do what needs doing," he said.

"But what needs doing? Do they make trucks? Grow tobacco? What do they all do?"

Daddy lit a cigarette and smiled. "People do all kind of things. Some grow, some make, some push paper around."

"Why would anybody pay you to push paper?"

He chuckled. "Things'll change in this country when enough people start asking that question."

"Do they at least draw something on it before they push it? Or write a story?"

"Nah. They just check some boxes and push it on to the next feller."

"What does he do with it?"

"He squints real close, to make sure the right checks went in the right boxes using the right color ink."

"That sounds worse than schoolwork."

"That's why they pay him so much for it."

"I'd rather be poor and grow potatoes."

Daddy laughed around his cigarette. He tousled my hair. "I imagine you'll figure out how to make a pile of money doing something."

I took his hand in my two hands. I ran my fingers over the wrinkles, the rough patches, the scars. "Will my hands look like yours one day?"

"Your hands will show the work you've done."

"I hope they look just like yours."

Daddy took back his hand. We drove in silence and there was nothing wrong with the silence. Sometime later he steered us into a Sunoco station set between a laundromat and a liquor store.

"Are we there?"

"Almost. Fill them cans with diesel."

I dragged the canisters from the truck bed, maneuvered the nozzle into one, and flipped the pump latch. The rushing fuel glowed dirty orange in the fading light. Its sweet oily scent billowed upward. Daddy whistled on his way into the Sunoco. A bug flew too close to the lit sign overhead, sparked, and drifted to the pavement a cinder. A dump truck pulled in, obscuring my view of the liquor store. I capped one canister and started the next as I listened for the bell over the Sunoco door. When the second canister was full, I wrestled it and its twin back onto the truck bed, ran a rope through their handles and the truck's eye hook, and tied a lineman's loop like my father had taught me.

"Good knot."

Daddy clutched two brown paper bags by their rolled-up mouths. He tossed one to me, and tucked the other behind his seat. I opened my bag as we drove away. Inside were lollipops—the round, layered, powdery kind that turn to sugar in your mouth. There were also Twinkies, a Yoohoo, and a Batman comic. Daddy slapped my arm. "Your mama didn't think of everything."

The lollipop's sour sent an ache through my jaw. I watched the road's yellow centerlines race past. I glanced behind my father's seat. I tasted the sour. "Daddy, did you buy liquor?"

His jaw began to clench and release, like he was chewing something tough. "Your mama tell you to keep an eye on me?"

The sun was behind the trees now, and soon we were more shadow than flesh. Daddy turned onto a long dirt drive which ended at a narrow brick house set under wide-canopied oaks. We parked, and a thick-chested man in wader boots and riding pants met Daddy midway between house and truck. He had wavy gray hair and big teeth. He nodded and grinned as he pointed out various pastures beyond the close-drawn trees. They shook hands. The farmer waved at me, and I raised my hand. My arm was small and thin, nothing like my father's.

Daddy drove us down a bumpy track to a grove of cedar. He set up our tent while I gathered rocks and kindling for a fire pit. The sun was just a glow on the horizon when I sparked the kindling. "That-taboy," Daddy said. We settled back onto our respective duffels and bit into our sandwiches.

"Daniel."

"Yes sir."

"Go fetch that bag from behind my seat."

I walked on clumsy legs back to the truck. Mama had said to leave if Daddy started drinking. I dreaded the thought of walking

back to the farmer's house. What if he was a Baptist? Would he throw
Daddy off his land? I thought about chucking the bag into the woods
as I carried it back to the fire. But there's no hiding anything from my
father. Nothing on this earth can hide from his gaze.

"Open it," he said.

I unfurled the rolled top. Inside were boxes of cherry cough
drops, packs of gum, and a fat pouch of chewing tobacco. A package
of marshmallows lay at the bottom. Daddy eased the bag from my
hand. "It goes better when I have something sweet." He said this to
the fire, his eyebrows knitted together.

I gathered some sticks and snapped their ends into sharp points.
Daddy laughed when I made a grab at the marshmallows and pointed
at my sandwich. While we ate, he told me about how he got kicked off
the high school football team because he wanted to fight anyone who
hit him. I asked if he'd known Mr. Beasley back then. He smiled at
the corner of his mouth and told me to respect my teachers no matter
who they are. He told me about the switchings from Granny Watts
and how it was usually she who did the crying afterward.

"She's never even sniffled when she spanked me."

Daddy laughed from his belly. "I reckon she's gotten cranky in
her old age. A body can give out, trying to whip sense into a Waterson
boy."

We lanced marshmallows and held them over the fire. They released puffs of steam as they shriveled and blackened at the edges. The
firewood popped, sending constellations of sparks skyward. Around
us crickets seethed as a pair of frogs called to one another. In the
distance, a horse nickered.

While I blew and nibbled at my marshmallow, Daddy devoured
his in one bite. He followed it with a cough drop. I loved him for
buying cough drops instead of whisky. I liked how the worry had
fallen from his face. I wished Mama could see him. Later we lay side
by side on our backs in the tent. I told him about some of my visions,
but called them dreams so he wouldn't worry. I fell asleep telling him
stories I can't remember now.

I woke to a high moon that filled our tent with a phosphorescent
glow. Daddy's breathing was deep and rhythmic. I scooted closer, until
my arm was pressed against his. I imagined his arm was mine, his
breath mine, every part of him me, even the fissures running beneath
his skin. He mumbled something in his sleep and covered my hand
with his own. I wondered if he was going to scream like he sometimes
did at home. Branches creaked overhead. The wind pressed the side

of our tent with a hiss, then snatched at the other. The wind was a dream-wraith prowling the dark, seeking whom it might devour. I held my father's hand and drifted back to sleep. He did not cry out.

The next day he strode freshly cut fields while I read my new comic book under an oak. After a time, I looked up to see him standing in a slight depression, arms spread, sun shining on his thick black hair. He turned to me, like he knew I was watching, just as I'd known before looking up that the strange sight had come over him. He waved me over, drove his knife into the ground, and told me to wait while he got his truck.

An electricity from the witching lingered on him, like a wire was shorting beneath his skin. When he had his truck backed up to the spot and was pulling rods and machinery from the bed, he tore a strip of skin from his hand. He slumped on the tailgate as blood welled in the wound and sprinkled the grass. He seemed surprised to discover blood fills him as it does every man. I took the cleanest rag I could find in his toolbox and tied it around his hand, jumping when the electricity passed between our flesh. He placed his bandaged hand on my head and regarded me as if he'd asked a question and was awaiting an answer, but I didn't know what to say. He slid off the tailgate and finished prepping his rig.

Soon water shot up through the pipe like it was boiling just beneath the topsoil. The farmer laughed with his big teeth. "Don't it beat everything?" he said. He slapped my father's back and tunneled into his pocket for a wad of bills. Daddy helped him sink the remainder of the steel pipe links and attach a Baker hand pump. The westward sun had begun to shatter in the tops of oak and sweetgum. Daddy asked if we could camp another night. The farmer pointed toward a stream bordering one of his pastures and told me it held trout if I knew how to catch them. He offered to loan me a pole, and I proudly told him we always carry our own, just in case. He laughed so hard I thought his big teeth might fall out. Daddy put a wrench to the pump's rod coupling and torqued it snug. That electricity still ran beneath his skin.

Later I met him at our cedar clearing with a string of fish. He already had meat sizzling in his skillet over a fire. "Had my mouth set for pan steak," he said, "so I ran to town real quick." He nodded at the fish. "We can fry them too. They're a good size." He offered a river of words while I cleaned fish. I tried to look him over without seeming to. He lifted the steak dripping blood and fat from his pan and placed it onto a tin plate. He dropped a handful of new potatoes in the pan grease. Then he wrapped my fish in foil and lay them beside the embers. We watched the potatoes sizzle. When the fish were ready, Daddy dished them onto my plate, divided the potatoes between us, and attacked his food.

"Did you see how strong that fountain is? You're good luck when I witch, boy."

I shrugged.

"You want more?"

I shook my head. Daddy scoured his pan with salt. He lit a cigarette with slightly shaking hands, then checked his watch. "Bout past your bedtime."

"You let me stay up last night."

"Which is why you should get to bed on time tonight." The light was gone from his voice. "Go on."

As I trudged to the tent he called after me, his voice softened: "A boy growing up fast needs his sleep." I wanted to cast myself into his arms and tell him why the nightmares had abated the night before. To explain that if he'd just stay close to me, he'd never need another drink so long as he lived. It was a childish thought, yet it's troubled me through the years. What if I had?

I lay down in the tent's stifling darkness. Outside, the intermittent rustle of a paper bag blended with the sounds of night creatures. It was such a small thing, that rustle. Like cards being shuffled, or the crackle of a tree limb breaking in the distance. I imagined the fire filling my father's belly, opening his spirit to the fire at the center of the world.

You can tell when the dead have drawn near by the sudden silence. Gone were the crickets and bullfrogs, the cicadas and night birds. The bag's rustling ceased as well. I rose to my knees, stretched out my hand, and pushed aside the tent flap. In terror, I eased my head forward until I could see them arrayed across the fire from my father, who now knelt as I did. There were bearded hunters and trappers, loggers and settlers and the women who'd followed them into the despairing wild. There were Tuscarora and Pamlico and Cherokee at quiet peace in their deaths. There were wanderers, hobos, haggard overborn men who suffer in every age.

My father eyed them over his bottle. "I got no business with y'all."

The dead considered my father through black eyes that glittered in the firelight. He downed a swig. The dead lifted dirty bottles and rusted cups and bug-eaten canteens to their whitened lips. He chuckled. "I seen worse than you." He toasted them with his bottle. They lifted bone-dry containers to their lips. My father shook his head and sighed. The dead leaned forward in anticipation. He stood, arched his back, closed his eyes, and a low hum emanated from his chest as his feet beat a rhythm in the dirt. His witching walk was only a shadow of this. He wasn't hunting water now. The gathered dead swayed as he danced about the fire.

I recalled my mother's admonition to run away. Surely this was to her a greater abomination than his drinking. If I ran, I would always be something less than my father. The river of power running from our people through his great-grandfather and now through him would bypass me. Or I could rise from this tent, step into the circle danced by Daddy, and receive the blessing or curse—not that I cared which, only that it would come from my father's hands and make me as he was. I knew all this just as surely as I knew Bobby Doyle was among us before I spied him.

He stood at the edge of the gathered dead in his funeral best, his blackened eyes not on my father, but on me. Daddy's head was back, throat filled with the groans of an ancient keen. He tilted his head forward, opened his eyes, and now he regarded me as well. I don't know if he saw only the boy crouching in the tent's entrance, or the man I might become, or perhaps all the possible fates awaiting me, but in his face was an admixture of sorrow and love. He extended his hand toward me.

Bobby Doyle didn't move, but I knew he too wanted me to come forth. How I wanted to run to my daddy. And how terrified I was. The other dead turned their eyes from my father to me where I knelt trembling at the tent's entrance. Urine filled my underwear and snaked down my thighs. How could I go to my father like this? I choked back a sob, retreated into the tent, and covered my ears against the sounds of my father's stamping feet, his grunts and moans and guttural humming. I fell almost instantly to sleep and dreamt the wind blew with gale force through the overwatching trees. I saw the landscape tremble before the advancing storm. I saw horses stamp and whinny in their stables, saw fish sway in their silt beds. I saw the watery black eyes of Bobby Doyle. I heard my father's voice calling from across a river, but I couldn't make out his words.

We packed in silence the next morning. I couldn't tell what I'd dreamt and what was real, other than the faint tang of my urine. I could glean no guidance from my father's gaze. He sipped water from a thermos and gripped the wheel as we headed home. We stopped for gas outside Hickory Shore, and he insisted on working the pump himself. He went to the restroom afterward, emerging with his face scrubbed, his hair slicked back. He sipped coffee around a wad of gum and gave me a weak smile.

Mama stood in the doorway as we came up the drive, as if she'd been standing there since we left. She came down the porch steps to greet us. "Ray!" she said when he kissed her cheek, "You smell like gas!"

"Spilled it filling up."

Mama considered his face as he told her how easy the water shot up, what a big help I was, my fine catch of trout. She turned to me. "Did everything go well, Daniel?" I nodded, knowing her greatest fear hadn't been realized. Whatever had transpired in that cedar grove, I was still just a boy.

Hickory Shore Messenger
Letters & Opinions
July 28th, 1975

I grew up in Hickory Shore, and I've lived here all my life. I've fished the Crow since I was knee-high to a tadpole, as the old-timers say. I also do some farming and am known in this area as a well-driller. I know they had experts look at everything going on with the Crow River Dam expansion, but being an expert is one thing, and knowing a place is an entirely different thing. A doctor can tell you if your leg is broken, but he can't tell you how it feels to you when you walk across your mama's threshold on that broken leg. He doesn't even know to examine your leg until you bring it to him and tell him something isn't right. That's how the river is to us down in Hickory Shore. Something isn't right. I'm no engineer or dam supervisor so I can't say exactly what's wrong, I'm just saying from how the river looks and feels, it's not right. It's gotten sick, and we've made it that way, and when I've tried to write and even gone to visit the officials up in the Crow River Watershed Authority, they don't want to listen. Now what kind of doctor doesn't want to listen when you tell him something doesn't feel right? Maybe it seems strange to some to compare a river to your leg, but to those of us who've lived by the Crow

all our lives, that's what the river is to us—a part of who
we are. Somebody needs to listen, because it's trying to
tell us something.

Ray Waterson
Hickory Shore

———————

"Ray Waterson," Granny Watts shouted from the top of her porch
steps, "you are a voice crying out in the wilderness!" I could almost
hear Mama's eyeballs roll. Daddy left us at the truck with Granny's
groceries and jogged up to her porch, where he got down on a knee,
took her trembling hand in his own, and kissed it.

"Good Lord," muttered my mother. "Would you look at the two
of them? It's bad enough I've got every octogenarian in the county
calling the house to commiserate on how the world's going to hell in
a handbasket because of that dam." Granny Watts placed her hand
on my kneeling father's head and prayed a benediction. "It's about to
stray into blasphemy," Mama said. "Those two were never more than
a half-step from black magic as it was."

"Now Ray, I made this sweet potato pie *special* for you and I
don't care if it's not suppertime yet, you're gonna *have* some." Granny
escorted Daddy by the arm into her house.

"I swear to you Daniel, I believe that hardheaded man is *her* son
and *I'm* the adopted child. '*Ray I made this sweet potato pie special.*'
Good Lord. Never a '*thank you Lee Ann for cleaning my rugs,*' or a
'*Lee Ann, I've never once had a tax audit even though every year I
hand you a shoebox of documents that looks like a pack of rats has
been mating in it.*' Well, I'll tell you what, that man can answer his
own phone calls from now on. They can all get a party line and talk
about that dam and the grassy knoll shooter and how we couldn't
possibly have put a man on the moon because the Bible says it's filled
with blood."

I helped Mama carry in the groceries. On the living room wall
amidst family pictures hung a framed copy of Daddy's letter. "Good
Lord. River's sick, he says. Why just last week didn't you bring me a
fish longer than your shinbone? *Prophet* my foot."

———————

Later that week, our chores done, Daddy took me fishing. We stopped for gas at the Esso, and he let me come inside to get an R.C. The old men quieted on their stools when we entered. Daddy handed a bill to Marty Giles at the register.

"Say Ray," one of the old-timers croaked. "We gonna get rain tonight?" The others volunteered conflicting reports coming from various radio and TV sources. "Sort it out for them, Ray," Marty Giles said. "You know those old coots don't believe anything a weatherologist has to say."

Daddy took his change and smiled. "Well, I'll tell you this: Me and my boy are getting our fishing in today, before that river runs brown for a week." I don't know how Daddy could tell without a cloud in sight that rain was coming, nor how much it would churn up the Crow.

"Say Ray, where y'all headed?"

"Aw now, c'mon boys—if I tell you where our honey holes is hid, you'll snatch the supper right out from young Daniel's mouth." Those old men could scarcely get up and down on their stools, let alone stand in the Crow. They pretended great offense.

"Hey now Ray, fellow veterans ought not treat one another thataway."

"Respect your elders now, sonny."

Marty Giles snuck a Baby Ruth into my hand. "Say now, Daniel," he said, "how about you tell us where the Great Ray Waterson likes to cast flies?" The old-timers turned their chapped and crinkled faces my way. I would have withstood bamboo sticks under fingernails before divulging Daddy's secrets, but he winked, so I told them we were headed down to the bend below our property, just below a stretch where the Crow churns through boulders. Where it runs rough, but not too deep for a man to keep his purchase. They shook their heads.

"Why you like that rough water, Ray? Why make it so hard on yourself?"

Daddy's face got serious. "It only seems harder. In smooth water, a smart fish like a trout can see everything you do. He can see your presentation—hell, he probably even reads your lips while you're talking to yourself about which fly to use. Your prey is always easier to take in a state of confusion." They all seemed to ponder the dreadful applications of what he'd said. He stood for a moment as if considering it himself, then came to. "Well." He considered their distant faces, nodded, turned to me. "Daniel."

Instead of fishing below the rapids, Daddy took us to the bend above our property, where the river met a tall granite face and bent to cradle Doc Moore's land as well as our own. He stood on a rock outcrop to cast, while I stood in slow-running water up to my hips. I cast and re-cast the fly he'd chosen for me, mindful of my arm and wrist. My father was lost within himself.

I too quieted myself in the way of a fly fisherman and was startled when he caught my rod on a backswing. He put his finger to his lips and gently pried loose my rod. "Close your eyes," he said. "Now listen."

"For what?"

"Just listen."

I heard water lap against rocks on our side and the thrush of deeper water along the far shore's granite face. I heard squirrels arguing overhead. I heard cinnamon rolls and orange juice gurgle in my stomach. I squeezed shut my eyes and leaned forward, straining my neck until the blood pounded in my head. I willed my ears to hear the river's secret.

"Do you hear it?" My father asked.

"I think so."

"What do you hear?"

"I don't exactly know."

"It's like a whisper, Daniel. Behind the usual noise. Do you hear it?" I leaned further forward. We stood still as the dead. "It says it can't be what we're trying to make it be," my father whispered. "It's grieving over what we're going to make it do. When the moon is full, you can see it writhe like a snake beneath a boot."

My blood ran like deep water whenever my father spoke such things. He put his hand on the top of my head. "Do you want to hear?"

"Yes," I whispered.

A hum came from deep in his throat. His hand suddenly felt warm. I was not afraid. The water beneath my downturned gaze rippled in the way of a shallow puddle when a horse walks alongside it. The water was suddenly richer in color, yet more translucent. It trembled with the rhythm of my father's voice. I was not afraid.

"Daniel!"

My mother stood on the riverbank, quivering with fury. "No!" she shouted. "I forbid it!"

Daddy took his hand away. "Get on to your mama, boy." His eyes were downcast.

"But Daddy, I—"

"Go!" He gathered up our tackle as I splashed to shore. Mama took hold of my arm and marched me homeward along the bank. I looked back at Daddy where he tarried, as if listening to the river, or perhaps speaking with it about me. I turned back to my mother. Her face was mottled and small moans escaped her throat, as if she were stumbling along the last mile of a very long march. I looked back, and my father was gone.

"Mama, I want him to baptize me the way his great-grandfather did him."

My mother stopped, drew back her arm, and slapped me hard in the face. I reeled with the blow as she grabbed my shoulders. I began to cry from the sting and more so from the savagery in her face. "You listen to me, boy! That was no baptism, you hear? It was an obscenity, and that man has been haunted ever since!"

"Mama!" I was sobbing.

She slapped me again, then brought her face so close I felt flecks of spit as she spoke. "I would sooner drown you right here than let you follow that man's path. Do you understand me, Daniel? Look at me! Do you think I don't mean it? I'll put you in the grave before I let you forfeit your soul."

"Mama!" I cried.

"Next time," she said through gritted teeth, "I'll have a gun. I'll kill you both where you stand, then I'll shoot myself. Do you understand me, boy?" She put her arm around me and walked me home.

I've kicked so long my legs should be burning but instead they're so cold and I kick against the goads. My God my God, why have you forsaken me? And yonder the watching eyes of Ray Waterson—his eyes, sweet Christ, his eyes.

See them gather on the shore, gather and into the rushing current come the dead brothers and sisters so long in the ground and yet so tired come to the river come with me we are going home we are all of us going home. Oh Lord my God remember me in thy kingdom, and see that child ashore. Please Jesus my savior, don't let me die in vain. I am not afraid will not be afraid but if I could just have one more breath see the sun once more, please, once more.

I can't

Can't kick any more

Into thy hands my God
Into thy hands
My God

———✂———

Hickory Shore Messenger
August 14th, 1975

WILKESBORO, NC—A dozen people staged a protest at the Crow River Dam yesterday. Hickory Shore resident Lenora Watts told reporters that the Watershed Authority is ignoring the long-term impacts of the dam's ongoing expansion. "Everybody's so excited about more electricity that nobody's asking who plans to use it. It certainly won't be we the people."

When contacted for comment, Crow River Watershed spokesman Marlin Connors said that greater electrical capacity will benefit all residents in the watershed area, and many across North Carolina besides. "People need jobs, and low-cost electricity is essential for the companies that will bring those jobs."

In her remarks to the small band of protestors, Ms. Watts alleged that the dam's taxpayer-funded electricity will support large companies without local ties. "They'll drive up the price of our land, then rent it back to us," she said. "And let's not forget the safety risks, which the industrialist kingpins running this operation continue to ignore."

Mr. Connors said that the Crow River Watershed Authority is a public agency not beholden to industrial interests, and that the dam expansion has gone through extensive engineering analysis to determine that it represents no risk to residents downriver.

———✂———

Granny's dining table became HQ for the Crow River Resistance, as they called themselves. Thankfully, Mama said, not many radicals lived in Cantwell County. Granny's ragtag comrades carefully removed pictures from her dining-room walls and tacked up topographical maps, hydrological surveys, and press releases. Granny kept her table larded with sandwiches and coffee. Clay Tompkins and his seminary buddies were regulars, as was Daddy, who sat sober and silent in his chair by the window. The rest were farmers from along the river or others with ties to the land.

Other resistances across history could probably condense their cases to a single page, but Granny was born with a manifesto on her lips. In pamphlets she elucidated the grand conspiracy: an ostensibly public agency, the Crow River Watershed Authority, flush with cash and permits from the U.S. Army Corps of Engineers, which intended to dam every river, stream, and gulley east of the Mississippi, had come under the sway of corporate interests. Originally built to electrify homes and farms, an expanded Crow River Dam would yield enough taxpayer-subsidized juice to power corporate facilities. It would end occasional lowland flooding, which was nature's way of keeping the soil fertile. Now, Granny said, Big Ag would come in with their Deutschmarks and Francs freshly converted to U.S. dollars and douse the soil with chemicals. "When they say flood control benefits the farm community, they don't mean *our* people," she said. "*Our* people have managed fine for generations. They mean the community that meets in board rooms to game prices and extract checks from Uncle Sam in the name of the family farm."

Granny warned against field agents representing anonymous real-estate developers. "They harken to the time-dishonored role of scalawag," she wrote, "with speech that betokens allegiance to community, springing from rootless hearts bound to their paymasters." She winked at me when she read this part aloud, and I glanced at Daddy, fearing he could read our minds about Harlan Carver. But his face remained passive, his eyes maybe on us, maybe on some other people at some other gathering in some other time. Clay Tompkins peppered Granny's recitations with more "Amens" than he gave Reverend Hardison's sermons.

A science teacher at Hickory Shore High churned out Granny's screeds on the school mimeograph machine. Granny said he did this at great risk, being the only black teacher in the school and one of the few to live in Hickory Shore. It seemed to me that the greatest risk any of us faced was being laughed at. Calvin, however, conspiratorial by disposition and weaned on stories of local politics and business, believed everything he heard at Granny's table. His father let him take poster boards and other supplies from the Red and White, so I suppose whatever version Calvin spun for him at home sounded believable enough. Or maybe Calvin Senior was privy to his own intelligence.

One of Clay's college friends tracked down business records revealing that the American arm of a German-owned brewing company had purchased dozens of acres in Cantwell County to the west, not far from Granny's land. And there were rumors that a Japanese conglomerate was scouting land for a toy-making plant. "It's the goddamned Axis invasion all over again," Granny muttered. While it is the universal duty of churchmen to scowl at blasphemy, Clay just put his arm around her shoulders and told her the Lord is master of all. I don't think Granny doubted this; in her mind these local predations were all tied to a historical world narrative and the inborn struggle between good and evil waged across the terrain of every man's heart.

Not long after I turned thirteen in the fall of 1975, Clay Tompkins baptized me in a rusty trough behind the church. It was a rare moment of pastoring authority for Clay, made possible by Reverend Hardison's bout with the flu. Clay was especially out of favor now that people knew of his association with my grandmother's band of dissidents. My father was there with trimmed beard, his arm steadying Granny Watts, who wore house slippers because her church shoes had long ago ceased to fit. The water was tepid and my face was hot with embarrassment as Clay laid hold of my head and dunked me, new J.C. Penney suit and all. I looked up through the rippling water into Clay's unusually grave face, then past his shoulder to the pale and quivering sky. There was no shaft of light, no still, small voice. Everyone crowded close in the fall's gray gloom and sang as Clay brought me back up into the air. I wondered how my father's initiation in the river by his grandfather all those years before had felt to him. Was there still time for me? Could he even do it now, wasted and withdrawn as he was becoming?

The next Explorers camp-out was downriver from our property, past where Daddy and I told the old-timers we aimed to fish, where the Crow runs over thick flat slabs of blackened rock, churning itself up and crashing runnel into plume before tumbling over a series of falls. Clay Tompkins brought two seminary friends, one of them with longer hair even than some of the girls. We roasted hot dogs, had a treasure hunt, and after the sun went down we crunched wintergreen mints between our teeth to see the sparks. Clay mentioned Jesus plenty, but he didn't watch your face for a reaction. He didn't make you feel like he needed you to feel something about Jesus for him.

Julie Moore came too, but still it wasn't so bad.

We played Stump the Preacher beside a pool of water bordered by a high granite wall. Calvin asked about the origin of the tribe Cain joined after killing his brother. "If God just made Adam and Eve," he said, "and they had just their two boys, where'd all those other people come from?" Clay's eyebrows rose. He looked to his seminary buddies for help, but they just laughed and shrugged. The long-haired one played a dramatic chord on his guitar. Calvin strode to the pool and waited on Clay.

"Well, hold on a second," Clay said, "I think I have an answer."

Calvin put his hands on his hips impatiently.

"The Bible is only partly a history book, okay?"

"What does that mean?"

"I mean it's also a storybook."

"Are you saying it's made up?" Eddie asked. His parents suspected Clay was not only a radical but a heretic.

"Not any more than a story your mother tells you about the day you were born." Eddie squinted skeptically. Calvin sighed.

"She may mention the pain, and something funny a nurse said, and what she felt when she finally saw you for the first time. Every bit of that is true, but it's not a history, you see? It doesn't include the exact time of your birth, or the doctor's name, or whether you needed a slap on the fanny to get your lungs working." Some of the kids laughed.

"So you're saying God made lots of people at the very beginning, but the Bible doesn't mention them?" Calvin had the look his father adopted when a salesman tried to gouge him.

"I'm saying that neither the Bible nor our parents mentions every fact. They tell us the parts that matter most, like how we belong to them and how they love us. That's the kind of storybook the Bible is."

"Sure has a lot of blood for a love story," Julie said.

Clay nodded. "Sometimes love is brutal."

Calvin trudged back to where he'd been sitting and pulled a Bible from his duffel. He'd marked it with several likely stumpers. His mother had made him bring his violin because Clay had asked her if he could, and when Clay's friends saw the case, they cajoled Calvin into bringing it out. Calvin's mother and teacher favored classical, but his father paid the bills, so a few staples like "Foggy Mountain Breakdown" and "Twilight Waltz" had come to populate his repertoire.

Calvin winced and shook his head, but Clay and his friends gathered round and riffed their challenges until he had no choice but to retaliate, drawing his bow back and forth faster than any Bach I'd heard him practice.

The circled guitarists strummed waves of chords in response, laughing and shouting at him to *go on* and *cut her loose*. We children cheered for Calvin as if it were a competition, though it wasn't at all; it was a river of music and he borne like a steamboat captain. I thought to myself that you never do know anyone fully. Just when you think you do, a moment like this arrives, and you see him with new eyes. You never know someone fully until you've seen him to his last day.

No, not even then.

———

Mannheim-Brock was headquartered in Munich. Its American subsidiary was in Boston, which was no easier for the threadbare Crow River Resistance to reach. Clay suggested demonstrating at the company's Winston law firm, but Granny insisted the place to stand was the swath of land Mannheim-Brock had quietly accumulated not far from her home. "People need to see that the Krauts are in our back yard," she said. "And we taxpayers giving them water and electricity."

There was little press, just a reporter from an environmentalist newsletter and, of course, our own *Hickory Shore Messenger*. Rather than spark a revolt, the news just alerted landowners to hold out for higher prices. Mama tried to help Granny see the bright side. "Consider all that extra money going into our community now that everybody knows who the real buyer is," she said. "You're probably putting someone's grandchild through college. And think of all those jobs!"

"It must surely be the end times," Granny said, head in hands, elbows on her dining table. "A brewery in a Baptist town, and my own goddamned neighbors lining up to sell them the land. You were right, Clay. We should have protested the lawyers. People still hate lawyers." Clay put an arm around her shoulders. "Don't fret, Sister Watts. The Lord shines brightest when times are dark."

"I'll be damned if they get this land," Granny said. "And damned if their beer trucks don't run over nails every time they pass by." All this Daddy watched from his chair by the window, his eyes elsewhere, his thoughts shrouded.

Cantwell County Sheriff's Department
Arrest Report

Date: 10-30-75

Time of Arrest: 8:15pm

Time of Intake: 9:35pm

Arresting Officer(s): Deputies T. Wilkerson; AJ Woodruff; F. Meakins; D. Cunliff; A. Mills; M. Daniels; J. Morgan; Hwy Patrol Off. R. Chilton; T. Boyd; Hwy Patrol Off. JD Williamson; Hwy Patrol Off. W. Mason.

Suspect Name: Ray Waterson

Address: 4819 Old Hwy 421, Hickory Shore, NC

Charge: Public intoxication; misd. disorderly conduct

Reporting Officer: T. Wilkerson

Incident Report: Suspect was in attendance at Cantwell County Board of Supervisors meeting in Room 105 C of the Cantwell Municipal Services Building. Suspect approached microphone during public comments and accused Board members of not returning his calls or responding to his letters. Suspect said Crow River Dam is causing problems. Board Chairman Miller explained to Suspect that this is not a Cantwell County matter and Suspect became agitated. Suspect began cursing and telling the Board that they would be held accountable for the dam. Board Chairman Miller indicated to officer in attendance T. Wilkerson that Suspect should be removed from building. Officer Wilkerson, noting that Suspect was armed with a knife, requested back-up. When supporting officers arrived, one of them with knowledge of Suspect indicated that he is a highly trained military combat veteran and requested more backup. When additional support arrived the officer with knowledge of Suspect indicated that backup was still insufficient. When informed that

there were no more officers available, Officer
Wilkerson issued a request for Highway Patrol
support. When these personnel arrived Officer
Wilkerson led them in subduing and disarming
Suspect. Suspect came peacefully.

"It was for his own safety," Sheriff Wilson told my mother as they
stood on our front porch in the middle of the night. "I hate to think
what could have happened if he'd got this knife out."

"Thank you," Mama said in a flat voice. I gathered the sheriff
had handed her the knife.

"With him as he is right now, he really ought not to be carrying
it. Think you could hide it from him?"

Mama chuckled bitterly.

During my father's time in the Cantwell jail, Harlan Carver and Fred
Ledbetter came to my grandmother's house. Calvin and I were rum-
maging in the dump for trap parts when we heard Granny shout. We
came to the fence and saw her brandishing a soup ladle as she hobbled
down her porch steps. Ledbetter had returned to the passenger's side
of Carver's Cadillac, red-faced and scowling, but Carver backed
away more slowly. Once Granny was down the steps and lurching
toward him with her ladle overhead, he slid into his car and gunned
the engine. When she drew close, he backed up a little and waited. My
grandmother called him a *chain-gang carpet-bagging kiddy-diddler*
and Ledbetter a *scallywag turncoat* and stumbled after the Cadillac
as it backed and stopped, backed and stopped. Carver hung out his
window and laughed. He kept his fender just beyond her ladle swings.
"C'mon grandma!" he shouted.

"That sonofabitch," Calvin said. He broke into a run, shouting
Sgt. Rock threats and waving a rusted tire iron. I scooped up a handful of rocks and followed. Fred Ledbetter's eyes widened when he saw
us. He said something to Carver, who backed the rest of the way out
as Calvin slung the tire iron. It sailed over the hood, eliciting a whoop
from Carver. He grinned, yanked the car into gear, and hit the gas. I
peppered his fancy car with rocks as he passed. He skidded to a stop

and put it into reverse, but didn't move. He and Ledbetter seemed to be arguing.

"Daniel," my grandmother called, "get into the house!" Calvin stooped beside her, gathering the biggest rocks he could find. Carver and Ledbetter drove away as we helped Granny inside. In between wheezes, she denounced interloping corporatists who think they can wave around a checkbook and buy whatever they please. She locked the door and told me to fetch the shotgun from under her bed. I brought it downstairs and she unclenched her fists to receive it. "There's my baby. Carries like a twenty and hits like a twelve." She winked at Calvin. "Just like you, short stack."

She turned to me. "Lord-a-mercy did you see those heathen tear outta here once they saw y'all coming? My guardian angels!"

"What did they want?"

"Hoowee, I got to sit down! Daniel, go to the cellar and fetch a six-pack of root beer. Calvin, double-check the lock and hand me that deck from under the coffee table."

When I came back upstairs, Granny sat at her dining table shuffling cards. A pouch of Beech-Nut and a spittoon rested by her hand. Her shotgun was propped in a chair beside her. She dealt three hands and eyed us. "Well c'mon boys—crack open them suds and let's play some cards."

"Granny, what if they come back?"

She patted the chair holding her shotgun. "Then they're gonna get *all they want*." She offered a smile. "Don't you worry about those fools, sugar. They won't be back after this. And don't go worrying your mother with it either."

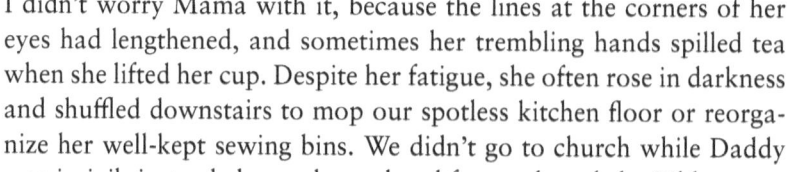

I didn't worry Mama with it, because the lines at the corners of her eyes had lengthened, and sometimes her trembling hands spilled tea when she lifted her cup. Despite her fatigue, she often rose in darkness and shuffled downstairs to mop our spotless kitchen floor or reorganize her well-kept sewing bins. We didn't go to church while Daddy was in jail; instead she made me breakfast and read the Bible to me as I ate.

Daddy came home a few days after Christmas, ten pounds lighter and steady-handed. He sat quietly in our kitchen and let Mama pare back his beard and hair unsparingly, as if he were an apple tree in springtime. He made no mention of the river, nor did he occupy his chair at Granny's during gatherings of the Crow River Resistance. It was just as well, they couldn't conjure what to do other than write letters to officials who would never respond.

He worked through the daylight hours, even witching a well three counties over, where they didn't know anything about the dead boy or jail or how people in Hickory Shore eyed him when he passed. At night, he stoked a fire in the woodstove and we watched whatever was on TV, my parents on the couch and me on the rattan rug with Bailey hanging off both ends of my lap. If we talked, it was about anything but the river or the dead.

And I didn't mention what had happened at Granny's, not to either of them. I know this belongs on my ledger. That there will be a reckoning one day.

———⌐

Clay Tompkins took the Young Explorers to McGalliard Falls in early spring. One of his seminary friends took a position atop a fall with a nylon rope and Clay showed us how to use it as we made our way up. "It's here to steady you, not carry you," he said. "Every man and woman has to carry their own weight. But you never have to bear it alone."

It was beginning to sound suspiciously like a Bible lesson, but he left it at that. The weather turned cold that night, so he showed us how to use leaves and sticks to insulate our tents. "You could survive a night in this with just three sticks and a little rope," he told us. He proceeded to prove it by giving his pup tent to one of the kids who'd forgotten his own and lashing two sticks to a longer one with his rope, the other end of which he tied to a tree. We helped him scavenge rows of sticks, which he leaned against either side of the rope until he had two angled walls. We covered these with leaves and brush and layered the ground inside with pine needles. Clay had us take turns crawling inside to see how warm it was. "They say the old monks slept inside their coffins to remind them where they're headed," he told us. "If I'd known it would be this cozy, I'd have taken up the practice sooner."

Later that night, I heard Julie crying in her tent, which Calvin and I had agreed was much too close to our own. Clay and his friends sat around the fire, which was now just crackling embers, quietly strumming their guitars. I heard the music stop, then footsteps to Julie's tent, then Clay whispering: "What's wrong?"

"I had a nightmare. I want to go home." She sobbed.

Clay tugged my tent line. "Daniel," he said. I didn't answer. Calvin lay fast asleep beside me, fingers twitching on his belly. "Daniel." Another yank on my line.

"What?" I tried to sound like I'd just woken up.

"I need your help."

I didn't see why he needed my help, what with two Bible-trained seminarians within earshot. I wiggled out of my sleeping bag and crawled out. Clay knelt before the opening to Julie's tent, from which her head protruded. She was wet-eyed behind a mess of tangled hair. She wiped her nose with the back of her hand. "Ever hunt spiders?" Clay asked.

"Huh?"

Clay led us to a silvered field. Julie reached for my hand, which I yanked away. Clay stopped, took out his flashlight, and motioned for us to crouch beside him. He turned on the flashlight and held the handle's end to his nose. He peered along the shaft of light that extended from his face, sweeping his head left, then right. "We're surrounded," he said. He offered Julie the flashlight. "Hold it like I did." He directed her gaze toward the grass. "Do you see?" The light beam jerked along the field. "Slow down and look. Just look."

"Hey, it looks like a bunch of little . . . green jewels."

"Those are spider eyes."

Julie squealed. She turned to look at me with the flashlight still at the end of her nose, and I hissed that she'd blinded me. She handed me the flashlight. Clay directed my head and I saw them—scores of tiny, paired emeralds in the grass.

"Do they know we're looking at them?" Julie asked.

"I don't imagine they care very much what we do," Clay said.

"Where'd you learn all this about spiders and shelters and everything?"

"My father."

"Is he a preacher too?"

"No." Clay offered us each a wintergreen mint. Julie crunched it and tried to see her sparks.

"You look like a cross-eyed badger," I said. She punched me in the arm. Clay took her fist in his palms. "My father has a furniture store in Thomasville," he said. "He'd rather I help him make $300 chairs than show children how to find spiders."

We started back to camp. "I thought parents are proud of sons who become preachers," I said.

"I think he'll be proud one day."

"Why's that?" Julie asked.

"Because every father wants his son to find his place in the world. Some just need time to accept what that place is." We helped Julie zip herself inside her tent. "Thanks," Clay whispered to me. "We have to look after the littler ones." I didn't tell him I was only a year older than Julie. "You and your dad camp a lot?" he asked.

"Used to."

"Can I tell you a secret?"

"Sure."

"Our fathers will disappoint us for the rest of our days."

"Huh?"

Clay smiled, and, with his moon-silvered hair and this grim news, he looked like a messenger angel, patience-worn by the frailty of man. "It hurts to see their flaws, on account of how much we love them. It's hard not to hate them for letting us down."

"Do you hate your father?"

"Sometimes. I'm only able to hate him because of how much I love him."

I'd never heard a preacher say such a thing. "Do they ever get better?" I asked. "The broken ones, I mean."

"Some do." He put his hand on my head, and I remembered how he'd prayed over me the day we killed the boy. "Never forsake your father, Daniel. Don't close your heart to him, no matter the pain he puts there."

I could scarcely bear the intensity of his moon-sapphired eyes.

"I'm glad you're here. Now git." He nudged me toward my tent.

"I'm glad I'm here too." I meant it.

———⌇———

The mailman found Granny at the foot of her porch steps, soup ladle near her hand. Sheriff Wilson took her straightaway to the hospital in Winston, while one of his deputies came out to give us the news. The three of us sped to Winston in our truck, my parents saying very little save for Mama asking several times, almost like she was irritated, what in the world her mother was doing outside with a soup ladle.

In the hospital bed, she looked scarcely like Granny Watts. The doctor explained that her hip was broken, some ribs as well. On the subject of consciousness, he explained that it was a wait-and-see situation. At this, Mama sat on the chair beside Granny's bed, clutched the hem of its blanket, and bowed her head. As the night darkened, Daddy drove me home.

Fred Ledbetter was waiting on our porch when we arrived. "Ray," he said as soon as we stepped from the truck, "I want you to know I gave a full report to the sheriff just a half hour ago. Everything I know about that sonofabitch."

"How's that?"

"Once I saw how he did Lenora that day we visited to ask about her property, I told him to get the hell out of Hickory Shore, that he wasn't closing any more sales if I had anything to do with it."

"Fred, what the hell are you talking about?"

We stood at the base of our porch steps now, Fred Ledbetter up top, as if this were his home and we paying a visit. He gave me a long look.

"Fred."

Ledbetter shook his head. "Ray, I just assumed your boy told you. Harlan Carver."

I felt my father's eyes settle on me.

"He's been scouting real estate for out-of-town developers. He told me he needed a local connection. I just made introductions for the man, that's all."

"For a commission, I expect."

"Well of course, Ray. I got to make a living same as anyone. But when he disrespected Lenora that day, I ended it with him."

"What day?"

"Sometime last fall. You were in jail. I just assumed your boy told you."

Daddy considered me like I was something he'd stepped in. "You were there?"

"Aww now Ray. It's no more the boy's fault than it is mine."

"Uh-huh."

"Now, I gave Sheriff Wilson everything I know about the man. If he's still around these parts, they'll pick him up."

"So you're saying he did this to Mother?"

Ledbetter shrugged. "I haven't seen nor heard from the man since that day I told him to leave town. But I know he's been slinking around, and I know he was especially interested in Lenora's land."

"You put a goddamn rattlesnake on her front porch is what you did."

"Now Ray, that's not fair. I had no way of knowing he was low-down."

"All you need is five minutes with Harlan Carter to smell the rotten on him."

Ledbetter's eyes widened. "So y'all *both* know this joker? Then why the hell am I standing here?"

"I'm asking myself that same question."

Ledbetter tromped down our steps, giving Daddy a wide berth. He opened his car door and paused. "Regina's organizing meals for y'all and for Lenora if . . . when she comes home. I'll take my boys over there tonight and keep a watch out for that sonofabitch."

Daddy nodded, barely perceptibly. We stood at the base of our steps and listened to Ledbetter drive away. I was cold, but I dared not go in while Daddy stood there. I waited for his reproach, pondering what I might say that wouldn't sound like I was blaming Granny. He went up the steps and into the house without a word. It was the worst punishment he could have contrived.

<hr>

Granny came home a few weeks later. She was frail and thinned and needed help to get up her steps. Inside she went straight to her couch and asked Mama for a shawl. Mama cooked, and we watched TV, and I knew how bad it was from the fact that Mama didn't fuss at her mother once. Granny asked me several times to make sure the front door was locked, the back door, the windows. She'd told us and the police that she'd slipped on her steps, that she was just an old woman who'd fallen. Daddy had no more to say about it to her than he'd said to me. He sat on the couch with Granny's feet in his lap and said nothing except to thank Mama for the plate he barely touched.

The police didn't find Harlan Carver, and as Granny's strength recovered, her spirits improved and she was able to stay alone in her house. She needed a cane and slept on her couch. Sunday suppers entailed more clattering of pans and fussing as she and her cane and Mama all maneuvered about her small kitchen. And still Daddy was silent.

I felt anger growing in me, for how easily he'd forgiven Fred Ledbetter, let Harlan Carver slip away, and shuttered the windows of his spirit against the river's call. For how easily he'd abandoned the notion of baptizing me in its waters. He kept his head down, planted gardens on our property and Granny's, and witched wells as summer came. My mother kept eyes on him like an overseer, and I hated this even more.

I wasn't supposed to take my Case knife to school, but not long after seventh grade began I did. At recess, I held its polished bone in my palm like a jewel on display for my friends. "My dad says Case is the best," Eddie confirmed. Calvin concurred, settling the matter in the minds of the other boys.

A hand shot between our conferring heads and sent it cartwheeling from my grasp. Carl Ledbetter grabbed my wrist and yanked me toward him. "Don't you know Injuns aren't allowed to carry knives?" I hit him full-knuckled, square on the nose. I was probably more surprised than anyone when he dropped like his legs were jelly. I waited for him to pop back up and level me, but he just lay on the asphalt holding his nose, a look of betrayal in his eyes.

"Holy shit," Calvin said.

I was suddenly furious at Carl for lying there helpless. I knelt and started punching wherever I saw an opening. I beat him like a rented mule, as Granny Watts might have said, though she'd have been ashamed to see me do it. The gathered children shouted. Eddie tried to stop me. "Daniel, he's crying!"

Two teachers yanked me to my feet. I tried to twist free, my knife no longer in sight. I screamed, and the gathered children grew silent. In his office, Principal Blevins pushed a box of tissues my way and told me about boys who veer down the Wrong Track. Then he called my mother, at which point I knew all hope was lost. He directed me to wait on the bench outside his office. A few minutes later Calvin appeared, bathroom pass in hand. "We couldn't find your knife. Me and Eddie looked everywhere."

I put my face in my hands.

"They had to put a big towel to Carl's nose."

"Good."

"His daddy came to get him."

I looked at my red knuckles.

"I didn't know you could punch like that."

"Me neither."

We heard my mother's church heels striking the hallway linoleum.

"I better get back to class."

My mother walked past without acknowledging me and introduced herself to the secretary. It sounded like a stranger's name. Mr. Blevins invited her into his office, and the two of them conferred regarding what to do about Daniel Waterson.

That night my father started on my rear with a yardstick, but when I didn't cry, he switched to his belt. Braced against my dresser,

I watched his face, haggard and splotched, in my mirror. His anger became fury, so that his belt was like a whip. I resolved to die rather than give him the satisfaction of a single cry. My mother stood with eyes glistening in my doorway. My face in the mirror belonged to some other boy.

My father's breath grew ragged. "You broke that boy's nose."

"Sorry," I said dully.

"Now I got to find money to pay the doctor bill. First your grandmama and now this."

"I've got sixty dollars you can have."

"You're goddamned right I'll have it. All that's going on and *this* is the fight you pick." I looked him full in the eyes through the mirror. It wasn't at all like Clay Tompkins promised; I had inside myself no love for him at all. My father looked away from my hating eyes and went downstairs.

"Daniel," Mama said, "you're not the only one who's angry."

"Well at least I did something about it."

Mama fixed me with a cold stare. "Boy, you don't know anything about anything, do you?"

Asheville Gazette
April 11th, 1976

SWANNANOA, NC—Police are investigating suspected foul play outside a truck stop on I-40. Employees of the Black Mountain 40 truck stop noticed a blue Cadillac with open door and engine running in the parking lot, and notified authorities. Investigating officers reportedly found a fully loaded revolver on the ground beside the car, along with what appears to be blood. A spokesman for the NC State Police said that they have not yet located a victim, nor can they locate the registered owner of the vehicle.

A couple of weeks later I crouched by the river, filling my father's empty bottles, while Julie watched from the rocks above. "Are you going camping this weekend," she asked, "or are you still grounded?"

"I can't go anywhere but church and school for the rest of my life."

With her shoe Julie nudged a rock from her perch. It struck the shore with a thump. "Hasn't your daddy heard of Alcoholics Anonymous?"

"I don't think he's very anonymous." I threw a can into the river. "Why don't you go away?"

"I need to make sure you get all that mess off our property."

"This is *our* property."

"Not if your daddy keeps drinking like he does."

"Go to hell."

Julie rooted in her denim satchel and dragged out her spell book. "I'm gonna curse you good."

"I hope you know you don't have any friends."

"Yes I do."

"Well I'm not one of them."

Julie pulled my pocketknife from her satchel. "Then I guess I don't have to give *this* back."

"Give it here."

She took a step back as I came up the bank. "Finders keepers."

I came to the edge of her outcrop. "Give it, thief!"

"I picked it up so nobody else would take it!"

"And then you kept it." I stepped toward her.

"Ask nicely."

I slapped her. She put a hand to her face, which seemed frozen in a yawn. A sob lurched from her chest. "So help me God, I'll hit you harder."

Julie screamed so violently I raised my hands to ward off her rage. She turned and threw my knife toward the river. It cartwheeled end over end, like a shotgunned bird, and struck the water where I'd almost drowned years before. Julie wrapped her arms around herself, sat down on the rock, and bawled. Even after I was well into the woods, I could hear her crying. My palm burned.

In my sleep was the barking of dogs along the river. They bayed through the night, black-eyed and hungry, and I dreamt they chased me. They loped behind me like rushing water, pouring over rock and log.

The call came early Sunday. Rain had been pouring from the blackened sky for hours, rattling our roof, drumming the windows. Mama and I picked at biscuits in the kitchen, Daddy dozed fitfully in the living-room rocking chair. I heard Mrs. Moore's trembling voice through the phone pressed to Mama's ear. "Oh my God," Mama said. She'd always claimed that saying this was taking the Lord's name in vain.

The rocking chair creaked as my father came out of it. Mama looked at me. "No," she said. "We kept him home. Is someone going to warn them?" She listened, her eyes welling.

Daddy stood in the doorway.

"Lord Jesus. I'm coming right over."

"Lee Ann," Daddy said as he yanked on his boots.

"The dam," she said. She looked at him like he'd done it. "Clay Tompkins and those children . . ." She choked back a sob. "They're camped by the river, Ray. A few miles down from the dam."

"Goddammit."

There was nobody near them to call, so half the Cantwell County Sheriff's Department was roaring up the river road. Mrs. Moore's nephew was a deputy, which is how they knew. "He told Carla the river's already seven feet higher at the bridge," Mama said. She slumped into her chair and began to pray.

"Lee Ann," Daddy said. "Lee Ann!"

Mama raised her head and looked at him with eyes of shattered green glass.

"Where's Doc Moore?"

"Carla said he was headed upriver."

"Go sit with her. Mind the creek when you cross. You sit with her, and you *stay* there." He turned to me. "Get on your boots." He pushed through the screen door and clomped down the porch steps. Mama ran to the back of the house. The kitchen was silent but for the slap of my bootlaces and the rain striking our roof. She returned in her slicker, clutching her Bible. "C'mon, child." We descended the porch steps, heads down against the rain, and started for the Moore's when Daddy halted us. A thick coil of nylon rope hung off his shoulder. He pointed at Mama. "You go. He's coming with me."

"Ray, absolutely not."

"Lee Ann, I can't do it without him."

"There's plenty of men headed upriver."

"I'm not going upriver. The river already has them."

Mama regarded him with horror. She glanced at me. "Ray, no."

"We might be able to save some. But I need his help."

Mama touched my head. Her face turned cruel. "You keep him out of that river. I don't care what it costs." She turned and left.

Daddy handed me a bucket of shop rags. "C'mon." We set out for the river. Bailey followed cautiously, wincing at the rain.

"Stay here, Bailey." I shooed him with my foot. "I said *stay*!" Daddy slung a rock, and Bailey yelped and trotted back to the porch. I ducked and scurried between branches, the bucket thumping against my leg as I tried to keep up. Daddy loped ahead, a chant under his breath. I could see the Crow much sooner than normal. Its moving mass of brown was loaded with trash cans and lawn chairs and other things scoured from the land overlooking its banks. It tugged at rain-weighted branches drooping overhead. Calvin and Eddie were upriver with Clay, so was Julie. I imagined a wall of water crushing their tents.

Daddy stood atop what used to be a steep bank. Water rushed about a foot below his boot. He looked out at the river and sang the first verse of the 23rd Psalm, slow and ululating in the style of the Old Regulars:

The Lo-ord i-i-s my Shep-herd! I sha-all-ll not want!

I did my best to respond. A shiver overcame me at the stanza about the valley of the shadow of death. As Daddy sang, he knotted his rope around a birch. He tied the other end around his waist. He finished the psalm, then nodded at the coils of rope at his feet. "Start tying rags at the middle, spaced apart."

"How do you know the river won't wash over the bank?"

"It won't." He considered the sky. Thick, lazy drops spattered his face. "Least not before they pass." He nodded upriver. "The bend yonder slows her. If we're gonna save any of them, it'll be here."

A large ironwood branch downriver cracked and tumbled into the water. Daddy shucked off one boot, then the other. It dawned on me that he intended to cross to the other side. I grabbed hold of his arm to stop him and felt a shock, like I'd grabbed an electric fence.

"I'll be fine, bud."

"At least take your boat!"

He pointed. The stand of trees that had cradled his boat was submerged, their tops shredded. His skiff was gone. I gritted my teeth. "No."

He peeled free my hands and took them into his own. Cold air blew from the river. "Son, this is the only place to snatch them up before the rocks." I sat in the mud and started tying rags to his rope with my cold fingers. "Current should be with me once I get halfway." He pointed to the far side, where waves sloshed through trees and lapped at the rise. "Anything big'll take the rope, so I'll hold it higher up the bank and come down when we see them."

"What if something big comes while you're still in the water?"

He pointed to the water lapping at his discarded boots. "If it carries away them boots, you get uphill to your mother, do you hear? Current's stronger than it looks." And then he leaped into that very same current, inciting the water to rage against him. He batted aside a trash can, a length of cardboard. A wood pallet threatened to entangle and sink him, but he fought free. He did a one-armed backstroke as he clutched the unspooling coil of rope in his other arm. A broken tree branch snagged the rope and tried to drag him downriver. I seized the rope lying on my legs, wrapped it around my arm, and dug my heels into the mud. A moment later, it wrenched my shoulders toward the river. Daddy whipped the rope up and down until it snapped free. When he reached the river's midpoint, he turned and struck for the far shore. He didn't see a floating pine, bristling with shattered branches, cut loose from its hidden anchor. The Crow hurled it at my father like a battering ram.

I cupped my hands to my mouth and screamed so loudly it felt like all the little muscles in my throat were tearing. He turned as the tree bore down on him, and the great weariness carved into his face was transformed into fury. The tree's frayed wingspan was too wide to evade, so he dove underwater. Rope slipped through my hands as he kicked downward, down towards the rocks and silted bottom and whatever might be waiting there.

The pine shot through the place where he had been and crashed into a stand of firs huddled in the risen water downstream. Daddy resurfaced, gasping, and made for shore. He moved up the bank and I climbed the rock plateau from which Julie had hurled my pocketknife. Ordinarily well above the river, water now swirled just a couple of feet below it. I thought about how small Julie was. I'd read that the Crow River Dam restrained acres of water, as much weight as a fleet of airliners. I imagined my friends tumbling in its froth like clothes in the wash. Across from me, Daddy stood deathly still, his gaze fixed upriver.

Mist swirled above the treetops. The rain stopped and I heard Daddy chanting where he stood barefooted across the river. People had thought him crazy when he'd tried to warn them. It didn't matter now that he was right, it never would. People would rather you be wrong the correct way than right a strange way.

At first I thought the body floating with downturned head was an uprooted sapling. I thought of the mothers praying throughout town. Who prayed for this boy eyeing the river bottom with a glassy stare?

Daddy came down the bank, tied his end of the rope to a tree, and pulled himself along it to intercept the body. The shirtless boy wore pajama pants with some kind of patterned print. Daddy stretched out his arm and snatched the boy's foot. He pulled him ashore, turned him over, and shook his head. He looked across the river to me, then cradled the boy and stepped carefully to higher ground, like a man carrying a baby. The boy's thin arms swung like pendulums. Daddy found a place at the top of the ridge and lay him down.

The river began to agitate as if in response to Daddy's theft. Water breached the bank on my side, sending tendrils into the field between my rock and the woods. Daddy's boots began to float and turn in lazy circles. Branches and clumps of brush sped downriver. Cardboard boxes, firewood, a battered refrigerator with its mouth gaping open to the sky. Suddenly Daddy splashed back down the slope. Upriver was Clay Tompkins, one arm over a log, the other clutching Julie Moore. Her face was white and she had her arms locked tight around his neck. A cross-cutting wave rolled over their faces. They shook their heads and spit. Daddy waved his arms and shouted. "Grab the rope!" I yelled.

Clay saw Daddy, and made as if to kick toward the far shore, but he didn't appear to have strength for anything but holding Julie and clasping that log. The mid-current bore them swiftly past slower-moving flotsam. Daddy jumped into the river and pulled himself along the rope, straining to reach them because of what waited around the next bend: the rapids and the falls like a cruel staircase, the river's narrowing that served as a gun barrel littered with boulders, rock faces rising fifty feet on either side. Drowning would be a mercy. Daddy kicked furiously, but he wasn't even going to come close.

Clay knew what waited downriver as well; he'd taken us there himself. He shouted at Julie, then let go of the log and raised her with both hands over his head, which disappeared beneath the churning water. The rope caught her across the chest and bowed downriver until Clay let go of her. She hung from her underarms, legs bobbing on the surface of the fast-moving water.

Past the rope, Clay's head came up. He turned to see that Julie had held on, then he looked skyward. There was no sun awaiting him there. I remembered the day he'd stood with Mama and me in our front yard, praying after Daddy killed the boy, and how none of his prayers had done any good. Now his lips moved in prayer again. Or maybe he was just trying to breathe. I suppose for the holy, there's no difference between the two. Clay's head bobbed downriver as his eyes strained heavenward, then he rounded the river's bend and was carried from our sight.

Julie cast her wide-eyed face from shore to shore. She called out something, then Daddy had her. He held her with one arm and worked along the rope to my shore. He struggled into the soggy field where I now stood, Julie's bare legs dangling against his own. She was shivering, her eyes distant. Daddy bent to set her down, but she wouldn't let go of him.

"Daniel," he said, eyes downriver.

"He might get through the rocks."

"Daniel."

"We can hang a rope from the McAllister bridge."

He turned his face to mine, and I felt that electric current pass through the ground between us, up my feet, along my thighs, into my gut, my throat, my brain. My father's eyes that had been brown all the days of my life were a bright smoky blue. I knew that in this moment he could see all that is known to man and the dead and every creeping thing beneath the river, visions I would only learn the substance of later: Calvin with a blanket around his shoulders in a deputy's car; three children being pulled from the current upriver; others tumbled and torn and crushed; an unbattered girl curled like a baby and stuffed under sunken tree limbs; Mama and Mrs. Moore and the church-women praying in the house on the hill; a clench-jawed Dr. Moore searching the river's edge by the dam.

And Clay Tompkins, clawing at the rock walls downriver.

I wanted to run through the woods up the hill into the arms of my mama, but Daddy's eyes gone blue were full of despair and I couldn't leave him. He pried Julie loose and guided her to me. She shivered and made a keening noise. "Take hold of her, now. Lead her home."

I couldn't look away from his spectral blue eyes.

"Hustle," he said. "She's going into shock."

"What about Clay?"

Daddy snatched up his boots and sloshed across the field toward home. Julie pressed her head against my shoulder as I guided her toward her house, shuddering when she inhaled and moaning as she exhaled. She had become an instrument of mourning. I told her my daddy might board horses again and that if we got a pony I'd show her how to ride. I said if the school flooded we'd likely be liberated for weeks. I said her mama was just through the trees and up the hill, that the water couldn't rise that high, that soon she'd be dry and warm.

Julie quieted as I guided her uphill through the dripping trees. She moved her feet in concert with mine. Her arms were a tight-drawn rope around my ribcage. I told her we could be friends so long as she didn't tell anyone at school. "I'm already your friend," she whispered.

I had run out of things to say, so I just patted her shoulder. We hadn't gotten far into her yard before there was a yelp inside the house. Julie's mother threw open the screen door and ran across the soaked grass praising Jesus. Close behind came other women praising Father, Son, and Holy Ghost. None of them had children in the Young Explorers. Mrs. Moore fell on her knees before her child as if in worship and enveloped her in her housecoat. The women gathered close and someone began a prayer.

Mama stood outside their circle. She knew some mothers would not be praising Jesus this day. I went to her and whispered about the rope, the swollen river, how Daddy had known where to be. I told her about the boy laid unbreathing atop the riverbank, and Clay Tompkins clinging to driftwood and letting go and holding Julie overhead even though that meant going under, under the water, into the arms of the deep, into the valley of the shadow.

Clay Tompkins once played with Johnny Cash. It was April 11th, 1958. Clay's uncle, a part-time sound man, took him along to a Hickory radio station where Mr. Cash was appearing and had him bring the banjo he'd been learning to pick. Mr. Cash couldn't help but notice, and he ushered Clay into the sound booth, where he played "He Leadeth Me" in stilted clawhammer while Mr. Cash sang along. So far as I know, it was his only live performance of that hymn.

Today that radio station broadcasts political commentary and late-night infomercials about home refinance and weight loss. I haven't been able to find the recording of Clay Tompkins and Johnny Cash, but I want to believe it still exists somewhere.

The next time Clay's name appeared in a newspaper was for winning the regional spelling bee in 8th grade. Julie Moore won the same region two years after the flood. When I told her what she had in common with Clay, she asked me if he'd been state champion. I told her he hadn't even placed. To the chagrin of her mother, who drove her all the way to Raleigh for the state bee two weeks later, Julie misspelled "contradiction" in the first round.

I have no way to discern whether Clay Tompkins was crafted from the beginning to be given over to the Crow. I know he was a speller and a Carolina Tarheel; I know he and his seminary friends recorded a folk music record that sold 173 copies in Denver and which isn't half bad; I know he got his golden hair from his mother, whose people came over from Norway. I know his father sold that furniture business in 1984 and retired with Mrs. Tompkins to Asheville. I know Clay was an Eagle Scout and briefly a park ranger and he knew how to hunt spiders under the moon. I know he mustered the strength to survive nine miles of churning river with Julie Moore in one arm and a slick length of driftwood in the other.

I've learned all I can about Clay Tompkins, you understand, but I don't know what he saw when he looked heavenward.

An emergency crew found him soon after my father did. Daddy had dragged him to high ground below the McAllister bridge and was blowing into his lungs even though the back of his head was beaten to pulp. Daddy insisted he'd gotten his heart beating for half a minute, that there was still life in him. When the paramedics told him there was no point, he told them to go to hell if that was their attitude. So they congregated on the road above, smoking cigarettes and waiting for him to run out of breath to push into Clay's lungs.

As for Johnny Cash, he wandered through Tennessee caves a decade after singing alongside Clay Tompkins. He was hoping to disappear and die, but he couldn't stay lost. Did you know that? He couldn't stay lost.

———✦———

The Crow took its time retreating, and the streets of Hickory Shore lay as mirrors underneath a sun that seemed not to care what had become of us in its absence. The National Guard appeared with shovels and pumps; the Red Cross brought blankets and sandwiches. Politicians came to stand on our bridge with concerned looks while photographers snapped pictures. Everyone knew someone taken by the Crow. Most of us knew all of them.

Sheriff Wilson asked Daddy's help finding the last missing child. Hundreds of National Guardsmen and deputies and firemen and fathers from every church along the river had searched river, fields, woods. They'd found not even a shred of the girl's clothes. Sheriff

Wilson had stopped caring what anyone thought. He motored his outboard down to our stretch of river, and Daddy climbed aboard in ragged jeans and Army jacket and crouched up front. I watched them disappear upriver, a wake of muddy froth fanning out behind.

The reason so many saw is because the girl was tucked under debris just beyond the bridge and its congregated onlookers. From above they watched Daddy spread his arms to become like the carved prow of a sailing ship. Some Old Regulars had trickled down from the hills to stand clustered on that bridge as well, and they echoed in their way my father as he cried out the verses in Matthew about the lost sheep. For some people in town it was the first and only time they ever heard an Old Regular chant. Then Daddy pointed unlooking to a spot not far from shore, and the sheriff anchored. He and Daddy sat wordlessly smoking cigarettes until divers arrived to wrest the child free.

People still recount how my father prophesied the fate of that dam. Others have noted that he kept his own son home from camping that night. Some recall how he saved Julie Moore from the Crow. Others will never forget it was he who sent Bobby Doyle to the grave. I suppose the history of any man is just what we choose to remember about him.

My friend Eddie Gilchrist was the boy Daddy had pulled from the river. People said it was a blessing he'd been saved during Don Dunwoody's revival, that it was part of God's plan for Eddie. We buried alongside him seven other children caught up in the plans of God. Men had to knock down the graveyard's back fence to make room.

Clay Tompkins was taken to his people in Thomasville. Mama and I rode with the Moores to his funeral, part of a long train of cars from Hickory Shore. My father was nowhere to be found. Julie and I sat in the back with one of her brothers. She wore a black dress and clutched a purse containing a Nancy Drew book and M&Ms, which she quietly ate. When she noticed me watching from the corner of my eye, she held an M&M over my lap until I opened my palm. Her brother shifted his long legs from side to side and sighed a lot. Eventually he fell asleep, his head thumping the window with every curve. Julie and I quietly crunched M&Ms and listened to her brother's head. Our parents spoke little.

In the church, we immediately knew Clay's mother by her golden hair. His father had the look of a man just awakened from sleep.

Clay's people drew close to Julie as if she carried something of their boy in her pockets. His mother fell into Julie's mother and their weeping silenced the murmurs in the pews.

Clay's parents insisted we sit with them up front. Behind us were whispers, the barks of men clearing their throats, complaints from children who did not understand a dead man lay in the casket before us. Another wordless appearance by Clay before an assembled church. Reverend Hardison was silenced as well on this alien terrain. He was getting a taste of his own medicine is what I thought as I considered him where he sat at the end of our pew, rolls of skin gathered at the back of his collar, sweat beading along his hairline. He was shaking his head like he disagreed with everything happening here. When the congregation began "Amazing Grace," he covered his face with his hands and shook so violently his wife had to wrap both arms around his shoulders to keep him from falling off the pew.

In the small silences I heard Julie's grinding teeth. Her body was like a slab of rock set against my own. She started shivering when Clay's father shuffled forward to eulogize his son, and a tiny snap came from her mouth. She retrieved the tip of a tooth and pushed it around her palm with her thumb. I put my hand over hers so nobody would see.

———

In the months that followed, investigations were launched, scapegoats were cast out, laws were passed. Money flowed into Hickory Shore from Raleigh and Washington. Money to repair riverbanks, rebuild barns and houses, replace business inventories, compensate victims. Nearly every family who lost a child moved away, and this was a relief to those who remained. Money poured in as well to build parks, to put in sidewalks and electric streetlights that looked gas-lit, to re-brick and paint old buildings. To beautify. To beautify.

———

Halloween night I woke in shattered moonlight to the sound of a traveling host. From my window I watched them journey east toward the river. In the stable, horses we'd boarded whinnied and nickered. I gathered a blanket about me and opened my window to the cold. The wordless song of the gathered dead was as wind passing through hollowed bone. Though the moon wavered in its cloud-strewn sky, the light within this host was steady, as if illuminated by some earth-laden mineral, or by the energy of their own decay.

Bobby Doyle attended the dead. Alongside him walked a boy with a crooked neck and several others who looked like his kin. In the center was a broad-shouldered man proud even in death, though half his face was stove in, his riding coat riddled with holes. A long-haired woman walked just as proudly on his arm, a sickly boy in tow. Behind these came Harlan Carver, whose newly blackened eyes suited him.

Bailey huffed from our front porch. He waddled down the steps to join my father, who stood between our home and this close-passing host. Daddy rubbed him behind the ear. All the passing dead cast their black eyes on my father but for Bobby Doyle, who looked up to where I stood shrouded in shadow. His gaze was an invitation. *There is always a place in the river.* I felt no compulsion this time to follow the dead boy, but I hoped my father would. *Go with them to the deep, Daddy. Lay with them in the depths, and then we living will find peace.*

The dead passed by us into the woods and the last of these was Clay Tompkins. Though the rest bore wounds and decay, his head was healed and he walked as a man filled with breath. His hair shone golden. The earth-haunting dead walked before him as a bridal procession, and the wind tunneling their bones was a wail. Daddy saw him and sank to his knees as our whimpering dog licked his face. Clay looked at neither my father nor me; his face was set eastward toward the river, eastward toward rest and what lay beyond rest. Just as I knew those who escorted him had not ceased their journeying, I knew that Clay was striding homeward and would not look back.

Somehow, lunchtime when I worked at Doc Moore's had become almost enjoyable. Mrs. Moore fueled the conversation with benign gossip, which Doc Moore enjoyed rebutting. No, Barley Whittaker did not break his leg dancing on his truck bed when East Carolina beat NC State; he slipped loading feed. Yes, Mandy Sanders went to live with her aunt for the remainder of the school year, but she was a patient and so no, by God, he would not speak to the rumors.

Julie had taken to wearing ribbons in her hair and in each earlobe a false pearl. I stacked wood behind her house one afternoon after lunch while she nestled yellow and blue pansies into a planter. Her hands were covered in soil, and she crooked her wrist to push back a lock of hair that hung well below the line of her old soup-bowl cut. When she did this, she looked so unlike the drowned rat of a girl my father had fished from the river that I found myself staring. "Do you ever have nightmares in the day?" She asked this without looking at me.

"Everybody who sleeps gets nightmares."

"I mean when you're awake. Do you see things. People who shouldn't be there."

"You mean because they're dead."

"Do you see them?"

"No."

She sighed.

"Do they talk to you?" I asked.

"No. But I know they want things."

"What do they want?"

She shook her head. "It's just daydreams." Her voice brightened. "You should join the after-school Bible study."

"I get plenty in church."

"That's just listening."

"Did you really bury your spell book?"

"Magic is for heathens and children." She looked me up and down as if to discern which I was.

"So I can give up worrying each night whether I'll wake up as a frog?"

"You never did apologize, you know."

"For what?"

She touched her face and turned back to her flowers.

"I haven't heard an apology from you, either."

She stood and faced me. Here were the squinty eyes I was used to, the slight overbite, the balls-of-the-feet stance that hinted at imminent attack. She tugged a strand of hair from her mouth and her eyelids mashed together in that deliberated blink of hers. "That's okay, Daniel Waterson, because I forgive you anyway." She looked me up and down again. "My daddy isn't paying you to stand around."

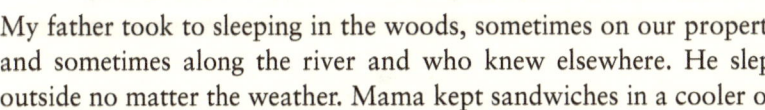

My father took to sleeping in the woods, sometimes on our property and sometimes along the river and who knew elsewhere. He slept outside no matter the weather. Mama kept sandwiches in a cooler on our back porch and beside this a stack of clean clothes and a thermos of coffee she made fresh every morning. I took on his chores with my own. In the evenings, Mama and I talked as if it had always been just us, a mother and son with no memory of Ray Waterson.

At night I did push-ups. I imagined I was pushing the earth away and with it this house, my parents, every preacher and teacher. When my arms tired, I fell to the floor and felt the cool boards against my belly. As the fatherless weeks wore on, I felt my muscles thicken and find their rightful places alongside one another. I pushed away the earth longer each night, and though always it ended in collapse, I imagined that one day I might break free of gravity and weariness altogether.

HICKORY SHORE TOWNSHIP
Water & Sanitation Department
January 11th, 1977

* * * FIRST WARNING * * *

This notice is issued to inform occupants and legal owner(s) of the residence with the address of 776 Hannaford Road within the township of Hickory Shore that pursuant to H.S.M.C. 118-1457 ("Blighted Residential Lots and Living Structures") the aforementioned property could be subject to fines and/or condemnation. The following conditions have been observed:

- Inoperative and/or unregistered vehicle kept or stored on the premises within view of street
- Damaged siding
- Rodent infestation

These conditions are in violation of H.S.M.C. 118-1457 and if not remedied within 21 days from the date of this notice are subject to fine. Continued failure to remedy will result in a second warning and possible condemnation.

. . .

Granny Watts stood trembling with anger in her living room, cane in one hand and letter in the other. "Blighted," she said. "*Blighted*, like I live in a goddamned potato patch." She fought back a coughing fit.

Mama took the letter from her. "*Rodents?* We don't have rodents."

"Well now, I do get the occasional rat from the junkyard."

"Abandoned vehicle? They mean Daddy's tractor?"

"I reckon."

"And as for siding, why that's just a fascia piece. They make it sound like there's a hole in your bedroom wall."

"Child, it's like I've been telling you. They're trying to take this house."

"Oh Mama, the boomers went floating down the Crow with that dam."

"Just because the money flowing into this county comes from the government instead of corporations doesn't mean the game is different, Lee Ann. It's the same type of men lined up at the trough."

"Conspiracy or no, this letter is ridiculous, and we'll just tell them so. If they start condemning every house with an unused vehicle in the yard, they'll have a riot on their hands."

"First the taxes, now this. This is how they do it—take a piece of you at a time." Granny began coughing so hard she had to sit down. She clutched her ribs where they'd been broken. A shadow passed across my mother's face. "Mama," she said, her voice gentler, "your taxes are still less than your newspaper subscription."

"A little piece at a time, so we don't start shooting."

My mother folded up the letter. "I'll talk to someone. They probably just have an overzealous new employee who's not worked in a small town."

"Talk all you want—if they don't get me this way, they'll find another."

Mama rolled her eyes, which compelled my grandmother to roll *her* eyes. She put her withered hand on my neck and asked me about school, and how many girls were chasing me, and if I knew how to be careful as a sailor. She laughed through her wheezes as Mama lit into her. After supper we hugged Granny where she lay on the couch. She tucked some money into Mama's hand, kissed her downturned forehead, and whispered something that made a tear fall from my mother's face onto her own. Mama made to wipe it away and Granny stayed her hand. The whole ride home my mother fussed about Granny's

stubbornness and paranoia, but all I could think about was that full
and rich and silent tear lingering on her mother's face.

It wasn't just Granny Watts being pressured: the whole county was
in thrall to a purifying spirit. The town bought out a tract of trailer-
home owners and committed their property to a memorial park. A
cinder-block brake shop was torn down to make room for a new post
office; a daycare run out of an old woman's home was shut down; a
whole row of shops were ushered away to make room for a new fire
station. All this rejuvenation seemed to operate according to the same
principles that animate tornadoes: some buildings were obliterated
seemingly at random, while others with no greater apparent worth
were spared. Some of these were even declared part of a new historic
district to be refurbished at state expense.

Granny bemoaned what happens when governments presume
to define beauty and history. "We're in the court of the Red Queen
now," she muttered. "Expect neither reason nor justice."

Calvin's father was wary of the forces behind these changes as
well, though he accommodated himself to them by expanding into
building supplies. The summer after 8th grade, he hired me to bag
groceries and stock shelves alongside Calvin at the Red and White.
Doc Moore filled up my spare hours with jobs on his property. Only
now do I realize that both men were trying to make sure we had
enough money at home. I didn't even think to offer any of it to my
mother. Nor did she ask.

My father sobered up enough to tow Grandfather Watts's rusted
tractor into Granny's barn with his truck. She made a pot of coffee
and then he patched her siding, and the next few nights the two of
them sat chewing tobacco and passing her Sweet Sixteen back and
forth to obliterate every four-legged creature they saw venture from
the junkyard. We accepted this sober spell the way one enjoys a little
sunshine in winter.

The pneumonia took Granny Watts quickly, which Mama said was a
mercy. It's more truthful to say that Harlan Carver killed her slowly,
and the only evident mercy was hers; she went to her death thinking
she'd protected Carver from the grave and Daddy from prison. I want

to believe this accrues to her ledger the same as my own silence accrues to mine.

Reverend Hardison eulogized her as if she'd been a famous personage, and in her way I suppose she was. I'd never seen our church so full, many of them the very men she'd persecuted. I imagined some came not just to pay their respects to a lifelong adversary but to confirm that she was really and truly no longer able to hound them. My mother sat proud and straight and wept not a tear, having spent them all at her mother's bedside. My father, reeking of whisky, could scarcely take his hands from his face.

Fred Ledbetter drove his family to her funeral in a new red Buick. The reconstruction and beautification business was treating him well. I saw no shame on his face for having partnered with the man who killed my grandmother. He sat towards the back in a nice suit, feigning piety alongside his thuggish sons and longsuffering wife. Afterwards he stood in the churchyard talking business, likely as not sorting out how to take Granny's property now that she was out of the way. My father walked past Fred Ledbetter and his cronies without a glance or word, across the road and into the woods.

Another warning came from the town while the soil was still fresh on her grave; this one indicting her diseased trees, the antiquated septic system. Mama hired a lawyer who did little quickly except cash her checks. I lay in bed nights, fuming about Ledbetter and excoriating my father in my mind for not dealing with him, which I understand now was a cheap way of absolving myself for my silence about Carver.

Late one night in the spring of 1978, I worked up the nerve to take action and hiked into town with a handful of tools. The streets were empty, and thick-painted hydrants in the new historical district gleamed beneath faux old-fashioned streetlights. Ledbetter's new Buick sprawled on his freshly paved driveway, but it was blocked by his old work truck. I slipped into the truck and quietly closed the door.

Shoving a screwdriver into the ignition and turning didn't work, so I sank to the floorboard and unscrewed the steering column panels. I stripped the ignition and battery wires, twisted them together, and was rewarded with dashboard lights. With trembling hands, I stripped the starter wire and touched it to the exposed metal of the pigtailed wires. The engine shuddered. I sat up behind the wheel and gunned it. Ledbetter's porch light snapped on. I threw the truck in reverse and barked the tires as I shot down his smooth black driveway. Down his street I raced, taking the first turn followed by another and then another, alternating left and right, my eyes more on the rearview mirror than the road. There was no one behind me. I found the eastbound road and really opened up the throttle. The engine on Fred Ledbetter's old truck ran smooth. I knew a half-dozen places I could leave it in gear and watch it purr itself into the Crow.

Not far out of town, a car closed on me with unnerving speed, brights on, blue light flashing. I put the gas pedal to the floor, but the police car reached my back bumper like I was sitting still. In the distance behind, I saw another police car gaining fast.

We passed my driveway doing eighty-five. The pit in my stomach was replaced by a wild elation. I shouted what I thought sounded like a war cry. I knew they were radioing ahead, that soon I'd be met by more deputies, perhaps even highway patrol. I decided that I would drive Ledbetter's truck off a cliff past the McAllister bridge. In my mind's eye I saw myself jumping free as it plummeted, like in the movies. Striking the dark water and swimming away undetected. Hopping a train to Florida.

I saw the turnoff, braked, and tried to wheel into it. I turned the steering wheel in the direction I thought it should go, but so far as the rest of Fred's truck was concerned, we were heading east to Tennessee. We compromised, the truck and I, by broadsiding a yellow pine.

I was arraigned in a white-walled courthouse room. The paramedics said nothing was broken, but my body disagreed. Mama had brought my suit and an egg sandwich; she sat in the row behind me, as if this were church and I getting married. The wrinkled white of her handkerchief spilled over her hands. Across the aisle from her sat Fred Ledbetter in the same suit he'd worn to Granny's funeral.

A sheriff's deputy read his report. The magistrate evaluated me from beneath unruly grey eyebrows. "Stand up, young man." My chair scraped the linoleum as I stood. "You understand I have the authority to send you to the Cantwell Juvenile Facility until you are eighteen?"

"Yes, sir."

"Any reason I shouldn't?"

"I don't guess so."

"You admit to the actions described in the deputy's report?" I nodded. Mama stifled a sob. "Mr. Waterson, I do not like thieves. Neither does the state of North Carolina." He stared until I felt the silence as a weight. He waved a stark white page. "Your school disciplinary record tells me that you do not know how to live properly in a community." He lifted a handful of papers varied in color and size.

"These notes from teachers and others in this township tell me your community does not yet wish to give up on you." He leaned across his desk. "Now. To whom should I listen? Them, or you?"

I couldn't imagine who might have written notes about me.

"That was not a rhetorical question, son."

"I don't know."

"That your mother behind you?"

I nodded.

"Daniel," he said, voice softening. "How do you think all this makes your mama feel?"

My mother leaned forward and grabbed my limp hand. Her sobs made my lifeless arm shiver. The magistrate looked from me to my repentant mother and I hated both of them. He sighed. "This court assesses the stolen truck to have a value below $1,000 and thereby finds the accused guilty of Class One misdemeanor auto theft."

Fred Ledbetter stood. "C'mon Frank! That truck is worth two thousand if it's worth a penny!"

The magistrate yanked off his glasses. "You want a full accounting for everything that's gone on in this town of late, Fred?"

"Now, Frank—"

"Shut your mouth and sit your ass back down in that seat, or you'll be spending a night in the very cell this young man vacated."

Ledbetter looked about for support and found none. He sat down, muttering.

The magistrate turned his attention back to me. "Daniel Waterson, you are sentenced to three months in the Cantwell Juvenile Detention Center. One year probation. Restitution in an amount to be approved by this court." He tapped a wooden disk with his gavel. Mama thanked him between sobs. Ledbetter shook his head in disgust.

"Listen here, young man," said the magistrate. "Plenty of people have it harder than you. Get to know some of those boys where you're headed if you don't believe me. And don't let me see you again unless you're bagging my groceries."

There was paperwork in a nearby office, where they told me I had twenty-four hours to report to the detention facility. They gave me a piece of paper explaining what I could and could not bring, as if my mother would soon be dropping me off at a summer camp. We walked out in silence. The sun had disappeared behind dull, flat clouds that stretched to the horizon in all directions. At home, Mama parked and took hold of my arm, her eyes on something in the distance. "Daniel."

It was as if she were a blind woman trying to confirm my identity. "I'm stretched to breaking."

"Sorry."

Her jaw tightened. "I didn't humiliate myself playing the tender-hearted mother back there for *sorry*. I need someone in this house to be a man. You think about that while . . . ." She gave my arm a shake and, still without looking at me, got out and walked to the house. Her frame looked strung together with wire.

That night she fried potato pancakes and link sausages and piled them steaming on a plate beside a pitcher of fresh lemonade. She kissed the top of my head and went upstairs to pack a duffel bag for me. The air was thick but unable to rain, the trees silent under its weight. Our kitchen door was open, and nightfall came to the edge of our steps. I listened to the sound of my fork against the plate, my chewing and swallowing, my mother upstairs, opening and closing drawers, humming a hymn like her own mother used to do.

April 17th, 1978

Daniel,

They say you tried to kill Fred Ledbetter and his boys with your granny's shotgun and then stole their truck, but I figure if you'd intended to kill them there would have been a triple funeral and we all would have been excused from school for it. I'm sorry you're in prison. I keep a list of people to pray for and I wrote your name on it. I wrote it in pencil because I know things will get better for you and your family someday soon.

It's not all an act, you know. I really do pray and believe in the Lord and try to do His will. But you know what it's like to be mad at everyone sometimes, even God. I can't tell that to anybody in Bible study. And I can't tell them about the waking nightmares. They're people I've never met, some with terrible wounds and some just broken down, but all of them with awful black eyes. They want me to follow them to the river. They don't speak, but I know that's what they want. I remember once you told me not to go down there by myself. But sometimes I think maybe it would be alright. Maybe if I just did what they want, they'd let me rest.

Be careful in there, and don't get any tattoos on your face.

Your friend,
Julie

Every kid in Hickory Shore harbored some exquisite piece of knowledge about three storied locations in North Carolina: the juvenile detention facility, the haunted house on Payne Road, and the nut house in Butner. Most of it was embellished, yet somehow it was less rich than reality. Maybe that's true of every myth.

I expected shankings and shower rapes, but instead it was remedial classes and pick-up basketball and daily counseling sessions. Troublemakers were quickly culled and isolated. Some boys looked in your face for trouble, others kept their eyes down. Most treated the place like something between high school and a hospital. The best part was not wondering if my father was sleeping down the hall.

May 9th, 1978

Dear Daniel,

I hope prison food isn't as bad as in the movies. Mama says not to call it prison. I can call it the Big House if you prefer. You know I'm kidding, right? I have to say I'm kidding a lot because nobody gets when I'm being funny. I think it's because I don't remember to smile at the right times.

Do you have any friends there? Kids here say you have to join a gang to survive. Most kids here are idiots. I try to pray for them because I'm supposed to.

Do they teach you practical skills there, so you won't lead a life of crime? I mean woodworking and engine repair and things like that. Mama says I'm terrible for wondering if you're making license plates there, but I think it's a legitimate question. Are you?

Don't tell your mother I asked, or she'll tell mine and then I'll have to hear about it. Mama thinks if you talk about things then you traumatize people. Are my letters traumatizing you? Maybe I should wrap them around rocks. See, that was also a joke.

So here's something to look forward to: when you get out I'm making you a cake. I was going to make one and send it to you but Mama says that's not allowed. I bet it is allowed and she's just worried I'll stick a file in it. She says I don't behave right. Daddy has her worried because he thinks something's wrong with me. I got upset at a really bad daymare and he had to inject me with something so I would sleep. It was the first time I've slept eight straight hours in a long time. Since all that happened at the river. Calvin says "hey." He saw me writing this letter at lunch. I figure he doesn't know how to read or write so I'd best pass his "hey" along. Be careful in there.

   Julie

Calvin did write me letters, but they were mostly dirty jokes and move-by-move breakdowns of his matches. We'd joined the wrestling team that fall, reasoning that years of practice behind the Red and White made us naturals. We soon discovered with no small bitterness that our best moves—Sammartino's abdominal stretch, the suplex slam, even the gentlest of full nelsons—were illegal. Calvin had persevered; I suppose he liked having a reason to stay after school that wasn't detention-related. Now he was wrestling freestyle in tournaments all over the state. He was turning out to be a formidable opponent when the opposition was limited to kids his own size.

Mama visited each Sunday, serving as mail courier. I frustrated her by not opening Julie's letters in her presence. She knew I knew this bothered her and refused to give me the satisfaction of hearing her admit it. No doubt she and Mrs. Moore were peeved that Julie sealed each envelope with wax and her St. Christopher medallion.

"It'll just be Bible verses," I told Mama when she let slip a curious glance. Twisting the knife, I added: "I might read it later." Mama raised her eyebrows and pretended to consider a row of sketches hung on the visiting room wall, a product of never-ending arts and crafts classes. "I've never known anybody to get a letter and not want to read it. And that poor child writing you almost every week."

"Calvin? He's barely written twice."

"You know *exactly* who I mean, you devil boy."

"You want to read it?"

"I get all the mail I need, thank you. If you want to ignore your friend that's your business. But it's not very good manners." She shook her head and smoothed a curl on my head. "Do you ever write back?"

I shrugged.

"Just like your father. I don't know why I wrote to him when he was overseas, except maybe I had this idea that my letters were like prayers and that if I didn't keep sending them he might not come back." She slapped my arm. "But at least he read them."

———✦———

June 19th, 1978

Dear Daniel,

Some kids are saying you stabbed a guard and tried to break out. Jeff Gilkey says his cousin knows somebody who says you grabbed a guard's gun and started shooting and they had to tranquilize you. At least you know nobody's forgotten you. All the rumors make you sound dangerous, except for the one about how you tried to kill yourself and got sent to Butner. Mary Taylor started that one, because Mary Taylor is a hateful little bitch.

I shouldn't have written that. But this letter's in ink and I'm not starting over.

Your mother thinks I'm your girlfriend. That's probably the most horrifying rumor of all. I can tell by how she smiles at Mama when I give her a letter. The last time I got so mad I told her I just write because the Bible says we're supposed to remember those in prison. Your mother got tight-lipped at that, and Mama let me have it later. I hate when people think they know me. Do you ever feel like that?

I don't think anyone really knows you, Daniel. Maybe Calvin. But even he doesn't know all of you, does he? Nobody knows all of me, either. Daddy took me to a doctor last week. A head doctor. A shrink. I think he thinks I'm going crazy. I might make some things up just to freak out the shrink. If you start getting my letters in crayon from Butner, you'll know it worked.

Julie

———✦———

On the day I was released, Mama fed me a tableful of food. We didn't talk about where I'd been. My father's only presence was the accumulated evidence of small displacements: grain sacks piled for bedding in the tool shed, a sandwich plate in the kitchen windowsill, curls of dried mud left by boot soles on our back porch.

Sometimes I went to watch Calvin wrestle. I'd sit at the top of the gym bleachers, no matter how small the crowd below. Sometimes Julie would show up, always with a book, and sit up top with me. "Why don't you just read at home?" I asked her one afternoon.

"I'm home enough."

"I don't understand a girl who brings a book to a wrestling tournament."

She put her hand over my eyes. It was warm, her palm moist. "What's the score in Calvin's match?"

"What?"

"You heard me."

"3-2," I guessed.

"Wrong." She withdrew her hand. "He's still on deck. I don't understand a boy who comes to a wrestling tournament and doesn't know who's on the mat." She settled back, pulled a half-empty bag of M&Ms from her purse, and held it up to me without looking. Below us, Calvin strode onto a mat. I took an M&M.

"You're gonna get more squinty-eyed than you already are reading all the time."

"You could stand to read the Bible, Daniel Waterson."

"What makes you think I don't?"

She squinted at me. "'We are the clay, you are the potter. We are all the work of your hand.'"

"Isaiah."

"Anybody who goes to church can name the book."

"Isaiah sixty-four eight."

"We're memorizing the book of James," she said. "You could join us."

"I don't think your friends want me in their Bible club."

Calvin scored a takedown and tilted his opponent to his back.

"Maybe it's you who doesn't want to be around them."

"You don't either."

She shrugged.

"Why do you read the Bible? It's not like we haven't heard it every day of our lives."

A shadow passed over her face. "It helps keep the spirits away."

⸻

HICKORY SHORE TOWNSHIP
Department of Public Safety
October 19th, 1978

Please be advised of our determination that
the residence with the address of 776 Hannaford
Road within the proper border of Hickory Shore
Township has been found to be unoccupied, and
is therefore subject to condemnation. This
is not a notice of condemnation, but is a
notification of the revised status of this
residence.

If you believe we have reached this determination in error or wish to discuss either
remediation or options for release of re-
sponsibilities in regards to this residence,
please call our offices at . . .

⸻

Julie liked to put down a blanket wherever I worked on her father's
property. She'd call out passages from Pablo Neruda or William Blake
and ask me what I thought. I'd tell her I didn't understand why they
couldn't get to the point, and she'd roll her eyes, cry out, and flop
backward as if shot. Lying prone with the contested verse on her
chest, she'd berate me for being the smartest boy she knew who had
not an ounce of imagination.

"I thought you were done with spells," I said to her one afternoon as I set posts for a well shed. She put down a book whose pages
she hadn't turned.

"Huh?" She was like this more and more. Lost inside herself.

"That log with candles stuck on it, at the bottom of the hill."

"You mean my personal property on *our* side of the line?"

"Don't worry, I'm not gonna mess with your voodoo shrine."

She fingered the spine of her book. "It's not voodoo. They're
prayer candles."

"What does that mean?"

"Churches used to light candles for people. Each thread of smoke
was a prayer rising to heaven."

"I never heard of that."

"Daniel Waterson, if I had to limit myself to what you've heard of, I'd be reading comic books and tying fishing lures."

"That sounds like a great life."

She gave a frustrated cry.

"How come you put your candles by the river? Why not your windowsill?"

Her eyelids mashed together. "Mama and Daddy worry enough."

I set a beam and knelt to fill around it with crushed rock. Julie watched me and I did not mind that she watched me.

"You want help?"

"No." I cut open a bag of cement mix with a pocketknife from my grandfather's toolshed and poured it over the rock.

"Aren't you supposed to add water?"

"There's water enough in the soil. Who are the candles for?"

"My brother, who's flunking chemistry at N.C. State. My grandmother who has shingles. Your granny." She looked toward the river. "One for Clay."

"What good are prayers for dead people? They don't need our help."

"Maybe we need theirs."

I set a level on the post top. "Who else?"

"What?"

"You named four people. There's six candles." I knew one of the candles was for me.

"How come you notice things like how many candles are on a stump, but you can't get better than a C in English?"

"I don't do well with rules."

Julie laughed. She picked up her book.

"Is one of them for you?"

"No."

"Who, then?"

"A girl."

"Who?"

She gave an exasperated sigh. "I don't *know* who. I just know she died near here, and she's not like the others. Her spirit is kindhearted."

I didn't tell her it was my sister. Nor did I tell her I sometimes saw Bobby Doyle standing in the deep shade of an oak, or at the corner of our porch, or in the recesses of our barn. I thought if she could come to believe that her own visions weren't real, she might get better. I think she knew nonetheless that I sometimes saw the dead as she did, and that like her I wondered in my disquieted heart: Mustn't every watching thing breathe?

```
        HICKORY SHORE TOWNSHIP
        Department of Public Safety
           January 22nd, 1979

This notice is to inform you that the Township
of Hickory Shore intends to initiate eminent
domain proceedings regarding the land parcel
with current township address of 776 Hannaford
Road. This letter serves the purpose of fair
notice as described in Chapter 70 of the N.C.
statute authorizing the Township with the Pow-
ers and Procedures of eminent domain in ac-
cordance with state law. From the date of this
letter you or your authorized representatives
have 21 days to file a response . . .
```

One summer night in 1979, my father shook me awake. His eyes were glassy. "C'mon, boy. It's time you were made to see."

I got out of bed and put on my jeans.

"Don't lace them boots. We'll take them off at the river." I shivered with fear and gladness. He stepped to my doorway, then turned to me. "Hurry up."

The gun barrel Mama pressed against his temple gleamed in the moonlight. Her words were as weathered gravestones. "You get out of this house or I'll paint the walls with you."

"Jesus Christ, Lee Ann."

"I told you what I'd do if you didn't let him be." She glanced at me. "Get back in that bed."

"God*dammit* Lee Ann! It's already in him! He needs sight to make use of it!"

"What use? Witching wells the rest of his days? Drinking grain liquor by the gallon just so he can get an hour's sleep?"

"It doesn't have to be that way."

"You're goddamned right it doesn't. Not so long as I draw breath."

"Mama—"

"You be quiet! I *warned* you, Daniel. Would you make me a murderer in my own home?"

"You can't keep him a boy forever, Lee Ann. You can't pin him down the rest of his life."

She drew back the hammer. "I don't have to forever, dear. Just so long as you walk the earth." I closed my eyes. Instead of an explosion, I heard my father sigh, then shuffle down the hallway, down the stairs, out the door. I heard my mother uncock the gun. "Daniel—"

"Get out!" I shouted. "Or shoot me. I don't really give a damn."

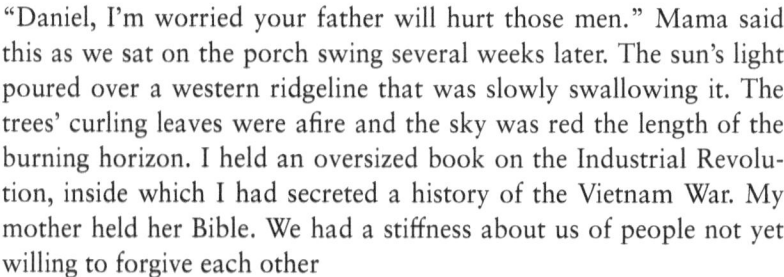

"Daniel, I'm worried your father will hurt those men." Mama said this as we sat on the porch swing several weeks later. The sun's light poured over a western ridgeline that was slowly swallowing it. The trees' curling leaves were afire and the sky was red the length of the burning horizon. I held an oversized book on the Industrial Revolution, inside which I had secreted a history of the Vietnam War. My mother held her Bible. We had a stiffness about us of people not yet willing to forgive each other

"You could hide that gun."

"When has he ever needed that?"

"Is Ledbetter behind them taking Granny's house?"

"Him and some others."

"I should have killed him instead of taking his truck."

My mother sighed and paged to the Psalms.

"Will they tear it all down?"

"For a landfill. It and the junkyard beside and two hundred acres stretching to the southwest. People will pay the town to take their trash."

"I thought they were trying to beautify everything."

"There's nothing more beautiful than money."

"Aren't there laws about it being by a river?"

Mama chuckled. "Mrs. Moore knows Ronda Showalter, wife of the councilman. She says the state's pressured them for years about farm run-off. They'll pack the garbage tight and tarp it and some bureaucrat will declare that soil conservation."

"They'll tear down her house?"

"The house, the barn, everything."

"So she was right. All along she was right."

"I wish I could tell her so myself. That would have pleased her."

"Daddy knows?"

"Your father is like my mother. Stealing land, to them, is like cutting off a limb."

"You going to warn them?"

"Warn who?"

"Ledbetter. The rest of them. Sheriff Wilson."

Mama pondered her Bible. "I don't know, Daniel." She pressed half-moons into the page with her fingernails. She closed her eyes and I knew she was praying. I pretended to read as I watched her pray for the strength to do whatever was right. I prayed my father would kill Ledbetter and every son of a bitch on the Town Council and that they would lock him in prison and never let him out.

⎯⎯⎯⎯⫤

Daddy didn't kill anyone; he went to Granny's shuttered house with his bottles and his knife and slept in her bedroom. Her shotgun was up there with him. I guess he intended to make a last stand just like he'd promised her. Not long after he moved in, Mama sent me over with a box containing a tin of ground coffee, a rectangular sleeve of crackers, and a tureen brimming with chicken broth. His snoring poured from the open bedroom window. I left the box on the dining table and dropped a garbage bag filled with his empties into the truck bed, where they shattered with muffled explosions. I took satisfaction from the moan that emanated from the bedroom.

The county court had granted a thirty-day appeal, but Mama's lawyer said we had no grounds to fend them off. When he said this, my mother stood from her ladder-back chair and denounced agents of town and court as antichrists. She stood Bible in hand and a rope of hair hanging before her God-fired eyes, and seeing the spirit of my grandmother rest on her quaking shoulders filled me with love and with grief, for Elijah was taken up into heaven, but to what end do all other prophets come? I helped her to the supper table that night, as I'd seen my father do so many times for my grandmother.

⎯⎯⎯⎯⫤

In the gathered dark, sleet peppered our roof, the fields, the bent and enduring trees. It scaled the limbs, the leaves, and every outstretched thing. I woke to the thrum of a fallen power line casting savage electric fire that inhabited a maple amidst the battering sleet. The tree's branches burned in a world gone to ice and it was an awful, holy thing. Power spilled from the severed line and gouged a blacked and smoking hole in the earth until someone, somewhere, threw a switch. The retreating din echoed as Gabriel's trumpet.

I stood at my bedroom window in a blanket and watched sleet sapphire the dawning landscape. The first thunder came minutes later, only it was not thunder, it was the crack of a limb tearing loose, a long and remorseless crepitation trailed by silence, then a thump. Some minutes later came another crack, another thump.

All day long Mama and I listened to the sky fall. There was no predicting which trees would break, nor how they faltered. A tall and straight pine in the eastern field simply fell over, as if killed by fright. A stoop-shouldered redbud was bent to the earth without breaking, shouldering the weight as a burdened beast and within it something like faith that this too would pass. Some trees shed branches as a rebirthing, others lost not a limb. Several were sundered to their roots, as if a rotten core had crept up through the center of them or had been birthed within them to be finally revealed in this testing hour. A pin oak overseeing Mama's garden cast down a dozen widow-makers whose branches speared the earth. A stately magnolia at the end of our driveway fell into itself, becoming a grotesquery as the day wore on. Mama insisted later the shattered among her apple trees had borne only bitter fruit.

The ground thawed the next day, and power was restored the day after. That afternoon, a Chatham County sheriff called Mama to say they needed my father's help at Ore Hill. Mama sent me to fetch him home. It took some work convincing him this wasn't a ruse to evacuate him from Granny Watts's house so the authorities could claim it. Finally, he sat bleary-eyed with a pot of coffee and an aspirin bottle at our kitchen table. Before the Chatham sheriff arrived, Mama helped him into his boots and took me aside to whisper that if I let him fall into one of the abandoned mine's vent shafts, I'd best cast myself in after him.

They came for my father because a boy had gone missing and dogs were no use where holes plunge a hundred feet and more. Daddy walked among the frost-mouthed and hell-stretching throats, and I stayed close. He tried to keep his arms extended in a witching as he wandered, but they fluttered like the wings of a struggling bird. I stumbled along at his back, bearing his failing and bone-sharp limbs, smelling his scent of coffee, whisky, and smoke. I waited for the power to inhabit him. Prayed for it to pass to me while there was still time.

The sheriff shook his head and spoke to his gathered men from the corner of his mouth. I stumbled as my father stumbled, and more than once I feared we would be cast headlong together into a hole so deep they wouldn't even try to reach our bodies. After a time, he shook me loose so he could venture alone into a copse of trees and piss. He walked about the holes again, shoulders slumped, boots scraping the steaming grass. I followed, arms at my sides. Finally the sheriff called us back in disgust and ferried us home. He left us in our driveway and my father disappeared across our western field.

⊰

"Don't worry about your Granny's house, man—worry about what your daddy will do to the first poor sonofabitch who comes through the door."

"I know that." I did know it, and I didn't like having Calvin tell me like I didn't know it. We sat in Marjean's Diner, math books open, a plate of fries between us. "And hold your damned voice down."

Calvin looked around, then leaned closer. "What are you gonna do?"

"What the hell am I supposed to do?"

Calvin shook his head and returned his eyes to a quadratic equation. He stuffed a fry into his mouth. He nudged his head from left to right, a kind of wrestler's stretch he'd acquired.

"I mean, do you want me to go over there and place him under citizen's arrest?"

"Just forget it. There's no talking to you when you're ornery."

Sherry, a curvy waitress not much older than me, brought us Cokes. "Marjean says I'm supposed to charge for refills, so just keep this between us." She winked.

Calvin shook his head at me as she walked away. "What women see in you I will never understand."

"She flirts with everyone."

"She didn't flirt with *me*."

"She dates guys with cars."

"Then that's our next project. After we take care of your granny's house. My dad says we ought to get a petition together or something."

"Newspaper says it'll bring fifty new jobs to the county. Nobody's signing a petition against that. Especially for some Watersons."

"Well, Wattses, technically. Daddy says those fifty jobs are bullshit, too. He says the only new jobs we'll see from a trash site is when truckers turn around in the parking lot."

"Ledbetter and those others will get paid. That's for sure."

"My dad is thinking of running against Showalter for Town Council. He says this whole thing is an arrogation of justice."

"Abrogation."

"Whatever. It's goddamned criminal is the point I'm making here."

"Elections won't fix anything. There's only one way of stopping people like them."

"That kind of thinking is what got you locked up."

"Yeah and I'm not afraid of it, either." My face was hot.

"You know I've got a 30-ought-six."

"Meaning what?"

"You know goddamn well what it means. If you decide to be a stubborn jackass and hole up with your daddy, I'm bringing my gun." He drained the last of his soda.. "I mean, Daddy will kill me if the deputies don't, but don't think just because I'm trying to talk you out of it that I won't be there if the shit hits the fan."

The lawyer encouraged Mama to begin packing Granny's things and she'd penciled the deadline on her wall calendar, but she trusted the disposition of her parents' house to Ray Waterson, and the disposition of Ray's body and soul to God. I roamed Granny's house during his sleeping hours with a vague notion that someone needed to preserve something of its history.

Arrays of shoeboxes and folders held decades-old electric bills, deeds to vehicles, pages torn from phone books, letters from her out-of-state daughters. There were reams of correspondence with various industrial and governmental entities regarding their overpriced items, their unhealthy practices, their destruction of community and family. There were invoices and draft budgets for my grandfather's engine-repair business, each more meager than the last. Several boxes contained hand-scribbled notes from hard-luck men or their wives, many thanking him for the loan or free repair, others apologizing for abusing his trust, others beseeching him for more money. I could almost hear my grandmother muttering about his disastrous mercy, even as she saved every letter.

And here was a photo of Mama, pigtailed and four years old, defiantly standing on the bottom porch step. Her sisters and brother stood to either side, and Grandpa and Granny Watts flanked their straight-backed and stubborn brood, posed before their house that would become nothing more than an obstacle to other people's garbage.

And here a fading photo of a dark-haired, solemn boy in rent-collared shirt, scratches on his arms, eyes peering into and through the camera. Beneath this photo was an article in *The Hickory Shore Messenger* about how he'd discovered a dead boy in an unused well on Doyle land. The day we killed Bobby Doyle wasn't the first time my father brought that family grief. I wondered if perhaps his eyes, darkened in the photograph, had blued for a spell after that witching, and if anyone had noticed.

Sometimes my father was not in Granny's house, but always he was near. He moved mostly through dreams, as I waded through history. We haunted both sides of the veil and were separated by it. One night near the court's deadline, I sat on the sleeping porch with a hatbox of documents between my legs, blood thrumming with coffee, synapses frayed and electrified. Upstairs my father moaned and the bedsprings creaked as he turned from side to side, as if to avert his eyes from something. I cursed and threw the hatbox across the room. Its papers spun and fell like leaves in autumn. What use was history against the machinery of injustice?

"Your master's bell has rusted through." My father stood in the moonlit kitchen looking through the window to the back yard. He was dulled by sleep or perhaps was moon-dazed. Stilled in this whited light, he was like the dead boy. I was filled with terror that he would gaze on me with the unblinking black eyes of the dead. I did not move and neither did I breathe.

"You've no call to rise." He trembled. "Go back to your rest."

Despite my fear, I went quietly to the window. I saw nothing but moonfired grass, the barn aglow, trees swaying in their gathered dark.

"I'll not come out tonight." My father bumped into me as he shuffled from the kitchen. I felt the electric current of his power, though he moved like an invalid. He took the stairs slowly, heavily. Upstairs the bed springs relented beneath his weight and were quiet.

The grass chilled my bare feet as I walked to my grandfather's weather-bitten barn alight as with holy fire. There was mystery in the trees and beyond them the river. I knew that about me stood a gathered host. They had come from the quiet of the woods, and to its darkness they would return. They were hidden from my sight. Even freshly scorched by my father's power, I could not see them.

I rolled open the barn door and moved through its caverned dark to the back wall, which demarcated my grandfather's workshop. I found a switch and stood beneath hooded glass rods that popped and hummed and bathed the workshop in a light brighter and thinner than the moon's. My eyes were drawn to a battered file cabinet, in the top drawer of which was a house plan penned on curled brown paper. With it was the original property map and maps of the surrounding domains. I cleared detritus from a worktable, laid the maps alongside one another, smoothing their rebellious edges. They depended for their surety on the interrelation of things, relying on a history of acres walked side by side, on the shared narrative of witnesses.

Walk fifty paces to the bored fir stump, an accompanying document declared. It was a command and a testimony. *Turn due east and walk one hundred paces to the sycamore. The property is bounded on the west by the cattle fence.*

These words were inexact to modern courts, to anyone who hasn't seen this sapling take root and grow, heard that creek chuckle as it swelled with rain. *A hundred-foot pin oak stands here. This field is graded to shunt runoff to the river. In that hillside before the ash grove is where I buried the slave families.*

It may well be because they descend from Ham that they are our chattel or it could be their cursed luck or perhaps our own, perhaps our owning them is a curse on us as well as them, and me cursed as the rest for I've kept them just as my daddy did. I've owned them but as the Lord witnesses I've done them fair as can be done short of setting them free to starve or be chained on some other man's land, or paying them and getting my throat cut by my own brother.

And no matter their origins they are God's children, perhaps more so than we, for the kingdom of heaven belongs to such as these and when they sing and bring in their young'uns from the fields are they not as children themselves, and we overwatching with our clubs and scatterguns, are we not as Pharoah's men?

And just today Ezekiel came hat in his hands white on the working side as any white man's, and he asked please could he bury his mama in sight of that well he dug for me because that's where she always told the children to meet her for prayers and surely she'll be confused to rise up when Jesus calls and not be able to find it.

They are children of God and they are families and they love one another just as fiercely as we love our own, and so when they pass they deserve to be buried side-by-side, the better to find one another come the Resurrection and the Judgment. And now with the diphtheria sweeping our county like the dread merciless scouring brush of God stirred to wrath by our iniquities, and so many black and white falling, how can we deny a Christian burial and a family plot to any of God's creatures?

I cannot, and though it be a white man's heresy, God has seen fit to prosper me, and to send many a man for a loan in these hard times, and I'm willing to share out from my storehouse but I will ask this in return, that they bring their slaves to me when they pass, that they might all be gathered between Ezekiel's well and yonder ash grove, that they might lie resting near their loved ones as all we hope to do.

People have taken to calling it the Slaves Rest, which is suiting, for they've earned it more than any. We lay them with their feet aiming westward and if their kin so desire they can drop in a trinket — a favored bowl or spoon or a carving — and I don't care what anyone says about that, for Harold Climber, still owing me 110 dollars in hard specie, prays over them the same prayers his own congregation receives, and if those prayers aren't enough to erase a spot of errant paganism then I suspect there's a whole passel of white folks who'll be surprised to wake up in Hell alongside their new African neighbors.

If I'm right then Lord you are my justice and my vindication, despite my brother's mutterings. And if I'm wrong, then Lord I can't understand what hardness in your heart would cause you to bear in yourself such cruelty, indeed I can't imagine it. I'm trusting that my heart is as yours, Lord, for surely it wasn't borne of this wicked world we've made for ourselves.

Two days later I arrayed on my grandmother's dining table what I'd found in the barn alongside census records from the library and names

I'd collected in a notebook. I didn't yet know how many slaves lay beside and now within that ash grove, but I knew they were there; I knew because of these pages like upturned faces and because my father had spoken to them in their midnight gathering. Whether he had conjured them or they he, I didn't know. But I knew of their existence less because of these pages than because of him. My neck tingled with this knowing, and the pages regarded me with expectation.

"Somebody walk on your grave?" Daddy leaned against the dining room threshold, a glass of stale water in his trembling hand. His eyes were bloodshot and squinted in defense against a waning light that set the living room shades aglow. I rubbed the back of my neck. He surveyed the quiet testimonies which were as impenetrable to him as he was to me. "She always did keep everything scattered from hell to breakfast. Him and her both."

I wanted to tell him I'd found something, that in my own way I had sight. I wanted to ask if this is what witching feels like, your skin electrified and you filled with a knowing that makes all other things you thought you knew seem rumors by compare. But to ask would have been like asking him to camp with me or to take me with him, to stand again beside that river and strain to hear it speak as he assayed me and found me wanting. I rose from the table and brushed past him toward the front door. "Don't mess with those papers," I said.

If forgetting a person is a kind of killing, then surely remembrance is a resurrection. The dead changed everything.

———

After three days of calling sick to school so I could go to the courthouse record room, I'd counted over eighty slaves who were almost certainly buried on that ash-shadowed hill. I knew it wouldn't matter to Ledbetter and the rest, so I showed the papers to Julie and Calvin. We went to my grandparents' house and walked beneath the shadow of the ash trees. Calvin crouched in the grass and moved his hand over the ground. "I think this is one of them."

"I don't see anything," Julie said.

"Here's another."

"You're seeing it because you want to see it."

"You have to feel it. You're just standing there with your arms crossed."

Julie crouched and moved her hands over the earth.

"See?"

Julie shivered. I didn't need to see or feel grave mounds. I knew as my father knew. Calvin stood. "What do you want us to do?"

We wrote letters to newspapers in Winston, Charlotte, and Raleigh, as well as to our own *Hickory Shore Messenger*. The school librarian helped us look up our state representative and senator, and we wrote to them too. We sent letters to the governor and the state historical society. We sat at Granny Watts's table after school and wrote them: Julie in thin, spidery strokes, her back straight, hair in a barrette; Calvin in unsteady script, tongue trapped between his teeth as he transcribed the master letter that was our template. I used my grandmother's Underwood, on the certain bet that my handwriting would only confuse and irritate people. Its ribbon was faded, so I struck the keys with enough force to embed each typebar face in the paper's grain.

We ferried our letters to the new post office and passed them one at a time through a slot in its brick wall. We believed they had a better chance of reaching their destinations if nobody saw who was mailing them. We stood looking at the slot as if we expected an immediate reply, then wordless and exhausted we parted—they to their homes and me to Granny Watts's house.

The court order had expired and I assumed this meant the city could send in Pinkertons and bulldozers whenever they pleased. My father was more sober and had taken to sitting evenings on the front porch, shaky from coffee and cigarettes, Granny's Sweet Sixteen propped against the rail. And my mother hadn't boxed up a scrap.

<hr />

Raleigh News & Observer
Feb. 11th, 1980

A Hickory Shore family fighting local officials who want to turn their property into a garbage dump claims their town's plans will not only destroy a home that has been in their family for generations, but despoil a newly-discovered 19th-century graveyard for slaves—possibly one of the largest of its kind in the state of North Carolina. The young man at the center of this fight is 17 year-old Daniel Waterson . . . .

In response to claims that the township's plans will benefit the economic well-being of the community, Mr. Waterson replied: "A place that can erase the history of

its people is no community at all." Town officials declined to comment.

All I did was speak words I'd heard from my grandmother a thousand times and her daughter after her. And do you know the very day
that article was published, I found my father's handgun—the one my
mother had threatened to murder him with—nestled in our truck's
glove compartment? I'd assumed it was for when Mama worked late,
because she'd started waitressing at Marjean's. Only now do I com-
bine the memory of that gun with the recollection that she'd taken to
driving slowly past Granny's house several times a day after the court
stay expired. If anyone had come to take that land, they would have
had bullets coming at them from two directions. I suppose I shouldn't
have expected any less from a woman willing to kill a preacher with
a ladder-back chair.

I only saw the article quoting me after it was clipped out, framed,
and lying on our kitchen table, same as Granny had done with my
father's letter to the *Hickory Shore Messenger*. As I read it, Mama
pulled a supper plate and a pan of banana bread from the oven and
set them before me. She leaned over where I sat, wrapped her arms
around my neck, and laid her head atop mine. We said not a word.

Mama, I'm sitting at that very same table, and when I close my
eyes I can almost feel your arms around me again.

That article briefly upended Hickory Shore. The Town Council held
closed-session meetings, our phone rang at all hours, and we were
deluged with letters from concerned citizens, conspiracy theorists,
and lawyers who didn't realize we were broke. The magistrate who'd
sentenced me sent a letter containing just two handwritten words:
"Well done." Newspaper articles posed questions about the unusual
attention town officials had paid to the hygiene of Granny's yard and
business entanglements between Town Council members and out-of-
state corporations. Fred Ledbetter had to hide inside his house for
weeks, so easily could journalists spot his copper hair and dented
forehead. Eventually the governor issued a statement saying that bal-
ancing the need for growth with maintaining our cultural heritage was
every North Carolinian's duty, but without explaining which side he

was on. Calvin's father said this was exactly what could be expected of him.

All this became the occasion for a reunion of what remained of the Crow River Resistance. Clay Tompkins's seminary friends came with college students from Winston, and they held a memorial service at the graveyard hill. Calvin and I said we didn't understand any of the speeches, which frustrated Julie to no end. Television stations were there, and the footage ran on stations across the state. Someone said it was even on national news, just a few seconds of it. Afterward everyone ate cookies Mama and Mrs. Moore baked in Granny's kitchen.

My father continued to sleep in Granny Watts's house, his hands now steadied, a lucid shine returned to his eyes. "Don't put it past that sonofabitch Ledbetter to try and burn the place," he grumbled as we ate chicken at Granny's dinner table, he and Mama and me, along with a couple of professors from N.C. State who had come to see about—carefully, they stressed—excavating the site. Mama was so happy she didn't chide him for cussing.

She made a lot of pies in the days to follow. She made sweet rolls and more banana bread. She saw that I took some to Calvin, and to the Moores's house as well. She told people at church that her son had fought town hall and won and put an admissions brochure she got from the N.C. State professors on my pillow.

—————

Two days after the court issued an injunction that our state historical society hailed as victory, my father came home. He even came to church a few times, where the three of us caused Fred Ledbetter to squirm simply by our presence. Like many people, Fred assumed every Waterson could recidivate with the slightest provocation, but Mama was content to let her cup runneth over with Christian charity. She asked after the Ledbetters' oldest son Daryl, who was apprenticed to an electrician in Asheboro, and complimented Mrs. Ledbetter on her purse or her earrings or whatever she brought for potluck. She greeted Fred warmly every Sunday, and that was probably harder on him than anything.

Daddy labored dawn into darkness repairing fences, pruning trees, prepping the empty stable for more boarders. Sometimes I helped him. Out of the blue he would stop what he was doing and exclaim: "So you just found your way through all that paper right down to the facts that mattered, did you?" "Yes," I would say, eyes not leaving my work. "Must have your mother's head for books," he would reply. I never told him my discovery came from the dregs of his visions.

"Daniel," Mama said one morning as she moved through the stations of her kitchen cross, "did I ever tell you that I helped your father write over two hundred letters, back when we hunted your great-grandfather?"

I shook my head.

"He couldn't abide the taste of adhesive, so licking the envelopes fell to me. Lord, the paper cuts."

"He probably needed your help writing the letters, too."

She slapped the back of my head, but not hard. "Your father isn't stupid, Daniel."

"I meant his handwriting."

"He does write like a left-handed monkey, doesn't he?" She smoothed down my hair. "You need a haircut, child."

I rose and took my plate to the sink.

"No, he didn't hand-write the letters. He used my mother's typewriter. The miles he put on that ribbon."

"He was glad to have your help, I bet." I knew the point she wanted to make, and sometimes it was easier just to help her get there.

"Yes, he was." She took my hands in hers. "He took my hands like this, and he said: 'Lee Ann, I don't think there's another woman in the whole world who would have licked all those envelopes for me.' I didn't mention the paper cuts. And then he said: 'At least no other woman I'd care to have anything to do with.' He always did have a sideways manner of telling someone he loves them."

"I've gotta get your carburetor changed out so you can get to work on time." I pulled my hands away.

"Daniel."

I paused at the doorway.

"Don't take that girl for granted."

Mama was worried for Julie because of what Mrs. Moore had told her about Julie seeing things. She told Mama she'd found Julie's journals, which were filled with wildness and horror. What neither of them knew is that Daddy had found Julie wandering toward the river one night. He'd carried her to our house, lain her on the couch, and woken me. She was semi-lucid, voice dull, face haggard. She said she'd been following a boy who knew where she could get some sleep. Deep sleep, the kind she hadn't had in ages.

"Did he have on a black suit?" I'd asked. "Like he was dressed for his own funeral?"

Daddy had cut me a look. We'd settled her under blankets, and he'd led me onto the porch. "Do you still see him?"

"Not like her. He doesn't try to make me do things anymore."

"Goddammit. Goddamn me."

"Why do you think it's your fault?"

"You've felt it before. How it jumps into people."

"But why's it so hard on her?"

"She wasn't crafted to be that kind of vessel."

"It seems like it hates her."

"The earth-walking dead are lost, do you understand? Not in place, but in what they are—neither born nor reborn. Every woman holds within her the power of creation. The dead hunger for it, but they can only see those who see them. In that river, while I held her . . . she saw everything. And they all saw her."

"What's everything?"

"The gathered dead and the stairway. The room without walls."

"Is that where he wants to take her?"

"Did he ever try to take you there?" His voice was sharp, fearful.

"No. I don't think so. Daddy, can they hurt her?"

"Well son, how does she appear to be doing?"

"What can we do?"

"You can't do anything."

"Then what can you do?"

He'd lit a cigarette, taken a deep draw, and curled his lip in hatred. "Some of them need killing more than once."

———

We knew what we aimed to do. It was penance, for we all knew what Earl Ledbetter had been doing. We all knew, and did not a damned thing. Now the last memory those boys will have of their mother is she lying bloodied and unmoving on their couch. We all of us killed her, not just Doc Willard who patched her more than once without breathing a word, but every man of us.

And it weren't any more noble thing, gathering as we did at the Sheriff's, me with my Sweet Sixteen and others with their rifles and some with rope who made no effort to hide it, and Sheriff Cauley caring not one goddamn either, for he knew he was just as guilty as the rest of us. We gathered because we wanted to avenge Helen, but more so for our shame at letting this come to pass.

So we gathered, even Earl's own brother Earnest, and it was too many of us to fit inside, so Sheriff Cauley stood on a truck bed stamping his feet with a sound like a hollow barrel and deputized the lot of us. Off we went. I sided up with Earnest because none of the others wanted anything to do with him. I have in my nature this inclination to come alongside the off-casts, as Lenora reminds me at every turn.

A farmer had reported a Packard Coupe sitting in the place previously occupied by his mailbox, so some of us rode down his way and fanned out into the surrounding woods. Men who hadn't talked in ages hailed one another through trees and across the creek, and if we'd carried picnic baskets instead of rifles it would have been a fine time. Our calls lessened as the distances grew and I could tell by how Earnest gripped and regripped his Winchester that he knew just where he was heading, so I grew quiet and stayed a step behind, just in case he got in his head to side with his kin after all.

As we cleared the ridge we saw Earl below, set against a tree holding a cloth to his head. He looked up in fear, then saw it was his own older brother, so he rose in greeting, raised that cloth as a welcome, and Earnest shot him clean through the breastbone. A splatter struck the tree behind Earl. Earnest fired again and Earl dropped without rebuke.

Earnest set down his Winchester and knelt and turned his brother to face the sky and pushed back that wiry red hair of his. Earnest shook his head and his tears pelted his brother's face gone slack. "I loved you, but I had to put you down." Earnest whispered this and there was graveyard dirt in his voice and I pretended not to hear. He pulled a folding shovel from his pack and we took turns digging a grave. We laid Earl in the earth and covered him over. I said a few words about forgiveness and mercy, though Christ knows I can't remember them now.

We said not another word between us, Earnest and I. Some men went out the next day to look and fewer after that and I suppose they all assume one of the others has got to him and indeed that is the truth of it. But I'll bet no one suspects it was his own brother shot him down.

*And now the debt of the town has grown, because had
any of us been man enough to deal with Earl Ledbetter
before that day, we'd have spared those boys the orphanage and Helen an early grave and poor Earnest Ledbetter
the sure knowledge of how Cain must feel.*

———————

Things began to unravel as my father lost interest in carrying his load.
That's how I characterized it, though I knew that the horse-tending
and repairs and odd jobs fell to me because he was wandering the
river in search of Bobby Doyle. I don't know how you kill a dead boy
twice, and I don't know if he knew either. It was maybe heroic, in the
same way we say men who leave their wives and children for war are
heroes. A better son would have viewed it that way, but all I could
think, when I imagined him prowling the darkened hollows of the
river and spirit world, was that I could have this power too, if only he
would give it to me. I was growing stronger by the day, while he was
getting smaller, but still he thought I belonged home with my mother.

Doesn't every son tell himself lies about his father?

———————

Calvin finished fourth in the state wrestling championship at 119
pounds the following spring, and while I was not much of a wrestler,
I could do nearly any work my father could do but for well-witching.
Carl Ledbetter gave me a wide berth at school. Most kids did. They
kept their distance not just because of my reputation, or because I
wore one of my father's Army jackets, but because it fit my growing
frame. I could do 200 push-ups in a stretch. I could rock the punching
bag I'd hung in the barn until dust drifted in clouds among the rafters
and the roof threatened to collapse. I would pummel it until my jaw
ached from clenching, and fury filled me like smoke in a closed room.

My father kept his liquor in a burlap sack at the bottom of his
tool crib. One day while he was witching the dead, I hid it in the back
field. That evening, as a band of orange and purple lit the western
trees, we heard his boots on the porch. He pressed his face against the
screen door.

"What'd you do with my drink, boy?"

I leaned back in my chair, casually. The air hung silent and heavy.

"Daniel, please," my mother said. "Tell him where it is."

"How come nobody in this house ever says the word *liquor*?"

"*Daniel!*" Mama hissed.

"Boy," my father groaned, "please." His stubble against the screen made a sound like an old phonograph commencing play.

"Witch it, Daddy. Go witch up your liquor."

"Daniel," my mother whispered. "Ray, I've got some money in my purse. Walk on down to McAllister. Or I can drive you" She hurried to where her purse hung from a peg.

"You think I won't come through my own damn door, boy?"

I was as tall as him now. Taller, when he was stooped and drunk. *Come through that door, old man. Come through that door and see what happens.*

"Don't test me boy."

"If you don't want to walk to McAllister, maybe you can swim."

"Daniel!" A compact fell from Mama's purse and clattered across the linoleum.

He pulled the door handle. My body was hot and tensed. I imagined his hair in my hands, his Indian blood in splotches on the kitchen floor. He slammed the door back into its frame and walked down the porch steps. I mastered my shivering and despised my evaporating fear.

"Daniel." Mama's voice was stern. "What did you do with it?"

"Don't worry, Mama. It's safe."

"You think I want him drinking?"

"You've still got your hand on your money and your keys."

She crossed the kitchen like a whirlwind and clamped her hand onto my forearm. "It's better than seeing you fight."

"Sure, Mama."

"And it's better than seeing him get in that Jeep and drive himself."

"Maybe he'll do us both a favor and drive off the bridge."

She slapped my face. I pretended it didn't hurt. She slapped the table with her other hand, her eyes splintered glass. "Shame on you! You want him dead? You want him to drive like he is and kill another boy?" Her voice faded.

"Then hide his keys."

"There's no hiding anything from that man." She gazed out the kitchen window. She always seemed to know where he was. When she talked about him she would glance one way or the other and you knew that if you walked along a line from her eyes, through walls and trees and all intervening things, you'd eventually find him.

Outside he paced the garden, arms spread in his witching walk.

I chuckled. "He really is trying to witch it."

"Don't mock."

Daddy turned his back to us and walked past the shed, toward the stand of trees guarding our back field. He walked with steady stride, bent forward, like he could see beyond the trees, through the browning chokeberry and beneath the pile of leaves where his bottles waited. I stood, causing my chair to clatter to the floor. "Son of a bitch."

Mama grasped for me, but I was through the door, down the steps, past the garden. As I reached the field, I saw him approach the chokeberry bush. Its teardrop leaves stained the ground where he knelt. I heard the clink of his wedding ring against a bottle.

"You put it down!"

"Go on back to the house, boy." He swiped slick leaves from a whisky bottle and grunted to his feet.

"Put down that bottle or I'll by-god take it from you."

He turned to face me. "Go on now." His hand with the wedding ring wrapped around the cap and twisted.

I drove him into the bush, over it. I snatched the bottle from him as we hit the ground and raised it like a club. Mama screamed behind me. His wrist struck mine and sent the bottle flying. It tumbled through the waning sunlight and landed with a thump in the tall grass. Bailey emerged from the underbrush and barked at us.

I seized the loose flesh of his throat and tried to claw his face, to get at those dead brown eyes, but he floated from underneath me like vapor. His legs tangled mine, and his hand like a stone struck my ribcage and then he was on top, his blade poised over my sternum. I grabbed hold of his knife hand.

Mama was screaming.

My father's eyes were black now. I yanked his knife toward my chest as I bore my heart upward. I felt the blade press through my shirt and into the meat of me. His eyes came alive and he recoiled as if I were a snake. Blood ran past my ribs and armpit when he yanked his knife free. Mama was screaming *you've killed him you've killed him Ray god damn you you've killed him.*

He stuck his finger through the hole in my shirt, tore it open, and spread open the slit in my flesh. He assayed the wound's depth. He considered my face the same way, like I was myself a kind of wound. Mama knelt beside my head and prayed to Jesus. I felt pain flood into the wound.

"Ain't deep. Not even an inch. Didn't hit anything vital."

"God *damn* you Ray."

"I didn't . . . ." My father sheathed his knife, took up his whisky, and left us there.

Mama walked me to the house and washed my purpled wound, which wept a steady rivulet of blood. She pressed an ice-packed dish-towel against it, led me across our darkening yard to the truck, and drove me to Doc Moore's house, where she left me in the truck and hurried across his lawn. The fissure from my father's blade throbbed with my heartbeat.

Mrs. Moore opened their front door, considered my mother's face, and called over her shoulder. Doc Moore emerged, thin and grim, and hied to the truck, my mother and Mrs. Moore trailing. "What happened here, son?" He adjusted his glasses and peered at the wound.

"It was an accident," Mama said. "They got in a scuffle and it just happened."

Doc Moore scowled as he pressed below the cut. I winced as a fresh stream of blood spilled down my chest. "This from his knife?"

"It was an accident," I said.

He turned to my mother. "Lee Ann."

Mrs. Moore put an arm around her. Doc Moore glanced back at me, then led the two women away. He stood with hands on hips as they whispered at him. He shook his head. My mother's fierce and willful eyes did not leave his face.

"Daddy, what's happened?"

"Julie," her mother snapped, "get back in the house right now." Julie squinted at our truck, then ran across the lawn. "Julie!" her mother hissed. "Come here!"

Julie leaned her head inside the cab. "Are you okay?" I shrugged my shoulders, which made me wince.

"Jesus Daddy he's bleeding to death!"

"Julie!" her mother cried.

Doc Moore, head shaking, went back into his house. Mama and Mrs. Moore spirited me inside and up the stairs, Julie on our heels. "Is he shot?" she asked.

"Hush, Julie."

"He needs an ambulance!"

"Hush, girl!"

Mrs. Moore spread a towel across the bed of their oldest boy, away at college. I lay down and Julie pushed past her mother to wrap her hands around my forearm. Doctor Moore entered bearing a plastic basin full of bottles and implements.

"Y'all need to leave us now."

"Daddy, I—"

"Out."

Julie slammed the door. Doc Moore pulled the bedside lamp close and retrieved a flashlight from his shirt pocket. "If it's too deep there's just no way around it, you're going to the hospital." He wiggled his hands into thin rubber gloves and spilled iodine across the gouge, using gauze to intercept the purple-brown liquid that darted down my ribcage. He pressed his fingers against the cut and spread its lips. I sucked in my breath.

"I'm sorry." He trained the flashlight's beam on my wound and peered into it. He wiggled his fingers.

"Jesus," I said. I lifted my head and tried to see. "Do I have to go?"

"I can stitch it. When was your last tetanus shot?"

I lay my head back on the pillow. "Mama knows."

"Mama knows," he muttered. He swabbed his curved stitching needle with alcohol and fitted it with suturing thread. Once he'd sunk the first hoop, he worked the needle with an unvaried rhythm. He breathed in with each jab, complementing my sharp intakes of air. "I imagine that pinches a bit," he said. His eyes did not leave his work. He was as my father witching a well, all of him poured into the task, all that he was working in concert. The ease of his labor made its magic seem commonplace. I envisioned my father having one of his wounds sutured. "It's not that bad," I muttered. He finished the last stitch with an especially hard tug, his lips pressed tight. A thin stream of blood snaked along my armpit.

"I'm sorry about your towel."

"Daniel. Accidents don't look like this." He considered me with his pale blue eyes. "You love your daddy, I know that, but—"

"It was an accident. Ask Mama."

The door opened. "Philip," Mrs. Moore said. He met her in the hallway and pulled shut the door. There was murmuring, the floorboards creaked, and there was silence. I drifted to sleep, awakening briefly when my mother turned off the lamp. A crisp thin blanket settled over me like snowfall. She knelt beside me and prayed in a whisper, sentence after sentence, as if she'd been storing up a book of entreaties for God. I fell asleep before she finished.

I woke a second time when the house was stilled, the moonlight steady and soft. The doorknob was turning and for a moment I thought it was Bobby Doyle coming to show me the pits and scars across his earth-sunk body. The footsteps were soft and small, and there was a smell of lavender soap. Julie sat close and rested her arm on mine.

"Can I see it?" I lay quiet. "I know you're not asleep."

"Didn't your daddy teach you girls shouldn't creep into beds with boys?"

"He hardly notices I'm a girl." I didn't know what to say to that. Julie wore skirts and hair bows and polished shoes, but there was a girl-ness to her that ran far deeper than these. Maybe God had gotten things wrong. Maybe Daddy would have been a good father to a girl, while Doc Moore was better suited to raising boys.

"Is it true that you did it to yourself? That you pulled his knife into you on purpose?"

"I guess so."

"Why?"

"I don't know."

Her voice hardened. "Does that girl at the diner know yet?"

"Who?"

Julie sighed.

"Where's my mother?"

"Went home."

I curled my knees to my belly. "I'm tired," I said. "I've never been this tired in my whole life up to now." Julie stroked my hair. "*Shh*," she said. "*Shh*."

I woke later to feel her back against mine. Her breathing was a deep and quiet procession of sighs. Her sighs were a rhythm and I breathed within that rhythm and sank into a sleep beneath dreams. When I woke to the smell of coffee drifting from the kitchen, she was gone. The pillow smelled of lavender and I lay there wishing I could go back to sleep for years. Forever. There was a clean shirt on the bed and the noise from the kitchen told me I was supposed to get up.

In the kitchen, Mrs. Moore put eggs and pancakes and coffee and juice and a bowl of steaming grits in front of me. I did my best to push the food around on my plate so it looked like I was eating. My stomach felt like someone had poured lead into it, and my shoulder throbbed. "Where's Doctor Moore?" I asked.

"Oh, he had patients in the Winston hospital."

Julie shuffled into the kitchen and surveyed the bowls and pans. "Lord, Mama."

"Hush."

Julie rolled her eyes. She jerked the refrigerator door open and hauled out the milk bottle. "Daniel, you want some Fruit Loops instead of all that?" Her mother set down a frying pan with a clatter. "Julie *Moore*."

"Just making sure he feels at home, *Mother*." She sat down with an old whipped cream bowl and filled it to the brim with Fruit Loops and milk.

"Keep eating junk and your skin is gonna break out again," her mother said.

"Mama!" Julie stared at her bowl, furiously crunching. Mrs. Moore answered a knock at her front door; she and my mother greeted one another cheerily. They swept into the kitchen, spouting words about the sunshine and the crisp air. Julie looked at them like they were lunatics. Soon Mama was thanking Mrs. Moore for everything but nothing in particular and tapping my good shoulder to steer me to the door. Mrs. Moore wrapped her arms around me and I winced.

"*God*, Mama!"

"Oh! I'm so sorry."

"It's alright."

I said it not to Mrs. Moore but to Julie, who stood with hand on her chair back and that look on her face to which I'd grown accustomed, the look of someone waiting for an answer.

At home, a suitcase lay opened on my bed. "Where are we going?" I asked.

"If you stay here, one of you will kill the other."

"Where are you sending me?"

"Just to Mama's, child. Someone needs to tend the place anyway."

I sat on the bed. "Why can't *he* go live there?"

"He needs to be near me."

She pulled history books from my shelves. Herodotus on the Greek wars with the Persians, Geronimo's biography, a book about George Washington crossing the Delaware. She added *Crimson Moccasins*, though I hadn't read it in years. She tucked the books into the corners of my suitcase.

"I can't cook."

"You can make a sandwich. You can pour a bowl of cereal. You can come to the diner. Marjean will feed you when I'm not there."

"Does she know?"

"Just that you're not getting along with your father. You're not the first boy to have that problem."

"You could come too." My voice was small, and I hated myself for being afraid to leave my mother.

"It's getting worse. He walks about in a daze. Vomits blood."

I sighed. "I can catch a ride with Calvin when you need me to mow or something."

She gripped my wrist, sending a bolt of pain up my shoulder. "You're not hearing me. You cannot *be* here." She began to rearrange the books on my shelves to close the gaps. "Some days it's all I can do to stay in this house. It's like I'm at the top of a steep hill, Daniel." Her voice softened. "If I allow myself even one step, my other foot will follow, and I won't be able to stop until I'm far away from here." She turned, and a wistful smile pushed through the lines around her mouth. "It's not something I expect you can understand."

"How long?"

Her eyes shone like stones at the bottom of a stream. "I don't know, child."

"He'll never stop."

"You don't know that." Her mouth pinched closed as she struggled to fasten my suitcase. Beyond my window the trees stood in a timeless whited light. With my good arm I drew her to me, away from my wound. I wanted to tell my mother that though I stood taller, I was still a small and broken thing. But any words I might conjure would fall too heavy on her trembling frame, so I rested my cheek atop her head. "It'll be alright, Mama."

Father, you cannot see the dead and I am glad—for how could you bear to look on me now? Do you remember fishing with me on the river, how you said I was good luck for you that day? All the loach we caught, how some stood shivering on end like silver reeds and you told me that was because they knew a storm was coming?

I understand now how they know. I understand many things, Father. I know Mother weeps through the night. I know they tell you that I won't return, yet still you search.

You cannot see me beside this fokienia. He emptied me and lay me beneath its shade and already its roots nip my skin. They feel like the fish kissing our ankles when we drag our boat to ground. I know the fokienia's leaves will grow greener as it devours me, yet still will I see the earth the sky the moon silver like a loach scale and Mother crying and you searching without hope in your heart.

I don't want to know these things, Father. Will I forget them when you find me? Will you lay me down among our fathers and is that when I will sleep? You said many times it is wrong for the young to know so much about death but I think it is you who does not know about the dead, about how tired we become.

I was handy enough with engines that Marty Giles gave me repair work at the Esso that summer. Calvin interned at a bank in Winston to satisfy his mother's demand that he explore options beyond the Marines. He told me the aunt he stayed with went to church nearly every night and there was nobody else to do anything with but Mary Taylor, who had a job at Old Salem. "I figure her butt will eventually balloon like her mama's," he said, "but so far it's normal." I knew they were dating, but I didn't tease him for it.

Julie interned at *The Hickory Shore Messenger*, where she wrote about farmers trying to set the record for largest watermelon, old women who traced their lineage back to Confederate soldiers, and pets capable of interesting tricks. I imagined her reading her stories to me, the way she used to share her favorite authors. Her hair was falling out in places, which she tried to hide with creative barrette placement. This is how I knew Daddy's hunting of Bobby Doyle remained fruitless.

Some Sundays Mama brought a basket and we ate on Granny's screened side porch. She would smile toward the back yard and tell me about the acrobatics her brother did back there before his leukemia or the concerts she and her sisters played for their mother. "Daddy was our bandleader," she said, "but Lord have mercy, that man could not carry a tune." Her laughter at those recollections was that of a girl with unbowed shoulders. I loved her in those moments, but I wanted them to pass quickly so that Sherry, the waitress from Marjean's, could come over. Now, in my remembrance, those Sunday hours dwindling to dusk are a kind of Sabbath. I heard a preacher say Heaven is like an eternal Sunday, which I used to think sounded terrible. Now I understand. I understand.

Interview with Chief William ("Little Will")
Holland Thomas of the Qualla Cherokee
James Mooney, unpublished notes
June 1887, Facility for the Mentally Disabled
and Insane, Butner, N.C.

Q: And you also made "artifacts" for Mr.
Valentine?

A: What? Mann Valentine?

Q: From Virginia.

A: (Laughs.) Ah yes, that old fool. We all
did. He dug up the Cullowhee, then he migrated
to Cherokee and Swain. He and his assistants
were a cloud of locusts. They dug up our people wherever they could find them, stole the
necklaces from our children, the pots from our
women.

Q: And so you began manufacturing fake
artifacts?

A: (Laughs.) Oh, they were all in good working order. Arrows, water pots, axes. We made
well-working items, then rubbed them in dirt,
or buried them in the creek for a few days,
chipped off an edge or two, then we brought
them to his camp. He paid cash money -- two,
three times what they would have cost him new.

Q: And how long did this go on?

A: A couple of years. We sold him fakes and
took back what he stole from the graves.

Q: You stole the real artifacts?

A: We reclaimed them. The nighttime raids I
led on the Valentine storehouses were greater
than any victory I had during the war.

Q: What did he do when he found out?

A: Went slinking home. Opened a museum up
north, gave lectures about our savage ways.
He sold what we sold to him. Museums across
this country have "ancient" Indian artifacts
younger than you and me.

Q: Why was it so important to take back the
originals?

A: [Silent for a while.] Because our people
still had use for them. Tell me, who needs a
cooking pot more -- a woman happily stirring
stew for her children past the dark beyond, or
some old fool who believes eternity is spent
sitting in a heavenly church?

Q: So you put the tools back into the graves?

A: Of course we did. And what we could not get
back, we replaced.

Q: Replaced?

A: We went to every grave Mann plundered and
gave them something for the dark beyond.

Q: What did you give them?

A: Many things, and always with these something that gives light. What a cruel thing it
would be, to send a child into the dark beyond
with no light.

———————⟨

I knew it was my father at Granny's door by the scrape of his boots.
He slumped against the doorsill and slid to the porch floor to sit cross-
legged. Bailey was with him; he chuffed and lay his head in my father's
lap. Daddy pressed his face against the door screen and exhaled. His
hair spilling across his shoulders was thick and black, but his hands
jutting from the sleeves of his fatigue jacket were the hands of an old
man. He'd stopped wearing his knife.

"What do you want?"

He turned his face upward to where I stood inside the door.
I couldn't descry his eyes through the dusk-shaded screen; for all I
knew, they had gone blue again. He cleared his throat. "Daniel." He

succumbed to a coughing fit. "Daniel." Across the dirt road, pine and cedar shivered against the gusts of a gathering fall.

"Turning cold early this year. You'll freeze to death some night."

He sighed. "There's things." He rubbed his palms together, their rustle like a table being sanded. "There's these things."

"I'll get you a blanket."

"No," he croaked. "I'm fine." He pawed the screen, like he wanted to reach me through it. Bailey groaned.

"Mama will hide me if you catch pneumonia right there on Granny's porch."

He slapped the screen. "I'm fine, goddammit." He licked his lips, tried to cough, gave up the effort. "Can I have a glass of water?" I brought a glass and pitcher from the kitchen. He turned aside his head and withdrew his shoulder to let me open the screen door, and received the water. His trembling hands still held a faint current when they brushed my own. I made to join him, but he shook his head. "Just stay in there." I stepped back inside and let the screen door thump closed.

"Can you sit down for a minute?" I leaned standing against the door frame. He looked up at where I stood, waited, finally shook his head. He poured more water into his glass and gulped it down. The screen creaked as he pressed his head against it. "I killed eleven men I know of in them tunnels." His voice became dark and clear, like it was itself a revenant. "I didn't start out a tunnel rat, but I volunteered, after . . . well, they killed a friend of mine. Vietcong did. He was my only friend over there." He peered up at me, and something like a smile briefly cracked his face. "You might not believe it, but I've never made friends very easy."

I grunted.

"Anyways, they strung him up in a tree with his insides hanging across the branches like vines. I knew they'd come from those tunnels, and Command had been asking for volunteers to start rooting them out. I figured the vision would help me."

"You witched men."

"Killing a man makes you hate him. You hate him because maybe he would have killed you. Because you know the look on his face will be on your own face someday. You kill men because you hate them, and you hate them because you've killed them. That's why it gets so easy.

"Most times you didn't find nobody down there. They'd usually bug out while we were miles away. Their land told them things." He gulped from his glass. Skin and whiskers rustled when he wiped his mouth. "But when there were people down there, I found them." The screen bent inward where his head pressed against it. Illumined by crepuscular light, he looked like a weather-beaten sculpture of the man who had been my father. His breath was tunneled wind as he lifted the glass again to his cracked lips. He drank, cleared his throat. "My C.O. didn't believe me the first time. He said he didn't hear gunfire, didn't believe I knew how to do more with my knife than whittle. That's why I scalped the next one. It sheared off like a wet corn husk. After I dropped that at his feet, him and the rest gave me more space to stand in."

I shivered and slid to the floor. He shifted, groaning with the ache of movement. Bailey huffed at him. "Goddamn, I need a drink."

"There's nothing here."

"It's fine. Whenever you get free of it for a while, you feel like more of what you're carrying around is really you. That probably don't make no sense."

"I don't know. Maybe."

"Daniel I've looked in every hole and corner, and I can't conjure Bobby Doyle. I don't know how to help that girl." He closed his eyes and shook his head.

"It's okay, Daddy."

"I heard on one of your mama's radio shows that happiness means getting in touch with who you really are." He pushed out a weak cough and sipped enough water to release the raspy chuckle behind it. "I don't reckon, given who we are, knowing ourselves makes us any happier." His voice stretched thin, near to breaking. "Not me, anyways."

"You don't have to—"

"I killed eleven men over there, and one sonofabitch over here, and I killed Bobby Doyle." His breath left him.

"Ray."

He moaned. I smelled cherry and a metallic odor of blood or medicine. Bailey shifted, yipped at him, resettled his head. "There was another one. I never told a soul." His face pinched like he was bringing up bile.

"Ray. Don't."

"A boy. In the darkness." His voice was a whisper. "I always knew where they hid. I hated them for hiding. I witched this one through a tunnel, then another, then another. He was quick, but I could sense him. I could smell him. I crept to where he'd finally stopped to hide, and then I was on him. I was *mahihkan*."

Wolf. I looked out to the stirred and shadowing trees. I didn't dare look on his inward-peering face.

"I put that knife through his chest, and the tip come out the other side." He whispered it in a tumble-down voice. "I burst his heart. He was dead before I laid him to the ground. He couldn't have been more than seven or eight."

"Oh, Ray. Daddy."

"I watched over him in the darkness while his blood drained out into the dirt." Daddy sipped water and coughed. "We always blew the entrances when we were finished, so I took him to a hole some ways from where I'd come in. He was light as a bundle of clothes. Like a shell of a boy. I laid him just inside the entrance, curled up, like I was putting him down for a nap. I was covered in his blood." My father had a coughing spasm that made the screen door rattle in its frame. He sucked in air.

"I snuck outside the perimeter that night. Our C.O. was jumpy, kept saying Command ought to pull us back. He was always one for being pulled back. I knew they were gone. When men move through a forest, the trees kinda bend, in their spirits. That's one way you know where to look." He pressed his face harder against the screen, as if to ensure I was still there. "Don't make no sense, does it?"

"I don't have the sight like you do."

The screen scratched as he nodded. "There's other kinds of knowing, son."

I settled my own head against the frame. "You went back to that dead boy, didn't you?"

"That night I took along my field shovel, and I carried him to a tree. It was a kind that gets big, like those tulip trees we saw in the Pisgah Forest." He looked back at me. "You remember fishing out there?"

I nodded. He nodded as well. "This one was still small. Branches thick with leaves. It stood off from the others, where moonlight could get through. I dug a hole for him in its shadow and lay him in it. He didn't have anything to carry on his journey, so I put a silver Zippo your mama give me in his hand." My father held up his own quivering hand to the waning light. He glanced at me. "So he could light his way in the darkness. Their eyes go black, after. It's why some of them wander." He cast down his own eyes, as if he were ashamed to bear this knowledge.

"I covered him over with dirt and put a shank of bamboo in the ground over top of him. I carved the word 'boy' in Viet into a piece of bark and strapped it to the stake with a boot string. I figured somebody would come hunting him." He considered me from his shame. "Every boy has somebody, don't he?"

"I reckon they'd want to know."

Daddy took his head from the screen. "We only want to know because we don't understand what it costs. Not until it's too late."

I sighed. I felt like he'd handed me another key to a door I would never find.

"The next day I told my C.O. I wasn't killing any more. Not with knife nor gun."

"What'd he say?"

"He knew better than to say anything. I got shrapnel from a mortar round not long after, and they sent me home. I told your mama I lost that lighter."

"Daddy?"

"Yeah."

"How'd you get that scar on your arm, the straight white one. In the tunnels?"

He stroked the fabric of his jacket sleeve. "Bar fight in south Winston. I was half drunk, but the other fella was all the way drunk. He cut me, so I put him to the floor with my knife pressed to his throat. I hunched over him, watched his pulse ticking like a clock. I knew I was going to open his throat and end time for him. But some old boy crouched down beside me and whispered that I didn't want to throw my life away. He sounded just like your mama's daddy, so much that I looked away from that ticking clock of a throat to see if it was him. It was just some old-timer, but I guess he broke the spell. And that was the last time I ever drew a knife on a man. Leastways until Harlan Carver."

"And me."

Daddy released a long exhalation. I smelled the blood or medicine. "And you."

"Is that when you stopped drinking?"

"Your mama came down to the hospital where I waited to get stitched, and she said: 'Ray Waterson, I got two things to say to you.' She said it in that voice she has, you know. Nobody made a peep in that emergency room, let me tell you what. 'First thing,' she said, 'is I got another baby coming, and I'll be goddammed if you're gonna widow me in this condition.'"

"She didn't really say *goddammed*."

"Coming from her mouth it didn't sound like cussing. It sounded holy."

"What was the second thing?"

"She said I was gonna promise her, in front of all those witnesses, that I wouldn't drink ever again, or so help her God she'd kill me herself."

"What'd you do?"

"Well what would *you* do?"

I chuckled. "Did she believe you?"

"I might could have kept that promise, if I'd kept the doors closed."

"What doors?"

"The doors to the room."

The room without walls. The trees across the road shivered against the strengthening wind. "You can sleep here tonight if you want. It's a long walk home for Bailey." My father scratched Bailey under a jowl. "He's had more life in him lately. Follows me everywhere." He pressed his face back into the screen, which creaked in response. "I never told nobody about that boy, Daniel. Your mama can't ever know, you hear? Not ever." He looked across the road. "It would break her heart for good."

"Daddy."

"Yeah."

"Reverend Hardison would say God forgives you. For all that happened in those tunnels."

"How? God doesn't see what goes on in hell." His stomach gurgled.

"I can make you a sandwich."

He grunted as he struggled to rise. I went to the kitchen, calling over my shoulder, "Come on in while I get the fixings out." I heard him clump down the porch steps, the click of Bailey's nails beside him. I returned to the screen door as he pushed through the fence gate. Bailey stood on hind legs and pawed at his hip, as if to hurry him along. My father shambled across the dirt road and between the swaying trees. He entered among their shadows and became a shadow and was gone. The gate clattered into place between us.

I wondered how many times that gate, since the day my grandfather hinged it, had pinched shut like a throat swallowing a word. It was as the world itself, groaning and dying on its axis, and all we with it, none knowing until his last breath that he is coming to rest, that we are all of us coming to rest. Later that night my mother brought me clean clothes and a pot of soup. "Have you seen your father?" she asked.

"He was here earlier."

She shook her head. "I've had an eye out for him a couple of days now."

"What's wrong?"

"Bailey died. Went to sleep in the barn a few nights ago and never woke up. Your daddy loved that dog." She stroked my shoulder. "I know you did too." She scrubbed the kitchen counter with a sponge.

"Mama."

"Yes?"

"Are you sure about Bailey?"

"Buried him myself, in that back field where he was so fond of dozing. I came to regret not fetching you. It took me a while to dig a hole deep enough to keep the possum and coyotes away." She considered the back yard through the kitchen window. "You should plant tomatoes come spring. That soil has always been good for them."

"You know I'm leaving next summer."

She nodded. "Yes."

"Mama."

"What?"

"Don't tell Daddy about his dog."

The night before Julie Moore found my father, the wind had tormented treetops shattered by ice all those months before. I was mauling logs behind her father's house when she came to me, wordlessly took my hand, and led me to a copse where my father lay impaled through the belly by a thick branch of pin oak.

"It's bad, isn't it?" she said. "I knew by the boots it was him, but I couldn't look." She stared at his boot toes pointing skyward. Smaller branches sprouted from the limb like the splayed hand of a god, gouging his chest and legs and pinning him to the earth.

"I heard Bailey pining for him." She looked about for our dog. "It's bad, isn't it?" She brought her eyes to the branch impaling him. "Oh my god."

His neck was stretched and gaunt, his muscles thinned. He looked as if he'd been scoured by some awful whetstone. I considered his opened eyes gone blue and his worn, sharpened hands, and I heard

Julie's quiet weeping, and all of these confirmed that this impaled corpse was my father. His face was calmed, though the knots of grass in his fists and the blood coagulated on his belly belied any hope of a quick death.

But was it a good death, Daddy?

Suddenly I was thirsty. "Julie, can you get your daddy? Tell him to bring a saw and a wash bucket. Mama can't see him like this." She sprinted up the hill homeward, her footfalls like a diminishing heartbeat. I crouched in the quieted glen beside my earth-pinned father. He wore a dirty white t-shirt and over this a long-sleeved flannel shirt. His eyes were open and they were blue and they were staring at the sky and at me leaning over him. I took his cool hand and slowly rolled up his sleeve, neatly folding each turn. I ran my fingertips along his straight white scar that was like a taut string beneath the surface of his skin, smooth as new-formed flesh. My other hand went absently to the scar below my shoulder. The rest of his arm, his neck, his face were wrinkled and overtaken by a yellowed, whiskey-stained pallor. A breeze worried his tangled beard.

I tried to think of words to pray, but I didn't know words a boy can pray for his father who has gone. Doc Moore trudged through the brush, Julie behind him. I expected him to put his fingers to Daddy's throat like in a movie, to verify with medical finality that my father was dead. Instead he stood beside where I knelt and put his long white hands on his hips. "How are you, son?"

"I think he's dead." I nodded assent to my own claim. "He's dead." I looked up at Doc Moore. "Isn't he dead?"

"I'm sorry." He knelt to open his toolbox. "Julie, how about you stand over there and keep watch for Mrs. Waterson." He used a hacksaw to remove the branches pinning my father, cut the main branch flush with his belly, and chucked it aside. He took my father by the boots and grunted as he lifted him off the stump. He took down my father's jeans and told me to look away and with a washrag he cleaned him. Then he put back my father's pants and bound the hole in his belly with a cloth. He called for Julie to bring the Army jacket which lay nearby.

As she carried it to us, my knife, the one she'd hurled into the Crow years ago, tumbled from a pocket. But for a deep gouge in its stag-bone handle, it had been polished to a shine. The blades, though rust-flecked, had been burnished, and their action was unimpeded by river-bottom grit. "Oh my God, that's . . . that's . . . ." Julie put a hand to her mouth. I put the knife in my pocket. It felt heavier than I'd remembered. "How'd he get it?" Julie whispered through her hands.

"No telling, with him."

She started to cry. "I'm sorry," she said. "I'm so sorry."

"For what?"

"He probably thought *you* threw it in. He was carrying it all this time thinking you—"

"Hush, Julie," her father said.

The funeral was small and my mother sat throughout with her Bible open to the book of Romans, where she'd underlined a verse:

> *O wretched man that I am! Who shall deliver me from the body of this death?*

Some people said no Christian church should host my father's funeral. I knew most of those who came did so for my mother. Fred Ledbetter was also there, his thinning red hair slicked back. Uniformed old men from the VFW sat near the back, and behind these a half-dozen hard-looking men my father's age. I wanted to ask what they knew about my father and why they'd come now that he was dead. I didn't look at them long because arrayed between us were the people of my mother's church and Calvin's sickened face and Julie's weeping face and all of them regarding me with my face turned against them.

Reverend Hardison stood briefly and read from his Bible, then sat while someone sang about crossing over a river. He rose again to deliver his eulogy, his eyes flitting between my mother's face and the page on his lectern. I didn't know what he could say, but surely it couldn't be the truth, not with my mother sitting ramrod straight in her black funeral dress, hands clasping her own Bible as if she were its author, hard shining eyes pinned to him.

I expected him to hew to the verses about the thief on the cross, the prodigal son, the laborer who comes late to the harvest. But Reverend Hardison surprised all of us, perhaps himself most of all. He began reading from his penciled notes, then paused. He looked at my mother, then his notes, then my mother again. He removed his glasses and laid them upon the page. He leaned on his lectern, almost over it, as if to penetrate with his bald and sweating head a veil between shepherd and flock.

He said that God apportions some people harder lives. He looked about the congregation, daring anyone to contest this. He said that if any man thinks he gets by, come Judgment Day, because he's done better than another, he's in for a rude surprise. He said God shows mercy where we do not—perhaps *because* we do not—and if God can't bring a man like Ray Waterson into heavenly rest, then he just didn't see the point of standing up one more Sunday to preach, because if that is the way of things, that those who draw the hardest lots receive no more mercy than those with unburdened souls, then this is a godforsaken world, and a preacher's time would be better spent fishing.

Praise be to God, he said, that this isn't the way of things, which is why he stood before us with a Bible instead of a tackle box.

Praise be to God, he said, that heaven was made not for those who deserve it, but for those who need it.

Praise be to God, he said, that a man who needed it so dearly could finally take his rest among hills that have no end, which stretch on forever and ever without end, which stretch upward into golden light that does not burn, *hallelujah*, the light of God that will not burn the man who comes humbled into its glory. The Reverend cried out these words and my mother nodded approval. In the back of the church a man wept, and this is always, where I come from, a harrowing sound.

I kept my eyes on Reverend Hardison because I was afraid that Bobby Doyle, whom I had not seen for many months, would march past our windows with his graveyard host. He was not yet buried but still I feared my father would be numbered among them. If I saw the blackened eyes of my father, I would scream; I would scream and would not stop; my scream would be a serpent crawling up from the pit of my gut, and the serpent would have no end because its tail stretches past our time's beginning.

After the final hymn, I took my place with the pallbearers and we bore my father's coffin down the church steps and around to the graveyard where a fresh-dug hole waited. There were no congregating wraiths, only the gathered living and the dead man in his box and some workmen waiting to ferry him to his new family beneath the topsoil. They levered him into the ground while the preacher prayed and the women cried for my mother and the men blinked and cleared their throats.

Back at our house, church women uncovered casseroles and meat trays and fruit pies. My mother sat in our kitchen—perhaps the only time she'd ever remained seated there while others stood—and received the ministrations of friends and acquaintances, none of whom had divined what to do until now, when finally they could help, because women of a community, no matter how small and ignorant the greater world might judge them, know what to do when someone passes over, which is to heat food, and brew tea, and weep with those who weep.

The men gathered in the living room and turned on the game with the sound low. At varied intervals, someone would recall something about my father, like how he'd once witched a well under the sour observation of a county extension officer who swore there was no validity to witching, or how he'd earned several Purple Hearts, which is more rare than civilians appreciate. They spoke like he sat brooding in a corner, and they had an obligation to honor the man beneath whose roof they were about to eat.

Calvin and I sat on the porch swing and rocked it slowly with the balls of our feet. He was quiet, just as he would have known to make conversation were he someone else's best friend. Julie sat on a chair nearby, the soles of her feet pressed against the porch rail, and she too was quiet, though this was not her nature. I wondered if she understood that the last man who might have been able to help her was gone.

―⤙―

I walked the woods and river in the weeks after my father's passing. I'd helped lay him in the ground, yet still I felt compelled to seek him like I'd done so many times as a boy. I had not his witching power, but I feared I'd find him nonetheless, my father the fallen king under the shade of a shedding tree, he with his strong broken body splayed over the treasure of sunfired leaves, blind to his treasure's decay as he lay curled upon it.

Sometimes I saw Bobby Doyle as I wandered, always far off, beside a tree or atop a hill, watching me but with no inclination to guide me. My father was never with him.

Once, as the dead boy looked on, I saw amidst trees near the river's bend a man who looked very much like Fred Ledbetter, except that he was leaner and his wiry copper hair was thick. He was dead, I would have known by the lightness of his footfalls even had I not been able to see the blackened orbs in his eye sockets. He hunted his brother; I knew this because I saw a dead man who looked very much like him wandering that very same copse, seeking as his brother sought. The brothers traversed the woods, blinded to one another's presence. What a terrible damnation, to see with the godawful sight of the wandering dead yet be unable to find your own brother. To wander in the presence of another and feel utterly alone.

Toward the end of our senior year, Calvin and I drove to Winston and enlisted. Perhaps neither of us would have done it absent the other. My mother took the news at Marjean's with a nod and went back to serving tables. Mrs. Pruitt received Calvin as a Spartan mother being reunited with her son after the sorting—as if he were now a man and the boy he had been dead to her. He was state champion at 128 pounds that year and received his medal amidst boys from cities people had heard of. The recruiter told him he ought to go out for the All-Marine Wrestling Team once he got through Basic.

Marjean announced my enlistment to the applause of her diner patrons. I halfway hoped it would reignite Sherry's interest in me, but I could tell by the succession of guys who waited for her in their fast cars that she had no use for a boy with a hand-me-down Jeep and no more future than they.

Julie came to me at the Watts house the night before I reported to Basic. She stood barefoot at the door with arms wrapped around herself, wearing a white blouse and long black skirt. She opened the screen door and let it thump softly closed behind her. Moonlight tumbled through the windows and we stood in a luminescent pool. My hand was on the inner door, and with her own hand Julie covered what portion of mine she could. The question was in her eyes, the way it had been from the beginning, the question that held its own answer tucked deep, like a dangerous riddle. She guided my hand and we closed the door. Her hair fell over her face and she walked past me to the sleeping porch, slowly, wading through the moonlight flowing across the floors as a river. I followed.

"Storm coming," she whispered. She gazed out at the trees as they swayed silver under the moon. She considered my unkempt bed. "Will we get wet?"

"Maybe a little."

"I bet it feels good, rain on your skin, nobody telling you to close your window." She rubbed the sole of her foot up and down her shin, causing her skirt to flutter and fall.

"Your parents know you're out?"

"No." She wound the hem of her blouse around her fingers. Her hands trembled and goosebumps covered her arms. Wind pushed against the screens, then sucked them out. Moonlight bathed us in mercury. "Daniel."

I stepped across the distance between us and eased my fingers into her hair.

"I know you did things with that girl."

I kissed her. She unbuttoned her shirt with shaking hands. "I know you did things," she breathed against my neck, "but I never. . . ." She shook her head. "I never."

I undressed her as she stood shivering with eyes closed. When we both stood naked on the moonsoaked porch she crawled onto my bed, lay back, and closed her eyes. Her skin was warm and she shivered within its warmth. I covered her body with my own. She held me to her, pressed me into herself, into all that was her mystery, giving to me all that she knew and did not yet know. Afterward she curled her back against my belly and pulled my arm around her. "After the night I slept beside you in our house, I didn't have daymares for weeks," she said. "I wonder how long I'll be healed this time." Then she fell asleep. The rain-bearing wind was like the air above ocean surf, and I was a cave in which she hid.

I woke to darkness and quiet, penetrated only by the hum of a fluorescent strip in the kitchen. Julie was gone. I showered, shaved, poured coffee. I emptied the pot and washed it and set it in the drainer, thinking Mama would be happy to see I'd cleaned up. Julie's note was stuffed into my boot:

> You snore. We didn't talk about it because you didn't ask, but I'm going to Carolina after next year. I haven't been admitted yet, but I know they'll let me in because I met some kids who go to school there and they were just as dumb as everyone around here, just with fancier jeans.
> Remember how I wrote to you in the Big House? You never wrote me back. Mama told me that it's pathetic for a girl to write to a boy and follow him around like a puppy when he never shows her one bit of interest. I write because it's how I ponder, but I think words don't do the same thing

*for you. If nothing else, you seem smarter for not talking
so much.*

*Mama says you're a bad seed. She loves your mama,
but she's glad you're leaving. Daddy probably is too,
though I think he's partial to you in his way.*

*We're all like words on paper, Daniel. Most people are
newspapers, and that's why they bore me to tears, and why
I can't wait to leave this town. I need to unfurl, to become
a book.*

*Sometimes I think you're a book too. A book nobody
can open, not even you. Inside are all those pages and I
can't see what's written on them. Maybe I should just leave
you on the bookshelf and go out into the world. Maybe
you'll fight a war, marry some country girl, have ten kids,
and not speak a word the rest of your life.*

*I suppose I'll keep writing you all the same. I know
you won't write back. Mama says it's because you're all
shut down inside. That's fine—I hate emotional men.
That's why I won't see you off this morning, because while
I figure you'll be manly about leaving, I know Calvin is
going to cry like a little girl.*

*Please be careful, Daniel. And put the sheets in the
wash. I don't need to spend the next year with our mothers
eyeballing me like I'm the whore of Babylon.*

I folded her letter and tucked it into a book with the others. Outside the trees were blackening beneath a sky gone from night to blue. Mama arrived wearing her best pleated dress and carrying a basket. She smiled and I could tell even in this darkness that she'd been crying. "I came to see off my son," she said brightly. She swept past me into the house, set the basket beside my bag, and went to the kitchen to clean what I'd already cleaned. "You eat something?"

"I'm fine."

"Want an egg. Some toast?"

I came to the kitchen doorway. "No ma'am."

"More coffee?"

"It's starting to feel like I'm at Marjean's."

Mama whirled around, hair spreading out like swings on a carnival ride, eyes squinted in thrilled anger, the way they used to do. She pointed her finger at me. "Boy," she said. "Boy."

I put my arms around her narrow shoulders and pulled her head to my chest. "Mama." She pushed me away. "Oh, hush." She nodded toward the dryer. "You even did laundry!"

"I didn't want to leave a mess."

"Oh, merciful Lord, my boy has finally learned some manners."

"Maybe I could take another cup of coffee. If you think there's time."

We sat on the front step and sipped from steaming cups. Mama went over the schedule as if I hadn't been the one to explain it to her. She reminded me to call as soon as I could, and made me double-check my wallet for the diner number, though I knew it by heart. She tucked a roll of stamps into my shirt pocket with a melodramatic sigh.

"I'll write."

A louder sigh. She saw me to the edge of her mother's porch but no further; it was the most she was willing to concede to the U.S. military.

As we got on the bus in Winston, Calvin's straight-backed mother regarded her son with tearless pride. It was his father who cried into a handkerchief, his other hand waving us onward, as if our lives waited and we were late. We climbed aboard and rode south into the gaunt South Carolina pines. We thought freedom lay ahead. When I think on those fools motoring south and east to the sea, I want to tell them to slow down, to recognize that nothing they will ever know again will feel like this.

I thank God I'll never see what haunts you child, not this side of the veil. Nothing shook my mother. Her faith was so strong so present so absent and now lost to me, passed over with her to glory. Will you miss me one day, as I miss her? Will you know this longing? God forgive me that I hope you will.

My spirit is frayed and so it's best I can't see whatever it is you saw, what stirred you so often from sleep and drew you to your window, and me watching you some nights from your doorway, afraid to comfort you for fear you'd turn your haunted eyes up to me. Whatever it was that would wake you, that in daylight would stop you in the midst of weeding my garden or toting the milk pail, that caused you sometimes to gaze out the window or the door as if someone were knocking. Stopped you and set you

*to shivering in the dead of summer. How you looked like
him in those haunted moments. My son my child my poor
cursed boy.*

*Oh Daniel, would it have been better had you drowned
in the Crow? Or had your father drowned holding those
snakes, before I called him to shore? To whom would
you have been born then, heart of my heart? Whose child
would you be, and whose mother would I be?*

*I sent you away for fear he'd kill you. But also because
you were becoming like him in how you bent your head
to a bowl, how you settled into the couch with your head
sinking back past your shoulders, the sound of your boots
clomping along my fresh-swept floor. I never had the visions, his and yours, but the two of you child, the two of
you have been my haunting, and I couldn't bear to see you
become him. How can you ever understand this, craving
as you do, as every boy does, to become like your father?*

*What kind of woman can't bear the sight of her hus-
band, her son? What kind of woman am I?*

*I pray that in you somewhere is the priest that was in
him, that might have shone forth had the Lord who is Just
and Justifier not staked him to the earth. My God Ray, why
did you lay there? Why in that grove, why beneath that
earth-pointed spear?*

*Now my child goes to arms as his father before him
and with no clearer reason. God help me, I don't know if
I ever want to see you again, for in my deepest dread you
come home to me, home to this haunted land with your
hands covered in blood, death clinging to you like smoke.
Child, if that is to be your lot, I pray you come home to
me in a box.*

The Marines taught us how to tuck a shirt and clean a rifle and rappel
a wall, how to eat and sleep and obey, how to embrace the smallness
of ourselves and our small places in the midst of something that had
been before us and would endure after us. After Parris Island and
Lejeune, they sent Calvin to Quantico and me to the Philippines. It
was an easy routine for those of us who'd grown up without air con-
ditioning. On free days I went to a wharf that smelled of fresh-gutted
fish and stretched out on the nearby sand. I didn't think about my
father or Julie or the dead. Toward the end of the dry season I often

lay under lines of swollen gray clouds that marched over the islands to the sea like an airborne river. The shadows that spread under those coastal trees in moonlight sheltered their own ghosts, but they were not the ghosts of my home nor my people, and so they had no need of my attention.

✐

November 20th, 1981

Dear Daniel,

I'm sorry I didn't write from the end of the summer until now. Maybe you didn't notice. Coming to the School of the Arts was like being born again—but not in the church way. Everyone here <u>reads</u>. Can you imagine that? <u>Literature</u>. There's writers like me, and painters, and musicians, and the teachers are artists too. You know who would be the oddball here? Pretty much everyone we went to school with. It's like I've stepped through a mirror into a world where everything has flipped sides and I'm the normal one and the world I've left behind is the one that's backwards.

The only thing is every would-be writer seems to think you're supposed to be mentally ill to do it, so they're always going on and on about their depression and obsessive compulsions and melancholy, but I'm pretty sure none of them sees the dead standing in their closets. It's okay though, I just wear the same clothes a lot and talk about being sad, and nobody is the wiser. I didn't see anything terrible for weeks after our night together. I don't have the heart to tell my shrink that there's more healing in your man parts than in all his books.

But eventually they came back. The daymares.

You'd belong, here. You read more than you let on, and there were all those figurines you used to carve and leave where you knew I'd find them. So we can check the art box for you. Unless that was some other emotionally withdrawn river-wandering boy trying to win my affections and all those years I mistakenly thought he was you. Anyway, one of you would fit right in. And there's no carvers I know of, which means you'd fit in but <u>still</u> be an outsider people are a little afraid of because of all your carving knives and whatnot, and isn't that your heart's desire: to be in but not of?

Sigh. I know it's hackneyed and clichéd to write "sigh"
when I'm sighing, but there's a point in every letter I've
ever written to you where I sigh out loud, a real live clichéd
teenage girl sigh, and I kind of hate myself for doing it, and
a couple of letters I even started with no real idea what
I'd write to you but with a full and iron-clad intention of
not sighing no matter what, and then it came out all the
same. Sometimes it makes me mad that you could bring
such a noise out of me, this common girlish stereotypical
response, and there's a couple of letters that are buried in
the woods between your house and mine, because I was so
mad at my sighing and at you for making me sigh and for
your pathetic little shrubs of letters when I've written you
trees, entire goddamned forests of correspondence, and all
you can write back is what you did that week and what
you'll likely do next week and maybe relay a pathetic little
joke from Calvin, who as God is my witness I still can-
not understand how they let him into the Marines when
even the county fair has a minimum height requirement to
ride the tilt-a-whirl, and I guess it makes me mad because
I know you're in there, I've seen all the love and fury and
hurt spilling up out of your eyes, Daniel, your eyes which
sometimes are all I can remember of you, because heaven
forbid you should send a girl a picture of you in uniform.

Actually, don't you dare, because the Sighing Girl in
me would surely wedge it into the corner of her mirror, and
if I become that girl I may well exit Sylvia Plath-style in
my mother's stove at Thanksgiving, which would prove her
right on so many topics that I can't bear the thought of it.

There's plenty more to say but can you believe it I've
used up all my paper? (Paper is that flat white stuff you can
go down to any variety store and buy and it's for writing
these wonderful things called letters.)
Julie

Calvin earned a back-up spot on the Marine Corps wrestling squad
until a knee injury sidelined him for a few months. In the interim,
his unit got assigned, like mine, to Lebanon, where people we didn't
know were fighting for reasons unclear to us.

January 8th, 1983

Dear Daniel,

Mama says your mother told her they're sending you to Beirut, and then for the first time in our relationship she chastised me for not being in closer contact with you. Don't worry, I didn't recount all the letters I've written, and how you stopped writing back at all. I just took my lumps and said yes Mama I'll write to him now, and so here I sit with pen in hand, true to my word, the only confidence this will reach you being the massive amount of resources this country pours into its military machine.

Being at the University of North Carolina I am obligated to write things like that, though I happen to believe it, not that I'm inclined to give anyone around here the satisfaction of hearing me say so. I think I wrote to you once that the School of the Arts was like a mirror of high school but, this place is more so, because it's cliquish and judgmental and desperate for you to repeat all the Sacred Truths its overseers cling to, the only difference being those Sacred Truths are exactly the opposite of what we were desperately expected to believe in Hickory Shore.

I don't suppose I do well with authority of any kind. Which makes me wonder how you haven't been court-martialed and taken out back and shot by the Marines, given your own authority issues.

They put me in a hospital for awhile. There's medicine they want me to take, but sometimes I skip it because it makes me sleep all day, and I can't write when I'm on it. My writer friends talk about their mental illnesses like trophies they've won and I'd give anything to not feel the way I feel sometimes. To not see what I see.

I know you know what I'm talking about.

I don't expect you'll write me back. Maybe the way you keep from acting out and getting yourself executed by the Marines is by stuffing every emotion back inside your shriveled little soul. Maybe you eat a lot of aggression in the form of Marine mess hall cheeseburgers and are currently on some kind of Marine-imposed diet as a consequence.

I GUESS I WOULDN'T KNOW.

Anyway, I hope you're okay. Better than okay. I don't know why they want you in Beirut. We don't get regular news in Chapel Hill; I think they pipe it all through Moscow or something, so the best I can make out is that you'll

*be bayonetting babies and suppressing local freedom-
fighters. But whatever it is, please be careful, okay? Maybe
we won't ever see each other again and maybe eventually
I won't write another letter, but I want you to know that
most days I can't imagine I'll ever have a friend or boy-
friend or husband or whatever who is as close to me as you
are, even though you feel a million miles away, and have
always felt to me a little like that.*

Julie

They told us we were in Beirut to keep the peace. It was pointless, but
at least Calvin was there. His father was proud he was a Marine; his
mother urged him in her letters to practice violin, because wrestling
and radioing for the Marines wouldn't last forever. He grumbled, but
he complied, and newcomers who made fun of him for having a fiddle
in a war zone soon learned how easily a human body can get twisted
into a pretzel. Sometimes people change when they're apart, and when
they come back together there's gaps between them, like an ill-hung
door in its frame. But Calvin and me were plumb as ever.

They kept several hundred of us in a four-story building of glass
and concrete. It was held upright by pillars that looked like exposed
ribs. The guards at the checkpoints were told not to chamber any
rounds.

I had been taught history as a recitation of facts. A brief history
of explosives, for example, might read like this: The Greeks discovered how to hurl fire, and man became as God. Men bundled this
fire in clay pots and wooden canisters, they layered it in gleaming
bullet-headed shells big as railway cars, they seeded it in the atom's in-
terstitial spaces. The small and vindictive man-god turned his enemies
to ash and consumed them with his indrawn breath.

But sometimes, rather than hurling death from a distance, he
clasped it like a baby to his chest and rushed headlong into the camp
of his enemies, a prayer on his lips.

So here is the history of a particular explosion: A man stands
at a window, coffee cup in hand, and considers how the sunlight is
yellower here—yet somehow thinner—than back home. He watches
a water truck circle the parking lot and roar through concertina wire,
through sentry posts where guards hold weapons with bolts closed.
The man stands watching at the window because he has legs and a

spine, and the truck passes into the building below easy as a knife into warmed butter. If he had just a moment to reflect, he might remember a Bible lesson about the Lord shielding Moses as he passed, because the glory of God is too awful to behold. The truck bears a light that might have seemed like the glory of God, but the truck is no more, and the man with his coffee is no more; all that remains of him is a slick length of spine that juts like a wet fossil from the wall behind, even as the floors above and below are lifted in the air to collapse upon themselves like a deck of cards tossed to the floor.

A boy below me dies because he is shot through with bone fragments that spring like darts from his friend who stands in a doorway. His friend is telling about the time in high school when he recovered a fumble and won the game, and neither of them is afforded a moment to realize death has come to collect their wispy souls. A boy on what was the floor above remains intact and looks to be sleeping. Eventually a medic will lift his eyelid and for the rest of his days dream of the dark orb he sees nesting there like a fish egg. Boys all around us are confetti and ash, and we who have not been shredded wait in our graves. I can recall neither earth nor sun nor sky; there is only this present darkness.

As the sound like a gong diminishes, the screams begin, some muffled, some distant. One is very close, and it comes again and yet again, but it's like a watch winding down. The silences stretch longer between the boy's screams, and his screams become cries, and these become a question. He asks the question again. There is no one to answer the boy, and now he is silent.

Son it is a fearsome thing to be lifted up in God's hands and to see with his eyes. I wrestled him all those years, borrowing his sight but never looking fully, because to see everything would be to see the work of my own hands through his eyes. You alone know why I couldn't bear that.

You coveted my power because you knew no better, because I myself didn't fully understand until that glass of water, your hand on mine just an instant and you thinking any power would come from me to you and me fearing the same. Then my spirit was eased, for a time, enough time to give my confession, and it was like when you were a boy, my boy in my arms on my shoulders hand in my hand flesh of my flesh and how did I who have seen so much not see that God gave me the power to kill and balanced it by crafting my son to heal, to heal even the likes of me.

That chance at healing is gone now, squandered and gone, but maybe there's time still, even now in this tomb of stone and glass, to give to you your inheritance.

There is death on all sides but I am not dead nor even entombed because here is a crack between rock slabs and here is air and smoke rising upward within it like a prayer from one of Julie's candles. It rises upward and I will follow to heaven or God or whomever awaits me, for I feel the presence of my father same as if he held me like he once did. Daddy, are you here?

I will climb the stairway to the room without walls, the dread grieving center of his creation, and there I will show you what I see. Though it undoes me I will show you and you will know and you will live as you were meant to live, my son, my boy, my baby.

There is crying, there is screaming, they are dying, Daddy, they are dying, and Calvin somewhere here with them. Show me, damn you, show me. Reveal to me the hidden things though I be damned with you. Give me the power to hunt the men who did this. To slit them open, black their eyes, widow their women, leave their children wandering and fatherless. Set me to burn, Daddy.

See now boy the rubble the metal twisted skyward and smoking and here this stretch of side-laid wall and beyond it a precipice overlooking smoke and flame from which rises the sound of an enraged river bearing away all life it can snatch and here boy let your legs be guided by this wind this holy breath that moves through the smoke and ash but does not move it.

Turn your eyes boy, turn from the precipice and the fire below and beyond the plains of sand and indeed the whole earth in its misery and grieving, this sight is not for you. Turn your eyes downward and see his boot beneath that slab, now stretch out your hands to him that always offered his own to you. I can take life but I cannot heal it. That, son of mine, is your power. I name you blade-catcher, flesh-mender, fire-talker. Breathe into your friend what's been taken and hurry, for there are many others besides.

So close I feel your breath your hand on my neck, your scent healthy and clean like it was when I was your boy, your son you loved, your shadow. Let me come with you, Daddy, into the river, into the trees, up the staircase, into the room without walls. I don't need power nor glory just let me be with you, your boy with you as I was, as I was. Don't leave me again, Daddy, please not in this place, not now, not again.

Upward into the terror into the sight I go, away from him and away, for he would follow even now, seeing all he's seen. Lord God this child brimming over with fury and love. See how he seeks, how he calls out, so eager to plunge into this river of blood. Upward I go though surely I will burn to ash, upward where this boy cannot follow, upward that he might be saved.

Daddy you have gone again, are gone as you were, and no heart remains within my chest to break. Go on then, leave me as you always did. I'll carry this burden myself. I kneel and pull away the rocks and twisted rods and here is my friend who never left, not once, but I feel his spirit leaving now. What a cruel world that would kill even you, Calvin. I'll not allow it, not this day. I press these hands to your torn and bleeding throat and feel flesh knit, to your ribs and feel them swell outward whole as your lungs fill. You will live, brother. My father is gone, but we will live despite him, you and me and every mother's son I can pull from these catacombs.

I hear music feel it in my blood and it is the music of God pure and awful and mercy-laden and it draws me home-ward. Homeward I go to this music, and why was I ever afraid? You cannot follow me son, not for many years, be-cause the river of your life stretches before you and it will be good, Daniel. It will be good.

My Lord my Maker my King, what wonder is it that you will not turn your eyes from the likes of me?

＞

After Calvin I moved from crack to crevice and then among the wounded where rescuers laid them. All was chaos because the men normally called upon for such work were the men buried together, the living alongside the dead and little to differentiate them. I moved among the dying and the power moved through my hands to seal their wounds and spark their silent hearts until I collapsed there as a dead man myself.

I woke in a British Air Force hospital in Cyprus. Nurses moved about with brisk purpose as a chaplain prayed over a boy unmoving in a nearby bed. A nurse rewarded my opened eyes with a thin smile and warned me not to speak as she peeled bloodied gauze from my throat and scrutinized what lay beneath. I drifted for days in something like sleep, marking time by sunlight on the wall, the passage of gurneys. My skull had been fractured, along with a collar bone. Shrapnel had entered my throat, just missing my jugular but nicking a vocal chord.

This is why my voice has a rasp, why it carried through the church seven years later like my father's in his last days. It's why, I told them, I don't give speeches or any such thing, but they all said, in one way or another, the same thing: *Who else can speak for her but you?* And so I did, and a pitcher of water later it still felt like I'd swallowed a thorn.

Calvin would have delivered a better eulogy, were he not such a blubberer, because even though his throat was flayed open when I found him, his voice today is rich as the base string on his fiddle. His children sometimes play concerts for him on their own violins, sounding like a clutch of feral cats, but Calvin claps as if he's never heard anything more beautiful. Sometimes they ask about the raised bands of knotted flesh across his throat, and when they do he says, *Aw now,* and changes the subject.

Eventually they flew us to Walter Reed Hospital, which meant our families could see us. Mama screamed when she saw my eyes were blue. It wasn't until several guys came by to thank me that she believed me when I swore I hadn't killed anyone. I told her none of us had killed anyone over there, other than ourselves.

She talked about my coming home and staying with her for a time, and then maybe going to school. Or I could get work in town and take on Granny Watts's place. Maybe put in a new garden. I listened to her with no intention of going back to Hickory Shore. I had no intention of doing anything, really, but rise up from this bed as soon as my body would obey and go far as the longest road would take me. To someplace wide open, with nothing to remind you how easily everything crafted by God can be unmade by man, can be broken into sharp, gleaming pieces.

During one of Mama's visits, Julie appeared in the doorway. Her hair was more reddish-brown than I'd remembered, cut in a short bob that curled inward and kissed her throat. Her hands were shoved into the front pockets of her jeans and she squinted at me like I was the same puzzle that had confounded her since childhood. She considered me with her watering eyes and I looked away, which drew Mama's attention to the doorway.

"Why, Julie Moore!" Mama rose to embrace her. "Your mother said you'd headed up this way." My mother had not told me this. Julie leaned into my mother's hug and Mama pushed her away, held her by the elbows, and gave her the up-and-down assessment that older women give to younger women. I took in Julie as my mother must see her, the slightest makeup, small, jutting breasts, runner's legs taut beneath her jeans, scuffed canvas tennis shoes. I saw Julie through my mother's eyes, this girl who'd followed her son around, who'd been slight and spare and inconsequential but who now stood here in seeming possession of herself.

"Daniel, isn't it nice of Julie to come all this way?" She returned to my bedside and smoothed the front of her dress. "Did you drive yourself?" I knew my mother already knew the answer.

"Yes, ma'am." Julie took the chair beside my bed.

"How long do you intend to stay?" My mother's voice was bright and sharp.

"A while." I could hear the taunt in Julie's voice, the same voice she'd used with her own mother so many times.

"What about school?"

"It'll be there later."

"Won't your people miss you?"

"I honestly don't know, Mrs. Waterson."

My mother kept a smile plastered on her face. She asked Julie about her parents, even though she spoke to Julie's mother more often than Julie did. She asked after her brothers. Julie parried Mama's queries with the faintest smile on her face. Eventually Mama looked down at her hands smoothing the front of her unwrinkled skirt, and it was as if she saw the liver spots and wrinkles and reddened knuckles for the first time. She sighed. A nurse came in to change my I.V. bag. We watched her with feigned interest.

"Well," said Mama, "I need to go pack. I'm having dinner with the Alexanders tonight." The Alexanders were a Marine family who'd opened up their home like so many others in the area. She turned to Julie. "I'm taking the train home tomorrow afternoon."

"Please be careful, Mrs. Waterson." Julie stood. The playfulness left her voice. "I hope you get some rest."

Mama nodded, her eyes on her smoothed skirt. Julie put her hand on mine. "I'll make sure they take care of him."

Mama lifted Julie's hand from mine and embraced it with her own. "I believe you, child." She kissed me and left. "I'll be back in the morning," she called from the hallway.

Julie stood looking at the empty doorway. Her hand returned to mine. "How are you?" she whispered.

"Been better."

She sat on my bed and took my hand into her lap. She considered my bandaged throat and traced the bruises around my eyes. "Does it hurt?"

"Only when I'm awake." We sat in the quiet as the sun went down behind the hospital. A nurse brought food. "Guess I should eat so they'll take this line out."

"I should go," Julie said. She leaned across my tray of meatloaf and Jello and kissed me.

She returned the next day, after my mother was on the train. She came every day after that. We didn't talk about much. Words had never done me any good, and after seeing the world blown open, after learning how little man's flesh and life mean to God, I had less use for talking than I'd had in the first place.

Julie didn't need to talk either. She would slip off her shoes, prop her feet on my bed, and read. She read and I slept, or pretended to sleep while watching her, or watched her openly while she slept. She had a wisp of a scar at her eye's corner, and when she curled into a ball on the chair, I could see the edge of a tattoo at her shoulder. It was a word from a language I didn't understand. I envisioned her lying on a table as someone drilled paint into her secret flesh, her eyes closed as they'd been the night she offered herself up to me. Sometimes when I woke I found her watching. It was alright, being watched by Julie. We slept and we watched each other and we were quiet, and neither of us felt like we were on the wrong sides of our skin.

She took a job at a restaurant where lobbyists and congressmen ate. She explained how you could tell their pecking order solely by the way they held their drinks, how one night a congressman solemnly asked her to come to his apartment when her shift ended. She told me about working and stuffing tips into her pockets and coming back to her cramped motel room and reading.

Julie called the authors she loved by their first names. She told me how Flannery delighted in exposing the heresies of Protestantism, though none of the Protestants got it, she said, because Protestants don't read. I told her my Protestant mother read more than most anyone else I knew. Julie had decided to convert to Catholicism, or

Eastern Orthodoxy—something soaked in mystery and blood. Her mother, she quipped with a twist at the corner of her mouth, was incensed.

"Won't you flunk if you don't get back to school?"

"It'll work itself out," she said.

I asked her if she was better and her face darkened. "I don't know what that means anymore. But I'm no nearer the dead than you."

One day I rasped to her what happened, how everything was darkness, and I thought I was in hell and figured God wouldn't save me, and how my father came to me. I told her that for a time I had a power to heal flesh, to work miracles even, but the power had left and my father had left. She sat on my bed cross-legged between my knees, hands on my thighs, and she listened almost without blinking. She didn't try to soothe me. She listened, and when I finished she told me I was a fool if I thought my power to heal had only existed that day and that it had left me. She told me that she loved me, that she had loved me even when she hated me. She bent over me, weight on my belly, her scent of soap and sweat close, her unblinking eyes level with my own. "Maybe you don't comprehend what it feels like to love someone, Daniel Waterson, but I'm here to tell you that you love me, too."

"It's my bloodline that gave you nightmares. That day by the Crow."

"Maybe some part of you bears my affliction, yes. But you also bear the cure. You love me, Daniel, and that makes you mine." She kissed me. "The sooner you get that through your thick head, the better off we'll all be." She kissed me again.

"I'm all broken down."

"You're cracked, boy. Not broken."

"We're too young to know what we want."

"That's a lie and you know it."

"Your mama and daddy don't want you being with Ray Waterson's son."

Julie sat back on her haunches. That twist returned to the corner of her mouth. "Let me tell you what my mama taught me about men. She said a man is like a linoleum floor. If you lay him right, you can walk on him forever."

I snagged her belt loop and pulled her to me. She kissed me again, hard, and then gripped my hair. "Listen to me, Daniel," she whispered, "because it's real simple. I'll give you all of me. I'll love you and cook for you and have your babies. But I won't be like your mama, you hear me? You ever touch a drink, and I'll kill you myself."

"Sure thing."

She pulled my hair, hard, and glared with fierce and shining eyes. "I love you, but I'll fucking shoot you dead. I'm gonna be a writer. I can do that just as easily in prison."

"Okay."

She kissed me again. "I'm going back to school this summer. We can take this slow, and you can court me properly when I come to Hickory Shore from time to time, or you can come to Chapel Hill with me. Take classes, bus tables, I don't care. Marry me or not, it doesn't matter."

I shook my head. "Why would you love the likes of me, Julie?"

"Because you're mine to love."

I pulled her onto me and she settled her head on my chest. "Just don't expect babies until my first novel is done. I may be in love, but I'm no goddamned fool."

———

We got married the day the doctors released me, February 13th, 1984, in the hospital chapel. Our unit chaplain was pale and thin, and his hands shook from too much coffee and nicotine. He'd been in Beirut and then Cyprus and had grown accustomed to presiding over the ends of things. He steadied as he got into the rhythm, like a car leaving gravel for a familiar roadway. I borrowed some dress blues and Julie wore a short beige dress. Calvin was well enough to be there. "Your mama is gonna kill you," he said, "and me too for not telling her." Our other witness was my ward's head nurse, a big, red-skinned woman who went through half a package of tissues before we even got to the vows. Our chaplain spoke through a spreading grin, and Julie clasped my hand as she'd done all those years ago at Clay's funeral.

I got leave and we spent the rest of that week driving the Blue Ridge Parkway. We slept at cheap motels in little towns huddled at the feet of the hills. We hardly spoke, except for when Julie read to me from Eudora Welty. She decided we were going to have a girl, and we were going to name her Eudora. Each night in bed she closed her eyes like someone slipping into a warm bath. She clutched me as we slept, like I might fall. Even in deepest sleep she clung to me as a possession, and it was good.

I received a medical discharge, and we rented a little house in Hillsborough so she could finish school. At nights I worked security at an office complex, and she sold shoes in the mall. She had a Mall

Self. She would stand before me in a skirt with hair pinned back, face lit by the bright, toothy smile she used to give church ladies and her Bible study friends in Hickory Shore, and ask, with a Southern Belle accent, "Can I help you?"

"Yes, do you have shoes here?"

"You mean here?" She'd gesture about our tiny living room like Vanna White flipping letters. "In this shoe store that has shelf after shelf of shoes, and a big sign over the door that says: *Shoes?*"

"Yes, ma'am. Shoes that go on feet."

"No. Go away."

"Oh, you're a real charmer," I'd say. "Didn't your mama teach you any manners?" She'd drop her head and fall against me with a groan, or slap my arm and tell me to rob banks instead of guarding them. "We could be like Bonnie and Clyde," she'd say, "only with brains and libido." Then I'd kiss her, and we would leave our quiet house, me to guard rows of empty offices, she to squeeze shoes on the feet of women who insisted their size-eights were really sixes. To this day Julie prefers being barefooted.

Our mothers, God bless them, were appalled. They visited to cook and clean, and they quietly waited for it to end. The truth is that we waited for it to end, too. We waited for something terrible to happen—accident or illness or flood—because we both suspected God punishes you for being happy. And if we weren't happy we were at peace, which feels even more undeserved.

—————

The weekend before Julie's first novel was published by a little North Carolina press, she pounced on me. She was pregnant by Sunday or thereabouts. We had a son, and Julie decreed his name would be Cullen. "It means *good-looking*," she said.

"What if he looks like me?" I asked this as I tugged a strand of her hair where she lay sweating on the delivery bed.

"Then we'll call him by his middle name."

I became a paramedic, and I was good at it. Mama told me I should go to medical school, and I had no way to explain that what made me good at helping people would make me a terrible doctor. Julie followed her novel with a collection of short stories about southern women that earned her some small literary prizes and—to her chagrin and secret delight—invitations to speak at Junior Leagues all over the South. Our mothers compounded her misery by taking her dress shopping. Through this heightened exposure to the kinds of women she'd always avoided, Julie finally perfected the southern art of insulting someone without their knowing it.

———✦———

Two years later we had another son, and Julie named him Isaac, because his perpetually surprised face made her cackle. Doctor Moore passed that summer from a coronary, and Julie's mother begged us to move back to Hickory Shore. I told Julie I didn't care where we lived, that we could live wherever she wanted.

"I'm not going to bother moving anywhere with a man who doesn't care what patch of land he lives on," she replied. She was like this now, had been working up to this her whole life, to a conviction that every decision matters.

———✦———

One Saturday Marjean called to tell me Mama had dropped a coffee pot at the diner, and at first all I could think is how odd for her to track down my number just to tell me that. "It shattered and scalded her bare legs," she explained. "But she just stood there, Danny, gazing out the window. The ambulance is taking her to Winston, and you need to get there right away. I'm sorry, sugar-pie."

Even sleeping, with her mouth agape and the small fluorescent light over her bed casting an ugly illumination across her skin, Mama looked healthier than I remembered from all those years with my father. "She'll be fine," I told Julie. I considered my mother deeply breathing, her bandaged legs splayed across the bed, and it seemed to me that what was really wrong was that she was tired, that she had been tired for years and was only now having rest. "I'll take a night job so she can quit that diner. She'll be fine."

Mama woke the next day, blinked, looked at me, at Julie. She couldn't raise her head. Her eyes moved lazily over the striped wallpaper, the gray lump of a television hanging from the ceiling, the I.V. pump. "Mama," I asked, "can you hear me?" She closed her eyes, and her eyelids fluttered, like someone either waking up or falling asleep. I squeezed her limp hand and she tried to focus her eyes on me, like she'd been carrying a question to ask me for the longest time, only now that I was here in the flesh, she couldn't remember what it was.

A squat, bald-headed doctor entered the room. The corner of his mouth gaped in what passed for a smile. "She can hear you," he said, "but she can't talk back."

"We deduced that," Julie muttered.

The doctor put his thick fingers to what remained of the white hair on the side of his head, and twirled them about. "It's like the wires is crossed up."

"Haywire," Julie said.

The doctor jabbed a finger at her and grinned. "There you go!"

"Will she get better?"

He shook his head and looked at his shoes. "Well, these things are hard to put a finger on." He held his hands before his chest like scales. "On the one hand, them wires could go uncrossed and she'd be almost right as rain." He lifted his right hand and wobbled it to signify *almost*. "On the other hand, they could get worse, and affect her primary functions." He lowered his left hand, and the smile left his face.

"So she could wake this afternoon and be fine," Julie said, "or she could pass by nightfall."

"Yes ma'am." With his mouth pinned shut, the doctor looked suddenly intelligent. He patted my shoulder. "It's up to the good Lord, in cases like this." Julie pulled her chair closer to the bed and caressed my mother's hand.

The next day Mama could blink purposively, and the day after that she could raise her finger to point. Julie would tell her we loved her, and my mother would raise her finger and blink. Julie's mother brought Cullen and Isaac. They stood on either side of Mama's bed and stared. When she blinked at them, they blinked back, and she rattled out a wheeze in place of a laugh, though her dry lips stayed frozen in a snarl.

"Still waitin' to see," the doctor explained with his scale-hands.

Calvin visited, but he couldn't stay composed for very long and left red-faced. His mother sent an enormous flower arrangement. Reverend Hardison came though he was retired and sat with his knees pressed against the edge of her bed and read to her from his Bible.

On the fifth day, Mama could sit up and swallow soft food. She and the boys traded blinks. They had some kind of code between them that I didn't understand. On the sixth day, I came in with coffee and doughnuts to find my boys stuffing Mama's things into their backpacks amidst crayon boxes and *Billy and Blaze* books. Julie had

helped Mama to a sitting position. "I need you to go steal us a wheelchair," she said.

"You need to lay her back down."

"She wants to go home."

"Why are you putting shoes on her? She can't even stand."

"A lady doesn't want to be seen in public in bare feet. Are you
going to get me a wheelchair, or do I have to send one of your sons for
it?" Mama rested a hand on Julie's shoulder and patted.

I located a wheelchair, and after we helped Mama into it, Julie
took the boys and the doughnuts down to the nurse's station to dis-
tract them. I wheeled my mother to a service elevator, and we got lost
in the hospital's bowels for a while, each corner yielding only more
greenishly lighted hallways, until we spilled abruptly onto the sidewalk of a busy street. I slowly trundled her in the direction I thought
the parking lot might be, trying not to look like a man abducting
a stroke patient. The sun was warm, and a slight breeze lifted the
strands of her grayed hair. She tilted her chin skyward.

Julie pulled alongside in our faded old Suburban, and we helped
Mama inside. She turned her head and shoulders to survey her grand-
sons beside her. They blinked a greeting. We left the wheelchair on the
sidewalk and sped away.

When the Winston Police figured out what we'd done, they called the
Forsyth County Sheriff, who called Sheriff Wilson, who drove out to
Mama's house and told me he needed to see her. I took him upstairs,
where she sat in bed as Julie brushed her hair. The boys were on the
bed as well, playing with Legos. The sheriff took off his hat. "How
you doin', Mrs. Waterson?" he shouted.

"She can't talk yet," Julie said.

"Are you gonna arrest us?" Cullen asked. Isaac held up a stick of
Legos like a gun and trained it on the sheriff.

"Lord-a-mercy he looks like your grandmama." We went back
downstairs. "She need any medicine?" he asked.

"They were just giving her fluids. She can swallow well enough
now."

He nodded. "My mama had a stroke," he said, "back in '77.
They wasn't much help back then, either. I'll tell the Forsyth Sheriff
I talked to your mama, and she indicated to me that she came here

of her own free will." He stopped at his car door. "All the same, I wouldn't take her back into Forsyth County if I was you."

Between Julie's mother and women from church we scarcely needed to cook. I drove to Hillsborough for clothes, toys, and Julie's typewriter. I could tell she was itching to write. It was how she made sense of things. Calvin rode with me. He ran his daddy's stores now, and three more across Cantwell County besides. He'd married Mary Taylor and their girls were just like her. We hadn't talked much since I'd moved to Hillsborough, but that didn't matter. He'd lost most of his hair and gained a belly, and that didn't matter either, because he was always smiling and always confident, and everyone admired him because he was the man they'd wanted him to become. I suppose if Mary Taylor was going to be able to love anyone, it would be him. "Her butt got big like we always expected," he told me, "but God help me, I love it."

In the weeks that followed, Cullen and Isaac expanded their circle of exploration to the fallow garden, the barn, the blackberry bushes. I showed them where Calvin and I used to camp, and the flattened slate on the ridge that was always cool, even in summer, and the pond that shone on clear nights, the surrounding trees brighter in its reflected starlight than when you looked directly at them.

My mother began to speak in small portions. The first word she said was *river*, which she spoke as she gripped Julie's hand. I led the boys through the trees, across the broken field over which I'd followed the dead boy. We stopped at the muddy slope that stretched down to the bank, and I told them I would take a switch to them if they came here alone. I held their hands and we listened to the gentle chuck and slap of the brown water. "Is dead people in dat water," Isaac announced. His sweaty brown hair came to a point at the top of his head. He had blue eyes. "Mama almost drowned in there," Cullen said. Julie had told them the story of the flood one evening as we sat piled on the porch swing. "But Daddy saved her." I didn't correct him.

I got out my father's old rod and my little one and taught them how to cast flies in the shallows. I told them all my father had told me about catching a smart fish like a trout. I told them never to trust the river.

Mama relearned other words. She contorted her wrinkled face as she dredged them from memory and forced them from her mouth. She gripped the bedspread in her hand, returning to strength, and said *blanket*. Her trembling fingers tapped the hairbrush on her side table, and she mumbled *brush*. Julie picked it up and gently ran it through her hair.

My mother sounded like a simpleton, but Julie spoke to her like she was the only sane person in the room. She spoke to her about the boys, and me, and how she was learning empathy for her own mother, living as she had in a house with so many men.

When the boys realized Granny Waterson was naming things, they made it into a game. They would bring her some small item, press it into one of her quaking hands, and wait. She would screw up her face, then spit out *block*, or *cup*, and they would clap and blink their eyes at her. She would wheeze-laugh at them and stroke their heads. Often they sought me out, laid hold of my wrists, and led me to where she sat in bed or on the porch swing. They would hand over my wrists like I was myself a small thing and wait as she looked me up and down. Sometimes she named me *trouble*, or *stubborn*. Other times she said *son*, *baby*, *boy*. Once she said *Ray*, and I didn't know if this was on purpose.

One day she spoke in fuller sentences and was hungry. She asked us to take her to her mother's house. She could walk, slowly, and we helped her through the gate and along the worn bricks and up the steps. The boys ran around the yard, ecstatic to explore a new place. Inside we helped Mama shuffle from room to room. She touched the old grandfather clock in the foyer and made me wind and set it to the right time. She ran her fingers over the shade of an antique lamp, an anniversary gift her father had cradled in his lap on a train all the way from Richmond. She sat at the dining table, in her old chair, and patted the table top with her palms. "Everything needs dusting," she said.

"We'll do that tomorrow," Julie promised.

Mama smiled and stroked Julie's hand. In the kitchen she leaned against the sink to survey the back yard. "I'll mow it later this week," I said.

She nodded. She started to tell the story she'd told me before I left for the Marines, about she and her sisters and her father serenading her mother, but it took too much breath. "It's alright, Mother," Julie told her. Back home, as the gold began to fade from the late afternoon light, Mama was suddenly tired, so tired she could barely raise her head. She asked to talk with Julie alone. I left them in her bedroom and went downstairs to help Mrs. Moore make dinner.

"Daniel," she said. She blinked back tears and shook her head.

"I know."

Julie came down for me. "Sit with her."

I went up steps that glowed with evening light, to my mother's room. She smiled and held out a tremulous hand. It was strong, even now. I don't know what sons are supposed to tell their mothers who are dying. I stared at her hand clasping mine.

"Daniel."

"Yes?"

"Know something I loved about your daddy?"

"What?"

"He didn't try to fill space with talking." She reached up her other hand, which wobbled at the end of her uncooperative arm, and moved it about, like she was suddenly blind. I leaned to her and she found my face. She patted my cheek. "You'll be okay," she said. "You'll all be just fine." She turned her head to the window, where the sky was going purple, the sun's light spilling across the tops of our trees. "This is your home," she said.

"Mama." I wanted to tell her I was sorry for all of it, for being born and for falling in the river and for Daddy and for being spiteful all those years. I wanted to tell her that I love her, that all the other times I've said it aren't enough, because only now do I know how much, now that I can see what it is to fear night and day for your child, and to be bound to someone, and to be borne along this life's river with only your tired, kicking feet and your flailing arms to keep your mouth above water. "Mama."

"Hush now. Give me my Bible." I took it from the side table and laid it on her chest. She wrapped her arm around it. She smiled at the window, then furrowed her brow. "I need to tend the garden." She sighed. "But I'm so tired."

***

There's some as wander but I was never one of them because I'm one that can see. We see with the Shepherd's sight cause he gives all to the chosen and not even his sight does he keep from us. We see with his sight but we haven't his labor or the labors of the wanderers so we rest here in the between. It's ground but it's warm like a bed and you can see all the earth and sky as well as your mama and your daddy and though they cry you don't cry because you see also the day they come lie beside you and even the day we all rise up and that joy is in your belly even now where you lie.

*And that's how I saw you from the start standing over
your daddy's shoulder as he tried to breathe back into me
what he knocked out and standing at your window looking
down at what you thought was me and following it to the
river and almost beneath the river, saw you watch it walk
about your church watch it in the trees and in your room,
and every time you thought it was me but I lay right here,
have always laid here waiting on mama and daddy and the
Call. I lay here and you think you saw me black-eyed and
watching you all those years but it wasn't me, Daniel. It
was you.*

*Them with sight see the wanderers but sometimes they
see other things past and future and things that might be
and worst of all sometimes they see themselves as they are
inside and that's what you saw. You thought it was me but
I lay right here in this warm rest. What haunted you worst
was always you, Daniel. That broken wandering dark-eyed
boy was you.*

I didn't realize how many people knew her until this afternoon. The
pews were thick with regulars from her church, from the diner. Marjean came weeping on her cane. Reverend Hardison came and did not
cry, as if finally he was past grief and expectation and had settled into
waiting.

People I'd despised were there: Fred Ledbetter, stooped and
bald; his son Carl, who is fat, harried by three towheaded boys, and
a contractor like his father; even Mr. Beasley, my long-retired teacher.
There were boys I fought in school, now men themselves, and the
deputy who arrested me after I stole Ledbetter's truck, and Sherry,
plumped up with a toddler on her hip.

Amongst the pews were all those people who'd wronged me, or
who I imagined had wronged me, as well as people I'd wronged. And
now I remember the way Fred Ledbetter used to bow his head when
Reverend Hardison promised a coming resurrection; Carl Ledbetter
crying as a little boy when his mother left him in Sunday School; Mr.
Beasley gently wiping chalkboards at the end of a school day; Sherry
sleeping on my chest like I was something safe. It occurs to me now
that hating anyone is just remembering the wrong things about him,
the things he'd probably like to forget about himself. We should all of
us have the chance to forget some things, don't you think?

Julie won't share what my mother said to her in those last hours. I asked her about it again as we dressed for the funeral. "She just talked," Julie said. "I listened, and she talked, and if there was anything meant for you, one of us would have told you."

"I should think anything my mother said was meant for me."

"And that'd be where you're wrong. Besides, the mystery you need to be pondering is right in there." She slapped my chest.

And that is the thing some men struggle against all our days: to know what lies beneath our skin, what it is we see reflected in a mirror, or in a woman's eyes, or on the surface of the river. Some nights, when I've dreamed of the dead boy and wake up in a sweat with Julie's bare arm draped across my belly, I imagine she knows me, that my father and mother knew me and whispered what I am to her. I suspect Julie knows what I really am, as does the dead boy, and perhaps the river, the three of them knowing what I cannot name about myself.

And now Cullen and Isaac have gone missing while Calvin's family, Julie's relatives, Mama's two living sisters, and what seems like half of Hickory Shore are crammed into Mama's house and spilling onto her porch. We notice around the same time, Julie and I. She searches the house, but I've come to the river. They aren't here, and I know they haven't been here. I try to call them, but my throat is so raspy from the eulogy, even after a whole pitcher of water, that I can only croak.

I walk to the back yard, and Julie comes from the house to take my hand, and together we pass my mother's garden. We cross the sloping field where blackberries grow, to that fallowed field where my father sunk a well for no reason I could discern, and now we hear them, just beyond the chokeberry. They are arguing beside the hand-pump my father installed over his well. Cullen grips the faded red handle and strains to lift it. Isaac stands looking up at him with hands on hips. They see us and step away from the handle.

"Your grandfather dug this well."

They touch it with tentative fingers, and when they do this I know we will live here, that Julie and I will raise our children in this place and grow old on it and die here as our parents before us.

"It doesn't work," Cullen says. He again lays hold of the handle and tugs upward with a grimace. I put my hand over his and help him pull. The handle relinquishes with a groan. Sometimes I'm reminded that I'm as big now as my father. Bigger, Calvin insists. Long ago I realized he wasn't really any bigger than other men. He just seemed that way to me.

The handle creaks as we push it back down. I wonder if water still runs below and if the screen at the pipe's end kept it from clogging. We work the handle until a gusher of water hits my boots. The boys squeal and clap. I cup my hands and catch the water; it's icy-cold and sweet, just as Daddy promised Mama the day we killed the boy. I drink, and for the first time today my throat doesn't ache.

I lift my hands to the mouths of my children, and they drink. They smile up at me with wet chins, and I catch a glimpse of what it means to be a man, to be the shadow of my father and at the same time to have these little ones as my shadows, nourished by my hands but really by my father's hands, because even as the dead harangued him, Ray Waterson witched a fine well. All my life until now has been a search for the man who was my father, that I might deliver him—and thereby myself—unto judgment. And perhaps this is judgment enough: The well he dug for us yields good water still.

For the first time since I was a boy, I have the feeling of working Daddy's big arms and legs as a crane operator—only now they are my own, as are the eyes through which I see my sons, and this well, and the water that pours from it. Looking on my wet-faced children who smile guilelessly up at me as if I am something magnificent and even magical, I see for the first time what I must have been in the eyes of my father. You spend all your childhood looking up at him, you see, but the eyes of your father are filled with you.

I see my sons as Daddy saw me, and by this I know what I have never fully known until this moment, at the end of his story and the final beginning of ours. I know with certainty the only thing any boy needs to know, which is that my father loves me.

This book was set in Sabon, designed by the German typographer and book designer, Jan Tschichold, and released in 1967. Tschichold was inspired to design Sabon after encountering a sixteenth-century specimen sheet produced by the legendary printer and typographer, Claude Garamond (1480–1561). The typeface is named after one of Garamond's students and colleagues, Jacques Sabon (1535–ca. 1580–90). Additional typefaces include Chandler 42, designed by Steve Mehallo, and Old Newspaper Types, designed by Manfred Klein.

This book was designed by Shannon Carter, Ian Creeger, and Gregory Wolfe. It was published in hardcover, paperback, and electronic formats by Slant Books, Seattle, Washington.

Cover: Photograph by Jack B via Unsplash.

www.ingramcontent.com/pod-product-compliance
Lightning Source LLC
Chambersburg PA
CBHW020359030726
47496CB00007B/2212